Praise for The Medieval Murderers

'Monks, mists, madness, taverns: the evocation of a strange but familiar Other Britain shrouded in time . . . A must for Historical Crime buffs and an ideal starting point for any reader new to the genre' TANGLED WEB

'The writers really know their stuff . . . A variety of backgrounds, from the Holy Land to Oxbridge and Saint Bartholomew's Fair add to the colour and make this a truly entertaining historical mystery' GOOD BOOK GUIDE

'If your taste is for well-written crime and well-written historical fiction, they are combined tantalisingly here' CRIME TIME

Also by The Medieval Murderers

The Tainted Relic
Sword of Shame
House of Shadows

The Lost Prophecies

A Historical Mystery

By

The Medieval Murderers

Bernard Knight
Ian Morson
Michael Jecks
Philip Gooden
Susanna Gregory
C. J. Sansom

POCKET
BOOKS

LONDON • NEW YORK • SYDNEY • TORONTO

First published in Great Britain by Simon & Schuster UK Ltd, 2008
This edition first published by Pocket Books, 2009
An imprint of Simon & Schuster UK
A CBS COMPANY

3 5 7 9 10 8 6 4 2

Simon & Schuster UK Ltd
1st Floor
222 Gray's Inn Road
London WC1X 8HB

www.simonandschuster.co.uk

Simon & Schuster Australia
Sydney

A CIP catalogue record for this book is available from the British Library

ISBN: 978-1-84983-119-2

Typeset by Rowland Phototypesetting Ltd,
Bury St Edmunds, Suffolk
Printed and bound in Great Britain by CPI Cox & Wyman,
Reading, Berkshire RG1 8EX

The Medieval Murderers

A small group of historical mystery writers, all members of the Crime Writers' Association, who promote their work by giving informal talks and discussions at libraries, bookshops and literary festivals.

Bernard Knight is a former Home Office pathologist and professor of forensic medicine who has been publishing novels, non-fiction, radio and television drama and documentaries for more than forty years. He currently writes the highly regarded Crowner John series of historical mysteries, based on the first coroner for Devon in the twelfth century; the thirteenth of which, *Crowner Royal*, has recently been published by Simon & Schuster.

Ian Morson is the author of an acclaimed series of historical mysteries featuring the thirteenth-century Oxford-based detective, William Falconer, and a brand-new series featuring Venetian crime solver, Nick Zuliani, the first of which, *City of the Dead*, has recently been published.

Michael Jecks was a computer salesman before turning to writing full time. His immensely popular Templar series, set during the confusion and terror of the reign of Edward II, is translated into most continental languages and is published in America. His most recent novels are *The Prophecy of Death* and, the

26th in the series, *The King of Thieves.* Michael was chairman of the Crime Writers' Association in 2004–5 but balances that by Morris Dancing enthusiastically – and badly.

Philip Gooden is the author of the Nick Revill series, a sequence of historical mysteries set in Elizabeth and Jacobean London, during the time of Shakespeare's Globe Theatre. The latest titles are *Mask of Night* and *An Honourable Murder.* He also has written a 19th century murder mystery, *The Salisbury Manuscript.* Philip was chairman of the Crime Writers' Association in 2007–8.

Susanna Gregory is the author of the Matthew Bartholomew series of

mystery novels, set in fourteenth-century Cambridge, the most recent of which are *A Vein of Deceit* and *To Kill or Cure.* In addition, she writes a series set in Restoration London, featuring Thomas Chaloner; the most recent book is *The Westminster Poisoner.* She also writes historical mysteries under the name of 'Simon Beaufort'.

C. J. Sansom is the author of the bestselling Matthew Shardlake series, set during the reign of Henry VIII. The most recent titles are *Revelation, Sovereign* and *Dark Fire.* He is also the author of *Winter in Madrid,* a historical thriller set in 1940s Spain.

The Programme

Prologue – In which Bernard Knight lays the foundation for the murderous tales that follow.

Act One – In which Bernard Knight's Crowner John confounds a band of treasure-hunters.

Act Two – In which Ian Morson's Nick Zuliani dices with death in a Russian blizzard.

Act Three – In which Michael Jecks' Keeper Sir Baldwin and Bailiff Puttock investigate murder most foul in the abbey crypt.

Act Four – In which Susanna Gregory's Matthew Bartholomew and Brother Michael become embroiled in a bloodthirsty college feud.

Act Five – In which Philip Gooden's player Nick Revill receives a letter from a mysterious uncle.

Act Six – In which C. J. Sansom confronts the Day of Judgment.

PROLOGUE

The coast of Kerry, Ireland, October 574

In the early-morning light, the fisherman Guleesh ventured nervously from his hut above Banna Strand in the Bay of Ballyheigue. His wife watched him from the door-hole, one arm around her little daughter, the other holding a hand to her mouth in breathless anxiety.

All Souls' Night had been full of omens, starting with a huge ring around a ruddy moon. When the orb had set, flickering curtains of green light weaved eerily in the sky to the north, rarely seen except as portents of some great disaster. As if this was not enough, silent lightning flashed for the rest of the night, unsettling the dogs and making them howl in company with a vixen that barked in the woods above the beach.

Now, thankfully, the dawn seemed quiet, with not a breath of wind. The sea lapped innocently along the miles of sand that faced the great western ocean that stretched out to the edge of the world. But this virgin strand was broken by a black dot at the water's edge, directly below their mean dwelling.

It was this that had eventually enticed the reluctant Guleesh out of his house. With the tide only just turned from the ebb, he walked cautiously down across the wide expanse of sand, his bare feet marking the pristine surface as he went. His thin, careworn woman watched him as he reached what they both had thought was a coracle. All kinds of flotsam ended up on their beach and, if it were not for the eerie signs in the heavens the previous night, it would have caused none of these premonitions of unearthly happenings.

She saw Guleesh reach the object as it rocked gently on every new wavelet that hissed up the beach. He bent to peer inside, then straightened up and began waving to her like a man possessed, his arm beckoning her to come.

Commanding her daughter to stay by the cradle with her brother, a lusty boy of two months, the wife Deirdre ran down the line of her husband's footprints, looking ahead uneasily at the strange lines of grey cloud that hung over the sea, where the Seven Hogs of the Magharee Islands broke the horizon. A dozen large jet-black ravens suddenly dropped from high in the sky and wheeled in a circle close over her head, cawing at her to hasten. As she came to the surf, which barely washed above her ankles, she saw that it was indeed a common coracle, a round tub of greased hides stretched over a wicker frame.

'Look, wife, look inside!' keened Guleesh, his voice taut with awe, as he lifted aside a rough-spun blanket. Deirdre steadied the rocking craft with one hand and looked down, her eyes round with wonder, as the guardian ravens strutted behind them.

Nestled on the blanket was a naked boy-baby, still with a few inches of birth-cord attached to his navel. Motherly compassion banished all fear, and she lifted the infant in his shawl and put him to her full breast. As she crooned into his ear while he sucked greedily, there was a long, low rumble of approving thunder from over the horizon and a single large wave came to speed the coracle up the beach.

Clonmacnois Abbey, Ireland, May 608

'What is to become of him, Father Conan?' The abbot's voice was weary with despair as he contemplated the problem that had beset them now for the past eight months.

The aged bishop shook his head sadly. 'The High Council feels that there is only one solution, Brother Alither. He has been chained now for a dozen weeks. It would be kinder to return him whence he came, rather than to leave him like this until he is claimed by God – or the devil!'

Alither, the abbot of Clonmacnois, shuddered at the prospect and tears appeared in his eyes, running down the grooves in his lined face. 'But the man is but thirty-three years old, the same as Christ at his Passion!' he groaned. 'He has lived here almost all his life, since he was brought here as a mere babe.'

Conan shrugged, not without compassion but bowing to the inevitability of God's will. 'The High Council considers that he is possessed, and I cannot say that I disagree with them, though I have never actually set my eyes upon him.'

Alither shook his head in bewilderment. 'You must see him for yourself; he is most comely. Apart from his affliction, he is perfectly sound in wind and limb.'

'But it is not his earthly body that concerns us, brother. It is his mind and his soul, if he has one!'

The bishop picked up a thin book from the rough table at which he sat and brandished it at the abbot. 'Is this the product of a Christian brother – or the ravings of the devil that lives within him?'

Conan opened the covers of wood covered with black leather that were bound over a thin sheaf of yellow parchment. He held it out towards the abbot and riffled the pages under Alither's nose.

'What demonical evil is this? Who in Ireland has ever seen the like of this before? Can you doubt that Satan had a hand in this?'

Alither had no need to look at it; he was only too familiar with the weird volume that, along with its author, had been the bane of his life for the past few months. Though the script was neat and regular, the content of the text was beyond comprehension.

'Perfect Latin, beautifully penned!' continued an exasperated Conan. 'And what does it mean? Gibberish, blasphemous gibberish! Apparently claiming to foretell the future, blasphemously encroaching on God's Holy Will, which has preordained every action until the end of time!'

The abbot nodded reluctantly. 'It seems that way, bishop,' he agreed sadly. 'Compared with this, the Revelation of St John is crystal clear!'

Wearily, Conan dropped the book back on to the table. 'Tell me again, before I cast my eyes upon him, how came this Brân to be here?'

Alither refilled the bishop's mead cup from a small jug before replying.

They were seated in the bare room where the abbot slept, worked and prayed, one of a dozen wooden buildings clustered inside the palisade on a low gravel ridge on the banks of the great river.

'He was named Brân, as the simple fisherfolk who found him were besieged by his namesake ravens as they rescued him from the beach – and Brân is well known as the son of a sea-god!'

With little effort he mixed pagan beliefs with his Christianity as he continued. 'They took him straight to the abbey of Ard Fert, not two miles from where the babe was washed ashore. The women there cared for him for seven years, until he was brought up the Shannon to us here at Clonmacnois.'

Conan knew, as did every *religious* in Ireland, of the magical origins of this Brân. But as the years passed and the child grew first into a scholar, then a novice and finally a monk without any further manifestations of the Other World, it was forgotten for almost three decades.

'He was talented with a quill and was put to work in our scriptorium, copying the Psalms and the Gospels,' said the abbot. 'Then one night last autumn, when the moon was full, he suddenly fell to the ground and had great spasms of his limbs. When he eventually fell quiet, he slept for a whole night and a day, then woke as if normal.'

'Not quite normal, brother,' said Conan dryly. He knew all this from the deliberations of the High Council in Tara five days previously.

Alither nodded slowly. 'No, you are right, Conan. As soon as he awoke, he went like a man in a trance to the scriptorium and began writing these verses, with such obscure meaning.'

'He had never written anything like this before?' growled Conan.

The abbot shook his head. 'Never. His copying was perfection itself. Over the years he prepared a large section of the Vulgate of St Jerome which was a joy to behold. Others did the coloured illumination, but his penmanship was exquisite.'

'But the fits worsened, I understand? What did he have to say about all this?'

'He told us that he always knew when a seizure was coming, as he was transported to some ethereal place where a voice spoke to him, filling him with prophecy and commanding that he record it as a warning to posterity. Then he knows nothing more until, when he recovers from the spasms, he has an irresistible urge to seize his pen and write.'

The bishop frowned. 'Whose was this voice? Does he claim it was the Lord God Almighty – or maybe the Horned One?'

The abbot shrugged under the coarse brown habit that hung on his weedy frame. 'He does not know, he says. It is just a voice that must be obeyed. He has no power to resist.'

'And his chaining? That cannot control his convulsions, surely?'

Alither raised his hands in despair. 'The fits come more frequently with every week. Now he suffers one almost every day. Lately, he has taken to wandering off like a sleepwalker, when he is in the trance that precedes each seizure. We cannot watch him all the time, so he has been shackled to prevent him walking into a fire – or into the river, which is so near.'

Conan grunted. 'Maybe it would have been better to let him plunge into the Shannon – it would have saved us a painful task.'

He hauled himself to his feet with a groan. His journey here from Tara had been undertaken with reluctance, both from the distasteful nature of his mission and the effort at his age of riding a pony across the bogs of the Midlands.

'Let us see this man, if indeed he is a man?' He sighed, picking up the book again as they left the room.

Outside, in the circular compound that encompassed the wooden buildings and three tiny churches of the abbey, a group of monks and their women stood uneasily, watching the abbot lead this emissary of bad tidings across to a thatched hut on the extreme edge of the enclosure. Just beyond this, the low knoll on which the abbey stood sloped down to the oily waters of the

Shannon, gliding silently through its many lakes down to the distant sea.

As they walked through the new spring grass, Alither made one last attempt. 'Is there no other way, bishop? Can he not be hidden away in some hermit's cell on the Cliffs of Moher or somewhere even more remote, like the Isles of Aran?'

Conan gripped the speaker's shoulder in a rare moment of compassion. 'And how would he manage to live, in his condition? Maybe choke in one of his fits, all alone? It is better this way, Alither. Our pagan forefathers would have strangled him or slit his throat and buried him in a bog-pool.'

Outside the hut stood two burly soldiers, part of the High King's guard who had accompanied the bishop from Tara.

'These will do the deed, brother,' said Conan stonily. 'I appreciate that no one here should be called upon to take part.'

Men and women, monks, servants, mothers and even children were drifting towards them, to stand in a silent ring around the hut as the two senior priests entered through the low doorway, which was covered with a flap of thick leather. Their eyes adjusted to the dim light that came through a narrow slit in the walls of clay and straw plastered over hazel withies between oaken frames. They saw a man in a coarse brown robe squatting in a corner on a pile of dry ferns. A stool, a wooden bucket and a small table with writing materials were the only furnishings, apart from a long iron chain that was looped around the central pole that supported the rafters. The other end was riveted to a wide metal band that encircled Brân's waist.

The captive looked up as Conan entered and made the sign of the cross in the air.

'God be with you, brother,' intoned the bishop. 'I am Conan, come from Tara to see you.'

The man on the floor looked up, his blue eyes guileless in a face drawn with exhaustion. 'I know you, bishop. You were sent to kill me.'

There was no fear or loathing in his voice, just a plain statement of fact, lacking any emotion.

'Why have you written these strange words, Brân?' asked Conan, holding up the slim wood-covered volume.

'I had no choice, father. It could not have been otherwise. I was commanded to set down the voice I heard. I am but a device for recording these awful truths. They emerge not from my mind but only from my pen.'

He shifted a little on his heap of bracken. 'But it is ended now. There is no need for more writing.'

'Do you understand what is said in the words you wrote, Brân?' persisted the old bishop.

'It is no concern of mine. These events will come to pass far in the future. Maybe I will be there to see some of them.' He said this in an uncaring fashion, as if it was of no consequence.

'Who gave you these prophecies, brother? Or are they of your own invention?'

Brân, his dirty red hair embedded with bits of fern and straw, turned a face like a tired angel to the old priest. 'I know that you wish to discover whether it is God or Satan. But I cannot tell you, for I do not know.'

'Where did you come from, Brân?' persisted Conan.

'Again, I know not! My first memories are of the good people who cared for me as a child. My last memories will be of the inside of this mean dwelling!'

Suddenly, his eyes rolled up so that the whites showed, and he fell back against the wall, lolling inertly with his jaw slack.

'This is the prelude to a seizure,' said the abbot. 'He will be like this for a few minutes, then the spasms will begin. Maybe someone is speaking to him now, inside that head.'

Conan made a sudden decision. 'It would be kinder to get it over with now, when he is unaware.'

Pushing Alither aside, he went out of the hut to speak to the two warriors who waited outside. The abbot hurried after him in time to hear his commands.

'Release that chain, but leave the band around his belly – it will help to weigh him down! Bind his wrists in case he recovers, then carry him to the river and throw him well out from the bank.'

He turned to Alither, who was standing aghast and trembling. 'Must this be, bishop? Is there no other way?'

Conan shook his head as the two guards moved towards the doorway. 'From the waters he came and to the waters he must return!'

As the words left his lips, an ear-splitting clap of thunder crashed overhead though the sky was clear. On the river, a single high wave rolled smoothly up between the banks, splashing up on to the grass and sending birds squawking into the air. It passed as quickly as it had appeared, but now there were shouts from within the hut. Conan and the abbot pushed aside the leather flap and stared as the two soldiers pointed to the corner.

A metal band lay on the bracken, still chained to the post. Inside it was a brown habit, the coarse cloth crumpled into a small heap in the centre. On the table, Brân's black book lay as it was left.

Alither picked it up and, crossing himself, stared at the bishop, his eyes wide with fear. 'A miracle, Conan! But is it for good or evil?'

ACT ONE

Exeter, February 1196

When three golden beasts did reign by bishop's rule,
A bearded champion fought oppression's realm,
His secret horde defied the edicts cruel,
But all was lost beneath the budding elm.

It was an unusual case for coroner Sir John de Wolfe – not so much because it was a find of treasure-trove but that it occurred not a hundred paces from his dismal chamber in Rougemont Castle. He was more used to ranging the length and breadth of the county of Devon to view some corpse, sometimes riding for three days on a journey to the more remote parts.

His clerk brought the news to him on a winter morning when the frost lay hard on the ground and even the sewage lying in the city streets was frozen solid. Thomas de Peyne, his thin cassock swathed in a threadbare cloak of grey serge, pushed his way through the curtain of sacking on the doorway at the top of the winding stairs cut into the walls of the tall gatehouse. The little priest's narrow face, with pointed nose and receding chin, was blue with cold, but he managed to control the chattering of his teeth to blurt out the exciting news.

'Crowner, they have found money in the outer ward!'

De Wolfe, sitting behind his rough trestle table,

almost the only furniture in that spartan chamber, looked up irritably. 'What, has some man-at-arms dropped a penny?' he asked cynically.

'No, there are many coins, hundreds of them – and some gold too!' squeaked Thomas, rubbing an almost frozen dewdrop from the end of his nose. 'Ralph Morin is there. He asked that you come and look, for it will be coroner's business.'

There was a voice from the other side of the room, where Gwyn of Polruan, de Wolfe's officer and squire, was sitting in his usual place on the cold stone of a window embrasure, apparently impervious to the icy wind that whistled through the slit.

'What's going on, Crowner?' he rumbled in his deep Cornish accent. 'This is the fourth such find since Christmas!'

John rose to his feet and pulled his grey wolf-skin cloak closer about his long, stooped body. As tall as Gwyn, but much leaner, he looked like a great crow, with his jet-black hair, hooked nose and dark stubble on his leathery cheeks.

'After the first two hoards that were found, folk seem to have caught gold fever,' he growled. 'Half the town has found shovels and are digging into every mound they come across.'

As the three men moved to the doorway, Thomas added: 'This wasn't a mound. They were digging a new well for the garrison families living in the outer bailey. It seems they had not gone down more than an arm's length when they found it.'

At the bottom of the stairs, which came out in the guardroom at the side of the entrance arch, they were joined by Gabriel, the sergeant of the men-at-arms who formed the garrison of Rougemont. The castle was so called from the red colour of the local sandstone from which it had been built by William the Bastard a mere two years after the Battle of Hastings. Gabriel was a grizzled veteran of some of the same wars in which John and Gwyn had fought, and they were old friends.

As they walked down the drawbridge over the dry moat that separated the inner from the outer wards of the castle, they saw a small crowd clustering around a wooden tripod, fifty paces off the steep track that led to the outer gate. Most of them were soldiers, huddled in thick jerkins against the cold, but a few hardy wives were peering from behind them, and a brace of children, apparently oblivious to the winter chill, were racing around and shouting. The outer ward, meant to be the first line of defence for the castle, was where most of the families of the garrison lived, their huts forming a small village inside the city walls.

Striding over the sparse grass and frozen mud, de Wolfe and his companions reached the excavation, where the circle of onlookers opened up to let them through. Here, another large man was issuing orders to the soldiers who were digging the well. He was Ralph Morin, the castle constable, responsible to the king for the defence and maintenance of Rougemont, for it was a royal possession, not the fief of a baron or manor lord. A tall, erect man, he had a forked beard that gave him the look of a Viking warrior.

'Another box of money, Crowner! How many more?' he said, echoing Gwyn's words.

De Wolfe stooped to peer into the hole that had been dug, about five feet wide. The wooden tripod reached a few feet above his head, supporting a pulley and a rope to lift buckets of soil and rock as the well was deepened. However, it had had little use as yet, as only a small pile of waste lay nearby. The hole was barely three feet deep, and in the bottom he could see the broken lid of a wooden chest, with some coins glinting beneath the smashed boards.

'Have any been taken out?' he demanded, his first concern being to prevent any pilfering.

'Show Sir John what you found,' ordered the constable, prodding a burly soldier who was leaning on a pickaxe.

The man bent down and picked up a crumpled woollen cap, which he handed to the coroner. 'I put a few in there after my pick went through the box, sir,' he grunted. 'Bloody hard work it was, cracking through that frozen ground!' he added, eyeing the coins in his hat hopefully.

John ignored the hint and tipped the dozen coins into his hand for a closer look. All were silver pennies, with the exception of one larger gold coin.

'These are Saxon, I'm sure,' he said, but then held them out towards Thomas de Peyne, who seemed to have a wide knowledge of almost everything.

The clerk peered at them short-sightedly and poked them around with a spindly finger. 'Indeed they are, Crowner. From different mints and different monarchs – there's Ethelred and Athelstan.'

'What about the gold one?' growled Gwyn. 'That's a bezant, isn't it?'

'It's certainly a foreign coin, but I'm not sure from where,' admitted Thomas. Always keen to show off his learning, he added: 'Bezants are named after Byzantium, where lots of gold *solidi* came from many years ago.'

'Right, let's get that box up,' commanded de Wolfe, handing the empty cap back to the disappointed soldier. He pulled it on his head, spat on his hands and lifted the pick.

'Easy with that! Get it out in one piece if you can!' snapped the constable.

Together with another man, the soldier lowered himself into the shallow excavation, and between them they levered up the metal-bound box and in a few minutes had it on the ground at the coroner's feet. It had no lid or lock, being a sealed case bound with iron straps, which had rusted so badly that they could easily be snapped with the point of the pick. The elm boards had softened after more than a century in the wet soil, and once the bands were broken the smashed top could be pulled apart to reveal the contents.

'Must be a good few hundred in there,' muttered Ralph Morin.

The box was full of silver coins, many stuck together by the damp tarnish that covered them. When John dug his fingers into the mass, he saw a few more gold bezants and, at the bottom, some gold brooches and buckles. The onlookers gaped and drooled at the sight of such riches, which for most of them would equal several lifetimes of their daily wages.

'What do we do with it – the same as the others?' asked the constable.

The previous hoards had all been taken to the sheriff for safekeeping until an inquest could decide what was to be done with the finds. He had the only secure place for valuables, in his back chamber in the keep of the castle. One of the sheriff's main functions was to collect the taxes from the county and deliver them in person every six months to the Exchequer in Winchester, so several massive strongboxes were stored in his quarters under constant guard.

On the constable's orders, two men carried the box up to the keep, with Morin marching close behind them to make sure that it reached the sheriff intact – though like de Wolfe, he wondered if an odd coin or two had already found its way into the pouches of the men digging the well.

The coroner and his two assistants followed them to the sheriff's chamber, which was off the large main hall in the two-storeyed keep at the further side of the inner ward. Henry de Furnellis, an elderly knight with a face like a bloodhound, had been appointed sheriff the previous year as a stopgap when the former sheriff, John's brother-in-law, had been dismissed in disgrace. Now Henry looked with a pained expression at the muddy box lying on a table in his room. 'Another bloody burden to carry to Winchester and to explain to those arrogant Chancery clerks,' he complained to his elderly clerk, Elphin.

Together, the coroner and the constable sorted out the coins into piles and placed the bezants and the five gold ornaments alongside them. Thomas, who always carried his writing materials in a shapeless shoulder bag, sat with parchment, ink and quill and recorded the exact details of the treasure. 'Nine hundred and forty pennies, twenty-eight gold coins, three gold brooches and two gold cloak-rings,' he intoned when he had finished.

'A nice little collection, and not much doubt that it now belongs to King Richard,' declared Ralph Morin.

De Furnellis nodded his old head wisely. 'No, as it was found within his own castle! Can't very well belong to anyone else, can it, John?'

De Wolfe cleared his throat, his usual response when he had some doubts. 'I suppose not, but I'll still have to hold my inquest for a jury to decide if it was accidentally lost or whether the owner intended reclaiming it at some future date.'

The sheriff cackled. 'He'll have a hell of a job doing that now, John. He's probably been dead for a century!'

Gwyn pulled on his drooping ginger moustaches as an aid to thought. 'Why are we getting all these finds in and around Exeter?' he rumbled. 'Especially this one inside the castle itself?'

John de Wolfe managed to beat the know-all clerk to the answer. 'It wasn't a castle then, that's why. Almost all these hoards were hidden by the Saxons when they knew that Harold had lost at Hastings and realized that our Norman forefathers would soon be marching towards them. Many of them buried their money and valuables, hoping to retrieve them later.'

As he paused to draw breath, Thomas jumped in. 'King William put down the rebellion in Exeter two years after Hastings – then, to make sure it wouldn't happen again, he knocked down fifty houses to make room for this very castle.'

Gwyn nodded slowly. 'So these things today were probably buried in what would have then been someone's back yard!'

'A rich someone's back yard, by the looks of it,' added the sheriff. 'I wonder what happened to him?'

There was silence for a moment, as although the despoliation of Saxon England had been carried out by their grandfathers or even great-grandfathers, there was still some unease at the memory that a few thousand Normans had slain or dispossessed almost all the Saxon nobility and wealthy landowners. Even though well over a century of intermarriage had diluted the blood, all of them except Gwyn considered themselves Normans.

'As I said, he certainly won't be coming back to claim them,' grunted the sheriff.

After his clerk Elphin had added his signature to the bottom of Thomas's list as a witness to the exact value of the hoard, the coins were placed in a large leather bag, together with the ornaments carefully wrapped in a cloth. The whole lot was then locked away in one of the massive treasure chests, which carried clumsy but effective locks on the iron bands riveted around them.

'I'll hold my inquest this afternoon,' promised John. 'Gwyn, round up all those soldiers who were digging the well and get a few more to make up a score for a jury. We'll hold the proceedings in the Shire Hall – and I'll have to have that sack to show them, to make it legal.'

The coroner's trio left the keep and went back to the gatehouse, this time hovering over a charcoal brazier that Gabriel had burning in the guardroom, which slightly warmed the chilly air. A pitcher of ale was produced, and one of the men-at-arms stuck a red-hot poker in it and passed around some mugs of the warm but still sour liquid. Thomas declined his, as ale was not to his taste, preferring cider, even at freezing point.

'At least this last hoard was found by sheer chance, not from a message from beyond the grave like the first one!' said Gwyn.

The previous month, a few hundred silver pennies and some bezants had been found after the cathedral archivist had come across a sheet of parchment tucked between the pages of an old volume of chants. This bore a brief message from someone called Egbert to his son, indicating that, fearing the imminent arrival of the Norman invaders, he had buried the family wealth at the foot of a preaching cross in the churchyard of Alphington, a village just outside Exeter. The archivist, Canon Jordan le Brent, had reported this to his bishop, and a search soon revealed the truth of the claim.

Unfortunately, Bishop Henry Marshal immediately confiscated the hoard on the grounds that it had been found on Church property and even forbade the coroner to hold an inquest upon it. Unsure of the legal position – as few people, including the king's ministers, had any clear idea of the extent of a coroner's powers – de Wolfe had had to submit, though he intended complaining to the Chief Justiciar, Hubert Walter, when he had the chance. Unfortunately, the Justiciar, who now virtually ruled England since the king was permanently absent fighting the French, was also the Archbishop of Canterbury, so it would be difficult for the Primate of the English Church to overrule one of his bishops.

'Ever since that scrap of vellum came to light, we have been plagued by people wanting to search the library at the cathedral,' complained Thomas. He had a particular interest in the matter, since he worked part time in the archives above the Chapter House just outside the cathedral's South Tower.

When he had been restored to the priesthood the previous year, his uncle, Archdeacon John de Alençon, had arranged for him to be given a stipend for saying daily Masses for the souls of certain rich men who had left bequests for the purpose. Another task, which was dear to Thomas's heart, was to sort and catalogue the disorderly mass of material in the library, in anticipation of a move to a new Chapter House, for which the bishop had already donated a part of the garden of his palace.

'Do people come in off the street to search the records?' asked Gabriel, unused to the ways of the ecclesiastical community.

'They probably would if they could read!' replied the little clerk. 'No, it's the priests who seem to have caught this gold fever, especially since that hoard was found in a churchyard. We've had a few literate clerks sent by their merchant masters to snoop around, but they don't get admitted. Unfortunately, we can't stop the parish priests coming into the library.'

'I presume no one has found anything more since that one scrap of parchment?' asked the coroner.

His scribe shook his head. 'No, even though they've been through almost all the books and rolls now, often not reading anything, just looking between the pages or shaking them to see if anything drops out!'

Thomas shook his scrawny head in disgust, though it was not clear to his master if this was at the greed of his fellow priests or their failure to benefit from the wealth of scholarship that passed through their hands.

Just as the ale was finished, they heard the distant cathedral bell calling for Terce, signalling the tenth hour at that time of year. John de Wolfe reluctantly rose from near the brazier and pulled his cloak tightly around him, fixing the upper corner to his opposite shoulder with a large silver pin and clasp. He pulled on a felt coif, a close-fitting helmet that covered his ears and tied under the chin.

'Come on! Freezing or not, it's hanging day,' he said brusquely. 'We have three fellows to see off. In weather like this, they may be quite glad to go!'

They collected their horses from the lean-to stables against the wall of the inner ward and left the castle, their steeds treading cautiously on the icy surface of the steep slope down to the East Gate. With the coroner on his old warhorse Odin and Gwyn on his big brown mare, Thomas looked a poor third as he rode awkwardly on his thin nag behind them. It was not that long since he had been persuaded to give up riding side-saddle like a woman.

They went around outside the walls via Southernhay to join Magdalen Street and rode away from the city towards the village of Heavitree, near where the gallows was situated, a long high crossbar supported at each end by tree-trunks. Usually, there was a crowd of spectators, with hawkers selling pasties and sweetmeats, but today the icy weather had limited the onlookers to a handful of wailing relatives.

The coroner had to attend to record the names and property of those executed, as any land or possessions of felons was forfeit to the king. Today there would be thin pickings, thought John cynically, as one of the men was a captured outlaw owning nothing but the ragged clothes he wore and the other two were little more than lads, caught stealing items worth more than twelve pence, the lower limit for the death sentence.

De Wolfe and Gwyn sat on their horses to watch, glad of even the slight body warmth that came off the large animals, while Thomas shivered as he sat on a tree-stump at the edge of the road, his parchment roll and writing materials resting on a box.

The three condemned men did their own shivering in the back of an ox-cart, their wrists bound to the rail behind the driver as he drove it under the three ropes hanging from the high crossbar.

One of the half-dozen men-at-arms who had escorted the cart down from the castle shouted out the names to Thomas, as he untied the men and made them stand on a plank across the sides of the wagon while the hangman, who was a local butcher, placed the nooses around their necks.

A smack on the rump of the patient ox sent the cart lumbering forward, and in a trice the three victims were kicking spasmodically in the air. The relatives of the two younger ones dashed forward and dragged down on their thrashing legs, to shorten the agony of strangulation, but the lonely outlaw had to suffer the dance of death for several more minutes.

The sensitive Thomas always averted his gaze and concentrated on his writing, but John and Gwyn watched impassively, having seen far worse deaths a thousand times over, in battles and massacres from Ireland to Palestine. When the performance was over, they left the gallows and returned to town for their dinners, for it was approaching noon. The coroner went back to his house in Martin's Lane, one of the many entrances to the cathedral Close, and sat at table in his gloomy hall with his equally gloomy wife Matilda. In spite of a large fire burning in the hearth, the high chamber, which stretched up to the roof beams, was almost as cold as the lane outside, and his stocky wife wore a fur-lined pelisse over her woollen gown and linen surcoat.

Conversation was always difficult, as Matilda rarely spoke except to nag him about his drinking, womanizing and frequent absences from home, although it was she who had persuaded him to take on the coroner's appointment as a step up in the hierarchy of Devon's important people. He knew that his description of today's hangings would be of no interest to her, but he thought he might divert her with the news of another find of treasure. Matilda's main concerns were food, drink, fine clothes and, above all, the worship of the Almighty, but money was also acceptable as a topic of interest. Like the others, she remarked on the frequency of the discoveries in recent months.

'These are all part of the ill-gotten gains of those Saxons, I suppose,' she said loftily.

Although she had been born in Devon and had only once visited distant relatives across the Channel, she considered herself a full-blooded Norman lady and looked down on the conquered natives with disdain. One of her major regrets was being married to a man who, although a Norman knight and former Crusader, had a mother who was half-Welsh, half-Cornish.

'I hear that a number of priests have been searching the cathedral archives, hoping to find another parchment leading to a hoard like that found in Alphington churchyard,' said John, carefully avoiding the fact that it was Thomas who had told him. Even more than her dislike of Saxons, Matilda detested his clerk for being a perverted priest, even though his unfrocking had been reversed when the allegations that he had indecently assaulted a girl pupil in the cathedral school in Winchester were proved to be false.

'Good luck to them,' she declared firmly. 'The Church should benefit as much as possible from the riches of those heathens!'

Her husband forbore to point out that the Saxons had been Christians for centuries before the pagan Viking fathers of the Normans ever set foot in Normandy.

Mary, their cook and maid-of-all-work, came in from her kitchen-shed in the back yard to clear their wooden bowls of mutton stew and to place trenchers before each of them on the scrubbed oak boards of the table. These were stale slabs of yesterday's barley bread on to which Mary slid thick slices of fat bacon with a heap of fried onions alongside. In these winter months, the range of available vegetables and meat was very limited, and most were stored or preserved from the previous autumn, as were the wrinkled apples that were offered as dessert, supplemented by dried figs and raisins imported from southern Aquitaine.

Eating was a serious business, and de Wolfe did not attempt to reopen the conversation until they had finished and were sitting on each side of the fire with a pewter cup of Anjou wine apiece.

'This treasure today will certainly go to the king, as it was found inside Rougemont,' he said with some satisfaction. 'The bloody bishop won't get his hands on this lot!'

Matilda scowled at him from under the fur rim of the velvet cap she wore against the cold. 'It would do far more good in the coffers of the cathedral,' she snapped. 'It will be wasted on more troops and arms for

Richard to fight that futile war against France. Better if he came back to England and tended to his own dominions!'

John headed her off by mentioning the Chief Justiciar, as he knew Matilda revered the archbishop almost as much as the Pope. 'Hubert Walter does an excellent job in Richard's stead. He has been a good friend to us over the years.'

He knew this would mollify his wife, who loved to think that she was close to the high and mighty. Hubert Walter had been the Lionheart's second-in-command in the Holy Land, and de Wolfe had earned his friendship and respect there during the Crusade. Having adroitly warmed up his wife's mood, if not her body, he finished his wine and rose to his feet. 'I must go back to Rougemont now. There is an inquest to be held on that treasure.'

'And I will be at my devotions in St Olave's Church for much of today, John,' declared Matilda as he left.

'And after the inquest I will be down at the Bush Inn visiting my mistress!' said John – though he said it under his breath after he had shut the door behind him.

Unsurprisingly, the jury at the short inquest decided that the finds from the new well were treasure-trove, as the original owner must have buried them deliberately in the expectation that he would one day recover them – as opposed to an accidental loss from a hole in a man's purse or pocket. In that case, the booty would belong to the actual finder, but obviously this could not apply to a sackful of coins and jewellery. Thomas de Peyne had recorded the findings on his rolls, to be presented to the king's justices when they eventually arrived in Exeter to hold the next Eyre of Assize. When the proceedings were finished, he went back to the cathedral to get on with his other work. The archives and library were also the scriptorium and exchequer of the cathedral, where clerks laboriously wrote out all manner of documents, from orders of services to the financial accounts of the diocese.

The library formed the upper floor of the Chapter House, a wooden building adjacent to the huge church, where the daily meetings of the Chapter were held. This was the controlling body of the cathedral, consisting of the twenty-four canons, who included the four archdeacons, as it would be some years before Exeter followed other cathedrals in appointing a dean.

The benches for the members were on the ground floor, below the lectern from which a 'chapter' of either the Gospels or the Rule of St Benedict was read, giving the meeting its name.

In the corner was a steep stairway up which Thomas de Peyne now climbed to the large chamber that contained the mass of documents which he had the task of organizing. A dozen high desks filled the centre of the room, around a charcoal brazier which stood on a slab of slate on the wooden floor. Its heat barely warmed the atmosphere, as the shutters on the unglazed window openings were wide open to admit light to the handful of shivering clerks who were working at the desks. Around the walls were sloping shelves on which to rest the heavy books, the more valuable of which were chained to the wall, such as the Exon version of King William's Domesday Book. Other shelves and pigeonholes contained a mass of parchment rolls, and a number of boxes and chests on the floor were filled with more documents.

Thomas stood and stared at the collection with a mixture of pride and exasperation. An intelligent man, he had been schooled in Winchester and was unusually well informed about all manner of topics, from history to theology, from geography to the classics. He was delighted to be given a free run of all these literary treasures, but the task of putting them all in order was a daunting prospect. Many of the smaller tracts and loose parchments had never been listed, and Thomas suspected that some of the boxes below the shelves had not been opened in decades.

He had appropriated a corner desk to himself, where he had begun the marathon job of cataloguing each item before putting them in order on the upper shelves. One of his problems was that he could never resist reading through anything that seemed interesting, which slowed down his progress considerably, even though it added to his already compendious knowledge. Now he settled himself on the high stool at his desk and began sorting through the pile of documents that he had selected the previous day, working steadily for the next hour.

'How are your labours going, Thomas?' A deep voice dragged him from his efforts to read the crabbed Latin script of a long-dead priest who had listed the donations for the building of a shrine in the cathedral some sixty years before. The speaker was Jordan le Brent, the canon who acted as archivist and master of the scriptorium. He was an amiable, elderly man with a devotion to learning and history similar to that of the coroner's clerk.

'Well enough, sir, though slowly,' replied Thomas. 'At least we seem to have at last been spared all those who came searching for maps to buried treasure!'

The older man shook his tonsured head ruefully. 'Perhaps not, my son. This new find we heard about today might well fire up even more interest in hidden silver.'

Thomas crossed himself fervently. 'Dear God, I hope not! They have disturbed enough of my papers already, scrabbling through all this.' He waved a hand at the dusty shelves and the mouldering parchments.

'The lust for silver and gold seems ingrained in mankind,' pondered the old canon. 'No wonder greed is classed as one of the seven deadly sins. Even my own brethren are not immune, for I found one of my fellow canons rooting through the shelves yesterday, when you were away on coroner's business.'

He avoided naming the person, but Thomas knew that many of the canons were fond of an expensive lifestyle, far removed from the austere rules laid down by St Benedict and St Chrodegang.

'We should limit those who can have access to our archives, canon,' said Thomas earnestly. 'Some of these old parchments are brittle and faded. They could be damaged beyond repair and much information about olden days be lost for ever.'

Jordan le Brent nodded slowly. 'I agree that we should keep out the clerks of burgesses and merchants, but we cannot bar clergy in the upper orders. But I will ask the proctors to keep an eye on the place at night and make sure the door is locked.'

He wandered away and Thomas went back to his pleasant labours.

Meanwhile, down in the Bush Inn in Idle Lane, where the city sloped steeply down towards the river, John de Wolfe was enjoying a quart of best ale and the company of his mistress Nesta, the pretty Welsh redhead who owned the tavern.

He sat at his usual table near the firepit, where the cold weather was being defeated by a large heap of crackling logs, spitting sparks on to the floor rushes which had frequently to be stamped out by old Edwin, the one-eyed potman. Nesta was taking a few minutes off from harrying her two maids, who were cooking in the kitchen-shed at the back of the inn. John told her all the details of the find of treasure that morning, and inevitably she also brought up the curious fact that so many finds had been made in recent weeks. He explained about the Saxon panic of a century or more ago, when much of their wealth had hurriedly been hidden in the hope of saving it from the invaders.

'But why is it being found now, for it's been lying there for long enough, God knows!' she said.

They spoke in Welsh, her native language and one that John had learned at his mother's knee. In fact, Gwyn's native Cornish was close enough for all three to converse in the Celtic tongue, as did a sizeable proportion of the country people in both Devon and Cornwall, who spoke Western Welsh.

'Such hoards have been turning up regularly for many years, Nesta,' he said. 'The one just before Christ Mass was a chance find, but then this note being found in the cathedral that led to the discovery in Alphington has started a kind of madness amongst the population. A number of mounds have been dug into around the city, but all they found were ancient pots and a few bones.'

'Thomas tells me that many people have been hampering his work in the cathedral by demanding to search the books there,' she said rather indignantly, for the little priest was a favourite of hers.

'Thank God so few can read!' said John fervently. 'Otherwise half the population of Exeter would be rooting through the archives.'

Only about one in a hundred were literate, this being confined to those in holy orders, both ordained priests and deacons, as well as those in the lower clerical orders, who also provided the clerks to merchants and the authorities.

De Wolfe dallied at the tavern for as long as he could, enjoying the company of his vivacious lover, but as early dusk fell he had to tear himself away to go home, where he would be expected for supper, a newfangled idea of Matilda's, who always wished to be abreast of new fashions. The noon dinner was most people's main meal of the day, but she insisted on eating again in the early evening, as did the nobility.

As he left, he eyed the ladder at the back of the taproom which went up to the loft, where Nesta had a small bedroom.

'I'll try to get back later this evening,' he said hopefully. 'I'm sure Brutus will be ready for a walk by then!'

At about the eighth hour, Matilda went up as usual to her solar at the back of the house, to be prepared for bed by her snivelling French maid Lucille. This was the signal for John to snap his fingers for his old hound Brutus, who was his invariable alibi for nocturnal expeditions down to the Bush. They left through the heavy front door, which opened directly on to the lane, and the dog ambled off to visit his favourite smells and mark them with a cocked leg.

The coroner's house in Martin's Lane was a mere twenty paces from one of the entrances to the cathedral Close, the wide space around the huge church. The narrow passage connected the Close to High Street, and John's was one of the only two dwellings on the west side, a farrier's stables lying opposite. John had on his heaviest cloak and pulled a broad-brimmed pilgrim's hat low over his black hair, as there was a keen east wind. Though there was a curfew after dark, this 'couvre-feu' applied mainly to damping down domestic fires for the night, as in a city where most of the buildings were wooden, a severe conflagration was an ever-present danger. People still went about the streets, though tonight few ventured out into the icy conditions and the almost total darkness, as heavy cloud covered the moon.

As he entered the Close, the only light came from a flickering pitch brand stuck in an iron ring over the distant Bear Gate. However, de Wolfe was familiar with every step of the way and set off down the diagonal path that threaded through the grave mounds, open burial pits and piles of rubbish that disfigured the area. He could hear Brutus scrabbling after something a few yards away, where a rat was probably rooting in a pile of discarded offal. The only other light John ever saw here on his nocturnal adventures was the dim lantern of a cathedral proctor doing his rounds. These were men in the lower clerical orders who patrolled the precinct and tried to keep order, as the Close was ecclesiastical territory, a 'city within a city' where the writ of the sheriff and burgesses did not run, the ultimate authority being the bishop.

Tonight he saw no one and was past the great West Front of the cathedral and halfway to the Bear Gate when he heard a cry from somewhere on his left. Immediately, his dog gave a sharp bark, then a deep growl. John was familiar with every nuance of Brutus's voice and knew that something was seriously amiss.

Then he saw a faint flicker of yellow light from the direction of the South Tower and a crash as if something had flung a door back against a wall. He began walking as fast as he could in the darkness, being careful of obstacles as this was not one of his usual paths. Brutus had no such problem and bounded ahead, still growling. Suddenly, the growl turned into a yelp, and, somewhere in the gloom ahead, pounding footsteps hammered on the flagstones. They rapidly receded towards the far exit into Southgate Street, and all John could see was a momentary glimpse of a figure as it passed beneath the flaming torch and vanished from sight. Pursuit was pointless and instead he hurried as fast as he could towards the light, using it as a marker. With only a few stumbles, he reached it to find a horn lantern on its side, but the candle still lit within. Picking it up, he found himself at the door of the Chapter House, which was wide open.

'Brutus, where the hell are you?' he called, and almost immediately the old dog appeared at his knee, giving a whine that sounded almost apologetic. Holding the light closer, John saw that there was a bloody graze on the hound's flank, though it did not appear to be serious.

'The bastard kicked you, did he?' he asked, fondling the dog's ears. 'I'll make him pay for that when I find him!'

Brutus whined again, with a different note this time, and pointed his lean muzzle towards the door. John took the hint and, pulling his dagger from his sheath on his belt, held up the lantern with the other hand and advanced cautiously into the building. His feeble light failed to reveal all of the large room, where the canons and their vicars met each day, but as he moved towards the centre of the flagstoned floor Brutus whined again and moved ahead of him towards the far corner, where steep wooden stairs led up to the library.

As he approached, he saw that a crumpled shape lay at their foot, a man dressed in a black cloak over a plain clerical cassock. His legs were spread-eagled and his trunk was half-turned as if he was asleep. As John knelt by the inert body, he saw that the head had been shaved into a tonsure, but by the stout staff lying alongside the man it was clear that this was one of the proctor's men, a night guard who had been patrolling the precinct. On his bald patch, a deep gash ran from side to side, dark blood still welling slowly from the wound.

The coroner feared that the man was already dead, but when he gently turned him on to his back he heard shallow breathing, though he was deeply unconscious.

'He probably fell down the stairs,' he muttered to his hound, but Brutus made no comment. 'So who was that bloody fellow who kicked you and ran, eh?'

There was nothing de Wolfe could do other than go for help. Using the lantern, he loped off as fast as he could to find someone.

Unfortunately, this was the quietest time in the cathedral, being the hours between afternoon Vespers and the midnight Matins, when most priests and their acolytes were either eating, drinking or sleeping.

John went into the nave of the cathedral through the small door in the West Front, but he could see no one up in the dimly lit presbytery beyond the choir screen. He hurried out again and decided to go to the proctor's hut in the Close, between two of the small churches that stood in the cluttered precinct. Here he found another proctor's man, huddled over a small fire, and within minutes they had both returned to the Chapter House, the proctor ringing a brass handbell vigorously to summon help.

Within minutes, two vicars-choral and a pair of secondaries, who were young men aspiring to be priests, appeared from somewhere in the recesses of the buildings and began fussing over the injured guard.

'Better take him to the archdeacon's house,' suggested the coroner, who knew that his friend John de Alençon, one of the four archdeacons, was a calm, sensible man who would procure the best aid for the stricken man. Using one of the benches, the four younger men carried the wounded man away, the other proctor lighting their path with a pair of lanterns.

'I'll come after you very shortly,' promised John. 'I need to look around here first.' Left alone, de Wolfe told Brutus to lie down while he cautiously climbed the stairs, the lantern and dagger still in his hands. There was no sound from the scriptorium above, but he wanted to make sure that no second intruder was lurking there. He made a slow circuit of the upper chamber, holding the small lantern high in the air, but he soon satisfied himself that the place was empty. He noticed that a number of books had been pulled from the shelves on to the reading boards and that some wooden boxes had been dragged into the outer aisle, their lids open and the contents in disorder.

Near the top of the stairs he saw a larger lantern lying on its side, the candle extinguished. Picking it up, he opened the small door that formed one of the sides of thinly shaved horn that allowed the light to escape. John sniffed at it and smelled the pungent odour of recently burned wax, guessing that the lamp had been used by whoever had run away from the building. As he came back down the stairs, the feeble rays of his own lantern showed a pool of drying blood where the head of the proctor had lain, but now he noticed something lying on the flagstones nearby. It must have been concealed by the injured man's body when he lay there, but now de Wolfe bent and picked it up. It was a thin but heavy book, almost the length of two of his hands and about an inch thick. He brought the lantern close to it and saw that it was covered in worn black leather, with a dozen or so parchment pages inside.

As he could not read any of it, he put it under his arm and, having satisfied himself that there was nothing else to be seen or done until daylight, he pulled the outer door shut and with a rather subdued Brutus at his heels made his way to Canons' Row on the north side of the Close, where the houses of a dozen of the most senior clergy stood.

In one of them lived his friend the Archdeacon of

Exeter, one of four archdeacons that served the diocese of Devon and Cornwall under Bishop Henry Marshal. A wiry, grey-haired man, John de Alençon lived a simple, ascetic life, unlike some of his portly fellow canons, and John found that the injured proctor had been laid in the priest's spartan sleeping room, which contained nothing but a hard cot, a stool and a large wooden cross on the wall.

'How is he?' asked the coroner as soon as he entered.

The archdeacon and one of the vicars who had come to the Chapter House were there, standing over the bed with worried expressions on their faces.

'He is very poorly, John. I have sent the other proctor up to St John's Priory to ask Brother Saulf if he will come down at once,' replied de Alençon. The nearest thing Exeter had to a hospital was the small priory of St John near the East Gate, which had a sickroom that offered help to the poorer people who could not afford to visit an apothecary. One of the Benedictine monks, a Saxon named Saulf, was skilled in physic and was often called upon in emergencies.

There was nothing the two Johns could do to help, so they went into another small room, where the archdeacon did his reading and writing. They sat at a table, and de Alençon's servant brought them a jug of wine and some pewter cups. As they sat and drank while waiting for the monk, John told his friend what had happened and showed him the book that he had found.

'I'm sure this is to do with this accursed treasure fever,' he said. 'It looks as if someone was rifling the library and was disturbed by the proctor. Whether he was assaulted or fell downstairs in a scuffle remains to be seen, but either way there is a dangerous man loose somewhere in the city.'

The archdeacon took the book and looked at it with

curiosity. 'This is very ancient, John. I've never seen the like of it.'

'What's it all about?' asked the coroner, curious to know what was so important that it may have cost a man his life.

De Alençon slowly turned the pages, shaking his head slowly in bewilderment. 'It seems to be a collection of quatrains of some kind. Written in excellent Latin and beautifully penned.'

'What the hell's a quatrain?' demanded the coroner. He sometimes tended to act the bluff soldier, partly to cover up his lack of learning.

'It's a short verse containing four lines, which rhyme alternately. As these are in Latin, they wouldn't rhyme in our Norman-French, John – but the meaning is still just about understandable.'

'But what's the subject they concern?' persisted de Wolfe. 'Is it a religious tract of some kind? Gospels or prayers?'

The archdeacon looked wryly at his friend. 'They seem far removed from prayers – almost the opposite! From the couple I've glanced at, they seem like forebodings of catastrophe. God knows what they mean, and I say that most reverently.'

He turned the yellowed pages over again, shaking his head in wonderment. 'It reminds me most of the Book of Revelation of St John – and few clerics understand that, though many pretend to.'

'But why would anyone wish to steal this most obscure book – and maybe even kill for it?' asked de Wolfe.

De Alençon shrugged. 'In desperation, perhaps? If you are right and this is part of the treasure-hunt fever, then having broken into our Chapter House and discovered nothing definite to aid his search, these obscure verses must have been the best he could manage to find that might speak of hidden treasure.'

The coroner mulled this over for a moment. 'Is there anyone who can tell us more about this book? Perhaps knowing something of its origins might lead us to whoever wanted to steal it?'

The archdeacon handed the book back to de Wolfe and made the sign of the cross on himself, as if to ward off any evil influences from having handled it. 'The obvious person is Jordan le Brent, our worthy archivist,' he suggested. 'Perhaps he knows where the book came from, though the disorder in that library is shameful. I hope that my nephew Thomas is able to improve matters with his labours there.'

John nodded as he rose to take his leave. 'My clerk is another who may have some ideas about this volume – he is a fount of information on almost every subject under the sun.'

It was the next morning before the coroner could show the book to Thomas de Peyne, and by that time he had had the news that the injured proctor had died, so he now had a killing to investigate, whether deliberate or by misadventure remained to be seen. Together with Gwyn, they sat in his chilly room above the gatehouse, huddled over a small brazier that Sergeant Gabriel had sent up to them. After de Wolfe had related the story, he handed the book to his clerk, who took it almost reverently.

'This is very ancient indeed, Crowner!' he said, carefully studying the covers and the contents. 'The style of binding suggests that it must be centuries old, and the manner of the penmanship is also archaic. It somehow reminds me of several Gospels that I have seen which came from Irish monasteries.'

'But what the hell is it all about?' demanded Gwyn gruffly.

Thomas turned the pages of thin animal skin and read a few of the verses, his lips moving soundlessly as he traced the words written in ink that was still jet-black after all this time. 'Latin quatrains, about a score of them. But no preface or dedication, nor any hint as to who the author may have been,' he mused. 'But I can see why my uncle suggested that the thief may have thought that treasure was involved . . . listen to this!'

Thomas cleared his throat and read out two lines from the middle of the book:

'Where sand and rock prevail beneath the sun,
Then gold galore bedecks the shrivelled king.'

There was a silence, broken by Gwyn belching and announcing that it meant nothing to him.

'You great Cornish barbarian!' complained the clerk. 'I merely quoted it to show that someone feverishly searching in the light of a candle for clues to treasure might grab this as the best chance he was likely to get.'

'We need another opinion on this,' said John. 'Your uncle suggested that Canon Jordan might have some ideas.'

Thomas nodded vigorously. He was greatly beholden to his uncle for getting him the post as coroner's clerk after his disgrace in Winchester and more recently as a part-time archivist under Jordan le Brent.

'Perhaps we could have a meeting with him this morning, master. And perhaps I could suggest that Brother Rufus could be included, as he served for some years in Ireland and is very knowledgeable about religious matters over there.'

The monk he mentioned was the amiable Benedictine who was the chaplain to Rougemont's garrison, possessed of insatiable curiosity but also with a wide experience of the world. The coroner agreed, and

Thomas went out into the icy streets to arrange the meeting for an hour before noon, after the morning devotions in the cathedral had finished. De Wolfe and Gwyn made their way to St John's Priory, not far from the bottom of Castle Hill, to see if Brother Saulf could throw any more light on the nature of the dead proctor's injuries.

The body was lying on the floor of a small room off the single ward, awaiting removal to the cathedral.

'As he is in holy orders, albeit minor ones, they want him back there to lie before the altar in a side chapel until he is buried,' explained the monk. He pulled back the sheet that covered the corpse of the proctor to reveal the injured scalp.

John and Gwyn, well used to wounds, peered at the laceration running across the shaven tonsure.

'Right on top of his head,' grunted Gwyn. 'Difficult to land right there and not bruise himself elsewhere, if he fell down the steps.'

John felt the edges of the wound, which were reddish-black and turned inwards against the shattered bone underneath, which moved ominously against his probing fingers.

'Cracked like an eggshell,' he muttered. 'I'd say he was hit on the head first and fell afterwards.'

Saulf, the gaunt Saxon monk, had also seen plenty of violence and agreed with the coroner. 'Could be an iron bar or somesuch.'

De Wolfe rose to his feet. 'He must have used some tool to break the locks on those boxes in the library. That might have been the weapon.'

As the assault had been in the precincts of the cathedral – and upon one of their own servants – John knew that the ecclesiastical authorities, especially the bishop, would fight against interference by the secular power in the shape of a coroner's inquest. He was not inclined to fight tooth and nail against this and decided that the clear circumstances allowed him to concentrate on finding the perpetrator, rather than confirming the obvious nature of the proctor's death.

They left the tiny infirmary and went back to Rougemont, where de Wolfe related to Henry de Furnellis what had happened. The sheriff was concerned at the news of a violent death, but as usual was content to let the coroner carry on with the investigation.

'You feel that this was definitely related to this mania for seeking buried treasure?' he asked. When John confirmed his belief, Henry shook his head in wonderment. 'I can't understand the greed of common people,' he said sadly. 'I had a message only an hour ago that yet another mound had been dug into out Crediton way. That's the third this week!'

The belief that there was treasure inside the numerous piles of earth and stones that dotted the countryside had been translated into frantic, though futile, activity since the first hoard had been discovered.

Thomas returned to say that both Canon Jordan le Brent and Brother Rufus would meet them before dinner at the tiny chapel of St Mary in the inner ward of the castle, where Rufus was the incumbent. The sheriff decided to join them, and at the appointed hour they assembled in the little church. The earthen floor was surrounded by a stone shelf meant for the old and infirm to rest upon, and here they sat while the archivist and the chaplain inspected the mysterious Black Book.

Jordan le Brent, a large, slightly obese priest, studied the covers and carefully turned the pages with an expression of increasing disbelief.

'To think that this has been in my archives for many years without my being aware of it!' he breathed. 'True, I have never had the time to delve through all those boxes of muddled documents, but it was remiss of me to miss finding such a unique book as this.'

As he handed it on to the Benedictine, a rather impatient John wanted answers. 'Have you any idea what it is and where it came from, canon?'

'No, Sir John, I have no idea! I inherited all the mass of material in the library some ten years ago. Much of it has been there since the present cathedral was begun in 1114, but I know that some of the parchments and books are even older, inherited from the previous abbey, which stood since Saxon times where the Lady Chapel now lies.'

'But what of its contents?' demanded Henry de Furnellis. 'I hear that they are most mystical and prophetic.'

The canon shook his head in despair. 'I cannot make any sense of the few I read just now. They seem to be the product of a fevered mind. I even wonder if they are saintly or devilish.'

'But it must be a work of considerable antiquity?' persisted the sheriff.

'From my long experience of written missives, it has to be at least several centuries since it was written and bound together,' answered the archivist. 'But there is no clue as to who did it and when.'

By now Brother Rufus had had the chance to study the book, and he closed it on his ample lap with an air of finality.

'I'm sure I have heard of this before,' he said in his mellow voice. 'Brother Thomas here is right, I think it came from Ireland.'

He uttered this with such confidence that the others turned to him in expectation, as he continued. 'I spent three years with the troops in that miserable island and visited many places, especially religious houses. I heard a thousand stories from those garrulous and superstitious Irish, and one of them was about a mystical book from long ago.'

With such an attentive audience, Rufus was in his element. 'Some of the older monks I met looked over their shoulders and crossed themselves when they mentioned it, for it seems that it was suppressed by the Irish Church and hidden away for centuries, then vanished altogether. No one knew where exactly it came from, but it was somewhere in the bog-ridden centre of the island.'

Thomas listened with rapt attention, as a combination of history, religion and mysticism was like manna from heaven to him. 'Why was this book so shunned by the Church, Rufus?'

'It was called the Black Book of Brân, who presumably was the monk who wrote it back in the mists of time. No one I had heard of had seen it, nor even met anyone who had, but it was held in awe, being a compendium of prophecies, some of which had already been fulfilled.'

'Who was this Brân?' asked the sheriff.

Thomas de Peyne piped up to answer this one from his compendious knowledge of history. 'In Celtic mythology, both in Ireland and Wales, he was a giant, the son of Llyr, the sea-god. He waded across the Irish Sea, towing his enemies' ships behind him.'

'Sounds a bit like Gwyn here,' commented the sheriff dryly.

'The head of Brân the Blessed is said to be buried on Tower Hill in London, where it defends these islands against invaders,' added Rufus.

'Didn't do much of a job, then,' muttered Henry, thinking of the Romans, the Saxons and his own Normans.

Rufus appeared to have exhausted his knowledge of the mysterious Irish book and further questions could draw forth no more information from him. Jordan le Brent looked disturbed and took the book back from Rufus with reluctant hands.

'It sounds as if this may be a dangerous relic,' he said sombrely. 'I doubt if it should remain in our cathedral if it has this bad reputation from our Irish brothers-in-God.'

Thomas looked concerned, as he did not want to lose such an intriguing item before he had a chance to study it in depth.

'What should be done with it, then, canon?' he asked. 'Surely it has too great a historical value to be destroyed! It may be part of the heritage of our early Christian Church.'

The archivist shook his head. 'No, that might be sacrilege, but it is not for us to decide. I will suggest to the bishop that it be sent to Canterbury – let them ponder it and possibly send it on to Rome. The Holy Father has a secure vault in the basements of the Vatican where suspect volumes may be carefully hidden from the sight of man.'

Young Thomas had his own ideas about that, but at this moment he wisely kept them to himself.

In the Bush that evening, John de Wolfe sat at his usual table by the firepit, which on such a bleak night was full of glowing logs. He had his arm around his auburn-haired mistress, and on the other side of the table Gwyn sat huddled in his frayed leather jerkin, with a quart of ale and a large meat pie.

'So what help did we get today from that coven of priests, Crowner?' grumbled the big Cornishman. 'Didn't get us any nearer discovering who belted that proctor over the head.'

John had already told Nesta the story of the Black Book of Brân and as a strongly religious Celt herself, with a reputation for being somewhat fey in matters of magic, she was intensely interested.

'Whether or not it helped you, it is a miraculous find,' she said. 'I only wish that I could read, for there must be things of great importance written there.'

'It may be the work of the devil, not the angels!' grunted Gwyn, himself a superstitious Celt. 'But what use is it to us in finding a killer?'

Nesta contributed some of her usual common sense. 'Stealing such a book means that it was a person who could read Latin. Otherwise, the thief could not even see that treasure was mentioned in one of these strange verses.'

John squeezed her closer, proud that his mistress had such a sharp mind. 'It also means that it could not have been some rough villain sent by a more learned rascal, for as you say he would not be able to find useful documents unless he could decipher them.'

'So are we looking for some priest?' asked Gwyn before swilling down the rest of his ale.

'A clerk, certainly, but not necessarily a priest. Almost no one, except a few rich barons and knights who have been to a school, have the gift of reading and writing, apart from those in holy orders.'

Ordained priests and deacons were far outnumbered by a whole range of lesser clerics, ranging from sub-deacons and lectors down to mere doorkeepers. Many clerks worked not in the Church but in the courts and commerce, as they formed the elite five per cent of the population who were literate.

'I suppose it narrows it down,' grumbled Gwyn. 'But that leaves us with a few hundred clerks in the city alone – and God knows how many elsewhere in Devon!'

Nesta looked up at her lover's stern face, the jaws darkened by black stubble, as it was some days since his last weekly shave.

'John, how are you going to pursue this killer?' she asked, her big hazel eyes full of concern. 'As Gwyn says, you have so many possible culprits, but no clue as to where to start.'

De Wolfe tapped the fingers of his free hand on the edge of the rough boards of the table, his frown indicating deep thought. 'Something the sheriff said today gives me an idea,' he said at last. 'If you can't catch a rabbit by running after it, you must set a trap!'

It might be an exaggeration to say that Thomas de Peyne was ecstatic, but he was certainly blissfully content at being both back in the bosom of his beloved Church after his time in the wilderness – and with a literary problem before him. He was crouched over his desk in the cathedral library, reading by the light of a solitary candle, oblivious for once of the biting cold.

The whole Chapter House was deserted at this eighth hour of the evening, and normally the timid little clerk would have been nervous at being alone in a cavernous chamber where a man had been done to death not many hours before. But his absorption in the pages of the Black Book left no room for fear, as he avidly read through the pages of vellum which bore the strange verses.

Further discussion with Brother Rufus and Canon Jordan earlier that day had brought them to the conclusion that the book had probably been brought to Exeter in the early years following the Norman invasion of Ireland, which began in 1170.

'We were not all honourable men in that campaign,' the chaplain of Rougemont had boomed. 'There was a great deal of looting by foot soldiers, mercenaries and indeed the nobles themselves. The churches, abbeys and priories were not always immune, I fear. This book may have been gathered up during the pillaging of some religious house.'

The old archivist had agreed and said that he recalled that several local knights who had returned from that campaign had donated various gifts to the cathedral, probably spurred by a guilty conscience. 'Anything vaguely literary may well have been dumped up in the library and forgotten,' he said ruefully.

Now Thomas was going through the mysterious book, carefully digesting each obscure quatrain and trying to make sense of the messages they must contain. There were two verses on each sheet of parchment, neatly centred on the pages. The jet-black ink looked fresh, though the brittleness of the leaves and the patina on the leather casing of the wooden covers betrayed its age.

For several hours the little priest pored over the verses, and all he managed were questions rather than answers. Who was this Brân who had written the quatrains? Where and when had he done it? And, most important, *why* had he felt impelled to write them?

Thomas puzzled over the references to plague and Tartarus' hordes and catamite kings – all of which meant nothing to him.

Other questions slid unbidden into his mind. Were these actual prophecies and, if so, were they in chronological order? And what time span did they cover – a hundred years or a millennium or eternity itself? And how could any reader identify whether a disaster – for that was what they seemed to foretell – would occur in his lifetime, as opposed to in the past or future?

When he had finished reading the twenty-four quatrains through for the third time, Thomas closed the book and sat back, his eyes closed as he tried to assemble his thoughts. One thing was clear to him, even though he felt guilty about his possible duplicity.

Canon Jordan seemed adamant that this book might be an evil influence and so should be surrendered to higher episcopal or even papal authority. If that were done, the Exeter archives would lose something of possibly great religious and academic value. There and then, Thomas decided that he would make a fair copy himself, so that even if Brân's original was taken from them, the library would at least have a record of the quatrains for further study. Surely, he told himself, even if there were some demoniac properties in the Black Book, they could not be transferred over to a mere transcript on virgin parchment. Spurred by the thought that the archivist and the bishop might act quickly and dispatch the book to Canterbury before he had time to study every verse, Thomas set to that very minute in making a copy. There was ample parchment lying around the library, as the treasury clerks and those who had to write the timetables and orders of service for the precentor kept a store in their desks. Thomas went around the room and took a couple of sheets from each place, then settled down with a fresh candle to begin his copying. He reckoned it would take him until tomorrow evening to finish the verses, given his other duties next day, then he could bind them himself. The simple materials of wood, leather and cord were kept in the library for this purpose, and Thomas was quite capable of threading a dozen pages between two thin sheets of wood and gluing leather across them. Once he had a copy, then he could concentrate on trying to decipher their meaning at his leisure, for this presented a challenge that his nimble mind relished.

Late into the night, he remained hunched over his desk, the only sounds being the scratch of a goose quill and the occasional sniff as his sharp nose became even redder in the freezing air.

It was almost midnight when he gave up, to go across to the cathedral for Matins and then back to his lodgings before the next service at dawn.

The wide-ranging duties of a coroner included many events apart from investigating sudden and violent deaths. As well as having to hold inquests on finds of treasure, any catches of 'royal fish' – the whale and the sturgeon – came within his jurisdiction, as they belonged to the king. But on the day following Thomas's nocturnal labours in the library, John de Wolfe was called to yet another category of his responsibilities. Not fire or rape this time, but a serious assault. These could often prove fatal, given the lack of effective medical treatment, and sometimes coroners would commit the care of the injured victim to the assailant, the reasoning being that the latter had a powerful motive for keeping the man alive, as if he died within a year and a day the perpetrator would be hanged for murder!

However, this time the victim was badly bruised and shaken but not in any serious danger of dying. De Wolfe, with Gwyn and Thomas at his side, rode out a few miles east of Exeter to the village of Clyst St Mary in answer to a plea from the manor reeve, the man responsible for organizing the labour force of the hamlet. He had ridden to Rougemont that morning to report that the bailiff had been assaulted by three men the previous evening. The bailiff was the representative of the manor lord, in this case the Bishop of Coutances, who was far away in Normandy.

'The lad who herds the pigs raised the alarm,' said the reeve as he rode alongside the coroner for the last half-mile into the village. 'Simple in his wits, but he knew when something was wrong.'

'You say this was in a field where there was a mound?' demanded John.

'Well, not a field as such, but in the wasteland between the pasture and the edge of the forest. There's a grassy heap the height of a man – the old wives say it has been there since the days of Adam and Eve, though how they could know that beats me!'

'How could your pig-boy see what happened if it was dark?' objected Gwyn.

'He saw the flickering lights of a lantern and crept up to have a look. The moon was more than half-full last night, so he could see a fair bit. There were three men, digging into the side of the mound, so he ran back to the bailiff's dwelling to tell him.'

'What happened then?' asked de Wolfe.

'Walter Tremble, our bailiff, called me out of my cottage and we went up there to see what was amiss. Sure enough, there were three fellows there, two of them with a pick and a shovel, digging like rabbits. Walter has a short temper and he ran ahead of me, shouting fit to burst.'

As they came within sight of Clyst St Mary, the long-winded reeve came to the climax of his story.

'The one with the lantern straightway turned and ran, but the diggers stood their ground, and when Walter reached them they set about him with their tools. He's a big man, the bailiff, but he had no chance against a pick and shovel wielded by two desperate men.'

'Why didn't you go to his aid?' growled Gwyn.

'I did, but I've got a stiff leg and was way behind Walter,' he whined by way of excuse. 'My breathing's not so good either. I'm not much use in a fight. Anyway, these men after beating the bailiff to the ground ran off into the darkness after the first man. I was more concerned about getting aid for Walter than chasing them,' he added virtuously.

'Could you see anything of them?' asked the coroner. 'Were they local men, d'you think?'

'Too dark to see, sir, even with a bit of a moon. But I got the impression that the first one, the one with the lantern, had a long habit on, down to his ankles. I thought he might have been a priest.'

'We'll have to ask the bailiff. He obviously got a lot nearer than you, reeve!' growled de Wolfe sarcastically.

They had the opportunity a few minutes later as they were led to the only stone house in the village, next to the church. The parish priest had to put up with a meaner one of timber, but the absent bishop had installed his bailiff in a more substantial dwelling. In a small room off the main chamber, they found Walter Tremble groaning on a feather-filled pallet on the floor, his stout wife hovering anxiously with a hot poultice for the bruising on his chest. He looked a sorry sight, with livid purple bruising down one side of his face, puffy lids closing his right eye and numerous scratches on both arms.

However, his injuries did not prevent him from lacing his story with numerous oaths and blasphemies as he told the coroner what had happened.

'They set upon me the moment I approached the bastards!' he mumbled through swollen lips. 'Struck me with a shovel and the handle of a pick before running away into the darkness, the cowardly swine!'

He could add little to what the reeve had already said, apart from claiming that the two diggers were large men, dressed in dark clothing, one with a sack around his shoulders.

'What about the one with the lantern?' asked Gwyn.

'That sod was much smaller, but he ran off before I got to the mound,' replied the bailiff. 'He was dressed in black, a long tunic like the one your clerk is wearing.' He nodded painfully at Thomas, whose rather threadbare cassock was slit up the sides for riding a horse.

There was no more to be learned from Walter, and with some muttered platitudes about trusting that he would soon be recovered de Wolfe took his leave, asking the reeve to show them where the assault had taken place. On the other side of the village, past the strip-fields that ran at right angles to the track, was an area of meadow, the grass now short and stiff with frost. Beyond that was the wasteland, a large area where trees had been felled to increase the arable area but which still had trunks and roots sticking up as far as the edge of the dark forest. At the top of this slope was a grassy mound, disfigured on one side by fresh red earth thrown out of an excavation a couple of feet deep.

'They didn't get very far down, as we disturbed them,' said the reeve. 'Anyway, they were wasting their time, as my father told me that his father and some other men had dug right through it fifty years ago and found nothing but some old pots and bones.'

On the way back to Exeter, John de Wolfe mused on what little they had learned in Clyst St Mary. 'The bailiff will survive, but what happened is part of this mania that is sweeping the district. They'll be digging into molehills next in the hope of finding gold!'

Thomas had a question, as usual. 'Are these the same men who attacked the proctor, I wonder?'

'No reason to think so,' grunted Gwyn. 'Every jackass in the county is wielding a spade these days.'

'But they were very violent and both the reeve and the bailiff had the notion that one of them was a cleric,' objected Thomas.

'You may be right, young man,' agreed de Wolfe. 'I think it's time we set that trap I mentioned, but it must be done carefully to catch the right vermin.'

That night the coroner's clerk finished his copy of the Black Book and spent until the midnight hour stitching the few pages into the covers. Having spent much of his life with books and documents, he was quite adept at simple assembling and binding. Encasing Brân's book with leather would have to wait until another day, as he needed to get some more oxhide glue from a tannery on Exe Island.

After morning services had finished in the cathedral, Thomas could not resist studying the quatrains yet again and gave up his dinner to go back to the library and pore over the obscure verses. He was particularly anxious to see if he could recognize any that might have relevance to the present time, but another two hours' study left him as baffled as ever. Some of the other clerks were very curious as to what he was doing, and as they all knew of the circumstances of the ransacking of the library and the killing of the proctor Thomas had no option but to tell them of the Black Book and to show it to them, as clerics were more nosy and gossipy than most goodwives in the marketplace.

Later that day he returned with the glue to sheath the boards in thin black leather, trying to make the copy as similar as he could to the original ancient tome. With the book in a screw-press in the corner of the upper room, to allow the glue to set, he decided to take the original back to his lodgings in Priest Street[1], so that he could spend more hours on it that evening. With a couple of candle ends salvaged from a side altar, he once again sat to rack his brains over the strange verses. He shared the small room with a vicar-choral, for, as the name suggested, many of the houses in Priest Street were rented out as tenements to junior clerics. Tonight, his roommate had gone to visit his sick sister in the city, and Thomas was glad of the solitude to puzzle over Brân's prophecies.

[1] Now Preston Street

Once again he carefully read through the two dozen quatrains, searching for anything that might suggest a contemporary meaning. Eventually, he settled on one that with a stretch of imagination might relate to the present time. It was the fifth in the series, and his lips again whispered the words as he read them through once more:

'When three golden beasts did reign by bishop's rule,
A bearded champion fought oppression's realm,
His secret horde defied the edicts cruel,
But all was lost beneath the budding elm.'

Thomas huddled deeper into his thin cloak, as the only fire in the house was in a communal room at the back and the cold seemed to be addling his mind.

'Only the first line means anything to me,' he murmured to himself, wiping a dewdrop from the end of his nose with the back of his hand. '"When three golden beasts did reign by bishop's rule . . ." Surely that could mean the kingship of our sovereign Richard the Lionheart?' He reasoned that this could refer to the new heraldic device adopted by Richard, showing three golden lions couchant on a red field. And surely the 'bishop's rule' by which they reigned could be Hubert Walter's regency, as the Prelate of Canterbury and Chief Justiciar had been given absolute control of England by the Lionheart, who seemed uninterested in ever returning to his island kingdom.

But what on God's earth did the other three lines mean? It could be something that was going to happen during Richard's reign, but that might last another thirty years, if his father Henry's monarchy was anything to go by. And where would it happen, in England or abroad? Exeter was further from London than parts of France, so news of what was happening in the capital percolated slowly and imperfectly down to Devon. Maybe there was some bearded champion rampant at the other end of England, for all Thomas knew.

He had a faint glimmer of intuition about 'edicts cruel', as it was common knowledge that the harsh taxation imposed by the king through Hubert Walter was increasingly unpopular everywhere, especially in the cities, where the brunt of the levy was suffered. King Richard's insatiable demand for more money to finance his army fighting to regain lands lost to Philip of France by his brother Prince John was becoming so painful to barons, the Church and common folk alike that whispers of rebellion had been heard here and there.

But that still made no sense of the rest of the verse – the 'budding elm' meant nothing to Thomas, nor did the 'secret horde'. He sat brooding at the small table that, apart from one stool and two mattresses on the floor, was the only furniture in the room. Who else could he discuss this with, he wondered? Canon Jordan seemed almost frightened of the Black Book and wanted to get rid of it, let alone discuss its contents. Brother Rufus was happy to talk about it, but Thomas suspected that their already lengthy discussions had exhausted the chaplain's knowledge and ideas.

Perhaps the vicar who shared the room might be a foil upon whom he could bounce some ideas? Peter Quinel was not the brightest star in the cathedral's priesthood, but he was an amiable and willing fellow and Thomas looked forward to showing him the verses and asking his opinion.

Some time later he heard the outer door opening, one that led from the street into a common passageway to the several rooms. He looked up expectantly, eager to engage Peter in discussion, but the heavy leather flap that closed the doorway of their room did not swing aside. Instead, he heard voices whispering outside, and with some trepidation the little clerk got up to see who was there. As he did so, two men burst into the room, large and menacing in the dim light. With a screech of terror, Thomas backed away, but he was bowled over in the small chamber and fell flying, thankfully across one of the beds.

'There it is! On the table,' growled one of the intruders, grabbing the Black Book. Almost paralysed with fright and expecting to be beaten to death like the proctor, Thomas cowered on the floor, shielding his head with his arms. In a trice, the two men had vanished as quickly as they had come, still muffled up in dark mantles, hoods pulled down over their faces.

Whimpering with fear, for he made no claims to be a hero, Thomas staggered to his feet as he heard the street door slam shut. He waited a moment to make sure the assailants had gone, then pushed his way into the passage and started shouting for the other residents, who were all asleep, making the most of the few hours before they had to get up for midnight Mass.

A few minutes later, after telling his story of the violent robbery, a couple of the bolder young priests ventured out into the street, but all they could do was to stare futilely up and down the empty lane for the thieves, who had long vanished into the darkness.

Next morning the coroner was furious when he heard of Thomas's ordeal and the theft of the old book. He had no particular interest in it as such, other than as a possible lead to the murderers of the proctor, but as it had led to the attack on his clerk's privacy and person, he was angry that an inoffensive little priest should have been exposed to such a fright.

'Are these the same bastards who killed that

proctor?' asked Gwyn, who for all his teasing of Thomas was very protective of him against all comers.

De Wolfe was pacing restlessly up and down his chamber, his long face creased by a ferocious scowl. 'I saw only one man running away from the Chapter House, but that affair in Clyst St Mary suggests that three of the swine are involved. They seem to operate only at night and wear dark clothing.' He swung around to face his clerk, who as usual sat at the table with a quill in his hand. 'Was there any sign of a third man last night, Thomas?'

'Not in the room, Crowner. There may have been one in the passageway or at the street door, but I did not venture out until they had gone.'

'And nothing about them suggested a priest this time?'

The clerk shook his head. 'They wore black, as you said, but not clerical garb – though I admit my mind was not on such matters during the few seconds they were in the room!'

'You said one of them spoke,' grunted Gwyn 'Was it a voice you recognized?'

'All he said was "There's the book" or somesuch words. It was a local voice, but not particularly coarse like some labouring peasant.'

John paced a few more turns around the bleak room. 'The one who attacked the proctor must have been able to read, to pick upon that particular book with a mention of treasure in one of the verses,' he said. 'But last night any ruffian could have recognized a black book without being able to read it.'

Gwyn, who was sitting on a window ledge whittling a piece of stick with his dagger, raised another question. 'How could they have known that Thomas had taken the book home that evening?'

De Wolfe stopped loping around the chamber to

stare Thomas in the face. 'Did you tell anyone about it?' he demanded.

Defensively, the clerk stammered that all the other clerks in the scriptorium knew about it and any of them could have seen him put the book into his shoulder bag when he left for the day.

'So this is another priestly connection!' snapped the coroner. 'You clerks all gossip like fishwives in a gutting-shed, so any of them might be our clerical thief.'

Thomas shrugged. 'I doubt if any of the scribes in the library were involved, for they could have stolen the book there or even taken the copy that I left in the press. But, of course, they could have told others outside the Chapter House about it.'

John smacked one hand into his palm. 'I'm sure we're looking for a priest, one who has a pair of accomplices. Whether he is one of the cathedral crowd or a parish vicar from the city, there's a bloody priest behind all this!'

He stalked to his stool on the other side of the table and sat down, his face screwed up into an expression of deep concentration.

'Thomas, take a leaf of old, used parchment and write in Latin something to this effect!'

Half an hour later Thomas de Peyne left the gate-house tower with a creased and grubby palimpsest in his hand – and a sly grin on his face.

Later that morning Thomas returned to the library chamber over the Chapter House and took his newly bound copy of the book from the press. He was pleased with the result, the leather having bonded firmly to the boards without bubbles and the covers opening easily to display the neatly inscribed pages. He took it to his desk and began to study the verses once again but was soon disturbed by several of the other clerks, who sidled up and began enquiring about his well-being after 'the awful experience' of the night before. Inevitably, the word had got around about the attack upon him and the theft of the book, as several of the young clerics also lodged in Priest Street.

Though their protestations of concern were mostly genuine, Thomas sensed that they were also fishing for any news of his interpretation of the Black Book, all being well aware that he had made a copy. Conscious of the fact that any of them might have taken the news of the original, deliberately or inadvertently, to whoever had stolen it, he played the role that the coroner had suggested to him.

'I have made some progress, I admit,' he said rather coyly. 'I cannot divulge what it is, of course. It's a matter only for the ears of the coroner and the sheriff.'

Ignoring their wheedling to give them some hint of what he may have found in relation to hidden treasure, he went back to the study of his new copy, concealing the pages from their avaricious eyes by hunching his arm over them. Then, with the eyes of his colleagues flicking over him at frequent intervals, he covertly began writing on a sheet of parchment laid alongside the book – though no one could see that he failed to dip his quill deeply enough into the ink pot, as the document had already been written earlier, back in the gatehouse of Rougemont.

After almost an hour, during which he usefully employed his time by once more puzzling over the obscure quatrains, Thomas rose from his stool and, with Brân's copy ostentatiously tucked under his arm, moved to the head of the steps.

'I need the privy,' he murmured to a young secondary sitting nearby as he left the scriptorium for the nether regions. As he went, he made sure that the piece of parchment slipped from between the pages of the book and fluttered to the floor.

When he returned a few minutes later, the apprentice priest handed him the fallen sheet with a mumbled explanation that he had dropped it on the way out. Thomas knew from his furtive expression that he had read it and probably already shared the contents with the other clerks. With a secret smile, the coroner's scribe went back to his place and this time returned to his study of the verses in earnest, as they had by now become a challenge to him that he could not resist.

'Do you really think this is going to work, Crowner?'

Gwyn sounded grumpy, as faithful though he was he would much rather be sitting by the fire in the Bush, with a mutton chop and a quart of Nesta's best ale, than crouched in St Bartholomew's churchyard in the biting frost. Alongside him in the lee of the little wooden church were John de Wolfe and Sergeant Gabriel, who had hidden four of his men-at-arms at strategic points around the edge of the enclosure.

'We can but try, as I can think of no other way of catching these bastards red-handed,' replied John in a low voice.

It was about the middle of the evening and the moon was showing itself fitfully between the masses of cloud that an east wind blew across the sky.

The churchyard was mainly rough grass and a few trees, as no burials had taken place here since the cathedral had long ago appropriated all the lucrative funerals to itself. In the centre stood an old plinth on which were the remains of a Saxon cross and this John had used as his bait, reckoning that a similar one in Alphington was now well known as the hiding-place of treasure.

'But why tonight, sir?' asked Gabriel, his voice like a rusty file on a blunt axe. 'They may leave it a week before searching.'

'Never, not in this present mood of hysteria,' said de Wolfe confidently. 'By now those Chapter House gossips will have spread the news amongst all their priestly friends. If any clerical treasure-hunter in Exeter has heard it, he'll be down here hotfoot before any other thieving swine can beat him to it – and that means tonight!'

They settled down again to wait, shivering under their cloaks and jerkins. Gwyn had a striped woollen cap on his unruly ginger hair and a sack wrapped around his shoulders, while the coroner wore an old gambeson under his wolf-skin mantle. The gambeson was a legacy of his fighting days, a quilted coat of padded wool, worn under his chain mail to absorb the blows from a lance or sword.

St Bartholomew's was in the poorest section of the city, down in the north-western corner called Bretayne, named after the surviving Britons who had been driven down into a slum area by the invading Saxons centuries before. The churchyard was the only open space in a maze of sordid lanes and alleys, lined by mean huts and hovels, infested by rats, hogs and goats. Realistically, it was probably the least likely place in Exeter where a rich Saxon would have hidden his treasure from the next wave of invaders, but de Wolfe felt that the lure of gold and silver would overrule such logical appraisal.

An hour passed and, with limbs becoming cramped and frozen, John began to wonder if his reasoning might have been too optimistic. Gwyn was blowing on his fingers to get some feeling back into them, and the sergeant's teeth were chattering audibly.

The coroner was beginning to consider calling off their attempt to trap the treasure-seekers when he heard the creaking of the old gate that led into the churchyard from the lane. Nudging Gwyn and Gabriel to keep quiet, he stared into the blackness under an oak tree that overshadowed the gate, waiting until whoever it was came into the open, where a transient glimmer of moonlight fell upon the path.

Like moving shadows, three black figures glided into the light, one smaller than the other two. A tiny crack of yellow light revealed that this man carried a horn lantern whose ill-fitting door failed to mask every glimmer. Many less hard-bitten persons than the trio of old soldiers might have fled at the sight of these silent black figures flitting through an abandoned graveyard.

De Wolfe put a restraining hand on each of his companions and hoped that the hidden soldiers would obey their sergeant's orders not to move until commanded. The three ghostly shapes moved silently towards the centre of the overgrown area where the base of the broken cross was half-hidden in weeds.

Suddenly, a dim shaft of light fell upon the old stones as the door of the lantern was opened. Faint scraping noises began as shovels were used to push aside the rampant undergrowth around the cross. This was the signal for action, and de Wolfe rapped Gabriel on the shoulder as he and Gwyn stood up.

'Right, men! Seize these fellows!' roared the sergeant.

As they began running towards the centre of the churchyard, four other figures erupted from the bushes and converged on the startled men. They attempted a dash for the gate, but were met by solid muscles and were forced down upon the ground amid strident curses and protests. Gwyn grabbed the lantern and held it up as the soldiers pinned the robbers down.

'Who the hell are these knaves?' he roared, giving a hefty kick in the ribs to one who was wriggling violently.

The coroner hovered over them like some black hawk, as Gabriel pulled away the hoods from their faces. John did not recognize any of them, but he felt that they did not have the coarse features or rough dress of the usual violent robber.

'I know who this one is, sergeant!' cried one of the men-at-arms in surprise. 'He's the priest from St Lawrence's.'

John felt a glow of satisfaction as his theory about a thieving priest was vindicated. If the soldier was right, this was the incumbent of the church of St Lawrence, in the eastern part of High Street.

At that moment the man in question was unable to confirm or deny his identity, as Gwyn was helping to pin him to the ground with a large foot placed on his throat. When he was released, he began gasping and gurgling, then launched into a series of lurid oaths unbecoming of a man of the cloth, until the coroner snarled at him. 'What's your name, villain?'

'I am Ranulf de Fougères, an ordained priest of this diocese, damn you!' howled the man. 'Release me and my cousins this instant or the bishop will hear of this!'

Gwyn gave a roar of laughter. 'He'll hear of it right enough! Perhaps he'll also attend your hanging.'

De Wolfe was more interested in what Ranulf had said. 'Your cousins, eh? Are they both priests as well?'

The other two were still struggling in the grip of the soldiers, and John saw in the dim light that one had a shaven tonsure. They were both big men and had an equally large vocabulary of foul language.

At a sign from de Wolfe, Gabriel and Gwyn hauled the vicar of St Lawrence back on to his feet but kept a firm grip on his arms as he spluttered a reply to John's question.

'They are most certainly in lower orders of the Holy Church and like me claim benefit of clergy! We demand to be released at once; you have no jurisdiction over us.'

Ranulf was a narrow-faced weasel of a fellow, full of bluster and self-righteousness. 'We are on consecrated ground here in Church property. You are trespassing!'

It was the coroner's turn to laugh now. 'You bloody fool! Just accept that you've been caught! We'll gladly turn you over to the bishop. There are still enough proctors in the cathedral precinct to keep you locked up, even though you killed one of them!'

At this, one of the cousins let out a howl. 'It wasn't me, it was Simon here . . . though he says the proctor fell down the stairs.'

The other man struggled anew, this time trying to get at his relative. 'Shut up, you lying bastard! I wasn't even there. It was you that Ranulf sent to ransack the books!'

A barrage of accusations and insults began between the three miscreants, until the men-at-arms cuffed them into grumbling silence. De Wolfe, frozen to his bones and out of patience with the squabbling clerics, told Gabriel to march the prisoners back to Rougement and put them in the cells.

'A night in that hellhole under the keep will cool their tempers!' he growled. 'Then in the morning the sheriff can negotiate with the bishop or the archdeacon about what happens to them. They won't be very happy with a bunch of renegade clerics who have murdered one of their proctors!'

The next afternoon John called upon his friend John de Alençon to learn what the episcopal authorities had decided. As he had expected, the Church had closed ranks and refused to let the secular powers deal with the charges of murder and two assaults, as well as the theft of the Black Book and the illegal digging into a mound at Clyst St Mary.

Over a cup of wine in the archdeacon's house, the wiry cleric told the coroner of that day's meeting between Bishop Henry Marshal and the sheriff, which he had attended.

'It was fortunate that His Grace was present in Exeter today, for much of the time he is away dealing with his various political interests,' said de Alençon with a touch of sarcasm.

It was well known that the bishop was one of Prince John's supporters in his long-running campaign to unseat his brother Richard from the throne. Henry Marshal had come perilously near a charge of treason over the prince's abortive rebellion when the Lionheart was imprisoned in Germany.

However, today's problem was untainted by politics, and the bishop had no hesitation in requiring the sheriff to hand over the three clerical culprits to his custody for trial by his consistory court, instead of the usual machinery of the criminal law.

'So they'll not hang, that's for sure,' said de Alençon. 'But our court will undoubtedly be hard on them, for the dead victim was one of our tonsured servants – and, of course, they also assaulted a priest, your clerk Thomas. My poor nephew always seems to be in trouble of some sort!'

'He spends much of his time trying to make sense of that damned book that is partly at the root of this trouble,' observed de Wolfe. 'What happened to it, by the way?'

'It was found in Ranulf's house when it was searched early this morning,' replied the archdeacon. 'It proves that they were the ones who robbed little Thomas. The book is back in the archives, now locked away by Jordan le Brent, who seems frightened by it.'

'What will happen to it, I wonder?'

'Canon Jordan intends to dispatch it to Westminster

as soon as possible. It seems the bishop has decided that Hubert Walter should see it first, as he spends more time there running the country than attending to the affairs of God in Canterbury.'

Once again a sarcastic note entered de Alençon's voice.

De Wolfe drank some more of the archdeacon's excellent wine before ruminating about the men he had arrested.

'It seems odd that an ordained priest and two in lesser holy orders should have embarked on a campaign of violence and robbery,' he observed.

'As its says in Paul's epistle to Timothy, "the love of money is the root of all evil" ', replied the archdeacon sadly. 'Our calling is no different from any other trade or profession, John. We have all types of men, some saintly, others pushed into the role because they were orphaned into the care of the Church as infants, rather than being called by God.'

'Have these men confessed their guilt?' asked the coroner.

De Alençon shrugged. 'They could hardly deny being involved, being caught digging and with that Black Book in their possession. But they claim that the proctor accidentally fell down the stairs, though you say that his wound was a deliberate blow. They also protest that digging for treasure is no crime, as if they had found anything they would have declared it to the sheriff.'

'A likely story!' rasped de Wolfe. 'And what about robbing Thomas and assaulting the bailiff of Clyst St Mary?'

'They flatly deny being anywhere near that village, but I suspect that a few weeks in the dismal cells the proctors use will create such discord between them that one of them will start blaming the others.'

'And poor Thomas?'

It was so often 'poor' Thomas, as the woebegone little clerk seemed to engender pity wherever he went.

'They say they only wanted to borrow the book and that as it was Church property they had every right to see it. Once again, they claim that Thomas tripped and fell, quite accidentally.'

'Too many folk become accident-prone when those three are around!!' grunted the coroner cynically. 'It's fortunate for them that they didn't contrive their accidents in Tavistock, for the abbot there has his own private gallows!'

By the end of the week, Thomas de Peyne had had enough of the Black Book of Brân. Though restored to the library, it remained locked in one of the iron-banded boxes until such time as Jordan le Brent could arrange for it to be sent to London, so Thomas worked from the copy he had made. Poring over the text occupied all his free time, as he wrestled with the challenge of the obscure quatrains.

His initial enthusiasm to decipher the verses had gradually changed into frustration, as no matter what new ideas he applied to the meanings, nothing remotely satisfactory emerged. With no idea of the timescale over which the prophecies ranged and no clue as to whether they were consecutive in relation to the passing of the years, he had nothing concrete to work with.

His only conclusion, which was little more than an intuitive guess, was that the quatrain that contained the phrases 'three golden beasts' and 'bishop's rule' must surely refer to the present reign, but, even if true, which year was involved?

In irritation, for anger was not an emotion that came easily to the mild-mannered clerk, he closed his copy of the book and banged his fist upon the cover.

'This is sheer nonsense!' he muttered to himself. 'I am wasting the precious time that the Almighty gave me to praise Him and study His works in fretting over the ravings of an ancient madman! I could write such verses myself that would contain as much or as little sense as these pointless babblings.'

On an impulse he opened the book again to the last page and drew his pen and ink bottle towards him.

After a moment's thought he dipped his quill into the little well and began writing in his impeccably regular script.

Though portents dire do fill with dread
And great significance implanted here,
Take care to always use your head,
Seek out the lie, for then your way is clear.

When he had completed the last line, he laid down his pen and sat back, feeling slightly guilty but also elated that he had struck a small blow for common sense in warning off any future readers of this farrago of nonsense that presumed to anticipate the pre-destination that God had ordained for man.

Three weeks later, after Canon Jordan had insisted that his copy be sent with the original to London, Thomas wished that he had not been so precipitate in interfering with the prognostications of that venerable Irish monk.

Henry de Furnellis had been on his twice-yearly pilgrimage to Winchester, taking the county 'farm' to the Exchequer, the taxes that his agents had extracted from the reluctant inhabitants of Devonshire. This time, in addition to the thousands of silver pennies in panniers on the packhorses' backs, he had included the two valuable hoards unearthed in the recent wave of treasure-hunting around Exeter.

However, it was not news about this that the sheriff brought back but of sensational tidings that had reached Winchester from its twin capital, London. On the day that he returned, Henry called his friends and officials together in the hall of Rougemont's keep. De Wolfe was there with his officer and clerk, together with Ralph the constable, several archdeacons, Rufus the chaplain, the two portreeves who headed the city council, a number of the more prominent burgesses and merchants and several of the sheriff's senior clerks.

Though travel-weary after his days on the road, the old sheriff was still able to give them a dramatic account of what had been going on in London. The only way in which such news travelled across the country was by word of mouth like this, though sometimes it was conveyed by official heralds sent by the Curia Regis to inform the county sheriffs of important events.

With his audience sitting at benches around the trestle tables or leaning against the walls, de Furnellis stood with folded arms and delivered himself of a speech, his bloodhound face more animated than usual.

'England – or at least London and the surrounding counties – has just narrowly escaped a massive revolt of the common people against authority. It seems that only drastic and determined action by Hubert Walter, the Justiciar, averted a blood-bath! However, he has not come out of this well, especially amongst the ecclesiastical community, for the memories of old King Henry and Becket are still lingering.'

He stopped to gulp from the ale-pot in front of him, and there were some subdued murmurings of expectation from his listeners.

'To cut to the quick of it, the merchants and common people of London and nearby towns have been becoming more and more resentful of the increasing taxes imposed on them by the king and his council. They became even more hostile when a new tax, the *taillage*, was imposed – because the amount each citizen was made to pay was decided by a jury. But it seems this jury was made up only of the richer folk, who conspired to virtually exempt themselves and lay most of the burden on the more lowly citizens!'

There was a revival of the outraged murmuring in the hall, though some noticed that the two portreeves kept their mouths closed. Henry de Furnellis was now into his stride as a storyteller, though de Wolfe was not sure whether the sheriff, as the king's representative in the county, was more in sympathy with the oppressed Londoners than with his liege lord, King Richard.

'Well, a couple of months ago they found a champion, a strange fellow known as William Longbeard, though his real name was William Fitz-Osbert. He was a lawyer, but had followed the king to the Holy Land as a soldier. Anyway, this man, with a black beard down to his waist like some latter-day prophet, started rousing the rabble in London, holding meetings in the street and denouncing the authorities who were crushing the populace with their unfair taxes.'

There was a growling amongst some of the audience in the hall, especially from the clerks and servants. 'Maybe we need a man with a long beard in Exeter!' called an unknown voice from the back. Undeterred, the sheriff carried on with his tale from the big city.

'It seems that William began organizing resistance on a large scale, forming groups of rebels and secretly smuggling in large quantities of arms from outside the city. There were alleged to be fifty thousand in his underground army, with district leaders and secret codewords. Longbeard even went across to Rouen to lay their grievances before the king, but it seems that Richard took no heed of his pleas.'

'What was the Justiciar doing all this time?' asked Ralph Morin, a staunch royalist.

'He was well aware of what was going on, for Hubert has spies everywhere. He began secretly drafting in large numbers of troops from outside London and drawing up plans to fight any insurrection. He let Fitz-Osbert go so far, then decided that he was becoming a real danger to law and order. Just before the revolt was due to flare up, he sent a party of men to arrest him, and in a fight in the street Fitz-Osbert fatally stabbed the leader of the guards. Then they ran and sought sanctuary in the church of St Mary le Bow. The Chief Justiciar sent a large force to capture him, but they barricaded themselves in the church.'

The men in the hall were riveted by Henry's story; good drama was hard to come by in Devon, especially when true, like this one and from the new capital itself.

'Don't say that they broke sanctuary, as with Thomas à Becket!' shouted Brother Rufus, aghast at the thought that a repetition of the great scandal of the previous reign might be repeated. But the sheriff nodded gravely, as he continued.

'Even worse, he ordered that piles of straw be stacked around the church and set on fire! The rebels retreated to the tower, but eventually the smoke and flames drove them out, when they were attacked and Longbeard suffered a sword-thrust through the belly. Then Hubert Walter, who had taken up quarters in the Tower, ordered an immediate trial of the ringleaders and condemned them to be executed the very next day.'

He swigged another mouthful of ale as the listeners waited in dead silence for the end of his tale. 'William

Fitz-Osbert, wounded as he was, was stripped naked and tied to a horse's tail, then dragged from the Tower across the miles of cobbles and stony streets to Tyburn, a new execution site to the west of the city, where his mangled and dying body was trussed in chains and hanged from the branches of a great elm tree, along with all his accomplices in the failed revolt.'

Thomas de Peyne, who had listened breathlessly to the sheriff's account, was suddenly assailed by a dreadful revelation.

This was that quatrain come to fulfilment! It was the words 'the budding elm' that triggered his recognition, for it was April now, when the new shoots would be appearing on the trees. Now the words 'a bearded champion fought oppression's realm' made complete sense, as did the rest of the verse.

He crossed himself repeatedly as he bitterly regretted adding his own foolish sneer to the copy of Brân's Black Book, rashly warning other readers not to believe everything they read. If the warning from centuries ago about Fitz-Osbert's actions and the further desecration of sanctuary – by the Archbishop of Canterbury himself – was true, what other terrible portents were forecast and would eventually come to pass?

Shaking with remorse, he forced himself to listen to the end of Henry de Furnellis's account.

'Though the Justiciar had effectively destroyed the rebellion, he is being reviled in London by both common folk and churchmen alike for his high-handed actions, and there is talk that the king will be petitioned to have him removed from office.'

He shook his grey head in despair. 'This was a bad time for England. The hatred of the population for harsh authority and the ruthlessness of the king's officer have weakened the bonds of loyalty to a king, who appears unconcerned with what happens this side of the Channel. The feelings of the men of London were shown by the way in which they acted at the execution site, this place Tyburn, which was used instead of Smithfield as the traditional place for the dispatch of traitors.'

'What d'you mean, sheriff, what actions of the populace?' asked de Wolfe.

'During the night, the bodies of Longbeard and his men were taken down by the saddened citizens, and the very chains in which they were hanged were broken up and distributed to the sympathizers as talismans of their respect. Not only that, but hundreds of common folk came to retrieve handfuls of earth from under the elm, below where the men had died. By next day there was a huge hole under where they had swung, such that Hubert Walter had to station troops to keep more folk away.'

When the story was rounded off, with admonitions from the sheriff to watch for similar signs of unrest in Exeter, the coroner's trio went back to their chamber in the gatehouse and sombrely discussed the sheriff's news.

Thomas decided to keep his revelations about the prophecy in Brân's Black Book to himself, mainly because of his regret at having rashly added such a dismissive verse. With both the original and the copy now gone to London – and, who knows, perhaps onward to Rome – he felt it best to keep quiet about his stupid and immature action.

'Let other generations decide about the quatrains for themselves,' he muttered under his breath. 'Let God's will be done in His own time. We have no business in trying to anticipate what the Almighty has in store for us!'

He went back to sorting out the archives, a chastened but wiser man.

HISTORICAL NOTE

The abortive revolt organized by William Fitz-Osbert was the first of a line of rebellions in England rousing the common man against oppressive authority – later came John Ball, Wat Tyler and others. Much of the severe ill feeling against Archbishop Hubert Walter was not so much for his ruthless suppression of the revolt but for his breaking of sanctuary at St Mary le Bow, too reminiscent of the traumatic quarrel between Henry II and Thomas à Becket in 1170.

Some accounts claim that Fitz-Osbert was hanged at the Smithfield elms, but it was on the Tyburn elm that he expired, probably the first of thousands to die there for almost six hundred years up to 1783.

ACT TWO

Tartarus' hordes irrupt through Alexander's gate.
Six Christian kingdoms crumble in a breath.
Though Latin traders use long spoons to eat,
It won't protect them from a demon's death.

I snatch the kumiss from the Tartar's hand and, tipping the leather sack up, I throw my head back. The raw, milky-white fluid gurgles out of the sack and hits the back of my throat like a well-aimed arrow. I relish the sting on my tongue and the fizz as the kumiss gurgles down. Drinking half-fermented mare's milk is an acquired taste, but one to which I have adjusted. When you're thousands of miles from a good Rhenish, and the craving's on you, you'll drink anything that'll guarantee to get you legless. Too much of it, though, and you end up seeing stars. Still and all, that's better than sharing your quarters with a dead man.

I should explain. The year is Ren-Xu – the Tartar year of the dog – and the year 660 for Mohammedans. To you and me it is the ninth year of Doge Renier Zeno's governance of Venice, the second year of Pope Urban the IV's reign, and one thousand two hundred and sixty-two years since the birth of Christ. Or at least I think it is. I have been away from civilization for too long now. And I have lost count of the days that have passed, like a sailor lost at sea. The mare's milk brew hasn't helped in keeping my head straight either. All I can say for sure is that it is several months since Friar Giovanni Alberoni, a fellow Venetian (albeit from that sharp, shingle strip that edges the lagoon), picked me up out of the gutter in Sudak.

'Niccolo Zuliani? Is it really you? I can hardly recognize you.'

'No, I'm not . . . who you say. My name's . . . Carrara, Francesco Carrara.'

'Nonsense. I know Francesco Carrara. He's at least twenty years older than you, and considerably larger in girth.'

I was so addled at the time that I didn't quibble any further over my embarrassment at being found in that state. Nor about the friar's reinstatement of my real name, which I had avoided using for some time. In Venice it was the name of a wanted man. Alberoni always calls me Niccolo in that formal, stuffy way of his. My true friends use the more familiar Nick just as my English mother did, but for the moment I was glad to be Niccolo again at least. He helped me get to my feet and supported my enfeebled body.

'I'm glad I found you. I have a proposition for you.'

So it was that the gutter in Sudak became the crossroads of my life. Sudak is in Gothia, by the way – some call it Crimea – on the northern side of the Black Sea close to the icy fastnesses of Russia, which are controlled by the Golden Horde. Its main claim to fame is as a point of contact between us Latins and those mysterious Tartars of the East. It was there the good friar nursed me back to something resembling health and fired my imagination with the prospect of plundering the fabled wealth of the Tartar Empire. Well, to be honest (a trait some say I lack, though they tend to be prejudiced, having been outwitted by me in some deal or other) – to be honest, I was the one wanting to do the plundering. Alberoni wanted to penetrate the distant depths of the Empire in order to spread the word of God to the heathen.

Myself, I go for more modest scenarios in order to make a living. I had been living in Sudak, albeit rather poorly, off a scam that we Venetians call 'the long trade'. Don't ask me why. The trick is to set up a company in a false name, or with a gullible but reputable fool as a front. Using the fool's reputation, you then obtain goods on credit over a long period, paying small deposits to keep your creditors happy. Then you rapidly sell off everything you have stored very cheaply, and finally disappear in order to avoid those creditors. Leaving the front man to take the blame. Simple, as long as you can hold your nerve. I lost mine when I was threatened by a big bear of a fur trader from Russia and came out with nothing. I should have stuck to honest trading, especially as the only other time I had reached for the stars had been an unmitigated disaster too. You may recall that I tried to rig the Doge's election to no avail, ending up with a murder rap. In short, that's why I had been holed up in Sudak using fat old Carrara's name as my own.

But that's all in the past now. Tonight I have to set about saving my own neck from the noose in connection with another murder. Though neck and noose are not exactly precise references. If I am found guilty of murder, the Tartars whose company I am forced to bear in this snowstorm will either tie me up to two horses and thrash them until they fly in opposite directions, taking pieces of me with them, or, if they deem me sufficiently noble, will wrap me in a carpet and merely trample me to death. The carpet treatment is to prevent my noble blood from despoiling the earth.

I suddenly feel dizzy and take another pull from the skin of kumiss to drive such thoughts from my head. I think of the body lying in the snowdrift outside. When the storm abates, he will be interred, and all traces of his existence under heaven obliterated from his Tartar god, Tengri. But before that happens, the barbarous bastards who claim to be his comrades will make an end of me. Which, if you think about it, is pretty unfair as it must have been one of them who slaughtered him. So, the thing is, I wouldn't mind so much facing death, but I did not kill the man. Then neither do I have the faintest idea who did. Yet I must find out, or suffer the consequences of being named the murderer myself.

I reluctantly set aside the skin of kumiss and huddle down in the warm goatskins beside the fire in the centre of the stove-house. I stare into the flames as they crackle and pop and rue the reasons that brought me to this pretty pass.

Back in Sudak, the good Friar Alberoni had let me into a secret.

'I have a book of prophecies made ages ago by a Celtic priest. And if I interpret it correctly, there is a verse or two about the Tartars that guide my mission.'

He rummaged in the bundles that half-filled the floor in his lodgings overlooking the harbour. He seemed to have all sorts of gewgaws for trading with the Tartars – beads and furs mainly. As though they were primitives who could be bought for a few trinkets. I knew better. If the stories I had heard were true, it seemed that they themselves had more treasures than we could imagine. Items of great value like pearls, and precious stones, cloth of gold and silk, as well as strange items like black stones that could be lit and would burn for days. What would they want with beads and trinkets? But the stories were that they were interested in everything the West had to offer and were prepared to trade for the things they couldn't gain by conquest.

A cold wind ruffled the wave-tops in the harbour, and I stared out over the Ghelan Sea. I fondly imagined that my gaze could stretch through the straits at the sea's western extremity, across the ancient lands of the Greeks and into the Adriatic and Venice. Where fair Caterina Dolfin awaited my return. Or not, if my deepest, darkest moods were to be believed. Why should she wait for me, when I was as poor as a lagoon fisherman, and a marked man to boot?

'Here it is.'

I sighed and turned my gaze back to the confines of the room. Alberoni was waving a darkly bound tome at me.

'This is the Black Book of Brân – prophecies that go back hundreds of years. But still speak truths to us today. Listen.'

He proceeded to recite one of the quatrains, which were all in Latin. Now it may surprise you to know that I knew the Church language myself. It may shock you even more to learn that I know it because I studied once for the priesthood. That was before the jingle of money diverted me on to a more lucrative path and broke my mother's heart. She had been set on me being a priest. Anyway, the poem, if I recall went something like this:

Though lightning and bare skull his banner bear
And all the world is 'neath a storm confined,
When hands across the sea are joinéd there,
Then righteousness is brought to heathen minds.

This he took for justification for his holy embassy to the pagan Tartars, even when I pointed out that they rode under a banner of nine yak-tails, not a skull.

'Don't quibble, Niccolo. They have left enough skulls behind them for it to be true. And the rest fits – the storm of the pagan hordes sweeping across the world. And if the West joins hands – we can bring righteousness to them.'

I sniffed in disdain. 'You can make any events fit such vague ramblings. Have any of these prophecies actually come true?'

Alberoni's eyes lit up. 'Yes, yes. They say that at the end of the last century a rebellion in England was clearly prophesied. If the scribe of the book lived in Ireland in the seventh century, how could he know about such an event?'

A little mouse of doubt began to scurry across my brain. I needed to reassure myself that a book of prophecies written in a far-off land hundreds of years ago was nonsense.

'Let me see.'

I took the thin but oddly heavy book from his reluctant grasp, flicking carelessly through the pages. Scanning the verses quickly and choosing one at random, I stabbed a finger at a quatrain.

'Take this one, for example.

"When three popes all murdered lie,
And Christ's own kingdom desecrated . . ."

'Three Popes murdered? It's ridiculous. Or this:

"Tartarus' hordes irrupt through Alexander's gate.
Six Christian kingdoms crumble in a breath.
Though Latin traders use long spoons to eat,
It won't protect them from a demon's death."'

I had intended to pour scorn on the prophecies, but suddenly this quatrain struck a chord, as if my choice had not been random after all but directed by a hidden hand. 'Tartarus' for the Tartars? And did the '*Latin traders*' refer to me? Something had made me shudder when I read the last line too. It spoke of a personal foretaste of doom. Outside, a chilly wind whipped across the window opening, and I pretended my shivering was all to do with the plummeting temperature.Then I started to examine the book more closely. I could see straight away that it was not several hundred years old. The pages were relatively crisp and the illuminations bright and clear. I chortled.

'The book is not ancient at all. No wonder the faker could insert a verse about an event sixty-something years ago. It was already in his past. This is like the letter that some claim to have seen that Prester John wrote to the West. The one that would make him over a hundred and fifty years old.'

Alberoni's face went red. Though I didn't realize it at the time, he had good reason to believe in the well-known Prester John myth. It centred on a letter purporting to come from the Far East, where a Christian ruler awaited his call to come and save the West in its hour of most need. To me, it was a neat forgery by an expert who made his money selling hope to the fearful. My mother had told me fairy tales of a similar king hiding under the earth in England. I didn't believe that either. But lots of people are gullible when it comes to forlorn hopes. And a good con man can make plenty of money pandering to them. This Black Book looked like a similar scam.

Alberoni snatched it back from my disbelieving hands.

'It's not the original book. Did I ever say it was? No. It's a copy made in the west of England by a scribe with a fair hand, which was then taken to Rome to add to the glories of the library at the Vatican. That is where

I . . . found it. Languishing in a dusty corner. Unread and unappreciated.'

'And they just let you have it?'

I had an inkling that Alberoni had not obtained the book legitimately. He scowled.

'It was cast aside because there was some tale that the scribe was possessed with evil.'

That was all he would say, and I knew then that he had stolen it from under the nose of the Vatican librarian. His hesitancy over revealing the book's recent history – when he realized he had gone too far – spoke volumes to me. And that was when I decided to steal this Black Book of Brân from him in my turn. His offer of a long and arduous journey to the ends of the earth, even with the possibility of profitable trade at the end of it, didn't stack up against a quick buck. I was still recovering from my drunken bingeing over the failure of the long trade. A fast and dirty deal appealed to me more at the time. I knew I could sell it to make some money, and so start trading again. I mean, if it had fooled Friar Alberoni, then it would fool another priest eager for its contents. And how could he object or protest, if he had filched it himself in the first place? So I hope you're now beginning to understand how I came to be stuck in a Russian stove-house with a drunken Orthodox priest and a dead Tartar.

As soon as Alberoni's back was turned that day in Sudak, I grabbed the book and was off on my toes. I know, you're telling me that a trader like me should have planned it more cleverly and waited for the best opportunity. But don't forget I had not heard the jingle of coinage for a while, and I was thirsty. I didn't have the time to plan it more neatly than that. However, I did have a good idea whom I would sell this little treasure to, so the theft wasn't completely stupid. I had first heard of this mad priest who lived on the banks of the Dnieper river from a gang of Russian traders in fur – one of whom had later threatened to detach my head from my body if I didn't return the furs he had given me on a sale-or-return basis. He had got wind of my long trade scam and caused the collapse of the whole deal. But before that, I had been his drinking companion. Him and a bunch of the hairy giants. I had spent a drunken night with them in Sudak planning how I might find an opening to trade with the Tartars.

Everyone else west of Sudak thought the Tartars were hounds from hell. But here on the wild frontier – the entrepôt where West met East and anything was up for sale – these fearful demons who held the yoke of Rus's slavery were just another possible business partner. And a Venetian never passed up a chance for a deal. The Russian traders, all as hairy as the furs they dealt in and as smelly, swore that a certain Father Kyrill was well in with the local Tartar lord. He had a reputation not only as a wise prophet but also more practically as a healer. For these reasons he was welcomed at the court of the local khan. It seemed the Tartars loved a heady mixture of religion, magic and prophecy, and Father Kyrill obligingly supplied it. He thus held the key to lucrative trading with his master based at Sarai on the Volga. When he wasn't at Sarai, the priest lived in a cave above the banks of the river Dnieper near Kherson. And positively drooled over anything to do with omens and prophecies that came his way. He could use it to impress his Tartar overlords. I reckoned I could kill two birds with one stone therefore. I would use the Black Book of Brân to buy Father Kyrill, who would then lead me to the Tartars' main encampment and the boss of the Golden Horde. I didn't know then that I would encounter the Tartars sooner than I had anticipated.

*

The howl of the wind outside the shack stirs the heavy cloth covering the door, causing a series of sharp cracks. It makes the flames of the fire flare up and brings me back to the present. The little band of Tartars now sits stony-faced across the fire from me. The Tartars are a moon-visaged breed at the best of times, with a sparse sprinkling of hair on their chins. Their narrowed eyes give the impression that they are always gazing in suspicion at whatever they see. And at this very moment they are staring suspiciously at me. I am a stranger, and therefore at the forefront of suspicion of the murder. I need to say something to ease the tension, but I don't know what. Drink is passed, and I am reminded of earlier that fateful night, before the murder took place.

It was just my luck that the weather changed for the worse soon after I set out for the riverside cave of Father Kyrill. By the time I got to the Dnieper, a blizzard was raging, and the river had frozen over. I later learned that even the Ghelan Sea had frozen for three leagues from its shoreline. Father Kyrill was not in his cave, which was lucky for him. If he had been, he would have been a slab of frozen meat by then. As I would be if I didn't find shelter. Even wrapped in furs as I was, the Russian winter is so intensely cold that a traveller can die in minutes if he remains in the open. That is why rich magnates had built stove-houses along major highways to act as refuges for themselves and other travellers. These square houses were made of great beams of wood that fit so snugly that no wind or cold could penetrate. The only openings were a small door to enter by, and a vent-hole for the smoke of the fire. Struggling through the biting wind that drove the snow into my face, I was lucky to spot one just before I froze. It stood out as a dark patch in an unrelenting vista of white. And someone else had beaten me to it. A thin plume of smoke was sucked from the vent-hole before it was whipped away by the blizzard. I pushed hard on the door and stumbled into the warmth. The fire was the only thing in the gloomy room that exuded any heat.

Seated in a bunch on one side of the central hearth was a gang of hard-faced slant-eyed men I knew immediately were Tartars. And on the opposite side of the fire, completely on his own, squatted a hairy-faced Russian whose fur hat merged as one with the lank, black, greasy locks of his head and beard. When he realized the newcomer was one of his own breed, a grin broke through the forest of hair, exposing yellowed, broken teeth. He spoke a few words in Russian, which I roughly understood from my days carousing with his countrymen in Sudak. I responded in kind.

'Kak dyela, stary durak.'

I could see he was a holy man from his black garb, so to ask how the old fool was doing was a sort of compliment. They liked being considered simpletons for God. He thrust out a grimy fist.

'I could be worse, young man. I could be frozen meat. So sharing the warmth with these hounds from hell—' he cocked a thumb at the silent and suspicious Tartars '—is at least preferable to freezing in my cave. My name is Kyrill.'

I have long given up marvelling at the strange ways of coincidence in my life. I prefer to call it luck. A commodity my life had been short of for a long while. So I merely took the presence in this sanctuary of the very man I had sought as a sign that my luck had changed. I squeezed his hand vigorously and immediately wished I hadn't. His fist was as filthy and as greasy as his locks. After I had recovered my hand, I surreptitiously wiped it clean on my furs. I noted that he wiped his own on his long, grey and greasy beard. I proffered him my name and jerked a thumb at our enforced companions.

'I'm Nick Zuliani. Trader. Who are they?'

'The devil's brood,' he grumbled.

As he settled back on his haunches, a stone jar slipped from the stinking folds of his clothes. He grabbed it before it shattered on the floor and, leaning across to the upper shelf of the stove, carefully placed the jar on it. I fancied something lurked in the jar, for it rocked slightly even after he had set it down. But then, it could have just been my fertile imagination. He wiped his beard and continued his story.

'Though the old boy's not so bad. His name's Sartakh, and he says they have been escorting Prince Alexander back to Kiev. They were returning to Sarai when the blizzard caught them out. That's all I've got out of them so far.'

I had heard of this Russian prince, Alexander Nevsky. He alone in Russia had dealt with the Tartar overlords, rather than try to fight them. And so he had saved his lands from devastation for years, where other princes and their subjects had fought and gone under. His pragmatism would have made him a good trader. So these Tartars were from Sarai and had been ensuring the prince's safe return to poor old Kiev. An old city ruined in the Tartar invasion years back, and not much restored now. My luck had definitely turned. They might now be my passport to the heart of Sarai, and Berke Khan, the boss of the Golden Horde. I slid my hand inside my furs and stroked the smooth leather binding of the Black Book of Brân. Maybe I wouldn't have to bribe Kyrill with it after all. I put on my best business manner and turned to face the Tartars. My smile was met with frosty suspicion, and my offered hand ignored. I saw I would have to work hard here.

I reckoned the only way to break the ice – no pun intended – with this bunch was to draw them into a little game of chance. All soldiers liked to gamble, and who knows? Maybe I'd even live long enough to spend my winnings. I reached slowly into my furs to ensure they didn't think I was producing a knife and pulled out a couple of dice. I shook them with an inviting rattle and tried the Tartars with a little crude Turkish.

'Gentlemen, the game is Hazard. As the caster, I will call a number between five and nine and put a stake on the table. You will cover that, and if I throw my number – my main – I have nicked it and win the bets. If not . . .'

They may not have understood a word I had said, but my intentions were clear enough. I had the complete attention of the little gang of round-faced men, agog at the two dice rolling around in my fist. The Russian priest disdained to play the game, naturally. But then he'd probably got no money anyway. Having gone over the rules again with a lot of waving of hands and holding up of fingers, I threw the dice. Of course, to draw the rubes in, I played it straight for openers. One of the younger Tartars got on a winning streak, and the pile of winnings moved his way. Then I started tapping the dice on the ground before each throw, as though in exasperation at losing. Soon the pile of coins shifted its location and grew on the rug in front of me. The session began to draw out long into the night, and they started to teach me Tartar words as we gamed.

When Eldegai arrived, he came like a demon out of the wilderness. We were still playing at dice. The leader of our band, the wizen-faced old man Kyrill had named Sartakh, suddenly pricked up his ears.

'Wait.'

Our game stopped abruptly. I mimed an enquiry to one of the Tartars, who explained. Now I am a quick study when it comes to tongues, but at first I thought

I had misunderstood what he had said. But he repeated it more slowly for me.

'Sartakh was born in a distant country where the females are of human shape and the men of a dog's. He can hear the slightest sound before anyone else.'

His companions sniggered, but the object of their humour stopped them with an abruptly upraised hand. He grunted in his guttural tongue.

'Someone approaches.'

His companions tensed, reaching for their swords. I belched and grinned inanely at the old man. A harmless fool lives longer than a curious meddler, and I didn't yet know what was afoot. Soon enough, though, we all could hear the sound of a horse being ridden hard, muffled though the hooves were by the snow. It was coming towards our encampment. The youngest of our escort – Ulan by name – muttered fearfully. My understanding of what they said was now being stretched, and I moved to sit beside Father Kyrill, who interpreted for me.

'Ulan said that it's a demon.'

Sartakh rose and stood by the door of the stovehouse, opening it to let the firelight spill briefly into the darkness. It risked a loss of heat but, that way, whoever it was would know we were aware of him, and he would be aware of us. This way there would be no surprise reaction on either side. A surprise that might result in a fatal misunderstanding. The sound of hooves ceased, and there was a heart-stopping moment while whoever it was stabled his horse. Then a bundled-up figure appeared in the outer circle of light. Ulan hissed and stood towards the back of the hut. The figure spoke.

'I am Eldegai, a traveller.'

'Still on the road at night?'

The question was Ulan's.

'I saw the traces of your horses in the snow, and I decided to catch you up rather than camp alone. It's too cold to camp out anyway.'

'You followed our tracks in drifting snow? Don't take me for a fool, demon,' muttered the young Tartar.

The stranger gave him a puzzled look but did not question what the boy meant. The moment passed, but from that time Ulan continued to keep the closest eye on him, apparently unsure if the stranger were man or beast. Sartakh broke the impasse.

'Quick. Come in, or we will all freeze.'

The newest arrival to the stove-house stepped inside the room and naturally moved over to the left. That is where male visitors go in a Tartar tent, I later learned, the right side being reserved for the women. I recalled that Father Kyrill was sprawled on the floor on the right of the room. Which might have explained something of the disdain in which the Tartars currently held him. They saw him as no better than a woman. Our visitor, being of their breed, knew better how to behave.

Sartakh moved to the back of the room as if the stove-house were his home, and he the host. He invited the new arrival to approach the fire. The bundled figure hunkered down, loosening his outer fur coat for comfort. By the light of the flames I could now examine his features. He was very ordinary-looking for a demon. He pulled the heavy cap off his head, revealing a head shaved in the traditional way of the Tartar with long braids at the sides. His face was that of a middle-aged man, rounded and red-cheeked in the way of the race. But trackways of lines ran from the corners of his eyes, giving him a severe mien. His mouth was a thin gash, lined on top with a curving moustache. The mouth opened, and he spoke his name again.

'Eldegai. A poor traveller.'

At least, that is what I believed he said. His accent was somewhat different from those I had got to know while taking their money. It was harder to understand. Maybe it was because he came from some other remote region of the Tartar Empire. I opined that it made him a sort of provincial hick, in a way, and gleefully invited him to play at dice with us. I liked a dead cert and relished parting a fool from his possessions. Eldegai suddenly grinned and moved into the circle of gamblers.

It was soon afterwards that Karakuchuk introduced us to Sic Bo. I had been aware of this quiet old man sitting at the periphery of the group, and careful with his bets. He had been examining my dexterous hand movements, and his face had been more screwed up than usual. As if he was trying to work something out. I knew the look – all con artists know it – the look of a mark who was aware there was a fix on but couldn't figure out what or how. I knew I would have to deal very carefully with him.

Now, as Eldegai sat down with us, Karakuchuk uncharacteristically took centre stage.

'There is a game I learned on campaign in Cathay. It is called Sic Bo. Unfortunately, it requires three dice, not two. And a cup.'

He gave me a hard stare through his narrowed eyes. He thought by suggesting a game I didn't know, he would nullify any cheating that might be going on. And prevent me from using my hands by having the dice rolled in a cup. Smiling, I dug into the pocket of my fleecy jacket and produced a new set of dice. The other dice I ferreted away in the same pocket. They were tappers anyway, and would be no good in a cup. At their core was a hollow partially filled with wax and a stone. By warming the wax in my hands, and tapping them on the ground as I had done after playing honestly for a while, the stone shifted and weighted the dice on whatever side was at the bottom. Karakuchuk's game would require a different sort of dice if they were to be thrown from a cup. Dice such as I had now produced, some of which were shaved down one side. These I would palm in at the right moment. Sleight of hand was a particular skill that had stood me in good stead for some time. Remind me to tell you about the little matter of the purloined ruby some time.

I had played dice games with a cup before. But Sic Bo was unusual in that the dice were not thrown out of it. Karakuchuk explained slowly for me.

'After shaking, the cup is upended, hiding the dice. Bets are laid on what might lie below the cup. The simplest bet is with straight odds on the total being high or low – more than ten or less than ten. Understand?'

Now they do say that great gamblers can hear the side that the dice fall on. But I didn't need to worry about having ears as sharp as Sartakh's. I knew how they would fall, once I palmed in the shaved dice. I nodded.

'I understand. It is a risky game.'

Someone produced a simple wooden drinking cup, and we began. I let the unaltered dice roll as they wished to start with. And, of course, I won some bets and lost others. I could see the look of triumph in Karakuchuk's eyes. But more important, I saw the greed in our new companion's – Eldegai was suckered. Out of a sense of malice, I then arranged it so that he won several times from Karakuchuk, who was not best pleased. But it gave me a particular delight.

Soon, though, with the shaved dice, I was winning hand over fist from the newcomer. I won a rather nice dagger with a jewel embedded in the hilt, that fine fur hat he had worn on arrival, and some other trinkets he drew from inside his coat as he ran through his losing streak. I suppose I should have stopped, but I got carried away with his desperate eagerness to lose everything he had. And I had spotted a small gold tablet tucked in the folds of his coat. I wanted it, but it seemed he was not far enough gone to wager it. He did lose a spare pair of boots, though. But then, suddenly, he rose from the floor, where the little circle of gamers squatted, and stomped angrily to the darker corner of the room. Sartakh shook his head slowly.

'Enemy. You have made an enemy.'

I shrugged. Soon, I would be gone and never see this man again. Eldegai was just showing himself to be a stiff and ornery man, good at taking offence. Or, I soon saw, giving it.

It all blew up a little later, when Karakuchuk started delving in one of the large saddlebags the Tartars had brought into the stove-house with them. The ripening smell had told me already that the pack contained meat that was not responding too well to the warmth of the room. Now it appeared the old Tartar was proposing to prepare some of the stinking contents of his bag for everyone. I wondered if I would be able to stomach the food he prepared. Kyrill noticed my horrified look upon seeing the greyish slab that Karakuchuk produced, and guffawed. He pointed at the mysterious pot he had earlier placed on the stove. The one I thought contained something alive.

'Perhaps you would rather eat my leeches, though I would prefer you not to, as they are most excellent for bleeding the sickly.'

He had put the pot on the stove to prevent the contents from freezing to death. Leeches. I shuddered at the very idea of even touching the slimy beasts that lurked inside. I hated them, and would rather die of excess bad blood than have one attached to me. Kyrill smirked and pointed at the slab of meat that was being carved up.

'It's probably an old horse that no longer had the legs to run as fast as the devils required of it. I have watched Tartars like this Karakuchuk slice open the chest of some still-living beast, butcher it and then turn it into a well-stewed pottage. Mind you, it still looked grey and unappetizing even after cooking. So I have found that a good swig of kumiss helps me tackle it.'

He proffered the kumiss skin, and I drank deep – several times – while the old man stewed down the fatty slabs in water over the fire. So I was ready, if a little tipsy, when the boiled-down mess was grudgingly offered me. It had even begun to look appetizing to my growling gut. It wasn't so appealing to the more fastidious Eldegai, who I could now tell was rather more refined than the others. He wasn't the raw provincial I had first had him down as. Nor the poor traveller he professed himself to be. He fussily disdained to touch the stew and rose from the fire to turn his back on the fare. I could see that his superior attitude drove one of the others, in particular, mad. This was a short, stocky Tartar whose name I had also picked up while playing at dice. He was called Taulubeg. And when Eldegai turned his nose up at the food, his face grew red. He rose from his corner, stomped on his bowed legs over to Eldegai, and spat some Tartar comment into his face. The import of the words was obvious to me even without understanding the language fully.

Something like:

'Too well bred to dig in along with the rest of us, then?'

Eldegai's reply was clear too from the haughty way he responded to his shorter protagonist.

'Well, yes, actually. This trash is not what I am used to. Besides, I can't afford to get ill with food poisoning. I have important things to do. Things you couldn't dream of.'

He turned his back on Taulubeg, as though the other man was beneath his consideration. If our leader, Sartakh, had not stepped in at that moment, pushing Taulubeg away, matters might have got nasty. Ulan, perhaps sensing Eldegai might at last give away something of his true, demonic nature, sidled closer to the well-dressed Tartar. So only he and I heard what Eldegai then muttered.

'The Il-Khan's envoy to Sarai doesn't soil his hands on such provender,' Eldegai said under his breath.

Ulan's face paled, and he backed away from this man he had reckoned to be a demon in disguise. And what he had said, it looked as though it was something to confirm Ulan's opinion of him. I kept well clear, not caring what it was that upset Ulan so. But I did register that the man was on some sort of important mission. An envoy to Sarai, eh? I might be able to use that, but for the time being I would keep it quiet. I didn't want to give Eldegai cause to dislike me any more than he did. I reckoned his annoyance at being cleaned out at Sic Bo would soon dissipate. And he would be wanting to get back what he had lost. So I was not surprised when, a short time later, he shuffled over to me as I lay back licking my lips over the fatty feast. For a while he said nothing, then he tried me out with a few words of Turkish. He had guessed that, as a merchant from the West, I might be more familiar with that tongue than with Tartar. It was likely he had met other traders too, and found this common language useful. But it was another common language – profit – that I wanted to share with him. For now I said nothing. A good gambler knows when to shut up and let a mark do all the running. So I let him run off at the mouth for a while, until he came to the point.

'You will give me another chance to beat you at the dice.'

His tone was peremptory, but I knew it would soon be wheedling. I turned the grip of the vice.

'No. I am weary of gaming, and happy with my winnings.'

'But it is only fair!'

I shrugged my shoulders and lay back, closing my eyes as though dozing. But, of course, my brain was working at full speed, looking to the far horizon, and Sarai. Who said a gambler had to play fair, anyway? That rule was not in the vocabulary of a Venetian. Playing fair is for losers. And Genoans – which is tantamount to the same thing. Though I digress. Eldegai was nonplussed by my refusal to play, but I soon heard the scrabble of his feet as he hunkered down close by. We resumed our silent discourse, with Eldegai no doubt puzzling out how to tempt me into another game. I could almost hear his pompous brain churning ineffectually. I finally realized I would have to lead him by the nose or wait all night. I opened my eyes and cast a glance sideways at him.

'Maybe there is another way you can regain your riches. A way we can both benefit from. At Sarai.'

When I mentioned Sarai he bristled a little, but I wasn't worried. Like all the Tartars, he had a natural swagger, but a certain bulge around his waist betrayed him as someone who spent too much time lounging around a court. I had him down as more of a talker than a doer. And for an envoy, he was not very quick on the uptake either. His eyes showed he had no idea what I was angling for. I realized I would have to spell it out for him.

'If you could use your influence at court, in the matter of trade, then perhaps we could both profit?'

I had in mind a sort of long trade such as I told you of earlier. But this time I would make it work. Eldegai would supply the reputable front to the business. And be the gullible fool who would be left behind to face the creditors after I had skipped with all the profits. A hard lesson, but I was willing to teach it him. Eldegai pursed his lips and stared off at an imaginary horizon. I could see the greed in his eyes, though. Impassive he wasn't. In fact, he was worse at doing a deal than he had been at dice. But I knew he could see the opportunity I was offering.

'I would just have to recommend you?'

He was imagining clear profit for no effort; for just being a figurehead. He thought I needed him more than he needed me, and that it was he using me, not the other way around. And so he was eager. I even toyed momentarily with the idea of doing an honest deal with him. It might have worked, after all. But I didn't consider it for very long. Why work hard to gain a fraction of the amount you can grab with just a little subterfuge? As a token of my false honesty, I gave him back the dagger I had won from him. It was more ornamental than practical, anyway. He grinned widely, showing yellowed teeth, and accepted the gift. But then he grimaced.

'There's only one problem.'

'A problem?'

'Yes. I am not going to Sarai with good news, so I will not be the best of partners. Besides, I would advise you to seek your fortune in Cathay. There is a far greater prize to be had there. Ask the old man. He's been, and knows the score.'

Eldegai jerked his thumb over his shoulder, and I looked over to where Sartakh stood. I could see he was talking to the other old Tartar.

'He knows. I have spoken to him of the riches that await anyone in Cathay. Once my message is received in Sarai.'

*

The wind takes on a different character. Instead of gusting, it now becomes a persistent howl that tugs at the whole structure of the stove-house. We all instinctively huddle closer together despite the uneasiness surrounding the Tartar's death. Someone in the room has murdered him. And I am no nearer to working out who. For the time being I remain the chief suspect, and at least one of these Tartars will be happy to see me dead. The real murderer, that is. The logs that make up the framework of the stove-house creak in protest at the battering from outside. Out of the corner of my eye I see a Tartar reach up and dab some kumiss on the felt doll on the shelf over his head. It's the one called Tetuak. The doll is an image of the Tartars' god, Tengri. Making an offering to Tengri betrays the fact that Tetuak is obviously very nervous. He sees me looking at him and masks the fear that shines from his eyes. He grabs the skin from me and takes a slug of the kumiss with a show of bravado that only serves to amuse me. It reminds me of how his boasting also amused Eldegai.

The stew had been eaten by all but the fastidious Eldegai, and once again the kumiss sack was circulating. We were in for a long night, and the Tartars fell back on what all warriors do to pass the time. Bragging of past deeds.

'I have crossed the Great Desert of Lop,' averred the boastful Tetuak, seeking in others' eyes the awe that feat should occasion. 'They say there are sirens there, which can lure you from your path, leading you astray to a place from which you will never return alive.'

'All the more reason to pay attention to your companions and stick together,' observed Eldegai with a smile. 'If you believe such nonsense.'

Another man would not have risen to the bait.

Tetuak, however, could not leave it there, and retorted with what would turn out to be an ominous comment.

'Lucky that you found us, Eldegai, or you certainly would have perished in this blizzard. Death was at your heels.'

No one knew then how unfortunate those words were to prove. Murder was merely hours away, and the victim's only epitaph was Taulubeg's uncharitable next words, as he looked over at Eldegai, the outsider, sitting on his own.

'Saved by us, but still avoiding the common herd.'

'Enough.'

Sartakh's reprimand was sharp and abrupt. He had a look of concern in his eyes. The arrival of Eldegai in our midst had soured the mood of the little band of Tartars, but he was still Sartakh's responsibility. In his impromptu role as host, it was he who had welcomed Eldegai to his fireside. But the man had made himself unpopular with everyone, and a sullen hesitancy gripped the camp. It was Karakuchuk who broke the awkward silence.

'Sartakh is right. We are stuck here until this storm decides to release us. Let's make the best of it. After all, we have another skin of kumiss to get through yet.'

He tossed a skin from his own saddlebags into the centre of the floor, where it wobbled enticingly, announcing its fullness. The old-timer himself tipped the dregs of the previous skin down his receptive throat, gargling on the milky brew. The new skin began its rounds of our eager hands, and my perception of the evening became as hazy as one of those winter peasoupers that fog out Venice so much you can't even see the other side of the Grand Canal. Did I say evening? With no windows in this damned hut, there was no way of even knowing what time of day it was outside. And I didn't know how long we had been cooped up together. We were suspended in a fog of timelessness. We drank.

Suddenly something caused me to wake up. A voice, a gurgling sound – I don't know what it was that roused me from my drunken stupor. But something woke me, and I threw the goatskins back that I had pulled around me. The cold air struck me hard, like a blow in the pit of my stomach, and I wrapped my fur jacket around me tightly. The room was dark, and I realized there was no rosy glow from the stove. No one had attended to the fire recently, and it was nearly out. I pushed myself up from the floor, keen to keep the embers in the stove going. It would take a great effort to relight it, if it died. My belly was suddenly eager to throw back up the kumiss I had drunk last night. I swallowed hard against the stale, sour taste, quelling the queasiness, and longed for a good red wine. Belching acidly, I laced up the front of my new, thick leather boots. They were the Tartar pair I had won off Eldegai last night. If indeed this was now morning. My old boots had been worn quite through, as I had bought them years ago from the little cobbler in the San Silvestro district of Venice. Old times, good times.

I stood on legs as wobbly as that fresh skin of kumiss had been last night before we had all emptied it down our throats. Why did my head ache more than it had a right to? Sudak had turned me into a seasoned drinker of rot-gut, but this brew seemed to have had a strong effect on me. And looking around, an even worse effect on everyone else. All I could see in the darkness were bodies, scattered over the floor like the aftermath of a battle. But unlike a scene from a military disaster where not a breath passed dead lips, here stertorous snores emerged from several mouths in a tuneless counterpoint of noise. I began stepping over bodies. One

I recognized as Kyrill from the tangle of his beard – the Tartars were mostly hairless on their chins. I went to step over another recumbent figure face down on the ground and tripped on the fur-trimmed edge of his robe. As I fell, my hand went out to save me, and it encountered something wet and sticky on the hard-packed earth that formed the stove-house floor. I prayed it wasn't the man's regurgitated horsemeat stew from dinner. It wasn't, it was worse than that.

When I cautiously sniffed my besmirched hand, I smelled a familiar odour. Metallic, coppery. It was blood. I knelt beside the body I had stumbled over and turned it over. It was Eldegai. I could see that his elegantly decorated outer jacket was matted with black blood. His normally ruddy face was pallid and wax-like, his bloodless lips curled back in a fixed scream of horror. But more shocking were the eyes. They were gone, apparently gouged from their sockets.

I heard someone gasp behind me.

'Demon.' It was Ulan, who had just seen what I had observed of the damage to Eldegai's face. 'Only a demon would do such a thing.'

I groaned at the Tartars' fierce superstitions. First off, Eldegai himself had been dubbed a demon by Ulan. Now he was saying Eldegai had been killed by a demon. Maybe he thought that demon was me. Ulan's cries seemed to rouse the rest of the sleepers, who voiced their horror at what they saw. For a moment the room was a turmoil of groans and guttural sounds. Then it died away, and I looked up to find the Tartars all staring at me with suspicion. But then, what would I expect them to think? Here I was kneeling over Eldegai's mutilated body with his blood all over my hands. This didn't look good for me. The tension in the air was palpable, and Taulubeg spat out something unintelligible. Father Kyrill quietly crossed himself and muttered a prayer. I had been in worse fixes and survived. But not much worse. My brain started racing. I pointed to Eldegai's chest.

'Look. He has been cut open – gutted with a sharp knife. I do not have such a weapon on me.'

It was true. I had travelled into Russia with a hefty belaying pin from a broken-down boat as my only defence. My sword and dagger had been bartered for some cheap wine a long time ago.

It was Taulubeg who recalled that I had won Eldegai's own dagger from him at dice.

'You killed him with his own weapon.'

'No. I gave it back to him. Look. It is tucked in his belt.'

My command of Tartar was suddenly improving, as my position became more precarious. Still, I was relying more on hand signals than on words. I pulled his ornate jacket open and revealed the dagger. I bent over to pull it from its sheath and show it free of blood. Then I suddenly thought that maybe it had been the murder weapon after all, and I would be sealing my own fate. I began praying it had no blood on it. The Tartars tensed at my potentially hostile move, and Sartakh stepped forward to grasp my wrist. I moved back, and the old man leaned over the body himself, hiding what he did as he felt inside the jacket. He fumbled a little longer than I thought necessary, but then drew the jewelled dagger from its sheath. It was innocent of blood, and I breathed a sigh of relief.

Then the rising wind distracted everyone's attention from me. A great gust caused the stove-house to shudder, and mutterings about demons were cast around again. Sartakh told Tetuak and Ulan to wrap the body up and take it outside. We didn't want the corpse rotting in the warmth of the stove-house, after all. They moved to follow his command, and a gust of chill air blew in the opened door. I shuddered. Even then, after the evidence was out of sight, I still felt my companions' eyes hardly leave me. And they muttered suspiciously amongst themselves. It seemed I was not convincing them of my innocence. Even Sartakh – impartial Sartakh – was cooler than usual in his attitude towards me. I grabbed a goatskin bag and sucked the dregs of kumiss in it.

So here I am – prime suspect in a murder case. I recall in the words spoken by Taulubeg something like a name he has thrown at me at the beginning of this nightmare. I ask Sartakh what his comrade-in-arms was referring to. He ducks his head down towards where I sit sprawling on the ground and repeats it, this time more clearly.

'Zhong Kui – it's the name of a demon.'

It takes me a long moment to realize that the old Tartar has spoken to me in English. It is astonishing. I am half-English and have learned the tongue from my mother. It has been our secret language in the house of my Venetian father. But what is this Eastern barbarian doing speaking the language? He grins at me, full of pleasure at my shock, and pride at his own skill.

'I have waited long to meet someone who knows the tongue, and thought I would try it on you. I see you can speak it.'

'Yes. But how . . . ?'

It turns out that he has learned it from a renegade Englishman – some say a Templar – who ran with Chinghis Khan's army when it invaded Hungary. I have heard of him, because the Englishman was later captured by his own people and killed for his misdeeds. Sartakh has done more than merely hear of him – he has actually met him. It occurs to me that, just like with my mother, I have a secret language I can share with the old Tartar as I strive to prove my innocence. And someone else's guilt. Because now Sartakh is suggesting that I find out who did kill Eldegai.

'Proving another's guilt is the best way to prove your own innocence, after all. And the story of Zhong Kui is not inappropriate.'

I nod. 'Then tell me of this Zhong Kui.'

He explains in a low and guarded tone, not wanting to stir up his companions. Apparently, it is an old story from Cathay.

'The emperor's jade flute goes missing, and then his concubine's embroidered perfume bag disappears too. It's the work of a small demon that no one can catch. Until a larger demon traps it, plucks out its eyes and eats it. The emperor questions the big demon and learns he was once a man called Zhong Kui who killed himself by dashing his head against the palace steps on finding he had failed the palace entrance examinations. In gratitude for the demon's services, the emperor bestows posthumous honours on Zhong Kui, who continues to serve him, ridding the world of mischievous demons.'

It looks as though I am cast as the big demon, and Eldegai's murderer as my little prey. Ordinarily, I would have found the story amusing. I mean, why didn't Zhong Kui, while still alive, merely buy his qualifications like all self-respecting bureaucrats? Then he wouldn't have cause to bash his brains out. Still, I think the application of the epithet to me is almost flattering. But Sartakh's face shows that it is not intended as a compliment. A demon is still a demon, and I am still suspect number one in the murder. He leans forward, his eyes cold and impassive.

'Do everything you can to find the murderer soon, or I will be forced to kill you myself. My men will expect no less of me.'

I try to calm my nerves and return to applying common sense. Apart from seeking a motive, I have to assess who, amongst the Tartars, has had the best opportunity to kill Eldegai. I try to recall where everyone was sitting when the kumiss drinking bout progressed to its conclusion. But I soon realize that the task is almost hopeless. And pointless. Once everyone else had fallen into a drunken stupor, the murderer could have trampled right over the recumbent bodies and not disturbed anyone. I rack my brains to recall if anyone had passed on the kumiss sack a little more often than was reasonable. I immediately eliminate Kyrill. He had been like a pig at a swill trough with the brew, tipping it down his gullet and dribbling the excess down his greasy beard. Later, his stentorian snores had preceded my own descent into the blessed oblivion fed by alcohol. Besides, he had not known any of the Tartars before our forced incarceration and had done nothing to create any ill feeling. I strike him from my list. I am left with the original band of Tartars. The two older men, Sartakh and Karakuchuk, have certainly been restrained in their drinking. But then older, wiser heads often wish to keep their brains clear, where others fall into temptation. Maybe one day I will be able to say the same for myself. Taulubeg, the shortest and stockiest of the group, which is saying something in a band of Tartars, has drunk with a ferocity commensurate with his fiery temper. Perhaps he could hold his liquor better than the others – who knows? The two youngest men, Tetuak and Ulan, appeared to drink their share – Tetuak because it fitted his boastful nature to be seen to carry the booze. However, I recall at least once seeing Ulan tip the sack up to his lips but not swallow. As if he didn't want to appear weak, but also didn't want to drink too much. Was that a deliberate act to keep him sober for a later evil deed?

My mind buzzes with the aftereffects of the booze, and I can't get things into focus.

Then something happens that distracted my attention completely. Ulan, as if to confound my previous thought, brusquely demands the kumiss, which lies near to Sartakh's left hand. The old man leans over and grasps the leather sack. As he bends forward to push the kumiss sack to Ulan, I notice something gleaming inside the folds of Sartakh's fur jacket. He doesn't see my shocked look, but as he sits back upright he pulls his jacket tighter around his middle, once more hiding what I saw. However, it is too late. I have seen the golden tablet that had been Eldegai's and which I had coveted while gaming at Sic Bo. Now it is in Sartakh's possession. He has stolen the gold, and maybe killed Eldegai for it. I know then I will have to add the only Tartar I considered an ally to my list of suspects. My head is swimming. If I can't even trust Sartakh, my confidant and translator, can I ever escape from being accused and punished for the murder myself?

As I bend forward to pick up the kumiss sack, something digs into my ribs. I finally recall the Black Book of Brân that was to have been my passport to Sarai, and the prediction that I found in it. The one that jumped out at me, as if it wanted to be read. Doesn't it say something about demons and Tartars? I slide the book from the folds of my jacket. The cover is dark and shiny in the firelight, and it feels warm and alive in my grasp. Flipping through the pages of prophecies, I find the quatrain in question:

Tartarus' hordes irrupt through Alexander's gate.
Six Christian kingdoms crumble in a breath.
Though Latin traders use long spoons to eat,
It won't protect them from a demon's death.

I once joked about these prophecies and denied their significance. Now, in the straits I find myself, this particular one isn't so ridiculous. Its import doesn't seem to bode well for me. The first two lines are now clear enough. The West's first sight of the Tartars has been when they surged through the Pass of Derbend between the Caucasus and the Caspian Sea – the so-called Iron Gates of Alexander. And there must have been at least six dukes, princes and other assorted nobles who died in the Battle of Liegnitz alone. As for the last two lines, any other reader could take them as a general warning about consorting with the devilish Tartars. Usually, these prophecy books addressed the grand affairs of kings and nobles, their issues of state and world-shattering events. Not the meddlings of little men like me and you. But these lines are uncannily accurate. If I am the Latin trader, then this old monk Brân is saying I will be involved in a demon's death – Ulan has called Eldegai a demon, after all. On the other hand, he may be suggesting I myself, in the guise of Zhong Kui, would die a 'demon's death'.

I shudder, even though until now I reckoned I didn't believe in mad prophecies. This stuff all seems too accurate to be scorned as nonsense now, however. Anxiously, I flip the handful of pages over, but none of the other prophecies makes sense. I look at the last quatrain, perhaps in the vain hope that there is a happy ending. I notice there is a gap between the last two verses, bigger than that between all the others throughout the book. This final set of verses, written in the same hand, seems different somehow. It is expressed in a more modern style, though still in Latin. It seems to me as though whoever has copied the original verses has had a yearning to sneak his own predictions in with the older ones. But was not bold enough to include them fully with the original predictions. These lines are smaller and more discreet:

Though portents dire do fill with dread
And great significance implanted here,
Take care to always use your head,
Seek out the lie, for then your way is clear.

I peer closely at them, and smile. I grab the sack of kumiss and drain the slimy dregs. The words of the anonymous scribe have just given me an idea. And all this talk of demons means that a plan is beginning to form in my mind.

For its climax, I will need the services of the Russian priest. Any con artist needs a good accomplice – a 'shill', we call them – and the more trustworthy he is, the better. Well, who could be more trusted than a priest? Normally, the shill purports to be a complete stranger, who just happens to be passing by, when the con man is sucking in the victim. This chance stranger confirms what is being said by the con man and apparently goes on his way. That wouldn't entirely work in the circumstances, but Kyrill arrived at the stove-house before me, and the Tartars know we are strangers therefore. What greater confirmation could the sting's victim have of the con man's tale than from the mouth of a priest? Kyrill has already innocently affirmed his credentials as a man of God. Now I will have to risk bringing him into my confidence. In the meantime I will play it by ear, setting the mood. I turn to the group of sullen Tartars and smile confidently.

'Do you remember when Eldegai first arrived? Ulan, there, thought he was a demon. Then later Tetuak spoke of the sirens of the Great Desert of Lop. That they sometimes seize the horse and leave the rider. But sometimes they also rip the bowels out of the rider and leave the body on the horse. Of course, it wasn't a demon riding in – it was only Eldegai. Just another traveller, like us. And he wasn't dead. Then.'

Sartakh mutters a clearer translation of my poor mixture of Turkic and Tartar to his compatriots. Their eyes widen, and Ulan throws a sharp comment back. Sartakh translates for me.

'He says, then do you think Eldegai was killed by a demon?'

I'm not sure if Ulan is entirely serious, but all the Tartars appear to be hanging on my response. The storm wind rises, spattering a swirl of hail on the outside of the shelter. It sounds as if something intangible is scratching at the walls, seeking to enter. The young Tartar named Tetuak draws a sharp breath and glances nervously over his shoulder. All this talk of demons is getting to him. I'm glad – that is what I am playing for. I want the Tartars to be fearful and open to suggestion. Kyrill casts a look of godly disapproval my way, which I ignore, and press on.

'I cannot say, but all this talk of demons reminds me of a story I once heard of creatures at the furthest edge of the world who have no neck or head. Their faces are in the middle of their chests. I would not like to come across them on a night like this. Maybe then I would be convinced. Of demons. Have any of you ever come across such monsters in your travels?'

As Sartakh translates the story, I am aware of a communal shudder that runs through the little group. The very idea of headless men is horrific to them. They shake their heads in denial of ever having seen such monsters. But I can see it has stirred their fears and fevered imagination, which is my intention. It is Karakuchuk who now responds to my uneasy story of headless monsters. I don't fully understand what he says, but I will tell it to you as best I can with only a little of my own embroidery.

'I have seen monsters,' he says.

Karakuchuk is as old as Sartakh but a little more reserved. He has hovered on the edge of the group most of the time. That he should speak up so readily is a surprise. Maybe the eerie quality of the setting – all of us trapped by the storm with a body bundled up in the darkness outside, and talking of demons – maybe it has sparked off his recollection. Whatever it is, his face, normally squashed and wrinkled due to his lack of teeth, becomes animated and alive.

'It was a long time ago, when these things were more common than now. After the campaign in India, in the time of Chinghis's son. As we returned through the wastelands, we came across a tribe of women whose men were in dog's form.'

The other Tartars cast sidelong glances at Sartakh – he of the reputedly canine hearing – and grin. But this is no snide joke at Sartakh's expense. Karakuchuk is in earnest.

'I saw them. Dark-skinned, hairy women, they were, in the village that we occupied. And no sign of ordinary men. The men-dogs ran in packs, and I saw them attack one of our men and kill him. We tried to shoot them with our arrows, but they had rolled in freezing water, and their pelts were coated with ice. It rendered our arrows harmless. We ran after them, but they were too swift, and ran off into the night.' He shudders. 'We left there pretty soon afterwards.'

I would not have taken old Karakuchuk for a coward. Nor for someone who could not see that the menfolk of the village had merely disappeared into the wastelands for safety when they heard that the Tartars were coming. Still, I had not been there when the pack of dogs attacked. Maybe I would have believed the stories too, in the circumstances. He shuffles to the back of the group once more, brooding. There is an awkward silence.

Suddenly, Kyrill groans and stretches his limbs. He is still unused to squatting on the floor and expresses a longing for a good chair. While the Tartars are distracted by the thought of Karakuchuk's tale, I quietly speak to the priest. I tell him I need his assistance in determining the identity of the murderer.

'I have no idea who it could have been,' he hisses anxiously, casting a fearful glance around the tent.

When his eyes turn back on me, I wonder for a moment if he also thinks I am the killer. I return his look with a confident gaze that I have no right to display.

'Leave that to me. Just follow my lead, when I come to the crux of the matter. Oh, and have one of those leeches ready that you carry around with you in the water jar.'

'The leeches? What for?'

He listens hard while I whisper in his ear what I need him to do. As he then settles down to sleep in the dark outer edge of the stove-house, I see that one Tartar in particular has not taken his eyes off me. Young Tetuak is a moody individual, given much to drinking and boasting of his prowess with the powerful Tartar bow. Until, I suddenly recall, Eldegai poured scorn on his more fanciful claim of killing three men with one arrow. His face had been red with stored resentment for the rest of the night. Nor had he been so loud-mouthed again, when his comrades spoke of battle honours. The rest of the band were obviously veterans, apart from Ulan, who had nothing much to boast of, being no more than a boy himself. But Tetuak was still old enough to have campaigned somewhere in the growing Tartar Empire. I now wonder why he hasn't talked of any battle deeds. Is he less bold than he suggests, and did Eldegai hit a sore spot in his armoury? And hurt his pride hard enough to cause him to retaliate in the dark?

Suddenly, there is a gust of wind down the flue that causes the fire to flare. Tetuak squeals.

'There is a devil on the roof, and it won't come in because there are Christians present.' He stares at me, then gestures also at the somnolent Kyrill. 'We should get rid of them, and the devil will enter.'

I am curious. 'Why would you want the devil to come in?'

'Because it could tell us who murdered Eldegai.' He turned to his comrades. 'You have all seen a kham evoke a good devil before.'

'A kham?' I mutter an enquiry of Sartakh.

The old man shrugs. 'A diviner. A shaman. Anyone who wishes to seek answers of a devil has a kham place cooked meat in their tent. Then the kham invokes a devil and beats on a drum to call it. The kham enters into a fury and is bound. Then the devil comes in the darkness, eats the meat and speaks. I suppose a kham is like to that priest there.'

I grin to myself at the thought of Father Kyrill being compared to some wild maniac calling on the devil for answers. It is lucky he has fallen asleep, and so misses Sartakh's unflattering comparison. But then, bearing in mind his propensity for prophecy, maybe Sartakh is not far from the mark. I think fleetingly of the Black Book of Brân tucked in my jacket, and the copyist's own effort at prophecy. Has it not served up to me a clue to the murderer's identity? Tetuak, meanwhile, is still muttering about my unhelpful presence. Apparently, the devil sitting on the roof would enter if I leave along with Kyrill. And freeze to death outside as a consequence. I also have no doubt that such a result would then rapidly confirm my guilt in the matter of the murder. If Tetuak is the killer, it would be a good diversion tactic for him. But I don't propose to give him, killer or not, such an easy way out.

For a moment the roar outside the shack ceases, and everyone draws breath. The abyss of silence is more frightening than the constant battering of sound has been before it. Taulubeg licks his lips and looks shiftily around at his companions. The little man has a nondescript face, but one that is prone to revealing more of what is inside the man than any of his comrades' visages. Where such as Sartakh hides behind an impassive face, Taulubeg signposts his moods as soon as they come on him.

'Devils, demons,' he grumbles. Poking a short, calloused finger at Tetuak, he jibes at the younger man. 'You know nothing. South beyond Armenia there are real monsters who have only one arm and one hand in the middle of their chest. To shoot a bow, two of them stand together. And they have only one leg and foot, but still can run faster than a horse.'

Tetuak gives a short barking laugh at the absurdity of such a tale. Devils he is prepared to accept, but obviously not strange monsters.

'Run faster than a horse. With only one leg!'

Taulubeg's already ruddy features darken even more, as his face reveals his anger once again. He is not going to be derided in such a way. And especially not by someone who runs off at the mouth like Tetuak.

'Yes. They run by jumping on their one foot. And when they tire of this, they revolve in a circle on hand and foot. They are called the Ciclopedes.'

At this further elaboration on Taulubeg's story, Tetuak's amusement turns into a helpless guffaw of mirth. It is only stifled when Sartakh nudges him in the ribs to remind him to be respectful to his elders. The laughter is cut off, but the damage is done. Taulubeg continues to glare at his derider with pure hatred in his eyes. The message is clear – the boy will pay for his mockery later. And I am suddenly reminded of the incident between Taulubeg and Eldegai over the nauseous stew. Can Taulubeg have harboured a grudge, only to take his opportunity for revenge in the teeth of the storm that now rages around our shack? I feel the urge to look him squarely in the eye.

With the walls creaking and groaning around us, I rise as if to stretch my stiff legs. Several sets of eyes shift suspiciously, following me as I step around the edge of the flickering fire. Taulubeg leans conspicuously away from me as I bend down to retrieve the kumiss bag at his side. He actually avoids my scrutiny, and I wonder again if he could be the murderer. Shoving a hand into the small of my back, and bending to get some feeling into it, I move to drop down closer beside Sartakh. I murmur a question to him in English.

The Tartar's pronunciation is execrable, but using English gives us a secret, common language. To use it now means no one knows what I am saying. And I particularly don't want Taulubeg to overhear. Even so, I studiously avoid the use of names.

'Sartakh, my friend, remember earlier, when you had to come between the dead man and our quick-tempered friend over there?'

The old Tartar screws his eyes up and gazes at me hard. For a moment I think he has not understood my words. Or to whom I refer. Then he speaks in his garbled way.

'Think you that . . . the one you talk of . . . mayhap killed in revenge for such a slight?'

I shrug my shoulders, wanting his opinion. Valuing his knowledge of the man. Taulubeg, of whom we speak, is sitting hunched over with his head bowed, ignoring the desultory chatter that flows from his other companions. The storm continues to rip around the stove-house, pinning us all together in its confines. Sartakh understands my gesture.

'Perhaps right you are. But . . . he . . . is more likely to have harmed him at the time. Not later, when his mood has flown.'

I sigh, and acknowledge his reading of Taulubeg's hot and cold temperament. Quick to act when provoked, but quick to cool off also. Sartakh takes the kumiss bag from my grasp and tips it to his lips.

'Still . . . who can tell how troubles fester in a man's brain?'

He leaves this reservation hanging in the air and gulps down the heady drink, his eyes twinkling. I won't strike Taulubeg entirely from my list, then. Glancing over to the door, outside of which is the bundle that is the dead body of Eldegai, I wonder who else amongst the Tartars has reason to have killed him. Tetuak has been mortified by Eldegai, who showed up the emptiness of his boasting concerning his skill with a bow. I next consider Ulan, who has certainly had the opportunity, as it was he who first discovered me standing over the body. Had he already been awake, waiting to shift the blame for his own actions on to another?

I glance across at where he is now engaged deep in conversation with the erratic Tetuak. The confining nature of the storm outside seems to have animated the young Tartar. The enforced proximity has driven him to engage in more intercourse than I have seen before. Perhaps the feeling of being confined with a dead man – and his murderer – is unsettling. Or maybe it is the kumiss we have all drunk. In any case, Ulan is getting red-faced over something, prodding a finger at Tetuak. Who in return is shaking his head vigorously.

I again go over in my mind the aftermath of the

argument that had blown up between Taulubeg and Eldegai. The occasion when Taulubeg accused him of being too snooty. Ulan had been there too, and had been angry over what Eldegai said about being the Il-Khan's envoy. I had heard the words too, and now need the importance confirmed. I lean backwards on one elbow across the rough skins that insulate the ground inside the stove-house. Sartakh is sitting with his back against the bundles that are piled around the edge of the room. His eyes are closed, but I am sure the canny old man is as alert as usual. I speak to him in English again.

'Why would Ulan be angry to learn that Eldegai was an envoy going to the ruler in Sarai?'

Sartakh's face does not betray anything, but I can see his shoulders tense at the import of my question. He slowly raises an eyelid and glances my way. He speaks, hardly moving his lips.

'So, know you that he was more than a mere traveller? How clever of you. I suppose you saw the paizah.'

Through his half-closed eyes he observes my puzzled look. Paizah?

'The gold tablet you coveted when you were cheating Eldegai out of his possessions.'

'Cheating . . . ?'

I refrain from any feigned outrage, when I see the smile playing gently on Sartakh's lips. After the start of the gambling, when I allowed Lady Luck to dictate who won and build the confidence of my marks, he took no further part in the proceedings. I thought then that he was just maintaining a distance as the leader of the band. Now I understand that he had seen through my tricks immediately. But then he clearly doesn't care if I have duped his comrades. That is their business. I change tack and go on the offensive. After all, I suspect Sartakh of stealing this paizah himself.

'Paizah, yes. The tablet that now appears to be in your possession, Sartakh.'

His eyes open wide now and bore into me like gimlets in the hands of a Venetian shipwright. He gives a little barking laugh.

'I see. You are not sure whether or not I killed Eldegai for the paizah.' He shifts forward so his mouth is close to my ear. He whispers in it. 'Let me explain what it represents.' He slides his hand inside his coat, and though he doesn't bring out the gold tablet I know he is holding it firmly. 'This tablet is the authority of the khan given to him who carries it. Anyone who sees it must aid the bearer of the paizah. It is more than a piece of gold. It is the word of the khan himself. No Tartar would attempt to steal it, for to do so would mean certain death. The tablet told me that Eldegai was the envoy of the Il-Khan of Persia. Subordinate to the Great Khan, but an important khan nevertheless. No, I didn't steal the paizah. I took it from his coat after his death, when I checked the dagger for blood. Now I keep it safe.'

I ponder for a while, taking in this new information. It still doesn't provide the answer to why Ulan reacted so badly to Eldegai's revelation. I tell Sartakh what I heard Ulan say, calling Eldegai a demon in human form for going to Sarai. The old man sighs and throws another dung brick on the fire. The flames die for a moment, then flare up brighter than before, lighting everyone's face in an eerie glow.

'Devils, demons. I wish you hadn't mentioned monsters in the first place,' he grumbles. 'Anyway, mayhap you heard wrong. You are still inexpert in our tongue.'

I shake my head, gazing across the flames at the figure of Ulan, who has now slumped back and appears to be dozing. His altercation with Tetuak is apparently finished.

'No. I heard the words well. He said what he said.' I hesitate for a moment, watching Sartakh frown in annoyance. My gambler's instinct tells me that Sartakh's interest is piqued. Now all I have to do is make him believe he is cleverer than me. I don a look of total perplexity.

'I just don't understand what it all means.'

Sartakh's eyes gleam.

'Then you should have listened just now to what he was saying to Tetuak. You see, it's all to do with who is really the Great Khan. When the last khan died, there remained his three brothers to succeed him, though you can forget the middle one. Hulegu is the Il-Khan of Persia, of whom we speak, and has no ambitions to be the Great Khan. Though it matters who he will support out of the other two. Arigh-Boke is the youngest brother, but he sits at the seat of power in Karakorum. And despite being the youngest, he is . . . how would you say it in your dog tongue? He carries on in the old ways.'

I know the sort from my trading days – holding everybody in their enterprise back, while those with new ideas want to forge ahead. I can think of a choice word or two to describe them – prehistoric, stick-in-the-mud, fogey – but I choose to be polite.

'A traditionalist.'

'A trad . . .' Sartakh can't quite get his tongue around the word, waves his hand to acknowledge the expression, and presses on. 'Now, two years ago, the older brother, while still on campaign in Cathay, mind you, breaks all the rules. Without returning to our heartland, he goes and proclaims himself Great Khan. There's a big—'

I feed him the word he seeks. 'Rift.'

He nods. 'Big rift. All the lesser rulers – like Alghu, the Chaghadai khan – are scrabbling around trying to decide whom to ally themselves with. I suppose the fact that Eldegai was on his way to Sarai would suggest Hulegu has decided which way to jump. And that is along with the traditionalists. Young Ulan, however, favours the older brother.'

There is the sound of a rasping throat over my shoulder, and Karakuchuk leans forward out of the dark. He spits a yellowish gob into the fire, where it sizzles briefly and is gone. I am reminded of the time he interfered in my gambling to suggest a game of Sic Bo. He is once again poking his nose in where it's not wanted. He growls at Sartakh in their own tongue.

'Speak a proper language, Sartakh. Not the devil's tongue, so we know where you stand.'

I can see the fire in Sartakh's eyes, but he keeps calm.

'I was merely telling the traveller about Arigh-Boke and his brother.'

Karakuchuk growls again, wiping the remains of the saliva from his whiskery chin.

'The brother you speak of is no more than an impostor. How can he be Great Khan, when he doesn't even come to Karakorum for the kuriltai – the great gathering?'

It sounds to me as if this brother has taken a big gamble to win the crown. Not being at the traditional place to stake his claim, he breaks with the old rules and does it anyway. I am beginning to like him. Karakuchuk continues grumbling, however. 'The boy's gone native away there in Cathay; he's in love with all the effete ways of the Chins. I wouldn't be surprised if he doesn't move the capital there next.'

Ulan hears what the old man has said, and suddenly there is tension boiling in the stove-house. 'What's wrong with him? Arigh-Boke is a fossil, always hanging on to the old ways. And there's much to marvel at in Cathay.'

'Well, as none of us here's been there, how can you comment?' sneers the old man.

Ulan rocks back on his haunches.

'Well, no. But I've heard lots of stories.'

'Stories,' laughs Karakuchuk. 'I've heard stories about enchanted mountains, unicorns, and ants that dig for gold. It doesn't mean they're true.'

Ulan butts in again.

'I'll tell you a story I was told by a Chin. He told me of a province to the west which, at whatever age a man enters it, then that is the age he keeps. But you have to stay there to remain alive.'

Taulubeg snorts, staring at the wide-eyed wonder shining in the visage of Ulan. Then he cackles and spits a phlegmy gob into the fire.

'Hehe. A Chin. I bet he was a eunuch court official who sat on his arse all day. I don't know why you believed such nonsense. I would have opened his veins for insulting me with patent lies.'

He pauses, and his final comment is directed straight at Ulan.

'And that's what you want. A Great Khan who listens to lying eunuchs all day long. Give me Arigh-Boke any day.'

Tetuak has also gone as pale as a pewter storm cloud over Venice, and Ulan is rendered speechless. Only Karakuchuk nods as though he agrees with Taulubeg. The room falls silent, and the only sound is the whining of the restless wind outside. And the creaking of the walls as they buckle and swell like ancient bellows with the air soughing in and out. It is as though we are all sitting inside some monster's chest. I can see the success of my planting the idea of unnatural activity in the minds of those present. I have them scared, and uncertain. In fact, even my pragmatic Venetian brain is jangling in the heavy atmosphere. And the sense of unease that is tangible in the very air everyone sucks into their lungs. I wanted them to be unsure of each other, and they surely are now. Better that than united in their unease about me.

Besides, all has suddenly become clear to me. I now know who has murdered Eldegai. I just have to convince the others that I am right. And that I had no reason to kill him. In fact, I had every reason for him to prosper. I think back over my last meeting with Eldegai, just before his death. It is what he told me then that I now have used to figure out who the killer is. Along with a few more shrewd observations, and the prophecy of the mystery scribe. But I'm still going to have to extract a confession. And much as I might long for the dark and feverish confines of the Doge's palace dungeons back in Venice to assist me, I know I have to rely on my own wits. And a little sleight of hand.

I peruse my companions, sitting huddled around the flickering fire at the heart of the stove-house. The brightness of the flames has faded to a cherry glow that barely illumines all our faces. The outer ring of dark walls has disappeared into the gloom, making the sound of their creaking in the rushing wind more eerie and uncanny. We might as well be sitting in the open under some dreadful, starless sky with a horde of winged beasts flapping down to pick us off like carrion. The unease engendered by the gloom and the tales of monsters lodged in everyone's minds admirably suits my purpose. Instinctively, the Tartars have moved closer to the fire as the scope of its warmth and brightness has faded. I rise and stalk around the perimeter of the room, which is half in darkness. It is time for a bit of showmanship.

I kick Kyrill's skinny haunches to arouse him from sleep and make my voice as sonorous as it can be.

'Come, priest. I feel the soul of Eldegai calling me. It wishes to speak.'

There is a stirring amongst the Tartars as the import of my words penetrates their skulls. One or two are moved to protest, but Sartakh stops them with an upraised palm. His eyes twinkle with curiosity as he searches my face for the meaning of my actions. I put on my best gambling face and drag Kyrill unwillingly towards the door. When I open it, the blast of cold air hits my face like sand from the lagoon whipped up by a vicious easterly wind. We make a swift job of dragging the stiffened body of Eldegai into the stove- house once again. Sartakh slams the door closed behind us, sealing in the warmth. The body lies close to the stove, and I stand with my back to the door, preventing anyone leaving. I abruptly indicate that everyone should form a circle around the corpse. Then I push into the group and take up my position.

We are now all sat close together in a ring, with Kyrill at my shoulder. To my left sits the sour-faced Tetuak – the boastful but unproven Tetuak. To his left squats fresh-faced Ulan, like all youths, convinced of his own rightness, but untested in battle. And then beyond him I can make out the wrinkled face of old Karakuchuk, veteran warrior and canny gambler. Between him and me, to my right hand, huddles Taulubeg – believer in demons, whose nervous features betray the fact. He isn't sure whether he is sitting with a devil even now. Sartakh is sitting slightly back from the ring, as if aloof. I try not to be worried about this. I have discounted him as the killer. He retrieved the gold paizah only as part of his duty as leader of the group, not with theft in mind. But with him sitting dangerously close to my back, I only hope my estimation of his innocence is right.

I take a deep breath and begin.

'Some say Eldegai was a demon . . .'

Ulan looks startled and begins to protest. But I hold up my hand to silence him. He subsides back on to his haunches, still tense.

'Some say I myself am a demon.'

I pause, but this time there is no protest. My shock of red hair, my bushy beard that has been untrimmed for months, and my green eyes no doubt enhance my dubious reputation. And I am going to use it to my advantage. I grin wolfishly, and four pairs of Tartar eyes stare nervously back at me. In one pair I can see the eyes of a murderer. Only Sartakh's eyes are calmly indifferent. I make a large gesture with my right hand, encompassing Kyrill.

'But the priest I travel with is a great magician.'

Now I have them. They stare goggle-eyed at the figure behind me in the darkness of the tent. I pray Kyrill is alert to his cue. 'The priest is a fisher of souls.'

'Take care, Venetian,' mutters Kyrill. 'Do not blaspheme.'

I breathe a sigh of relief. At least I now know he hasn't fallen asleep again.

'Just pray for Eldegai's immortal soul, Father Kyrill,' I intone, keeping my audience entranced. 'And I will do the rest.'

All eyes are fixed on the black shape of the priest as he steps forward and kneels over the bundle that is the mortal remains of Eldegai. They watch as he makes the sign of the cross and says a prayer for the dead man. I myself am praying – that Kyrill has remembered what I have earlier coached him to do. And that he will do it well. The leech jar that I have picked up from the shelf above the stove stirs under my jacket. I tremble as Kyrill lays a hand on the body, then closes his fist as though he is drawing something from the mortal remains. Something like the dead man's very soul. I suddenly have a feeling that this is going to work.

With a powerful gesture that I didn't think he had in him, he casts the invisible contents of his fist to the mat at my feet, beside the embers of the fire. The Tartars stare through the glow, unsure if they can see anything or not. Then I make a pass over the spot, and there, wriggling on the matting, is the black and slippery form of Eldegai's immortal soul. A communal gasp escapes the lips of the band of Tartars, and they pull back in fear.

I pick the leech up from the floor by its tail and let it blindly rear its head. I am glad my sleight of hand has not failed me, when I quickly palmed it from the jar and cast it on the floor before it could attach itself to me. I hold on now despite my horror of the slimy creature. We are close to the climax of my performance. I mutter under my breath to Sartakh.

'Tell them Eldegai's soul is seeking his killer.'

Sartakh speaks, and even his voice is shaky at what seems to be taking place. But he speaks with conviction. I give him my next command.

'Tell them all to put their right hand over the fire.'

At Sartakh's command, four shaking hands are thrust out over the heat of the dying embers. I bring the wriggling worm to the centre of the circle of fingers. Its head probes the air. Tetuak's eyes follow the wavering form of the leech with horror, but he holds his hand firm. Karakuchuk's fist is steady too, and his wrinkled face betrays no emotion. His eyes are dead and glassy. Taulubeg's method of control is to close his eyes firmly, but his lips are still forming a prayer to Tengri. Ulan is the most fearful of all, and his hand trembles as the seeker of truth dips and weaves in the air.

I hoped to guide the leech towards the killer's hand

myself, but to my astonishment it suddenly goes unerringly for it. Ulan squeals, but the leech fixes firmly on another hand. That of Karakuchuk. I should have guessed the hand of our animal butcher would be irresistible to a bloodsucker. For I have already figured out that Karakuchuk's skill has also been used on Eldegai. The butcher's favourite method of slaughter is to cut open the animal's chest and to still its heart by squeezing it with his powerful fist. In just such a way did he end Eldegai's life.

Screaming, and feverishly trying to brush the harmless leech from the back of his hand, Karakuchuk staggers to the door of the stove-house and tears it open. The wind roars into the room, throwing everyone and everything into confusion. Mats and pots fly through the air in the gust, and it is some time before Ulan and Sartakh together manage to force the door closed again. Leaving Karakuchuk outside in the maelstrom.

I look into Sartakh's eyes, questioning what should be done. He shakes his head.

'Leave him to his fate. He will not survive out there on his own.'

After the confusion caused by the wind is rectified, an uncanny silence descends on the interior. Only Sartakh is moved to speak.

'Tell me, Zuliani. How did you know it was Karakuchuk? Once you had realized Eldegai was an envoy from the Il-Khan coming to Sarai, you should have suspected Ulan. Karakuchuk would not have killed someone who sided with Arigh-Boke and the traditionalists.'

'You really don't know, do you?'

Sartakh looks a little put out at my comment, but his voice is firm and unwavering. 'Know what?'

'That Eldegai was not offering Hulegu's alliance with

Boke. He told me himself that he was bringing bad news. The Il-Khan was throwing in his lot with the other brother. The older brother.'

'Why would Eldegai tell you that?'

I hesitate, not wanting to explain the little matter of a long trade scam and the opportunities suggested by Eldegai in Cathay. And how I was going to have used Eldegai. I do tell him Eldegai informed me 'the old man' knew his intentions. Sartakh's face breaks into a smile of comprehension.

'You thought he meant me. But then, when I told you Eldegai was going to Sarai to offer Hulegu's alliance, and clearly didn't know what his message was—'

'I had to think again. Ulan didn't know the true course of events either. So it could have been him who killed Eldegai. As indeed with Tetuak or Taulubeg, for other reasons. But there was one stumbling block. They all spoke the truth to me. Everyone spoke the truth to me, except one. And I was reminded of a prophetic bit of doggerel.'

In fact, it was that verse at the end of the Black Book written as a warning by the copyist to anyone taking the prophecies too seriously. It went:

Though portents dire do fill with dread
And great significance implanted here,
Take care to always use your head,
Seek out the lie, for then your way is clear.

'Only Karakuchuk lied. He implied he'd never been to Cathay, when Ulan spoke in admiration of the place. He had clearly forgotten about telling me where he learned Sic Bo, the game we played much earlier in the evening. He had fought on campaign in Cathay, and he hated the place and all it stood for. He would stop at nothing to aid Arigh-Boke's cause against his brother. He did stop at nothing, murdering Eldegai, and gouging out the eyes to make it look as if a demon had done it. He even hinted that I might be that demon. But to show I do not place my trust in portents and magic—'

I draw the slim black book from my jacket and with only a small hesitation toss it into the stove. The flames hungrily consume the dry pages, burning like the fires of hell. Each section flares up before curling into a blackened leaf that drifts up the chimney in the hot air currents. In truth, I am glad to get rid of the cursed book. Despite the aid the last quatrain gave me, I feel that no one should have an insight into their future. It is too dangerous and fearful a thing. As I watch the pages blacken, I briefly wonder if this is the only copy. Or if the original still exists, and whether it will continue to puzzle and vex others down the years. I turn back to Sartakh.

'You know, it would not surprise me if Karakuchuk also drugged the kumiss skin he offered up that had us all so drunk. I truly have never experienced so swift a response to such a skinful.'

Sartakh laughs and slaps me on the shoulder.

'You are a veritable demon. From now on I shall call you not Zuliani but Zhong Kui.' He pauses. 'Listen. The storm has ended.'

It is true. The hut no longer shakes and twists, and sweet silence hangs over the encampment. Sartakh unfastens the door, and we both stoop through the low entrance and emerge into a peaceful world. The sky has cleared, and the morning sun is staining the snow a blood red. It feels good to be alive and no longer suspected of murder. Sartakh is gazing out towards the sunrise.

'You will have to replan your route, it seems. Your real goal is further east than you had thought.'

He means the Cathay-loving brother's domain. And he is right. I have already determined to return to Sudak and Friar Giovanni Alberoni. I am certain I can wheedle my way back into his favour and convince him that the Black Book of Brân was no more than a faker's scam. I recall the place which the good friar wanted to go to from the very beginning.

'Yes. I am bound to the court of Kubilai Khan, to the summer palace of Shang-tu, that some call by the name of Xanadu.'

ACT THREE

When three Popes all murdered lie,
And Christ's own kingdom desecrated,
The third age then shall hasten by,
And Antichrist with bloody slaughter sated.

Feast Day of the Translation of St Thomas,[1]
Eighteenth year of the reign of King Edward II

When his fingers touched it, he grunted with satisfaction.

Teetering tiptoed, precariously balanced on three stacked chests that wobbled alarmingly as he pried each crevice, he found a moving stone. Even as his grin widened, the topmost step of his makeshift ladder moved, and the smile was snatched away. He clung to the great pillar, cheek pressed to the stonework in a desperate embrace.

Heart beating like a war-drum, he closed his eyes and blew out his breath, a shiver of pure ice running through his spine as he gently set his feet flat once more. Dear God, but this was fearsome. He daren't fail – and to fall *would* be to fail. He'd be damned if he'd do that.

[1] 7 July 1325

But there was no possibility of success up here like this. Brother Alexander relinquished his hold on the pillar and cautiously returned to the crypt's floor. There, he eyed the chests with a frowning contemplation. It was clear enough that they weren't high enough, all set square on the ground like that – but if he were to put the longest one on end, and a smaller on top of that, he may gain an extra foot of height, as well as being granted the comfort of knowing that the boxes were resting more squarely.

The longer chest was soon lifted, not without effort, grunting, and two curses for which he would have to make penance later, and then he lifted the smallest chest atop. Glancing up at the pillar again, he started to climb.

A few moments later he had it. The mortar between two stones of the pillar had been eased away, leaving a narrow gap into which his book would just fit.

It was a scuffed, tatty old book, yet if half of what Alexander had heard was true, it was one of the most dangerous tomes in all Christendom. If he could, he would have taken it to the calefactory and hurled it on the fire. The flames would quickly destroy its malevolent messages. Not that he could. Books were his life.

He remained for some while sitting on the larger chest, his hands on the ancient marked covers. He had his instructions, and he was keen to complete his mission, but, even as he tried to rise, his lips set in a stubborn line, he felt his hands move almost of their own volition towards the pages of pure, yellowed vellum. He shouldn't look. He'd been warned about the danger. Yet there was something that drove him on. His fingers felt the roughened edges, feeling how the years had scraped at them. Then his eyes caught the first quatrain, and he frowned in the lousy candlelight, peering to make sense of the words.

The first was incomprehensible; and the second and third. He began to frown with perplexity as he riffled through, searching for something that would make sense, but none did.

It was then, his bewilderment growing, that he heard the noise.

At first he told himself it must be rats. God alone knew how many of the cursed creatures lived here. The damned things were all over the place, coming in from the sewer that led out to the river Tyburn near the wall encircling the Palace of Westminster, right next to the abbey. Novices were told that the scrabbling sounds were excommunicated souls seeking an entrance so they might find their way to the altar, thence to heaven. It was ballocks, of course. They all knew the sound of a rat gnawing – but still, there were moments when even a farmer's son could almost believe he heard the voices of the damned in the middle of a wintry night when the wind blew and the rats gnawed more furiously. A little imagination was a terrible thing to a novice.

This wasn't a rat, though. It was a measured, steady tread. And – oh, Christ's cods – it was coming this way!

He hurriedly moved to the door. From here he would have to pass along the corridor, and a man coming this way must see him. He hesitated, and in that moment his life was forfeit.

It was some while later that his screams woke the community of the abbey at Westminster.

Sir Baldwin de Furnshill was breaking his fast in a leisurely manner when the young man appeared in Bishop Walter Stapledon's hall.

'My Lord Bishop!'

Motioning to the fellow, Bishop Walter indicated that he should approach the table. Baldwin cast a glance over the fellow. He was of middle height and clad in a worn habit. Baldwin assumed he was a clerk – but then he saw that the man had a tonsure. A young monk, then. Perhaps a novice. There seemed little of interest about the fellow, as he was introduced as a messenger from the monks of Westminster. Only a remarkable pallor about his thin, pinched features. But many monks were half-starved. It was no surprise that this one looked hungry.

Baldwin shot a look at his friend, Simon Puttock, who sat on the other side of the bishop. Lately the Keeper of the Port of Dartmouth under his patron, Abbot Robert of Tavistock, Simon had for many years before been Abbot Robert's leading bailiff on the waste known as Dartmoor. He was the chief law officer in that wild and dangerous land. Now, though, like Baldwin, he was bored. Neither wished to be in London.

They had arrived here in the bishop's entourage, helping him on his journey, and Baldwin in particular was itching to return home.

Bishop Walter peered short-sightedly at the messenger, who spoke urgently in a low whisper, his mouth almost at the bishop's ear. Bishop Walter chewed slowly but then stopped, apparently startled, and glanced up at him. 'Say that again!' he commanded in a quiet but firm tone.

The messenger, clearly numbed with shock at being sent to converse with the King's treasurer, stammered as he tried to respond.

'Very well. I understand. Please tell your abbot that I shall send him assistance as I may.'

The man was dismissed. He stood upright and glanced about him at all the servants eating, and was gone.

'Trouble, my lord?' Baldwin asked.

Simon looked from one to the other, then nodded to the bottler and held his empty mazer aloft. The bottler grinned quickly and hurried to the top table with a jug of the bishop's best wine.

The bishop eyed the level in Simon's mazer. 'You should drink that quickly.'

'Are we late?' Simon asked.

'No. But you will need to be fortified.'

'Why?' Simon chuckled.

The bishop turned to him, and now Simon could see how pale he had become. His voice was low, quiet, but certain. 'Because if what this messenger says is right, you are about to see something that will turn the strongest stomach, Simon.'

The Prior of Westminster Abbey, commonly called Old Stephen by the less respectful members of his Chapter, sat back at his desk and shook his head. His goblet of wine had already been emptied for the fourth time, and he set himself to refilling it from the jug, releasing the breath from his lungs slowly, trying desperately to calm his shattered nerves.

Alex. Poor, stupid Alex. He had been there to fetch the book. Well, no one would say that Stephen would be able to. Not now, not in his sixtieth year. A fall from that great pillar would incapacitate him. So he'd sent Alex. Bright, quick-witted little Alex. The boy who'd raised the intelligence of the whole abbey when he arrived here six years ago . . . and who was dead.

'It was terrible, prior,' the Franciscan said.

Ach, God! There were times when he was happy to entertain guests, but not today. Stephen nodded agreement as Friar Martin sighed. He was a tall fellow, this young mendicant. Not yet eight and twenty, if he had to guess, yet Martin's robes were already ancient and patched, his feet unshod, his face streaked with filth. Yet for all his outward signs of poverty, he had a quiet confidence. Quite unlike most of the humble beggar-types, he exuded calmness.

Stephen took up his goblet and slurped wine in the hope he could avert ... Too late! The shaking had taken hold of him again, and now his hands were trembling so much he thought that the cup must fall. There was nothing – *nothing* – that could have prepared him for that sight. The blood ...

'Can I help you, prior?' Friar Martin enquired.

Yes, Stephen thought. You can leave my convent. Right now. But aloud he merely said: 'No, my friend. I am just saddened to think of my assistant.'

In his room, the abbot knelt in prayer before his small altar, his forehead resting on his clasped hands, and as he muttered his prayers he shivered, the tears falling in a steady trickle down his sallow cheeks.

Friar Martin walked silently along the flags to the altar, where he saw the slim, stooped figure of Friar James.

James did not glance at him. 'How is the *good* prior?'

'As good as may be expected. Deeply shocked.'

'Hardly surprising.'

'Why do you say that?'

'There is gossip even here. You should know that. The men who live in grand institutions are often diverted from the path of contemplation and their order. Some form attachments with each other.'

'You mean the prior ... ?'

'Aye. The dead lad was his catamite. A vile practice. Some could almost say the prior is lucky not to be there with the lad. Are you not shocked and disgusted, brother?'

Friar Martin tilted his head a little and peered speculatively towards the altar. 'Yes. I think I am, rather. You will not speak of such matters before me again. You understand? *Never.*'

'Prior, my Lord Bishop Walter is here to see you.'

'Oh, my lord, I am grateful you could come!' Stephen said. He rose and gripped his staff before shuffling towards the bishop. 'I didn't know whom to call . . . and my abbot refused to call for the coroner or . . .'

His voice faltered as he noticed the men behind the bishop.

'My good prior, this is my good friend Sir Baldwin de Furnshill. He is the Keeper of the King's Peace in Crediton. I asked him to join me here to see if he may help.'

'Oh, my brothers will be most distressed if a king's officer were to invade our precinct,' Stephen said unhappily.

'Do not concern yourself,' the bishop said. 'Simon Puttock here has been bailiff to Abbot Robert for these nine years past.'

'Ah, a man who is used to discretion in dealing with religious offences?'

Simon glanced at the bishop and Baldwin before nodding slowly. 'I've had some experience.'

'That is excellent. Excellent! But my manners! Please, let me offer you wine?'

With surprising alacrity for a man who needs must use a staff, the prior moved to his table and picked up a small bell. It rang clearly, and a shuffling gait was soon heard outside. A young, tonsured head appeared about the door, and Simon recognized the young messenger.

'Robert, please fetch goblets and wine.'

The boy nodded – with his soulful eyes he reminded Baldwin of a mastiff deprived of its meal – and disappeared.

'Would you care for some food as well?'

'The body, prior,' Bishop Walter said gently. 'Where is it?'

Prior Stephen gazed down at his table. 'It's down in the crypt.'

'We shall need to see it,' Baldwin said.

The prior was clearly distressed by the death of this man. Violence was rare and naturally disturbing to a man like Prior Stephen. Few would expect murder in a great abbey – except violence was natural in any large foundation. It was not so many years ago that the Dean of Exeter had conspired in the death of a political enemy in the Chapter, hiring the vicars of Heavitree and Ottery St Mary to murder the cathedral's precentor. Where there was money, privilege and power, there were motives for murder.

Still . . . 'You are sure that this was murder?' he asked.

To his shock, Stephen began to laugh shrilly, like a man sent suddenly lunatic.

'Faugh!' Simon exclaimed. 'What's that?'

They were being taken down into the crypt along a dank, dingy corridor under the abbey's Chapter House when the smell caught at his throat. It was there, over the odour of burning pitch from the torch in the hand of the old lay brother who was taking them along the narrow stone passageways.

Bishop Walter had remained with the prior, and Simon could see why. Prior Stephen was in a dreadful state. He would say nothing about the dead fellow, only that he was most certainly murdered. More than that he would not say, but instead his eyes filmed over, and he started to shake uncontrollably, wine spilling from his goblet and showering his table and lap.

'Did the bishop say anything to you about the body?' Simon asked in a muted voice.

'No more than he told you. He was silent all the way here,' Baldwin said. 'It is most peculiar. I have never known him to be so close before.'

Simon wrinkled his nose in disgust. 'Can you smell that?'

Baldwin shot him a disdainful look. 'My sense of smell is fine, Simon. I can detect excrement – but that is no surprise. I dare say we are close to the sewers.'

'Not here,' the lay brother said.

'Then why that odour?' Baldwin asked.

'I was told not to say.'

'Who told you not to say?' Baldwin asked.

'The prior. You'll see soon enough anyway.'

'See what?' Simon said.

And then they turned a corner, and he saw a flickering light ahead of them. It glinted from the moisture on the stone walls, from puddles on the ground – and from something else.

'Sweet Jesus!' Simon blurted.

'Yes. The poor boy died badly,' the lay brother said tonelessly.

'I could not tell you. I didn't want the messenger to hear of it.'

'In Christ's own name!' the bishop swore.

'It was concealed. I swear by the Gospels, my lord, I did all I could to keep it hidden. No one knew it was there, so far as I can tell.'

'Someone clearly did,' Bishop Walter said. 'What was the lad doing there if he didn't know about it?'

'I asked him to fetch it to me.'

'Why?'

'The Franciscans. They are deeply spiritual men, I am sure, but one of them tried to engage me in conversation about books. He asked to see the abbey's works, and when I had shown him he enquired about others. Books that might be more . . . contentious. It made me anxious, so I sent young Alexander to fetch it. Someone found him there and killed him for it.'

'But he was not merely killed, was he?'

'I would that he *had* been!'

Scarcely a man, Baldwin thought. The youth's face was unlined, the flesh pale and smooth.

Simon called: 'Baldwin, I can't . . .'

'I understand, Simon,' Baldwin said with some asperity. In the last few years Simon had grown more accustomed to the reality of sudden, violent death, but with a murder like this even Baldwin felt more than a shade of queasiness.

'Did no one hear him?' he asked the torchbearer.

'Of course they did. Loads of us heard the screaming.'

Killing him in this manner must have taken an age, Baldwin told himself. 'Nobody sought him?'

'The man who did this knew his way about, I'd think. He knew how to get here, knew enough to close doors and all. And all the noise we heard, well, we heard it through the windows. All of us came piling out to help the poor soul, but we were in the yard outside. No one could hear anything through these walls.'

Baldwin looked about him briefly. It was easily believable. The walls down here were enormously thick. The crypt itself was beneath the main Chapter House, and so some distance from the sleeping accommodation. The monks would all have been sleeping in their dormitory some distance away, and although they could have heard a man's screams through their own open windows it was unlikely that the sound could have been heard through the walls. Here, they must have been three feet thick or more.

But considerations of how the noise travelled were less compelling than the sight of the dead man.

He was slumped with his back to the pillar in the middle of the room. The enormous stones were there to support the weight of the massive ceiling above, and it was not wide enough for the man's arms to span the masonry, but someone had done their best to make him, binding his hands with a thong so tightly that the leather had cut into both wrists.

As the bearer said, he had died badly.

A strip of leather on the ground showed how he had been gagged. The cloth holding the gag in his mouth had been wrenched aside at some point. Perhaps in the poor man's agonized struggles, trying to escape even as the skin was flayed from his living body and rolled aside like an opened shirt.

The bishop left the prior and marched to the abbey church. There, at least, he hoped, he would be able to gain a little solitude for contemplation.

Entering, he saw that there were already other men up near the altar, both kneeling in prayer, and he recognized them as Franciscans. So these were the men who the prior had said were strangers to the convent. Bishop Walter strode to the front of the church and bent to kneel, feeling his old joints complain as he did so. Always the same: as he grew older, his ancient frame had started to fail him. First it was the piles when he spent too many hours in the saddle, then his eyes had begun to weaken, so he must use spectacles to read even in good light, and now his legs were complaining at the regular kneeling on cold stone. Even the callouses on both knees did not help any more.

The other men had fallen silent as he walked in, and now, as he remained kneeling quietly, he was sure that at least one of them was eyeing him. But he would not be distracted from his communion with God. To his relief, soon after he had closed his eyes he heard the rustle as they both stood, then the firm slap of their bare feet as they made their way from the church.

That was when Bishop Walter began to pray in earnest for the return of the book, the cursed Black Book of Brân.

Simon was relieved when Baldwin had apparently completed his investigation of the body and they could leave the noisome passageway leading to that foul chamber.

'Who knew the lad best of all?' Baldwin asked the torchbearer.

'Don't know. I'm a lay brother, and they don't always tell us much. You know, we're just menials and servants. We don't matter,' the man said in a surly tone.

'You have served the abbey long?'

'No. I served the king, but now I am retired here. A corrodian.'

'A pensioner? And yet they do not treat you well?'

'The abbot has a book about all the things he wants and expects, and God save the man who gets it wrong. It's all listed in his book. And so are all the people who don't measure up to his standard.'

'Did that boy?'

'Hmm?'

'Come, now. I am seeking his murderer. A man who could do that either must have hated the boy a great deal or must have had some reason to want to punish him. What can you tell me?'

'The lad was a pleasant enough fellow. Friendly, but no slacker. Hard worker, from all I've heard. And he had a good brain on his shoulders. Could read Latin, Greek, French and other languages. He was a good student. No wonder the prior was proud of him.'

'Not the abbot?'

'The abbot has his own ideas about what is right and wrong.'

'What is your name?'

With a display of reluctance the man grudgingly admitted, 'Peter.'

'Thank you, Peter. You disagree with him?'

'No. Why should I? He is trying to bring back honour to the abbey.'

Simon was still wiping at his mouth. Now he looked up, his face still sour after the sight in that chamber. 'Why mention that? Has there been a loss of honour here?'

'Didn't you know?' Peter demanded. 'About the thefts? The insult to the king? No man would insult our King Edward, God save his soul! But they did his father.'

'Who would have insulted the king?' Simon scoffed. 'No man would dare offend a king.'

They had climbed a winding stair and now were approaching the door to the Chapter House. In answer to Simon's comment, Peter turned to it and pointed. 'See that?'

'It is a parchment, isn't it? Not good quality,' Simon said, studying the skins nailed over the door. There were three sheets he could see, stretched over the door's frame. He prodded them. 'It's pretty rough, though. No wonder it wasn't used for writing.' He leaned closer to sniff at it, but then withdrew sharply when Peter shrugged and responded.

'It's not very good, no. But I doubt many tanners wanted to cure the hide of Master Puddlicott once he was skinned.'

Bishop Walter left the church feeling a little calmed by his prayers. As he entered the passageway that gave out to the cloister, he glanced up into the Chapter House and saw the other men standing at the door.

'Had you heard this tale?' Baldwin asked as the bishop walked towards them.

'The skin? Oh, yes. I remember the matter very clearly. Twenty years ago, was it not?'

Peter nodded. 'Aye.'

'Were you in the old king's service then?' Bishop Walter asked.

'Me? No, I was in his son's household. Our present king. I was a man-at-arms. A sergeant,' he added proudly. But then he shook his head and sighed. 'I was hurt fighting the traitors at Boroughbridge, and that is why he bought my place here – to let me rest before my death.'

'Really?' Baldwin said, eyeing him doubtfully.

'I have been injured, and I grow lame sitting in a saddle or marching,' Peter said.

'Why was this flesh left here?' Simon demanded, his lip curled as he stared at the leathery hide.

'He had robbed the king,' the bishop said. 'What else would you have had him do? Puddlicott and others took the king's most prized possessions. King Edward used to leave them here in Westminster's crypt for safety. When the thieves were caught, he was determined to make an example. Puddlicott claimed to have benefit of clergy. He was held in the Tower for two years before he confessed that he lied. His skin, and the skin of the other robbers, was nailed here as a deterrent to stop other monks aiding felons.'

Simon winced. 'That was the old king, then?'

'Yes. King Edward I, our king's father.'

'You say the monks abetted the thieves?' Baldwin prompted.

'That was the suggestion. The king's treasury down in the crypt was secure, with locks on all doors, but the felons clambered in through a window. It took them days, I heard tell – they had to work at the bars first, breaking the sill to remove them, and then climbed inside, where they broke open the strongboxes and took all of value. The guards apparently heard nothing, the brothers said they heard nothing – and yet a mason worked two nights to break open the window! And some of the felons were harboured within the abbey.'

Baldwin was studying the door with a speculative eye. 'And last night another man was flayed alive. That is a curious coincidence, is it not?'

Simon coughed to cover his urge to throw up again. 'You call it "curious", Baldwin? I just call it *sick*. Whoever did that was mad!'

Abbot John of Malvern swore to himself as he marched from his lodgings along the pathway to the abbey, his arms wrapped about him against the morning's chill.

The fool! He had no damned doubts what Alexander had been doing, and for the abbot's money he deserved all he had got. No. No, that was too harsh. But the lad had taken the keys to the crypt, he'd gone in there at dead of night and according to that priggish twit, Prior Stephen, he *had* been looking for the book.

Damn the book! It should have been destroyed an age ago. The bishop himself shouldn't have brought it here. That was stupid in the extreme. As was sticking the thing down there under the Chapter House. There had been a number of attempts on that chamber in the past. Only a few years ago the crown jewels had been stolen from there. The blasted place wasn't secure. Who could have been stupid enough to leave that book there? Only the son of a hog – Prior Stephen. He was too dim to see the dangers, the idiot!

'Abbot.'

Bloody rudeness! 'Bishop.'

Bishop Walter peered at him short-sightedly. 'I am sorry to hear of the death of the fellow during the night.'

'It was a shame. Yes. Poor Alexander.'

The bearded knight at the bishop's right shoulder leaned forward. 'Have you found the murderer?'

'Me? Why, no.'

'Whom have you set to finding the killer?'

'That is hardly my responsibility. I have asked the prior to look into it. It is more his province than mine.'

The knight had the impudence to eye him askance at that. 'Not yours? Is this not your abbey?'

'It *is* my abbey. And as such I have a duty of care over all—' he held up a hand to cut off the knight '—over all the living within my community. As prior, he is responsible for the men within the abbey, the lay and the ecclesiastical, and maintaining order. I find your interest in the matter impertinent, master.'

'You do realize that the young fellow down there in the crypt has been *murdered* by having the flesh torn from his body?'

'Enough, Baldwin,' Bishop Walter said, holding up his hand. 'My lord abbot, I have spoken to the prior already. I would be very keen to ask my two friends here to help you to investigate the death. They would be most happy to do so.'

'These two?' the abbot said. He looked from the bishop to the knight, and then to the heavy-set man behind them. 'And what exactly could they do to help us?'

The bishop smiled thinly. 'They would at least be active in searching for the murderer.'

After they had gone on their way, and by some miracle Abbot John had managed to hold his tongue even when the bishop had been so insolent as to suggest that the two scruffy churls – being dubbed knight did not confer honour and breeding on a man, plainly – should aid him in seeking the killer, he stormed off into the cloister.

Seeing the novice Robert, he bellowed at the lad for a jug of his best ale and marched to the Chapter House.

The leather at the door had been there all his time here in the abbey. When he had been elected the leader of the community he had been here only a year or so. That, so he believed, was because he was untainted by the implications of the fiasco of the years before. He had been picked for his resolution and his integrity. No more would his monks be consorting with worldly fools from the king's palace over the walls, no more flirting with wenches and buying their own favourite foods. No, they were monks, and they had best remember that they should live by the holy order that was granted to them.

There had been many who had been hanged for those misdemeanours, so he had heard. Some for the actual robbery, others because they had received the stolen items. Like William of the Palace, William Palmer. He had been the procurer of women for the abbey back in those appalling days of misdeeds and misbehaviour. One of these strips of flesh was probably his. So John had heard, all the leading felons involved had been hanged and then flayed.

Interesting, he thought, running a finger down the nearest panel of leather nailed roughly to the timbers. Such a lot of emotion represented here. The rage of an elderly king, the anguish of the felons caught for the offence, the jealousy of those who sought to take the king's money . . . and the shame of the holy community when these obscene leathers were installed.

Prior Stephen had been here then. A young man, he

had ignored the obvious, just as had so many. Weak, ineffectual, a discredit to the whole community, he should be removed. The abbot wouldn't help him. He was a reminder of past shame.

And now there was cause for more shame and anguish, he told himself. And the prior was involved.

Well, the abbot would prevent any more rumours of an embarrassing nature from escaping. He would not permit anything to harm his abbey. Not again.

'Do you think you may be able to learn who was responsible?' Bishop Walter asked.

'Of course we can,' Baldwin said instantly. 'A man who is capable of such reckless brutality will be easy to find. My fear is that it could be someone motivated by ferocious hatred – perhaps a relative of one of those whose skin is nailed to the door? Can you tell me anything about them?'

'Do you really believe that a lad as young as poor Alexander could have been selected for such a punishment? That robbery was four years before our king began his reign. Twenty-three years ago.[2] And I would guess that the lad himself was younger than that.'

'You would be correct. How did you guess?'

The bishop smiled. 'I have my own methods of enquiry.' Actually, the prior had told him that Alexander would have made a good vicar but was still too young for a role of that kind, so he must have been less than two and twenty years.

'If that is correct, then why would someone seek to flay him?' Baldwin wondered aloud.

It was Simon who noticed the look in the bishop's face. 'Bishop? Do you know something about this lad which would help us?'

[2] The robbery was April/May 1303

'I greatly fear I may,' Bishop Walter agreed. 'I think that this is another robbery. But it is far more dangerous than the last.'

'Please tell us,' Baldwin said.

The bishop nodded, and the three continued walking slowly about the grounds between the abbey church and the palace wall.

'It is called the Black Book of Brân,' he began. 'It was given to me early on in my reign as bishop. My predecessors hinted that it contained foul predictions. I have to confess, I did not pay them much heed. I had enough to do with maintaining the building works at the cathedral. In those early days it was hardly certain that we would be able to finish the rebuilding started so long ago.'

'Did you look into it?' Simon asked.

'I did. And I saw at once what made the book so inflammatory. There are predictions in there, you see. Predictions that are so dangerous . . . well, I decided to bring it up here to Westminster and see that the book was locked away securely. There was nowhere quite so safe in Exeter.'

'Predictions such as what?' Baldwin enquired.

'You recall the name Joachim of Fiore?'

Baldwin frowned. 'He predicted that the third age of man was about to begin, did he not? He said that there were three ages, all defined by the span of years . . .'

'Yes. The first was the age of the Father, which was the period of the Old Testament; the second was the age of the Son, which was the New Testament. But he proposed that there might be a glorious third age, which would be the age of the Holy Spirit. In that, mankind would become ever more spiritual. It would be the age of monks, with all praising God and His glory until the end of the world would come.'

'And Joachim and his believers were disappointed,' Baldwin said with a small smile.

The bishop's face remained stern. 'They made calculations that said that the third age was surely forty-two generations after the birth of Christ. And because the average generation is thirty years, he saw that the beginning of the end of the second age must be in the year of Our Lord twelve hundred and sixty.'

'Which must have been a strange morning for Joachim's followers when they awoke and realized that the world was still all about them,' Baldwin said lightly.

'No. Because it was the end of the second age. There was not to be a great change overnight. First, Joachim foresaw that there would be a great ruler who would be the Antichrist, and he would throw down the existing corrupt order of the Church in order that a new, fresh, more holy church might be born.'

'Yes.' Baldwin nodded.

'Joachists believed that the great ruler was the Holy Roman Emperor, Frederick II. But I think that they were wrong.'

'So was Joachim. The end of the world has not come,' Baldwin pointed out.

'Except his teaching showed that for each age there must be a stage of incubation. He did not state how long for.'

'What of it?'

'Just this: he foretold that there would be three Popes murdered, Christ's kingdom desecrated, and then there would come the time of the third age.'

'Well, then,' Simon said, shrugging. 'There's no need to worry about that until three Popes have been murdered, is there?'

Baldwin was nodding slowly, his eyes fixed on the bishop.

'Well? Is there?' Simon said, looking from one to the other.

It was Baldwin who answered quietly. 'Pope Celestine V was murdered by Boniface VIII; Boniface was assaulted and died from his wounds; and then Benedict XI was himself murdered. And we have lost the Holy Land, Simon. Christ's own land, desecrated by the Moors.'

'"And Antichrist with bloody slaughter sated",' Bishop Walter quoted. 'That is a part of the prophecy, and why it is vital that we find that book. I think that someone sought to steal it for his own purposes, and Alexander happened to be in the way.'

Prior Stephen was in the cloister at a desk when Baldwin and Simon saw him.

'What now?' he muttered to himself as he noticed the two striding towards him. Reluctantly, he set aside his rule and lead.

'Prior, I should like to ask you some questions about the dead monk. I understand that you had a copy of the Black Book of—'

'Hush!' Prior Stephen flushed to hear Baldwin mention the *thing*. 'In God's name, Sir Baldwin, that is something I do not wish to hear even *named*. It is a hideous thing.'

'Can you tell us a little about it?'

'I would not.'

'The bishop himself told us that he brought it here. I would like to know what happened to it.'

'It was stored securely.'

'In the crypt?'

'Yes. It was supposed to be safe in there.'

'Who knew of the book?'

The prior looked away. 'It should have been me alone, but I didn't feel safe with so great a work as that.

I told the abbot, of course, and I think he made a note of it, for future abbots to be warned.'

'And then it was installed safely in the crypt. Except it wasn't safe, was it?'

'It was as secure as I could contrive.'

'This boy Alexander learned of it.'

'That must have been misfortune. The poor boy did not realize what a treasure – and curse – the book was.'

'What sort of a fellow was he, this Alexander?' Simon asked.

'He was a very bright boy. Clever, good with his hands, very astute, quick to see the best means of illustrating a point or . . . Look here. Let me show you.'

Prior Stephen reached under his desk to where he kept some sheets of parchment. 'Look – when a scribe is practising, he will use old offcuts of parchment. Only when he is sure of the illustration does he set to putting it down on vellum.'

Simon looked down and saw a magnificent picture of a dragon. It was green, with flames of red and orange that were so realistic he felt they might scorch him. Red, enraged eyes met his own, and he could see each talon on the terrible feet. 'My . . . It's so lifelike!'

'That was his skill. Look, here is another. A boar. Any man who has seen a boar suddenly appear from a thicket would see that and recognize the brute. The tusks, the coarse hair, the malevolent appearance . . . It is a marvellous piece of work. That was Alexander, though. He was capable of great artistic skill. That was his own means of honouring God. By setting down the things he saw in his head on to parchment or vellum.'

'Vellum is the more expensive?' Simon asked.

'It is the most prized material. It is the best calf's leather. Only the very best. Not sheep or goat, only calf. Four sheets of skin will make only eight leaves for a book, so sixteen pages. It is the rarity of perfect leather that makes it so expensive. Most leathers have some imperfections, but good vellum must be perfect. Like this.'

He held up a sheet. It had pinpricks running along each side, and connecting them, from left to right, were a series of pale lines. Baldwin nodded. 'Those are the lines for the scribe, so that he knows where to set the characters.'

'Exactly. It is vital that the lines be straight. To make them roughly would be an insult to the work within the book. An insult to God.'

'And the book of . . . which we discussed?' Baldwin said. 'Was that good quality?'

'For its age. About two hand-lengths long, with wooden boards covered in black leather. There were some inconsistencies in the quality of the vellum, but the writing was of very good quality – although some parts were hard to read, even for an educated reader. The characters were quite archaic. It was Irish, and very ancient.'

'Would Alexander have been able to read it?'

Prior Stephen looked at Baldwin very directly. 'He could perhaps read it. But it was not his place to do so. In the first place, the book was denied him. In the second, he was an artist. A marvellous illustrator, yes, but still only an illustrator.'

'So you do not think he could have read it?' Baldwin pressed him.

'I . . . If you push me, then, yes, I would think he probably could. He was a very well-read fellow. But that does not say he definitely could.'

'So you do not think he was there for his own benefit?' Simon said.

'What do you mean?'

'Simply this: what was he doing there? If not seeking

the book for his own purposes, was he there for someone else?'

'You suggest he was there for . . . ?'

Baldwin answered sharply. 'Do you propose to tell us that he was there on legitimate business? What is kept in the crypt? Cold meats? We have been there, remember, and seen all the strongboxes. But none was opened. Where was the book kept?'

'I have said enough on that. But I would swear that he was not a felon. Alexander was a good monk.'

To Simon's dismay, Baldwin was soon taking them back down into the crypt again.

'It is clear that if there is a clue to the murderer's identity, it will be down here, Simon,' he explained as he bent to study the floor.

'At least the body's gone,' Simon said. He looked about him in the glimmering light without enthusiasm. 'I will never forget how the man's flesh had been peeled away.'

'It reminded me rather of an execution,' Baldwin said, looking across at him, frowning. 'The men who have been accused of treason against their king are often treated in like manner, their breasts torn open so that their heart may be cut out and burned.'

'Yes. But his breast wasn't torn open. His heart remained. He was merely skinned and left to bleed to death, or die of shock and horror,' Simon pointed out. 'And there was nothing about Alexander to suggest treason, was there?'

'It is a consideration, nonetheless. There was something so appalling in the way that the man was left there to die that there must have been something symbolic about it. Perhaps he was viewed as a traitor by the man who killed him?'

'Because of this book? What on earth could there

have been about the book that would make someone kill him?'

'That depends on what he was doing here,' Baldwin said. He had stopped near the pillar at the middle of the room and was eyeing the ground with interest.

The blood had been left in thick clotting pools. No one had yet come to wash the flags clean, and there were two trails leading from the pillar to the doorway, where the lay brothers had dragged Alexander out, his heels making those sweeping lines on the stone.

'Look here, Simon,' Baldwin said, pointing.

Swallowing his revulsion as best he could, Simon walked to join his friend. 'Dust?'

'Too gritty. Mortar, I'd guess,' Baldwin corrected him, rubbing a pinch of the bloody mess between finger and thumb and gazing up at the pillar. 'A fair amount scraped from between two stones.'

'Your point?'

'I wanted to see why that fellow was killed. Now I feel sure that either he was unfortunate enough to come here and see the book being stolen or he himself had taken the book and was punished for his crime.'

'What of it?'

'Think! Simon, if another stole the book and Alexander merely interrupted the felon, why rip his flesh from his body? If another found him here stealing the book himself, then perhaps that would have deserved punishment, in the killer's eyes. The boy was here and must have somehow heard of the presence of the book, I assume.'

'What about the mortar?'

'If I had a precious item to conceal, I would not install it in a chest,' Baldwin said, nodding towards all the steel-bound boxes about them. 'Look at them! They would be astonishingly hard to open. A thief might spend hours down here and open only one or two. It would be daunting, but it would still be possible. And a thief who came here to win a prize, such as a cup of gold or a jewel-encrusted cross, might try any box to win something of that kind. It would be embarrassing were he simultaneously to find himself the proud discoverer of the Black Book of Brân! But a man who managed to acquire a key to the crypt's door may also find a key to a chest. So a prudent man may seek another place of concealment. Often when a monastery has an object so valuable and rare, they will install it in their own little hiding-place.'

'Somewhere more secure than a strongbox?' Simon asked disbelievingly.

'Yes. Somewhere where not even the most ardent felon would consider looking,' Baldwin said, pulling a couple of boxes over to the pillar. 'Like the interstices between stones. Look up there.'

He had climbed on to the largest box and was reaching up into the gaps between stones, testing the mortar and pressing and pulling, trying to see where one could be moved. 'Ach! They are all fixed!'

'There's a gap above you, there,' Simon said.

'Where?' But even as he asked, Baldwin saw the dark shadow. It was a good few inches higher than he could reach, but he was sure that he could test it with his dagger. He tugged the weapon free of its tight sheath and probed the gap about him. To his surprise the stone moved easily to one side, leaving a larger gap, and when he pushed the blade in it slipped inside for more than ten inches. 'Nothing there now,' he grunted, sheathing his knife and jumping down to the ground again. 'Whatever was there is certainly stolen now.'

'You think that's where they installed it for safety?' Simon asked, staring aghast at the narrow space.

'If you were a thief come to ransack the place, would you have looked there, or just kept your eyes to the obvious? It was a mark of brilliance to hide it up there,' Baldwin said.

'So now we know where it was, what do we do?'

Baldwin was staring at the ground. 'We ask who it was who came to take the body away.'

'For what purpose?'

'To see if the men who fetched him wore sandals, Simon. Because there has been someone in here without them,' Baldwin said, pointing to the footprints that led from the crypt to the main door. 'And who do we know who walks barefoot?'

'The Franciscans, if they are particularly pious.'

'That is correct,' Baldwin said. He was pulling the strongboxes away from the pillar, to place them back where he had found them, but as he set the first down he paused and stared. 'That is strange.'

'What?'

'Well, I don't remember seeing any strongboxes by the body this morning – do you? And yet one of these other boxes has also been set upright in the blood. The gore is all over the handle and side, as though this too has been standing there at the pillar for someone to look for the book. But Alexander wouldn't have been setting the box in blood if he found Brân's book. The blood was Alexander's own, shed when someone caught him with the book. So does that mean another man found the book and killed Alexander, and then put the box away, even though he knew the screams must have woken the whole community? That would show considerable courage. Or perhaps someone saw Alexander and pulled the boxes away before we saw him—'

'Or someone came here like us to see whether the book had gone?'

'Yes. Quite. Which may mean someone else is searching for the book too. And that could be dangerous.'

*

Friar Martin bent his head at the sight of the dead man before the altar. It was fortunate that the monks had already tidied up his body before installing him beneath the hearse here, but there were still streaks of blood showing on the man's face.

He could not feel much sympathy. The fool was meddling with things he'd no knowledge of, nor the intellect to understand. It was enormously dangerous for him. As he had learned.

At the end of the Mass the monks filed out silently, their leather soles crunching on the stone and tiles. The only men who remained were the prior, Friar Martin and Friar James, and as Friar Martin rose to leave he was surprised to see the prior approach them.

'Brother prior,' he said, ducking his head.

'Brothers. I am most sorry about this appalling desecration in our community.'

It was a dreadful event, there was no doubt. The church would have to be reconsecrated to take away the stain of murder, although fortunately it would not be long before such a ceremony would be held. No one would wish to hold up the reconsecration. The king was enormously proud of his church, and he was jealous of any who might seek to harm it.

'It was a terrible crime,' Friar Martin said.

'I am most sorry for the man who died. It must have been an awful discovery,' Friar James said.

'Naturally.'

'And yet it appears so motiveless. That is what is so truly alarming,' Friar Martin said. 'Is there any conclusion as to why the brother was slaughtered in so revolting a manner?'

'What reason could there be for such a foul deed?' the prior demanded, turning his pale eyes upon Martin.

Friar Martin smiled thinly. He was not so foolish as to attribute motives. 'Whatever the reason, it must surely lie within the abbey. Unless, of course, the felon has fled?'

'No man has fled the abbey that I know of.'

'Then beware!' Friar James intoned. He leaned forward, his hawk-like features fixed into a scowl. 'The man must still remain within the walls. And he is *evil*!' His lips parted in a sneering grimace. 'The man who killed the lad is the harbinger of slaughter. The bringer of death to all.'

Simon and Baldwin took a little while tracking down Peter, the lay brother who had earlier been their torchbearer.

He was sitting in the calefactory, warming his feet before the fire, a quart pot of ale at his elbow, while he rubbed some oil into his temples.

'I get these headaches,' he admitted when asked.

'We will try to be as quick as we may,' Baldwin said soothingly. 'It is about the dead monk.'

'Alexander. Poor fellow.'

'Yes. Was he particularly devoted to any master here? You know what I mean – was he . . . ?'

'He was the prior's man. No doubt about that. He was the man Prior Stephen trusted more than any other.'

'They had similar interests?' Simon asked.

'Yes. Both were very bookish. If Prior Stephen needed something, he'd always ask Alexander, because Alexander would always know which book he needed. They were natural allies.'

Baldwin nodded. 'Did they often work together?'

'Yes. Whenever there was a special book to work on. They'd often work together then. I think the prior looked on Alexander as being a natural copyist. Prior Stephen was himself an expert. Easily the best in our scriptorium.'

'I see,' Baldwin muttered. 'Tell me – you brought us to see the body. Had many others been there before us?'

'Almost all the brothers in the convent, I would say. It is not so common that we have a dead monk in the crypt.'

'No. And the fact that he was one of your own would mean that many would want to go to see him, I suppose.'

It wasn't a question. Baldwin had been a warrior monk, a Knight Templar, and he knew the tedium of living in a monastery. The early rising, steady days of prayer and work, always the same, with minor changes of emphasis depending upon the Church calendar. It was no surprise if something like this would attract some of those who had lived here for many years without even the hint of excitement.

'I would think so.'

'How many of them were barefoot?' Simon asked.

'I don't know – I wasn't looking at their feet,' Peter said with bemusement. 'But I will tell you this, though. There were plenty who'd have had bare feet in all likelihood. They'd all been woken from their beds. Not all would have thought to put on sandals.'

'That is fair,' Baldwin said, nodding. 'Another thing – do you know if anyone moved any boxes around in there? After the body was found, were the items in the crypt moved about?'

Peter stared at him for a moment. 'You think anyone would want to tidy up in there? We'd found a *body*, Sir Knight. We aren't all that used to finding our own brothers opened like that!'

Bishop Stapledon met them as they stood out in the yard before the Chapter House again, discussing the matter. 'Have you discovered anything new?'

'I'm afraid not, bishop,' Simon said. 'The trouble is, it could easily have been anyone within the abbey. The only reassuring factor is, it is unlikely that it'd be someone from outside. The guards all swear that there was no sign of forced entry, and the porters are content that their gates were not opened. So it is someone within the precinct.'

'Which is scarcely reassuring to those who live here,' the bishop pointed out acidly.

'What can you tell us of the Franciscans here?' Baldwin asked. 'Do you know them?'

'No. I do not think that I have met them . . . There are many thousands of Franciscans.'

'Yes. And many hundreds are Spirituals.'

'Who are they?' Simon demanded.

'An extreme faction of Franciscans,' Baldwin said.

'That is a harsh description!' the bishop protested.

'How would you describe them?'

'As highly dedicated aesthetes, perhaps.'

'I am not sure that it makes them sound any more sympathetic.'

Simon was baffled. 'What are you talking about?'

'These men, Simon, believed the Joachist view of the world – that the world's third age was coming. There would be need of a new religious order, one that was uniquely pure. These men believed in following Christ's path of poverty. Nothing could be owned and held by them – their food must be begged from others, they should labour and count on God's mercy to feed them, clothe them, give them beds at night. *Everything.* But because these ideas were so powerful, they were also unworkable.'

'Why?' Simon asked.

Bishop Walter sighed. 'Because the Franciscans were too successful. They began to infiltrate universities. They had to teach their men how to work, how to argue and debate, and most of all how to preach to the masses. But to do that they needed buildings. And they wanted many thousands of men to be out in the world doing God's work – well, how do you organize thousands of men without even the certainty of ink and pen? You cannot expect God to provide a bureaucracy. Friars need organization as much as monks. The whole argument has been debated ad nauseam, and the Pope has decreed that individuals can maintain their poverty while the order can hold property.'

'But the Spirituals, Simon, disagreed. They saw this as another step towards the end of the world. Because what they believe is that they will be needed to save the world in the third age. As the Antichrist takes on the Church and pulls it apart, so the Spirituals will be there to pick up the pieces and be the foundation of a *new* Church, one free from the corruption and profligacy which they say the existing Holy Church is guilty of.'

'I do not understand. You said that this Joachim predicted that the end of the world would have been sixty or more years ago. So surely these "Spirituals" will have no credibility?' Simon protested.

'A prophecy may be correct in its import, and be . . . hazy as to the precise time it will *become* so,' the bishop said.

'The Spirituals believe very firmly in the prophecy – but if the time is a little out, they will be able to manipulate the prophecies to suit them. It's been done before . . . but only by the unscrupulous, of course,' Baldwin added hastily.

'I am glad you added that,' the bishop said ironically. 'I should not like to think that you could accuse anyone in the Church of such heretical behaviour.'

'Of course not, Bishop,' Baldwin said smoothly.

'But why should this all become relevant now?'

'The prophecy about our king,' Baldwin said quietly. 'And his son.'

'What?'

'You have heard it – it has been about ever since Prince Edward's birth. The prophecy told of the six kings of England after John – Henry would be a lamb, Edward I a dragon, our king was a goat, his son will be a boar. All these have come to pass in their own way for the first three. Now we wonder what our next king may be like. But you know who was termed "the boar who came from Cornwall"? King Arthur. Some say our next king will be similar, with the heart of a lion, but strong, relentless and cunning. They already say he may become Holy Roman Emperor. Perhaps he will be the man to bring down the old, corrupt Church and help to set up a new order, based on the Friars Minor, the Franciscans.'

'You should be cautious to whom you tell that tale,' Bishop Walter said in a low growl.

'I shall. But first I need to speak to the Franciscans here to see what they were doing last night.'

'Very well. Go with God. And be careful, Sir Baldwin. Do not accuse these men of any crimes. You are on Church ground here. It is not safe for you to jump to conclusions too directly.'

'I am grateful to you for your warning.'

Baldwin nodded to himself as he watched the bishop stride away, peering about him with that short-sighted frown that was so habitual to him now.

'Sweet Christ's cods, Baldwin – is that right? You just accused our king's son of being the Antichrist.'

Walking about the cloister garth, his hands clenched before him, Friar Martin avoided Friar James's look.

He had seen that expression so often. The man had heavy lids, which gave the impression that he was contemptuous of others. Today he was watching Martin with keen attention, but Martin was not going to admit to being aware.

'Brother friars. Do you mind if we speak to you for a little while?'

Martin faced the men as Baldwin introduced himself and Simon. 'I am honoured you wish to speak with us,' Martin said. 'But I presume this is no social meeting?'

'We have been charged with seeking the murderer of the unfortunate monk.'

'A shocking thing. Especially here, so close to the palace of the king.'

'Yes,' James said. 'That adds a distinct ghastliness to the whole matter.'

'The only ghastliness lies in the cruel death inflicted on the man who was slain,' Baldwin said shortly.

'You think so? I should have thought that the idea that a religious man on this side of the wall is a savage murderer, while on the other is the king, who considers this house of God as his personal chapel, was itself quite appalling. The juxtaposition of the man who seeks to elevate this church, and here, subsidized by that same king, is a lunatic who can kill in that manner. That to me is ghastly. Or is it merely sordid that I can attach such mean thoughts to such a foul extinction?'

'You are too educated for me to comprehend,' Baldwin said shortly. 'Do you know of any reason why the lad should have been murdered?'

'Me? What would I know?' James sneered. 'I am a stranger here.'

'You have travelled much. You are a man of experience.'

'Perhaps. Well, I will tell you this: the boy was handsome.'

'You imply that he was—'

'You know what I mean. Repulsive, foul, evil sins were perpetrated. Perhaps his lover killed him.'

'Why do you think this?'

'I saw the look in his eye. I have been a monk and friar much of my life. I can recognize the signs. The prior and that boy were too . . . affectionate.'

'You have proof?'

James glanced at Martin. 'It is a matter for the abbot. You should tell him and demand that his prior makes a full confession.'

'Perhaps we should allow the rumour to die with the boy, eh?' Martin said with quiet firmness. 'This is gossip-mongering. I ask you to be more cautious with your accusations, Friend James.'

'I will—'

'You will please be silent.'

James subsided, pale with anger.

Baldwin glanced at Martin. The man had authority, which was surprising when used against a man so much older than him. 'Where were you when you heard the screams, Friar James?'

'In my chamber. The abbot has provided us with a pleasant room.'

'In his house?'

'No, in a room there.'

Here in the cloister they were surrounded by abbey buildings. North was the church itself, while west lay the abbot's house, the prior's standing next door to it. From the prior's stretched a long building that bounded the garth on the southern side.

'There?' Baldwin asked, following his pointing finger.

'That is the refectory, but the guest quarters are beyond that, yes.'

'So your room would connect with the corridor to the crypt's entrance?' Baldwin noted.

'Would it?'

'Were you both woken by the murder?'

'I was not asleep,' James said. 'I heard a shout, then a shriek. After that there was just a terrible sound of anguish. I think the poor boy went mad before the end, mercifully.'

'What did you do?' Baldwin asked.

'I went to wake Martin, and then hurried to see if I could help.'

'What of you?' Baldwin asked Martin.

'Me? I took heed of the screams and ran straightway to the source as speedily as I might.'

'You knew where the sounds came from?'

'The man's voice echoed along the passageways to the guest rooms, so I followed the noise until I came to the crypt.'

'By which time the killer had gone?'

'Yes. The boy was slumped there against the pillar . . . But you saw him, of course.'

'Who else was there?'

'No one. Only me. So I ran back to fetch help,' Martin said. He held Baldwin's gaze boldly.

'Interesting,' Baldwin said. 'Why was James not with you?'

James said: 'My legs are not so young, nor my blood so warm, as those of a man five and twenty years my junior.'

'What of others?' Simon interrupted. 'Surely someone else realized where the screams were coming from?'

'I think that because they sleep in the main dormitory, they heard the lad through their windows, which give out on to the pasture by the wall to the palace. We heard the noise from within, which was why we were so quickly on the scene.'

James added: 'The brothers were all scrambling about in the dirt out there. They had no idea.'

'I thank you for that. Tell me, Friar Martin, why did you drag the chest to the pillar?'

'Me?' Martin said calmly, but his world had tottered. How could this man have known that?

'There is still blood on your ankle. And at the hem of your robes.'

'I collected that as I tried to help the fellow, and as I tried to shrive him. I knelt at his side, in the gore. I had no boxes there. Why should I?'

'Was he alive?'

'His soul was there, but his body had failed. I did what I could.'

'I see. Is there anything else you would like to tell me?'

'I should like to help you, but no. I fear there is nothing I may tell you,' Martin said.

'And what of you, Friar James?'

'Me?' James said, and shot a look at Martin. 'There is nothing I can add to my young master's words.'

'That made little sense,' Simon said as the two left the friars in the garth. 'The older man deferred to the younger.'

'Yes. And there was little friendship between them, for all their protestations,' Baldwin said. 'I wonder why they are here? They are unlikely companions – one old and set in his ways, the younger more comfortable with his position. I wonder what set them to travel together.'

'Don't Franciscans have a duty to wander the country together?'

'As mendicants, yes. Yet surely James is a little old for such work?'

'He did not seem a very amiable man,' Simon noted.

'Hardly,' Baldwin agreed.

'What did you think of his observations about the dead brother and the prior?'

Baldwin was silent for a moment. Then he said: 'I dislike malicious rumours. But they can on occasion serve to help a man find the truth. Let us go and speak to the prior.'

'You dislike my sharing that with them?' James said.

Martin was coldly furious. 'If I hear you talking about catamites and homosexuals, I will have you transported to preach in the mountains.'

James shivered. He had travelled through the mountains, and the idea of remaining there in perpetual cold was hideous enough to silence him.

'You made it up, did you not?' Martin hissed after a pause.

'No. I was told by a lay brother. They all know it here.'

'Well, you will not mention it again. I won't have that lad's memory poisoned. Leave it, James.'

'Yes.' James bent his head, but if Martin had seen his eyes he would have noticed the resentment flaming in them.

So you would deny your own loves, would you? he sneered to himself.

It took little time for them to return to the cloister, where they found the prior bent over a bowl of sand. It was set upon a small brazier, and he was stirring a pot of milk in which two quills had been set.

'Yes?' he asked brusquely.

'Please finish what you are doing,' Baldwin said suavely. 'We would not wish to disturb you.'

The prior gave him a surly glower, then returned to a small basket of goose flight-feathers. He had a small knife, with which he stripped the quill, and then he cut off the top and the bottom, before throwing the long middle section into his pot of milk. From the milk he withdrew the two quills and held them carefully, plunging them into the hot sand to temper them. Withdrawing them after a moment, he studied them before setting them aside and turning to Baldwin. 'Well?'

Baldwin wrinkled his nose. The odour of scorched feathers was repulsive. 'The two Franciscans. Can you tell us what they are doing here?'

'Friar James and Friar Martin? They arrived here a couple of days ago. Why? They are surely above suspicion.'

'You think so? In that case, it must be someone here in the abbey who is guilty of the murder. That does at least narrow the field for us.'

'What?' In his surprise the prior almost upset his pot of hot sand.

'You are no fool, prior. You must know that unless you wish to explain the murder by means of some form of miracle, then a man from within the abbey last night must have killed the lad. And that means someone who was living here – so a member of your community or one of your guests. It seems unlikely that someone could have broken into the abbey overnight to do this and slip away while all the monks were outside.'

'You cannot be suggesting that monks or friars could have done something like that?'

'Persuade me how someone else might have done it and I will be keen to learn,' Baldwin said.

'But this is ridiculous!'

'Not ridiculous, no. There is some method behind this madness. Who on earth would dream of murdering a lad in so gruesome a manner, other than a madman? Yet there is some intellect behind it.'

'Why do you say that?'

'Whoever killed the boy did after all have him produce the book in the first place.'

'So whoever killed him didn't know where it was until poor Alexander showed him?'

'That is very likely the case,' Baldwin agreed. 'Which leads one to wonder: how did Alexander learn where he could find it?'

The prior pulled a face. 'I shall be candid.'

'I would be most grateful,' Baldwin said sarcastically.

'He put it there for me in the first place. But he swore he would tell no one about it.'

'Why? Because it was too high for you to reach?' Simon guessed.

'What was too high?' the prior demanded, glowering.

'We know where you hid it,' Baldwin said. 'And it was high in the pillar. So if the lad went there to fetch the book down, why should he have done so? Was he accepting a bribe to seek it out, or was there some other motive for him to get it?'

'What sort of lad was he, would you say?' Simon asked before the prior could answer Baldwin.

'Well, as I said, he was a good worker.'

'But was he fanciful? You often find that fellows of his age are daydreamers – especially those who spend much of their time drawing.'

'He had a wonderful imagination, yes, but his mind was fixed mostly on more serious matters. He was always looking for the next piece of work to illustrate, and his sketches and rough outlines were always of the highest order.'

'So he was reliable? He wouldn't be likely to take money for stealing the book?'

'No! Certainly not! He was always a most devoted lad, to the abbey . . . and to me.'

'Was he really?' Baldwin said quietly.

It was late that afternoon when Simon and Baldwin returned finally to the bishop's hall and sat at the bench, jugs of wine at hand, stretching their legs out towards the fire.

'Have you been fortunate with your enquiries?' Bishop Walter asked at last.

Baldwin wiped his moustache with his hand. 'It is intriguing, I confess. The dead monk was not disliked by anybody. He knew where the book had been secreted, but that means nothing. Either he went there to the crypt to steal it himself, to look at it, or he passed the crypt and found another man in there robbing the chamber. We cannot tell which. Yet it is certainly true that he was there in the dead of night, when he ought to have been in his cot, as the other monks were. Or most of them.'

'You have had no more joy than that?'

'I fear not.' Baldwin considered for a moment, wondering whether to tell the bishop of the accusation laid against Alexander and the prior by Friar James, but decided against. 'I should like to learn more, though. Perhaps it would help were I to find out a little about the Franciscans there at the abbey. Is it possible to enquire about them surreptitiously?'

The bishop eyed him narrowly. 'You think that there is something about them that rings false?'

'Perhaps. I know this: it would be peculiar for one of the monks to suddenly take it upon himself to steal this book. What would be the urgency? But someone who was here as a guest, now that would be different. A man who was visiting for a couple of days only, and who had only limited time in which to take the book – that is more likely.'

'I shall make my own investigations about them. Friar Martin and Friar James, they are called, I think?'

'That is right. Why are they in the abbey? That is what I should like to know.'

*

When Simon awoke the following morning, his head mildly sore from the bishop's good Bordeaux wine, he was surprised to see that Baldwin was already out of his bed.

He felt bad, but not because of his head. No, it was more than that. Gradually, his memory returned to him, and he had recollections of waking in the night, visions of a skinned man walking towards him holding a book that dripped with blood, the pages all made of fresh, human flesh, with no writing upon them, but only gorgeous, illuminated pictures that flashed with fire and violence. It was a terrifying memory, made still more fearsome by the eyes. Eyes that begged for aid, when none could be given to him. No. He had not slept well last night.

Simon hadn't wanted to go to bed. He'd known that he was going to suffer a sleepless night. From memory, he recalled sitting up until late with Baldwin, discussing the murder only briefly, mostly chatting about the book and the kind of predictions that could be held within it.

The picture that kept returning to Simon's mind was that of the boy's body, but at the same time he was afflicted by visions of the book itself. A work that must surely rank amongst the most foul in history, from its reputation. The way that the bishop had described it had been enough to make Simon averse to seeing it. If he were to come across it, he would not touch it, he decided.

The thought of the lad in that foul little crypt reaching up to the book and bringing it down, only to have it wrenched from his grasp and then . . .

That was where his imagination failed him. Alexander had been bound to the pillar in which he had hidden the book. Who could have done that to him? And how? The lad wasn't incapable. He had looked quite strong enough to protect himself. Perhaps the assailant had a partner? Again, the vision of the two Franciscans sprang into his mind. He could easily envisage one holding a knife to Alexander's throat, while the other gripped his hands and bound them behind the pillar, only to have the first begin to cut with his blade at the poor lad's breast, slowly slicing to peel back the flesh.

It was a repellent idea, and yet Simon was unable to eradicate it from his mind. He could imagine the poignant agony of the point of the knife settling on his breastbone, then slipping slowly downwards . . .

What had the lad done to deserve such a foul death? Merely pick up a book. That was insane! No one deserved death from touching a book.

'Ah, awake at last?'

'Baldwin, I didn't sleep very well last night.'

'Nor did I as a result!' Baldwin said grinning.

'My head feels a little strange, as though it has been filled with feathers,' Simon confessed.

'There is a strange thing, now. And you hardly finished your fourth jug of wine.'

It was a terrible thing to admit, but there were times, especially when Baldwin was at his most righteous, when Simon could dislike his old friend. This reaction had much to do with the fact that the knight preferred to avoid strong drink and only supped sparingly of wine. Last night Baldwin had drunk little, from the sight of him.

Suddenly Simon's belly felt uncomfortable. There was a feeling that his head was hotter than the rest of his body, and he had a roiling sensation in his gut. 'I think I need a little water,' he said.

After breakfast, which comprised bacon, cold beef, some thick slices of bread soaked in gravy and four eggs fried in the bacon's fat, Simon felt considerably better.

'You don't deserve to be able to eat all that,' Baldwin muttered after toying with his own cold meat.

'I have managed to learn a little about our friends the Franciscans,' Bishop Walter murmured. 'This morning I spoke to a friend who is close to the order.'

'And?' Baldwin asked, leaning forward keenly.

'It would appear that they have come from the Pope himself,' Walter said.

Baldwin's eyes narrowed as he absorbed this. 'Why should they be at the abbey, then? Are they on an embassy for the Pope? But then they would be going to the palace to discuss the matter with the king. Yet here they are, remaining in the abbey itself.'

'Perhaps they have business elsewhere?' Simon said.

'If that is the case, surely they would have continued on their way until they came to the place where they should conduct their affairs? There is no reason for them to break their journey.'

'Unless, of course, their business is to be conducted at the abbey itself,' the bishop said.

'Such as acquiring a book which the Pope wants?' Baldwin guessed.

'That is a thoroughly scurrilous comment,' the bishop said with finality.

'But what else could they be doing?'

'I do not know, but I have been told that Martin is one of the most highly regarded friars in his order.'

'What of James?'

'His reputation is more . . . ambivalent.'

'Interesting,' Baldwin murmured.

'Why?' Simon asked.

'If they are truly on an embassy from the Pope, surely he would pick two men of equal integrity? Not one above reproach and one who was less than spotless?'

*

They were soon at the abbey, and Baldwin led the way into the abbey's grounds. Once there, they crossed the northern tip of the abbey church and went down to the abbot's house.

The young novice, Robert, who had served them wine the day before, was at the abbot's door when they knocked.

'He is very busy, Sir Baldwin.'

'Ask him if he could make a little time to speak to us.'

The boy looked reluctant, but he did as he was bid and soon returned to take them up to the abbot's hall. Here they found the abbot standing near his fire, head jutting pugnaciously. 'Well?'

'Abbot John, we do not wish to make your life more difficult,' Baldwin said soothingly. 'As you know, we have been asked to find out who was responsible for the murder of Alexander. Is there anything you can tell us which could help us?'

'What on earth could I know? Do you suspect me of the murder?'

'Abbot, please. We have heard nothing but good about your ministry here. No, I do not accuse you.'

'That is good. I have spent all my waking hours doing the very best possible for this house since I was elected to the abbacy. I will not tolerate any insinuations about my work. How could anyone think that I would do anything to harm this house? I love it with all my heart.'

'It has been through hard troubles in the last years, I think?'

'Under Abbot Wenlock it was sorely tested. He was . . . well, he was a weakly man. Many of us are. He misused his position, and that meant his monks could misbehave as well. They were involved in frolics with whores, they consorted with gamblers and gamers, and then there were the robberies.'

'More than one?' Simon asked. 'We heard only of the attempt on the crown jewels.'

'Which attempt? There were many. Once a short while after the loss of Acre, again at the turn of the century. And did you know that a hundred pounds were stolen from the money given to the abbey for the chantry Masses to be held for Queen Eleanor on her death? Can you imagine that? Monks stealing from money donated for the good of a woman's soul!'

'Is that why the king had the men skinned and set their hides on the door?' Baldwin asked.

'Probably. It was a good reminder to the monks about the sort of treatment they could expect if they were to misbehave again. Not that the king trusted them after that, and nor did his son. The crown jewels were removed after the last attempt, and now they're stored in the Tower of London, I believe.'

'At least that must have been the end of the problems here, though,' Simon said.

'Would that that was true! After the disaster of the robbery, many of the monks were held in the Tower, and even when they were released the king never forgave them. They fell to internal squabbles. Disputes that could serve no useful purpose, but led only to the diminishment of the abbey. It did not stop until the old abbot died. Fortunately, since then we have had a period of calm and have re-established some sense of *purpose.*'

'Only to see it savaged by this latest disaster,' Baldwin finished for him.

'Exactly! How can I possibly hope to protect my community from news of a terrible murder like this?'

'You cannot save it entirely, but if the killer is located and brought to some kind of justice then at least there will be some resolution. If the killer is not found, matters will be a great deal worse.'

'Why?'

'All will think that the murderer remains here within your walls. Not only outsiders, but those within your community will remain distrustful of their own brothers. Lay brothers will look askance at the brethren in the choir; those in the choir will be doubtful of their companions; all those outside the abbey will wonder who was responsible. It will never be possible to clear the taint unless you help us to find the actual murderer.'

It did make sense. The abbot was silent for a period, staring hard at Baldwin. Then he turned away and gazed through his window. It was all very perplexing. The abbey was his responsibility, as was the community within. The book was very important. It had to be kept from the eyes of those who could not understand it. It was too provocative, too sensational. Too dangerous. But he had another duty. As the abbot, he had to protect the abbey itself. The abbey was more than merely a collection of monks – it was a small outpost of God's on this very tainted soil. Monks had a duty to serve and save souls, but the abbey was more than merely the sum of their efforts. Eventually, he sighed. 'Very well. I will do all I may.'

'We know of the book already. Do you think that Alexander could have been selling it for his own benefit?'

Now he had chosen the path of honesty, it was easier to answer. 'No. I think that the lad was incapable of such an action. I tell you plainly, I never acted as confessor to him, and so can be honest: he never struck me as particularly bright. He was a good illuminator, true, but no more than that. He would never have plotted anything, I believe, to the detriment of the abbey. He did not have the imagination, and he was not evil.'

'Unlike the man who killed him.'

'Quite so.'

'Why should he have been slain in so foul a manner?'

'The boy was skinned, just as the earlier thieves were. Master Puddlicott was the instigator of the robbery of the crown jewels, I believe, and he was hanged and skinned. One could almost imagine that poor Alexander was looked upon in the same light by someone who saw him in the crypt.'

'Do you mean to suggest that one of your monks saw him there and decided to punish him?'

'I make no suggestion. I merely reflect on the facts and wonder.'

'Is there anyone in the abbey whom you could suspect of such an offence?'

The abbot turned and stared at him. 'Do you seriously believe that if I knew a man here who was capable of such an appalling act I would conceal him?'

'He was speaking from his heart,' Simon said as they left the abbot's chamber.

'He gave that impression,' Baldwin agreed. 'And yet I am sure he has suspicions. I refuse to believe that he would not have his own idea about who could be guilty.'

'Perhaps he is fearful to admit to them.'

'Why should he fear any man here? Within the community he has full powers. Any man he thought could be responsible could be arrested in an instant and held securely in gaol.'

'That is true if he feared a death, but he could be more anxious about damage of another sort. The danger of the book, for example.'

'What sort of danger could that book hold?' Baldwin wondered aloud.

'If all that we have heard is true, and if it is thought to promote the prince as the Antichrist, do you not think that it could bring retribution upon the abbey itself? The king may accuse the abbot of harbouring the book to the detriment of his son and thus the realm?'

'That is possible. Although the abbot could hardly be blamed for something written long ago by someone in Ireland, surely?'

'When the king is involved, it is best not to be too confident,' Simon said.

Baldwin nodded. King Edward II had a reputation for brutality which was unequalled.

Simon noticed the novice Robert near the entrance to the buttery as they walked to the door. He nodded, and Baldwin peered. The novice appeared to have been weeping.

'Are you all right, boy?' Simon asked.

'Yes. Yes, I am well.'

'You knew the dead monk, did you?'

'Yes. He was a good man. Kind and generous.'

It looked as though he was going to burst into tears again. Baldwin beckoned him over. 'Is there anyone who could have wanted to harm him? He appears to have had no enemies here, and yet he was killed in a particularly foul manner.'

'No one in the abbey could have wanted him dead. All loved him. He was respected by the prior, and his work was highly praised by all who saw it. No one could have wanted to do that to him!'

'But someone did,' Simon muttered.

'It must have been someone from outside the abbey, then. No one in our community could have wanted to see him dead.'

'Do you mean to accuse the Franciscans?' Baldwin asked sharply.

'I accuse nobody!' the lad blurted anxiously. 'I am only a lowly . . .'

'Did you hear anything the night he died?'

'We all heard his screams.'

'You know that is not what I meant. Was there anything specific you heard which would lead you to believe that the Franciscans might have been guilty?'

Simon interrupted before the boy could respond. 'This is a matter of murder, Robert. Not some novice's prank. If I want I can ask the abbot to command you to answer.'

'I heard them.'

'Who?'

'The Franciscans. On the night he died. I heard them talking in the passage. They were talking about the book, saying that they must get it.'

'They knew about it, then?' Baldwin said.

Simon was frowning at Robert. 'You knew about it too, didn't you?'

'All of us know of the Black Book of Brân. It is not the sort of thing that could be kept quiet. How could you keep a thing like that secret? We all knew that it was there.'

'You all knew it was in the crypt?'

'Yes. In one of the boxes.'

'I see. What did the friars say?'

'They were angry that they couldn't find it. I heard the younger one say that they would have to search again.'

'What did his friend say?'

'I didn't hear,' the lad admitted. 'I suppose he spoke more quietly.'

'And this was in the corridor near the dormitory?' Baldwin said.

'Yes.'

Simon was frowning. 'But before or after the screams?'

'Oh, before. I went out with the others as soon as we heard the screams. They were terrible.'

'If that's so,' Simon said, 'you must have seen Alexander rise and go out?'

'I just thought he was going for a piss. It didn't occur to me that he was going to the crypt,' Robert protested.

'We accuse you of nothing,' Baldwin said soothingly. 'But tell me: it was after you had heard the voices?'

'Yes. He must have heard them too, I think.'

'Why?'

'It was almost immediately afterwards that he rose. He was as quiet as possible, and I looked at him, but he was going so quietly I assumed he didn't want to speak to me. And I didn't want to wake the others.'

'Where did he go? Straight out into the corridor?'

'No. Not at first. First he went to the prior's house. I could tell. I heard the doors over at the far end of the dormitory, and then the door to the prior's house.'

Baldwin and Simon exchanged a look. Both recalled Friar James's accusations about homosexuality against Alexander and the prior.

Simon said: 'You can tell that? It couldn't have been the abbot's house?'

'No. I've heard all the doors. The abbot's house has a door with a pronounced squeak in the hinge. It wasn't his.'

'What then?'

'He came out again, for I heard the door close, and walked along the corridor towards the church. I could hear his sandals.'

'So you heard him go to the crypt?'

'God save me, yes!' Robert said quietly.

'Was it long before you heard the screams?'

'A while, yes. But in the dark time passes slowly. You imagine things, don't you?'

'Yes,' Simon agreed, but then he frowned quickly as he remembered his dream of the night before. And there had been something else. 'Tell me, Alexander was a good illuminator. Did he share his pictures?'

'Sometimes when he was proud of a picture he would show it, yes. There was nothing wrong in that. He would ask for advice about making it more realistic.'

'I have had an idea, Baldwin. We need to speak again to the prior.'

Simon led the way at a trot, and Baldwin was forced to keep up.

'What is it, Simon?'

'The pictures the prior showed us yesterday. There was a dragon and a boar, you remember? And those are two of the animals which are held in the prophecy about the six kings you spoke of.'

'Of course!' Baldwin said with anger. 'Why didn't I think of that? So the boy was aware of the prophecy too, and was drawing pictures to illustrate it, you think?'

'What if he wasn't only interested in that prophecy? If the bishop is right, and there are prophecies in this evil book, perhaps the lad Alexander was seeking to bring them together into one, larger book?'

'Why should he do that?' Baldwin said, but he was not scoffing.

'Any artist likes to create work that will be important. If there are linked prophecies that affect our prince and tell of him pursuing a terrible destiny, wouldn't that fire an artist's imagination?'

The prior's desk in the cloister was empty, but Simon reached beneath it for the rough drawings he had shown them the day before. 'They've gone!'

'He must have realized what he had done and has hidden them,' Baldwin said.

'Let's—'

The rest of his words were forgotten as they heard the screams from the Chapter House.

*

They were not alone in running at full tilt to the chamber. Lay brothers and monks all dropped their work and pelted across the yards to the corridor and into the meeting place for the brothers.

'What is it?' Simon demanded as he came to halt at the entrance, but then his voice was stilled at the sight within. He had to swallow and turn away.

'My God!' Baldwin said, and then he was bawling for the monks and others to leave the room and not disturb anything. 'Simon! Simon, keep them all out. We don't want anyone in here.'

Simon agreed and stood in the doorway while Baldwin studied the room, an arm about his breast, his chin cupped in his left hand.

'Is he dead, Baldwin?'

Baldwin saw no need to respond to that.

The prior sat sprawled in a mess of blood and urine, his back to a pillar, both arms about it. His eyes were wide in a horrified stare, and were it not for the fact that his lips were stopped with a thick roll of parchment his mouth would have been wide in agonized terror, Baldwin felt sure.

He walked about the body. Like Alexander, his hands were bound tightly about the pillar, and there was a bloody mess where his belly lay. 'He's been stabbed in the gut and left to die,' he concluded.

'Why do this to him?' Simon spat.

Baldwin was pulling the parchment from his mouth. 'Because this fool and his friend Alexander were copying the Black Book of Brân. These are pages they were taking from it and, unless I am much deceived, these were some examples of drawings that Alexander had created to illustrate the prophecy of the six kings.'

'So who killed them both? Surely they were killed by the same man?'

'It seems most probable. And the motivation was

something to do with this copy of the book. And the original, perhaps.'

'So when we find the original, we shall also know who was responsible for both murders,' Simon said. 'But if the book is so dangerous and must be concealed, why leave the parchments there for anyone to find?'

'Yes,' Baldwin said, but more pensively as he leafed through the parchment he had taken from Prior Stephen's mouth. 'Why leave these here?'

Friar James was walking along the northern wall of the abbey, peering up at the great belfry, when he saw the two men. They were walking towards him at an amble, clearly involved so much in talking to each other that they had no heed for anyone else.

Well, he had little desire to speak to them. He bent his head and tried to avoid looking at them at all as he passed by them, and as soon as their legs had disappeared behind him he looked up again.

And found himself jerked backwards.

Before he could shout for help, a gloved hand was clapped over his mouth, and he was dragged, his arms gripped tightly, an arm about his breast, at enough speed to make it impossible for him to regain his footing. He was pulled so far that he began to wonder whether they would fling him into the Thames or the Tyburn, and he had just decided that they would when the hands supporting him suddenly released him, and he found himself on his back staring up at the knight and bailiff.

'Sir Baldwin, you will pay dearly for this assault,' he spat, struggling to rise to his feet.

'Calm yourself, James,' Baldwin said, planting a foot on his chest and pushing him on to his back with ease. 'You are not accused of any crimes yet. But I would hear more about the book. And Martin's and your plan to find it on the night that the boy died. And what you were doing this morning, of course.'

'I don't know what you mean. I have the protection of the Church and the Pope himself. You cannot keep me here against my will!'

'It will be your will, I am sure, to help the relevant authorities to discover who killed the prior and his monk? What other action would a man of God decide to—' His face suddenly hardened. 'What do you mean, you have the protection of the Pope himself?'

'That is none of your business.'

'You hear that, Simon? So he doesn't bluster, saying that the Pope's protection is always granted to a man of his order. No, rather he seeks to warn us off because the Pope has given him special protection.'

'Release me immediately, or you will pay a terrible penalty! You cannot hold me. You will feel the authority of my order, and I shall have no hesitation in demanding that you be held for—'

His voice was cut off as the knight drew his sword. It gleamed wickedly blue and came to rest upon James's throat.

'I am grateful that you have become quiet, James. Now, friar, I would know what happened that night, first. And before you invoke the power of the Pope, let me warn you that his writ does not run here just now.'

'You are a *heretic*!' James hissed, shocked.

'No. But I have the king's writ to investigate murder, and the king would be keen to know all about this book and the two friars who sought to remove it from his realm. Just as he would be keen to know about the prophecy of the six kings.'

There was a slow clap from behind them, and Friar Martin slowly approached. 'Very well, Sir Knight. An impressive display of force. Perhaps, though, you could release my companion? He is prey to piles, and the cold grass here will be sure to bring on an attack. Pray, let him up, else my ears will suffer immeasurably all the long walk home!'

There was a small alehouse a short distance from the main gate to the abbey, and it was to this that they repaired. Once they were seated, James still eyeing Baldwin with deep suspicion and dislike, Friar Martin ordered wine for them all and sat back on a stool, contemplating Baldwin with some interest and amusement.

'That was a most bold display. I was almost concerned when I saw you draw your sword.'

'I was in earnest.'

'I think not. There are king's officers who would take off a man's head, and others who profess to believe in the rule of justice. I feel sure you are one of the latter.'

'You think I *profess* to believe in justice?'

'I am prepared to think you may believe in it,' Martin said with a smile, and after a moment Baldwin smiled in return.

'Will you tell me what happened on the night Alexander died, then?'

'I cannot tell you all . . .'

'Then let me tell *you*. You were sent here by the Pope to recover a book.'

'Written by an astonishingly unremarkable monk in Ireland.' His tone betrayed his contempt for the Irish. 'He went mad and disappeared. Hardly surprising in a land like his. His book, however, is as remarkable as he was not.'

Baldwin nodded. 'And some believe the book is dangerous.'

'There may be consequences, were a book with prophecies that could be manipulated by the unscrupulous to be discovered just now.' Martin smiled.

'Quite so. And there can be few books of prophecies so easily manipulable as these. Add to them the still more inflammatory prophecy of the six kings, and you have a veritable Greek fire of incendiary forecasts. How is my guess?'

'Accurate enough. The Pope would prefer the book to be taken into his care. Here, it is possible that it could be discovered. If the king's jewels could be robbed from that crypt, a book could as easily be removed. And there are delicate negotiations afoot in France – the Pope wants peace between the English and French kingdoms, and this . . . *nonsense* could impair those negotiations.'

'How did the Pope hear of the book?'

'How? A copy was to be sent to him many years ago. We have known of it for many years.'

'And I expect the good abbot told of the book when it arrived here?'

'I should not be surprised. The Pope cares about inflammatory material of this nature.'

'*I* care about dead men appearing in the abbey.'

'We were seeking the book, it is true, but that is all.'

'Very well. What did you see, though? You were the first on the scene after Alexander's murder.'

'How do you know that?'

'Your footprints. No one else walks about without sandals all day long, friar. It makes your feet flatter and broader, and that makes the footprints wider and smoother too. If you want, we can go and test the theory – the prints remain there.'

'Prints hardly prove I was there.'

'They are not the only proof.'

Martin set his head to one side and smiled. 'I doubt it, but I have no reason to conceal the truth. Very well, I heard the screams and was quickly there. I had hoped that the book would also be there, but when I arrived there was no sign of it. I have to confess, I had made use of a little deception in the hope of learning where it was. I stood outside the dormitory, and spoke in a loud enough voice to wake the dead that I was desperate to find the book and would go and search for it that moment.'

'Where was James?' Simon asked, casting a baleful look at the friar.

'He was in our chamber. I left him snoring.'

'What of the prior?' Baldwin continued.

'You know as much of his death as I do myself. There is no reason for him to be killed, so far as I know.'

'Nor was there for the boy Alexander.'

'No, indeed. But the man who killed him clearly saw him bring out the book, and killed him to take it.'

'Perhaps.'

'What other motive could there be, other than theft?'

'Concealment? Punishment? The parchments in the prior's mouth were from the six kings' prophecy. None bore on the prophecies from Brân's book.'

'So?'

'Perhaps the man who killed both acted from an urge to conceal the book. Rather as you would have,' Baldwin said.

'But you cannot believe we were responsible for the deaths?'

Baldwin drank his wine and smiled. 'Do I not?'

'No, not seriously. Someone else must have killed them.'

'Who?'

James could not restrain himself any longer. He spat: 'They deserved it! The prior and his catamite! Sodomy is the worst sin for a monk. Unbridled passion . . . Any man could have killed them and be praised for his action!'

'So who do you accuse, friar?' Baldwin asked.

'The abbot himself, perhaps! He wants to protect his abbey from the poison of sodomy, I am sure! If he sought to defend his institution against such behaviour, he would be serving God!'

Simon strolled with Baldwin back into the abbey's grounds. 'Why don't you like friars, Baldwin?'

'It is not all friars, only the Franciscans. They are often untrustworthy. Some say that they will manipulate the truth in order to promote their own perfection.'

'I seem to recall that it was you who said that.'

'Really? Then perhaps it is my prejudice which is coming to the fore, then,' Baldwin said with a short grin. 'But it is still true, nonetheless. There are some in that order who consider themselves superior to everyone else. In their warped view, they matter more than all others, because they are hastening the third age of the world into being. That means they are sanctioned to do anything to bring about the arrival of the Antichrist.'

Simon shivered. 'Do you think that he is truly coming now?'

'Simon, Simon, do you know how many men have predicted the end of the world? Do you know how many have been disappointed in their predictions? There were those who thought the end of the world would come in the year of Our Lord 1000. More predicted it would be a few years later. Joachim said it would be 1260 when the Antichrist would appear. Others said that when Acre fell, four and thirty years ago, the end of the world was coming, because God had taken His lands away from His people and given them to the Muslims.'

'Don't you believe that Christ will return?'

'Of course I do – but I believe that it will be at a time of His choosing, and not predicted by a monk hundreds of years ago wearing a hair shirt and sitting in a draughty room on a bog in Ireland!'

'What do we do now?'

'It's clear enough that the two friars wish us to believe that the abbot was responsible.'

'Yes.' Simon nodded grimly. 'You are not sure?'

'No. But James is convinced.'

'Or he wishes to divert our attention from him. Let us go and confront the abbot, then. Perhaps he will confess?'

'I doubt it greatly,' Baldwin said. 'And yet there is merit in speaking to him again. If nothing else, to warn him of James's suspicions.'

They had come to the outer wall of the abbot's house, and Baldwin knocked.

'Of course, all we need to do is find the book, and we shall have our felon.'

'But who has it? That is the question,' Simon agreed mournfully.

They were ushered into the abbot's hall a few moments later.

'What now? I thought I'd told you all I could.'

'I wanted to enquire about the Franciscans. Are they here to take the book away?'

Abbot John leaned back in his chair and growled. 'They are not. They were sent by the Pope to discuss other matters. Matters of international importance.'

Baldwin nodded. Martin had said that the Pope was attempting to smooth over the diplomatic chasm that had opened in English and French relations. 'I see. And Martin is a papal envoy, then?'

'Yes. I have been discussing matters with him.'

'You realize he knows all about the book?'

'What if he does?'

'Perhaps he wished to acquire it for his own purposes?'

'What possible reason could he have for wanting it? No. He is here for other business which does not concern you.'

'His companion, James. Do you know much of him?'

'No, in truth. I know that he has been well regarded by his confrères, though.'

'He is old and experienced.'

'Yes.'

'While his companion is a great deal younger,' Baldwin said reflectively.

'What of it? In this age, men of ability will rise.'

'Absolutely. And there is greatness in a Church that rewards merit.'

'Quite so.'

'And yet ... To have a man of James's ability relegated to the post of clerk to a man half his age must surely be galling to his sensibilities?'

'He is a man who has grown old in the service of God. He will not feel such jealousy, if that is your inference.'

'Perhaps you are right.'

'And what of it? A man like him would scarce kill two because he wished for recognition.'

Baldwin was quiet for a moment, and gradually his eyes narrowed as though he had suddenly thought of a fresh and uniquely unwholesome aspect to the mystery. 'But would another man kill for that, I wonder?'

'What do you mean?'

Baldwin was suddenly on his feet. 'Simon, come! I have some thoughts I need to consider.'

Friar James could see his friend's eyes on him all the way from the refectory to the guest chamber.

'So, then. Are we ready to depart?'

'Oh, I think so. There is little more to discuss here, after all,' Martin said. He crossed the chamber to their bed and took up his leather scrip. 'We have done all we may here.'

'The abbey is in a ferment,' James growled. 'Should we not remain here for a little longer?'

'For what purpose?' Martin snapped. 'There are two already dead. Would you have us remain here? In faith, my friend, I swear it would be best for both of us to depart and report to our master.'

It was at that moment that Baldwin opened the door and entered.

'Sir Baldwin, you do have a habit of appearing when least expected.'

'You are to leave?'

'You overheard us?' James growled.

'You were not hiding your conversation. Now, tell me, to which master do you return to report?'

'We have only one master – God!'

'Ah,' Baldwin said and nodded sagely. 'That is true in general, but here on earth you make reports to the Pope – and to your own general, of course.'

Friar Martin was smiling now. 'And you suggest that this is unfortunate? We are loyal servants.'

'Loyal enough, perhaps, to kill in your service.'

'That is a disgraceful suggestion!' James blurted loudly. 'You dare accuse Friar Martin of murder?'

'You suspect it already, my friend,' Baldwin said mildly.

James opened his mouth to deny it, but then he slowly allowed his head to droop, and his eyes would not meet Baldwin's.

'Besides,' Baldwin continued, 'if I were to suspect you, I should only have to accuse you, and you would confirm or deny the crime. And no matter which the case was, you would escape punishment, because you are in possession of benefit of clergy. You could confess here and now and no English king would dare to take you. Not since the death of St Thomas has a secular officer brought justice to a priest. Neither priest, vicar, monk nor friar can be held under the laws of England, save by his own Church master.'

'So? Then why do you persecute us?'

'Hmm? I do not mean to. No, I merely wished to know what you would do with the Black Book of Brân were you to discover it.'

Martin smiled gently. 'You are an intelligent man, Sir Knight. I am surprised you never sought to ask me before. But I fear I have to be honest. I would take it. My general would dearly love to read it.'

'And amend a few predictions to more fully suit and benefit your order?' Baldwin asked cynically.

'Our order has a duty to help to bring about the new age, in which all the world shall be as a monastery, with all people singing the praises of God all day.'

'So you would be keen to bring about that blessed day, then,' Baldwin said.

'It is our duty.'

'Which is why you persuaded a young lad to seek it for you and bring it to you,' Baldwin said.

Martin's smile was frozen. 'You were not there.'

'You do not deny it. I believe that the suggestion was plain enough, that the boy should find the book and bring it, because it was so evil that it would pollute the minds of all who read it. And then you went to the prior and let him know by a deliberate slip of the tongue that you were here to learn all about it.'

'There was no subterfuge. I told the prior and asked for the copy, because my master wished to see it.'

'But you were sure he would not allow you to take it.'

'It was clear enough by his attitude that he did not consider us suitable porters for his prized book. He preferred to keep it hidden here.'

'How did you arrange for the boy to fetch it, then?'

'The prior was not very trusting. After we spoke to him, we rested, and we went to see whether we could find it ourselves. But there was no sign of it. We had to give up. James here returned to our room, after we discussed the thing a while in the corridor outside the monks' dorter, and then I walked back to the crypt for a brief search.'

'And Alexander appeared while you were there?'

'No.' And at last the mask of confidence slipped. 'No, I sought high and low, but no sign could I see. So I returned to our chamber to sleep. But as I was about to open the door, there was the scream, and it chilled my blood, Sir Baldwin. It chilled my blood.'

'So you ran there, saw he had placed boxes—'

Martin sighed. 'Yes. I saw the boxes and guessed at the hiding-place. I confess, my greed overwhelmed me. I clambered up and felt in all the cracks, but there was nothing there. The book was stolen. So I went to the poor boy and said the paternoster and prayed for him a little. And then moved the chests back with the rest.'

'Why?'

'If someone had been there, I did not want them to think that I knew where the place of concealment lay.'

'And you guessed that if the book were recovered, you may have another chance to seek it,' Baldwin reasoned. 'So from all you say, your companion could not have been the killer?'

'No.'

'But he did suspect *you*.'

'Did you?' Martin asked.

James had no need to answer. He hung his head like a whipped hound, then said: 'My companion was away from me for some while, and when I hurried to the crypt after the screaming I found him there with the boy. It was a great shock to me.'

'Perhaps. Well, Friar James, have no fear. You are

safe in your bed,' Baldwin said. 'It was not your master who killed these two.'

'Then who did?'

Baldwin grunted to himself. 'First, tell me: how did you gain access to the crypt? Where did your key come from that you may search the room?'

'There was a man who had a key. He let me borrow it,' Martin said, smiling.

'I see.' Baldwin considered a moment, then shook his head. 'It is a pathetic tale, in truth. I wish I did not have to tell it. But I think there is no merit in leaving matters to fester. Please, friars, come with us.'

He walked slowly along the passageway to the cloister, and thence to the abbot's hall. On the way he saw Peter, their torchbearer of the day before, and asked him to fetch wine to the abbot's hall.

'Abbot, I am sorry to disturb you once more,' he said.

'Of course you are,' the abbot said thinly.

'These are matters which require care. Bringing to justice a murderer is a serious matter. However, consequences can be serious even when lesser crimes are committed. Especially when the man who may be offended is immensely powerful.'

'Please, Sir Baldwin, come to the point and stop honing the edge.'

'Very well. You, abbot, wield power of life and death, within certain boundaries. You can arrest your brethren for misconduct, punish lay brothers and others, can you not? And were I to find a murderer in your midst, I should be powerless to capture and punish him. This is your precinct. My authority is left at your door.'

'I know all this.'

'Yes. And yet you have to be cautious in the presence of your neighbour, the king. His own father came in here and punished a thief by flaying his body and leaving the skin nailed to your Chapter House door as a reminder to your brethren that you should be more careful in future.'

'There were allegations that brothers from this abbey were complicit in the robbery of the crown jewels,' the abbot admitted.

'Just as they were in stealing this book,' Baldwin said. 'A brother from the abbey here allowed Friar Martin to use the key to the crypt to search inside for the book. How many keys are there?'

'Only one.' The abbot frowned. He reached under his robes and brought out a heavy key ring. 'It is this one,' he said, indicating a long, heavy key. 'It is always with me.'

'The crypt was open. Plainly another man has a key,' Baldwin said. Then he grinned. 'And I know who he is.'

Peter entered apologetically, a tray with goblets and jugs of wine in his hands. 'Sir Baldwin asked for wine, my Lord Abbot.'

'Bring it in, then,' the abbot said tersely.

'So, abbot, you have here a problem: the book, which this friar would be most glad to remove from your possession and take with him to his master; you may deny him the opportunity, but there is another key. So even if you find the book and return it to your crypt, you will still need to find that key. Or change the lock, which would be expensive.'

'I do not understand what you mean,' the abbot said.

'I had thought that the book was the target of the robbery. Now I think that it was an accident. It was not the book itself which was wanted. It was a copy being created, a copy that incorporated pieces of the strange prophecy of the six kings of England.'

'Who would want to kill to recover that?' Brother Martin demanded.

'Think of the two dead men. One killed and flayed

like the thief of the crown jewels, the other stabbed, but with works stuffed in his mouth as though the words and pictures were designed to choke him.'

'Well?'

In answer, Baldwin turned to Peter, who was serving wine to Simon. 'A man loyal to the king may take the prophecy of the six kings as an insult to his master. If he learned that this prophecy was to be bruited abroad, might he not take it into his head to prevent it? A royalist may well decide that this prophecy, which alleged that the present king was little more than a goat, while his first-born son would be an Arthur, bringing new realms under his sway, was a slur on his master. A man who sought to break into the crypt and spread such tales deserved to die in the same way as that earlier thief. Skinned.'

'What of the prior?'

'He had sought to have Alexander work with him on a copy of the Black Book of Brân and incorporate in it the prophecies of the six kings. He was guilty too. And because the killer was in the pay of the king himself, and the king possessed a key which gave access to the crypt – from the days when the crown jewels were stored there – it was easy for this man to open it for Alexander. You see, I was surprised that Alexander should be able to gain entry. Prior Stephen himself told me that valuables were stored there. Clearly, the door was kept locked. Yet Alexander entered. More, I was astonished that his voice was heard mostly from the open windows. Little sound penetrated from the crypt along the corridors. Perhaps that was because the man who killed Alexander had already locked them both inside, to prevent any risk of their being discovered until he was ready. That door barred the sound of the screams.'

Peter eyed him with a wry grimace. 'You accuse me?'

'Yes, Peter. I believe you are still in the pay of the king. You were never truly a corrodian. You are not old; you have no injury. No, you are a king's spy in here. And when you saw that there was a risk to his reputation, you took it upon yourself to destroy utterly those who threatened him.'

Peter gave a dry chuckle, then bent over Simon's goblet. Suddenly he whirled and hurled the heavy jug at Baldwin. He turned and pelted for the door, slamming it behind him.

The wine had drenched Baldwin, the heavy pewter slamming into the wall behind him, but he was already on his feet and making for the door. Simon got to it first and wrenched it open, and then the two were running along the corridor towards the cloister.

Peter was some distance before them, and Simon caught a glimpse of his heels as he rounded a corner. The lay brother was hurtling into a wall to slow himself, then setting off to the right, towards the lay brothers' dorter.

'This way!' Baldwin nodded, and the two pounded on, their heavy boots echoing on the slabs.

There was a door open. Simon saw it, saw movement, and drew his sword. Inside he saw Peter rummaging in a chest. He stood with a long knife in one hand, a heavy-looking book with ancient wooden board covers in the other. Seeing Simon and Baldwin, he rushed at them, knife held close to his breast, the book over his heart like a buckler.

Baldwin caught the gleam of steel as he reached the door and threw himself sideways, but his ankle turned on a loose stone. He hit the wall, his temple catching a protruding stone, and suddenly all went white, silver stars shining in his face as he slumped to the floor.

Simon leaped before him and, before Peter could stab downwards, Simon's sword clashed. Peter gripped the book tightly, but he could wield his sword with skill with his right, and Simon was reminded of his story of being in the king's host. This was a man who had fought before.

So had Simon. He was trained in the basic English fighting techniques, but his training had been supplemented by his years on the moors, dealing with the miners. They had shown him rougher methods of fighting with steel. More serious, more dangerous, more unexpected. When Peter suddenly dropped to one knee and thrust upwards, Simon was able to parry with ease; when Peter feinted a slash from the right, only to slip sideways and thrust again, Simon blocked and darted to Peter's right, trying to stab under his armpit. Peter was wily too, and retreated sharply, blocking the manoeuvre. But he brought up the book at the same time, and it snagged his blade for a moment. It left a brief opportunity, and Simon took it. He sprang forward and right, and thrust.

The first caught the book on the point. It skittered on the hard, age-blackened wood of the cover as though meeting steel and slipped over the cover, making a long slash, then slid over the top, where it met Peter's throat. The blade slid in effortlessly, grating slightly on Peter's spine, slicing through his windpipe, and on until Simon's hand was on Peter's chin, while he grabbed Peter's own fist and kept his blade away.

His furious advance knocked Peter backwards, Simon's sword rattling over the stone of the walls. And then, as Peter collapsed, dropping his own sword and clutching at his throat, Simon saw bubbles emerge from the huge wound, and he heard the rattling of breath gargling in Peter's blood. Simon rolled away and vomited.

Monday before the Feast of St John the Baptist,[3] Twenty-Second year of the reign of King Edward III of England (Ninth year of the reign of King Edward of France)

The prior leaned back in his chair and set down the spectacles. At his age it was unsurprising that he should need such instruments, for men of his age often did, but it yet rankled that he was forced to use them.

This chill morning it seemed as though the world was dying. Much as it had seemed all those years ago when the strange knight from Devon and his friend had found the king's spy and killed him. The man who had killed poor Stephen.

There had been so much pain and suffering in those far-off days. Prior Stephen being slaughtered just after poor Alexander, and all because that fellow Peter wanted to save the king from some little embarrassment. Not that the new king would have minded. From all that had happened since then, with the civil war, the irruption of King Edward III into the void left by the death of his poor father, the new war with the French, even the king's declaration that he was the true King of France a decade ago, his restless ambition had become all too clear. He had made all those events seem so far distant they were like a dream. And for a man who was almost fifty years old, with failing eyesight, sore limbs and a memory that was not to be trusted with matters that happened a scant five minutes ago, their dreamlike quality was more real than more recent events.

Peter had died, of course. There had been talk about skinning him like an ox and having his skin held up on the door, but the old king wouldn't hear of it. Refused

[3] Monday 17 June 1348

to accept that the man had been in the wrong – even tried to deny aiding him. But the presentation of the crypt's key, which had been discovered in Peter's room, had silenced his negotiator. Peter's body was removed, and the book remained where it had been left, in the safekeeping of the abbey.

Not that it was safe there. After that attempt, Bishop Walter of Exeter had suggested a safer place in which to store it, and it had come here, with the prior, when he was elected to this house. There were some who still wondered about it. No doubt those Franciscans would dearly have loved to have handled it, just so that they could copy the more outrageous prophecies and use them to the greater glory of their order. But no. Abbot John had insisted upon keeping it. If the Pope himself ordered it, he would give it up, he said, but no one else's command would be heeded. But the Pope didn't want to *command* that it be given up. And the Pope had more important matters to concern him by then. War between France and England – yet again. But there were some in the papal Curia who thought that the mad jottings in that book may have some relevance. It was not so heretical as to deserve destruction and should be kept safe in case it proved useful. The Franciscans were probably responsible for that. They always believed they could manipulate books to suit themselves. Maybe they'd try to get it again and rewrite pieces to better fit their view of the world.

Never mind. Here it was, and here it would remain. All those prophecies . . . Perhaps some had come to pass. Certainly, there was war enough to sate the most bloodthirsty Antichrist. But there was no man who appeared to fit that description. And what of the other prophecies? They were the merest nonsense.

Prior Robert stood and stretched, preparing for the Mass. Once a youthful novice in a great, bustling abbey, now he was prior in his own right in this little house at Hemel Hempstead, and he was content.

He left his room, and as he did so, unknown to him, the little taper, which had illuminated his work, fell. A spark alighted upon a fragment of dandelion seed lying amongst the rushes, and it combusted as he closed his door behind him, flaring into some dog hairs. They were enough, just, to light a few fragments of straw and rush.

The prior entered his priory church with his hands clasped, singing. For some reason, as his eyes caught a glimpse of the cross on the altar before him, he was struck with a shiver of horror. Into his mind came another prophecy from that damned book: *Then plague and war will scour the land.*

No, that was nonsense. Just like all the rest, he told himself. He was glad that the damned book was well concealed, down beneath the altar here, in a chest under a heavy stone. It would take a man of unusual foresight and wit to discover it there. Long may it remain, for no man should ever read it again.

ACT FOUR

As ancient foes do burn and fight,
And foul fair fields with their woeful dead,
The Hammer of the Unruly will show his might,
The glorious sun, the golden head.

And then, when war-blood stains the trading stones,
Will murder spoil the rock's most sacred place.
And while the King's house mourns its shattered bones,
Will blaze the traitor's sainted face.

When scarce a decade since the plaguey scourge,
Far worse than northern wars have ravaged sore,
Then kings and rock will clash and purge,
And strife will visit colleges once more.

I

Cambridge, November 1350

It was a good night for crime – dank, foggy and dark. The robber stood in the shadows cast by the college of Peterhouse and bided his time. The only light was from the lamp that hung above the gate, a pale, sickly gleam that did little to dispel the blackness. He smiled grimly.

Perhaps God had sent the mist to help him. It was not such a wild thought: the so-called Black Book of Brân, with its uncannily accurate prophecies, was considered dangerous by the Church, and God might well have decided He did not approve of what its current owner – William de Drayton – intended to do with it.

And He was right to be worried. Drayton was a despicable creature, who claimed to have rescued the book from a fire in Hemel Hempstead. The robber suspected that Drayton had set the blaze himself, ruthlessly ensuring that no one survived to accuse him. Of course, it was all Prior Robert's fault. The foolish, trusting head of Hemel Hempstead Priory had rashly taken Drayton – who by chance had been stuck there for a few days after his horse had gone lame – into his confidence one night, telling his visitor all about the strange and wonderful book that had been entrusted to him, stored in its special box of stone. The robber grimaced. Prior Robert must have been drunk, because *he* would certainly not have told someone like Drayton such a closely guarded secret. Perhaps the plague, which had been sweeping the country when the priory had burned, had addled Prior Robert's mind.

Once he had snatched the book from the smouldering ruins, Drayton had disappeared, scuttling from settlement to settlement in an effort to avoid the foul disease that was claiming one in every two or three of the population. It was almost two years before he had deemed it was safe enough to emerge and sell Brân's prophecies to the highest bidder. He had originally intended to hawk the tome in London, but then had decided to travel to the University at Cambridge instead, on the grounds that scholars loved books and were more likely to pay top prices than the book-dealers of London.

The robber grimaced a second time as he recalled

the interest Drayton had managed to drum up – the Black Book of Brân had been kept secret for hundreds of years, yet Drayton flaunted it as though it were an undergraduate textbook. At least a dozen academics had clamoured to buy it, and immediately began bidding against each other – the different colleges had always enjoyed a degree of antipathy towards each other, and no one wanted a rival foundation to gain the upper hand. Now there were only two left: Bardolf of King's Hall had offered fifteen marks, but Wittleseye of Peterhouse had managed to scrape together seventeen. The robber did not have that sort of money, but he wanted the book – or, rather, his master did, and no one liked disappointing *him*. So he decided there was no choice but to take it by force. He did not take pleasure from the fact that he would have to kill Drayton in order to get it; it was simply a necessary part of the plan.

The robber reflected on his master for a moment. He was still young but already showed the mettle and determination that would make him great one day – and he showed the cool ruthlessness that would allow him to succeed in all he did too. The robber had never taken a life before, but when his master had ordered him to do so, he had not dared demur: clearly, his master wanted the book at all costs, and as Drayton was unlikely to hand it over without demanding a princely sum in return, then Drayton was going to have to die.

The robber scratched his chin in the darkness. Perhaps Drayton's death would be foretold in the book – his master had told him that it contained remarkable predictions about all manner of events. And that was why he was so determined to have it, of course – to see whether his own destiny was announced by the ancient prophet, and to see how he might use the verses to claw more power and wealth towards himself.

In the distance a night-watchman called the hour, and the robber shivered, hoping that Drayton would not renege on the arrangements he had made that day. It had not been easy to stalk Drayton without being noticed, and it had been pure luck that the robber had happened to overhear Wittleseye agreeing to hand over his seventeen marks at midnight. Of course, Wittleseye should have been suspicious of the fact that Drayton insisted on trading at a time when honest men were abed, but the Peterhouse Fellow was so determined to have the book that he did not seem to care. The robber knew for a fact that Wittleseye had not told his colleagues what he was going to do – perhaps he intended to run off with it and make his own fortune. The book had a habit of bringing out the worst in people.

The robber wondered what Bardolf of King's Hall would say the following morning when he learned that the book had been sold while he was asleep. He allowed himself a second mirthless grin. Except that would not happen, because Drayton would be dead and the Black Book of Brân nowhere to be found. By dawn it would be miles away, en route to his master.

Just when the robber was beginning to think that Drayton must have decided against selling to Wittleseye, the man appeared. He had been drinking and was unsteady on his feet, no doubt celebrating the seventeen marks he thought he was about to acquire. Soundlessly, the robber left his hiding-place and padded towards him. Drayton had a bag looped across his shoulder; even in the dim light of the lamp above the gate, the robber knew it contained the book. Before Drayton realized what was happening, the robber slipped up behind him and plunged a dagger into his back. He used his other hand to cover his victim's mouth, to prevent him from crying out. Holding a man while the life ebbed out of him was not pleasant, but it did not take long. The robber dropped the body and grabbed the bag.

The book was inside, wrapped in oiled parchment to protect it from the damp. Deftly, he pulled away the wrappings, keen to see the thing that had led him down such a dark path. What he found made him gape in horror.

Drayton had brought Aristotle's *On Dreams* to the meeting instead. It was the same size as the Black Book of Brân and had the same crude wooden covers, but that was where the similarity ended. Filled with rage and frustration, the robber hurled the tome at Peterhouse's door. What had Drayton done with the real text? The robber knew for a fact that it was not in his lodgings on the High Street, because he had searched them thoroughly. And Drayton had no friends in the town so could not have left it with a third party. Had he sold it to King's Hall for fifteen marks, and planned to deceive Wittleseye and get Peterhouse's seventeen too?

The robber cursed softly in the darkness: the one man who could have answered his questions was dead. Would the Black Book of Brân disappear yet again, before someone else 'discovered' it and attempted to use it for his own ends?

II

Cambridge, July 1357

Matthew Bartholomew, Master of Medicine at the college of Michaelhouse and the University's official Corpse Examiner, only just parried the blow that was intended to deprive him of his head. He staggered, struggling to lift his sword to meet the next lunge. His opponent's face was infused with battle-lust, and

Bartholomew knew he could not deflect many more vicious swipes – he was a physician, not a warrior, and although he had acquired a modicum of skill with weapons through the years he was no match for a trained professional.

All around him were the sounds of affray: clashing weapons, war cries, clanging bells, the crackle of fire. It was not the first fracas that had raged in the little Fen-edge town, but it was certainly one of the most serious. He could hear the moans of the dying, and the sandy soil of the Market Square was stained dark with blood.

'Say your prayers,' snarled Hugh Bardolf, preparing for his final assault. 'I will show you what happens to those who declare an allegiance with Peterhouse.'

'I have not declared an allegiance to Peterhouse,' objected Bartholomew, ducking behind a cart of onions. Hugh kicked it out of the way as if it were no more solid than straw.

'Liar! The Master of your college made a speech today, swearing to fight against King's Hall.'

'He cannot have done,' protested Bartholomew, knowing there was no point in trying to reason with Hugh when the man was so inflamed but persisting anyway. 'He is away.'

Hugh ignored him, concentrating instead on driving him back with a series of determined hacks. Bartholomew's arms burned from the effort of defending himself, but then Hugh performed a fancy manoeuvre that saw the sword fly from his opponent's hands. Weaponless and exhausted, Bartholomew braced himself for the blow that would kill him, but even as he raised his head to look Hugh in the eye he saw the man's fury fade to shock. Then Hugh dropped to his knees, before pitching forwards to land face down on the ground.

'Lord!' murmured John de St Philibert, clutching his

bloody dagger with unsteady hands. 'Brother Michael told me you could hold your own in a skirmish, but I thought Hugh was going to kill you.'

Bartholomew retrieved his sword, knowing the danger was not yet over. Hugh had brothers in King's Hall, and it would be only a matter of time before one raced to avenge his fallen sibling. He pushed John behind him; the Junior Proctor was an even less accomplished warrior than he, and a vengeful Bardolf would hack him to pieces in moments.

But no one came, and a quick glance around told Bartholomew that the violence was ending as abruptly as it had started. The bells grew silent, the clash of steel petered out and calls to arms were replaced by the moans of the wounded. Eventually, Market Square residents felt it was safe to open their doors; they emerged cautiously, making disparaging remarks about the University's insatiable penchant for fighting. A month ago the friars had been at each other's throats over some edict from the Pope; now it was the turn of King's Hall and Peterhouse. The two colleges had suddenly taken against each other after years of peaceful coexistence, although the feud had been confined to sharp-tongued exchanges in the High Street until now.

John was still gazing at Hugh's body. The Junior Proctor was a handsome man, betrothed to the Earl of Suffolk's eldest daughter and so destined for a life of power and influence. Until the earl chose a date for the wedding, John was studying law at Cambridge. Afraid that academia would not prepare him for the rough politics of a baron's household, he had volunteered to serve as the University's Junior Proctor, which meant he was one of the men responsible for maintaining law and order amongst students. He worked hard at both, although neither peacekeeping nor scholarship came easily to him.

'I stabbed him in the back,' he said wretchedly. 'I should have told him to face me first.'

'Then he would have killed you,' said Bartholomew practically, knowing that Hugh would have thought nothing of pitting his great broadsword against John's slender dagger.

'What will Joan say when she hears about this?' John's voice was full of anguished remorse. 'She will not want to marry a man without honour.'

Bartholomew thought Joan was the least of John's problems. 'Do not tell anyone else what you did,' he advised. 'Hugh has brothers, and you do not want them coming after you for revenge.'

John was horrified, the courage he had mustered to save the physician dissipating now the danger was over. 'I did not think of that. Lord! What have I done?'

'Cut short a killing spree,' replied Bartholomew tersely. 'Hugh was an accomplished warrior, and he had no right sparring with Peterhouse's boys. I saw him kill three myself, and if you had not stopped him there would have been more. You did the right thing. Just do not discuss it with anyone.'

'Is that why you fought him?' asked John. 'You saw him cut that bloody swath through those hapless students, and you wanted to stop him?'

'They were unarmed,' said Bartholomew shortly. Witnessing such brutal carnage had been harrowing, and he knew it would haunt him for a long time to come. 'I had to do something.'

'You should have been unarmed too,' said John, eyeing the blade that the physician still held. 'And so should Hugh. Weapons are forbidden to scholars.'

Bartholomew nodded towards the corpse of a King's Hall student: Hugh's blind blood-lust had led him to kill a lad from his own side as well as 'enemies'.

'I borrowed his. Do you know how the fighting

started? As far as I understand, it is because my college has announced an alliance with Peterhouse – or so Hugh claims. However, our Master is away, so perhaps one of the other Fellows . . .'

'I did hear a rumour to that effect,' said John, nodding. 'However, I suspect what happened today had nothing to do with anything your colleagues may or may not have said. It was *meant* to happen – it was predicted in the Black Book of Brân.'

Bartholomew stared at him in confusion. 'In the what?'

John regarded him askance, as if astonished that he should have to explain. 'It is the text everyone is squabbling over. Surely you have heard about it?'

The physician had not heard about a book that was being squabbled over, but was not inclined to ask questions about it when there were wounded men who needed his attention. He pushed all thoughts from his mind except medicine and began the grisly business of stitching cuts, setting bones and pasting poultices over bruises. Most physicians declined to perform such lowly tasks, but Cambridge's only surgeon was an unsavoury character with a notoriously poor success rate, and Bartholomew disliked entrusting him with anyone's well-being.

As he worked he became aware that the ringleaders of the feud had declined to leave the field of battle. They were bickering with each other, their voices growing increasingly acrimonious. John tried to order them home, but they were disinclined to listen to him, and the Senior Proctor – Brother Michael – was chasing after some of Peterhouse's more feisty students, hoping to prevent them from embarking on another brawl.

'They started it,' a Peterhouse scholar named Wittlesey was declaring. He was an overweight cleric who liked to brag about the fact that he was the Archbishop of Canterbury's nephew. 'We came to buy bread, and they began baiting us.'

'They did,' asserted his colleague, another plump priest who claimed kinship with the archbishop. Neuton had hidden behind a cart the moment fists had started to fly, and he took a sip from the wineskin that was never far from his reach, to steady his nerves. 'Then Hugh drew his sword for no reason and started hacking at people.'

'He drew because Peterhouse called him a bastard,' explained Beadle March, one of the army of men hired by the proctors to keep the peace. He had a pink face, small eyes and an upturned nose, features that were redolent of a pig. Although he had more brains than the average beadle, he was vindictive and petty, and there was a general belief amongst the students, albeit without evidence, that he had enjoyed a criminal past.

'Well, Hugh *is* a bastard,' said Neuton, taking another swig of wine. 'The Bardolf clan share a father, but they all have different mothers. And we only mentioned his illegitimacy because *he* insulted *us*.'

'He called them thieves,' supplied March.

Bartholomew looked up sharply; the trouble was likely to reignite if the beadle insisted on repeating the barbs that had started it in the first place.

William Bardolf, the one member of the Bardolf tribe who was not illegitimate, shrugged indolently. He was vice-warden of King's Hall, a large, black-haired man with a beard. 'That is not an insult; it is the truth. You make no secret of the fact that you want to steal our lawful property.'

'The Black Book of Brân is *not* yours,' shouted Wittleseye. 'It is mine. I paid for it seven years ago, and it promptly went missing. *You* are the thieves.'

William's expression darkened. 'We have stolen nothing. The book came to us by the hand of God. Besides, you did not pay for it – Drayton was murdered before you could give him anything.'

Neuton glowered. 'And who was responsible for that? King's Hall! You killed Drayton and stole the text. Now you claim to have come by it miraculously. Well, your story is ludicrous!'

'Not as ludicrous as yours,' snapped William. 'Wittleseye went behind your back seven years ago, trying to buy the book for himself. Now you pretend you were all united? It is laughable!'

'Who told you what I did seven years ago?' demanded Wittleseye, looking decidedly shifty.

March began to whistle airily, looking anywhere except at the Peterhouse men. Fortunately for him, the scholars were more interested in each other than in gossiping beadles.

One of William's siblings, who looked just like him except for being twice his size, stepped forward. '*Peterhouse* murdered Drayton, not us,' snarled Roger Bardolf. 'Wittleseye did not want to part with his money, and murder ensured he got to keep his silver *and* the book.'

'Then why is it not in my possession now?' demanded Wittleseye, eyeing him disdainfully. 'If I acquired it by sinister means seven years ago, then how does King's Hall come to have it?'

'Divine intervention,' replied William when Roger hesitated uncertainly. 'God took it from the hands of thieves and gave it to men who will treat it with respect.'

'I do not care who stole what,' said John, speaking quietly to calm them all. 'Just go home. Brother Michael will hear your grievances as soon as he has seen to the dead. He—'

'There would not be any dead were it not for these … these *devil's spawn,*' yelled Wittleseye, incensed. 'But what can you expect from men whose mothers are French witches?'

Roger stepped forward menacingly, but his brother stopped him with a warning glance. Roger clenched his fists, clearly itching to use them, while Wittleseye hastily ducked behind his colleagues.

'The proctors will fine anyone who swings a punch,' said March, nevertheless grinning his delight at the prospect of more violence.

Bartholomew stood quickly, acutely aware that threats were more likely to aggravate than ease the situation. He gestured to John that he should send the beadle away before his interjections made matters worse, but the Junior Proctor did not see him.

'You speak without knowing the facts, Wittleseye,' said William. His voice was mild, but there was menace in it. 'Our *grandmother* is a French witch, but our mothers are all barons' daughters.'

'And we would rather be bastards than kin to an archbishop,' added Roger, wrinkling his nose in exaggerated disgust.

'I am not keen on archbishops either,' said March conversationally. 'They are invariably devious. Well, they have to be, if they are going to rise very high in the Church. Everyone knows that.'

'No wonder the Bardolf clan steals books,' said Neuton to Wittleseye, loud enough to be heard by half of Cambridge. 'Their French blood means they cannot help themselves. They are all villains.'

'You took leave of absence from your studies last year,' said William, smiling malevolently at the two priests. 'Remind me where you went.'

'They went to France,' supplied March helpfully. 'To see the Pope in Avignon, and they came back telling everyone how lovely it was, and how charming were the people. Of course, we are at war with the French, so these sentiments are hardly patriotic . . .'

'Stop it!' cried John, trying hard to be forceful. 'Everyone will go home immediately, or I will—'

'Our brother Hugh is dead,' said Roger in a dangerous growl. 'I am not going anywhere until his murder is avenged.'

'It *has* been avenged,' said John. He swallowed hard, and his eyes flicked towards Bartholomew. He was an uncomfortable prevaricator and felt guilty about what he had done, no matter how justified. 'Hugh is dead, but so are five Peterhouse men.'

'But unlike them, Hugh *deserved* to die,' said Wittleseye spitefully. 'He was an abomination with his over-ready sword, and the world is a better place without him.'

'I will tear your heads off,' shouted Roger, shaking off his brothers' warning hands and striding towards the Peterhouse priests. 'And then I will play camp-ball with them.'

'You need only one head to play camp-ball,' said March, thoroughly enjoying himself. 'Any more would be confusing.'

'Enough,' snapped Bartholomew, intervening when he saw Roger's dagger emerge from its sheath. John was apparently unequal to preventing a second brawl, and the physician did not want more wounds to stitch. He interposed himself between the two factions. 'Take your injured friends and go home before anyone else dies.'

For a moment he thought they were going to ignore him too, but the Peterhouse clerics were unnerved by the appearance of Roger's dagger. Wittleseye flashed an obscene gesture at his enemies – a vulgar sign that Bartholomew had never seen a priest make before –

and stalked away, pulling Neuton with him. After a moment, lingering just long enough to look as though they were dispersing of their own volition, the Bardolf clan sauntered off in the opposite direction.

'Thank you,' said John, relieved. 'I thought they were going to fight again, and the Bardolfs would have slaughtered the priests. It was the Peterhouse students who did the fighting before – Wittleseye and Neuton did not risk their own skins.'

'They urged them on, though,' said March. 'I do not like those cowardly clerics.'

'You should confine him to desk-duties,' advised Bartholomew, watching March strut away to join his fellow beadles. 'He is too poisonous to be allowed out.'

Bartholomew returned to the wounded, but there were a number of them and it was afternoon by the time he had finished. He was on his way home, disgusted by the whole affair, when he met March. The beadle informed him that the dead had been taken to Holy Trinity and, as Corpse Examiner, Bartholomew was required to inspect them and give an official cause of death. The proctors did not want bodies to act as rallying points for further bloodshed, and the quicker they were in the ground, the better. Bartholomew was in no mood for viewing more victims of violence, but went to do his duty.

Brother Michael was waiting for him. Besides being Senior Proctor, Michael was a Benedictine monk and taught theology at Michaelhouse. He was also the physician's closest friend. His face was grim, and it was clear he was both unsettled by and angry about the trouble afflicting his town.

Beadle March pointed to where the bodies lay in a row, his porcine features alight with ghoulish malice.

'Do you need help? I am excellent at identifying killers from wounds.'

'No, thank you,' said Bartholomew, suspecting that March intended to settle a few scores by naming men he did not like as the culprits. 'John will be here in a moment. He will help me.'

'Suit yourself,' replied March disagreeably. 'I will just stand here and watch, then.'

'He is not a performing ape,' said Michael curtly. 'And you have your own work to do.'

Just then, John approached with parchment and pen, ready to marry the name of each victim with the official cause of death. March slouched away, but it was clear he resented being omitted from the proceedings and did not go far. Bartholomew began his examination. There were seven bodies, including Hugh's. All were young, and Bartholomew did not find it easy to kneel next to them and inspect their wounds. John was oddly quiet, and when Bartholomew glanced up to make sure he was paying attention, he saw the Junior Proctor's cheeks were wet with tears.

'It is so senseless!' he blurted when Bartholomew raised questioning eyebrows. 'I know bloodshed was predicted in the Black Book of Brân, but I was not expecting this . . .'

'I know,' said Bartholomew kindly. He had no idea what John was talking about, but he understood his distress. 'Go outside for some fresh air. I can finish on my own.'

John did not need to be told again. He left as fast as his legs would carry him, calling out to Michael as he went that he would organize the beadles for the next patrol. March watched him go with an amused grin, but the expression faded when Michael glared at him. The beadle muttered something about joining his colleagues and made himself scarce.

'If I were not so short-handed, I would dismiss March,' said the monk, coming to stand next to Bartholomew. 'But I need every man I can get at the moment – at least until King's Hall and Peterhouse come to their senses. What can you tell me about these foolish young men?'

'I saw Hugh kill three, including the boy from his own college.' Bartholomew pointed them out. 'And the rest have sword cuts that make me suspect they were his victims too.'

Michael regarded him balefully. 'I watched you grab a blade and challenge him. What were you thinking? I was sure he was going to kill you – and then who would have inspected corpses for me? Thank God John was able to come to your rescue. Did you hear how it all started? A rumour that Michaelhouse plans to side *with* Peterhouse and *against* King's Hall. It is untrue, of course.'

'Do you think the gossip was a deliberate attempt to cause trouble?'

Michael rubbed his eyes. 'I wish I knew. I came as soon as I heard the two factions were yelling accusations at each other, but Hugh attacked Peterhouse before I could stop him.'

'Hugh started this fight?'

Michael nodded. 'Although I saw someone standing beside him, murmuring in his ear. I suspect one of his clan was determined to have a spat and used him as a means to start one. Hugh's temper was notoriously volatile.'

'Did you see who it was? He bears some responsibility for what happened – for Hugh's death, as well as these others.'

'It was raining, and he wore a hood that conveniently masked his face. However, I shall find him. No one disturbs the peace in my town and evades justice.'

'In the verbal squabble that followed the riot, when you were chasing those lads from Peterhouse, the ringleaders accused each other of stealing some tome – the Black Book of Brân. What is that about?'

Michael gaped at him. 'Are you jesting with me? The question of who owns the thing has been the talk of the town for the last two weeks. Surely you have heard of it? It lies at the heart of the Peterhouse–King's Hall dispute.'

'I have been busy. There are student disputations to organize and I have patients to see.'

'Where have you been doing all this? The moon?' Michael waved away the physician's objections and began to explain. 'The Black Book of Brân is said to be eight hundred years old and was written by a monk who either went mad or vanished – the explanatory notes are difficult to decipher, apparently. It comprises poetry that predicts the future.'

Bartholomew was disgusted. 'No one with a modicum of sense believes in that sort of nonsense.'

'And therein lies the problem: the scholars of King's Hall and Peterhouse do *not* have a modicum of sense. They are convinced that the book is a powerful tool for predicting future calamities, and each group maintains it is the rightful owner.'

'What sort of future calamities?'

'Well, the verse that has them all clamouring about the book's uncanny accuracy mentions strife visiting colleges. Of course, there is an air of horrible inevitability about the whole business – that trouble was predicted, so someone has ensured that trouble we shall have.'

'Which college has the stronger claim to the text?'

Michael frowned and shook his head slowly. 'Neither, as far as I am concerned. It came here seven years ago, brought by an unsavoury character called

William de Drayton, who said he had rescued it from a burning priory. I doubt he came by it honestly, and there was a suspicion that he had set the inferno himself. Despite this, two colleges expressed an interest in buying the book: Peterhouse and King's Hall.'

The tale rang a bell in Bartholomew's memory. 'I remember Drayton. He was stabbed not long after the plague. We investigated, but we never found his killer.'

Michael nodded. 'What we were not told then, but seems common knowledge now, is that he probably died because someone wanted the book he had been carrying in his bag.'

That did not fit with what Bartholomew remembered. 'The book was one of Aristotle's, although I cannot recall which. We wondered what kind of killer would have left such a valuable tome behind, and it led us to conclude that the culprit was probably not a scholar.'

Michael's expression was bleak. 'Well, I am told now that Drayton's bag was *supposed* to contain the Black Book of Brân. He was taking it to Peterhouse, where Wittleseye was ready with seventeen marks. Wittleseye waited in vain for the delivery that night – or so he says.'

Bartholomew frowned. 'But I was under the impression, from the quarrel in the Market Square, that King's Hall has the book. Does that mean someone from King's Hall murdered Drayton?'

'Peterhouse certainly thinks so. But King's Hall says the sale was never made – that Drayton died before Peterhouse could pay for it.'

'So where has it been these last seven years?'

'That is what I would like to know, but no one seems able to enlighten me. According to King's Hall, it simply appeared in their chapel one morning. I am not one to believe such fanciful notions, but no one has stepped forward to offer a more plausible explanation.'

'Why did no one mention this when Drayton died?' asked Bartholomew, a little angrily. 'We might have found his killer, had we known he was peddling crooked goods. We spent days trying to uncover a motive for his murder but were forced to admit defeat in the end.'

Michael nodded, then sighed unhappily. 'I do not want more bloodshed. Will you come with me to King's Hall and Peterhouse, to ask questions about this damned book? If we can solve Drayton's murder and learn where the tome has been these last seven years, then perhaps these two colleges will stop sparring with each other.'

The streets were unusually empty as Bartholomew and Michael walked to King's Hall. Townsmen and scholars alike were unsettled by the uneasy atmosphere that pervaded the place, and rumours about the bloodiness of the most recent brawl warned sensible folk to stay indoors. Churches were locked, shops were shuttered and colleges and hostels posted extra guards on their doors. The pair had not gone far when they heard the sounds of a violent scuffle. It was coming from St Michael's churchyard, and a sharp yelp of pain prompted them to go and investigate. When they arrived, the Junior Proctor was lying on the ground, clutching his middle. He pointed with an unsteady finger when Bartholomew and Michael approached.

'He ran that way,' he gasped urgently, trying to struggle to his feet. 'Quickly!'

'Who?' demanded Michael, hurrying forward to help him.

'The man who attacked me,' shouted John, agitated by the length of time it was taking them to understand.

'Go after him before he escapes. He has a dagger, so be wary.'

Knowing he would make better time than the fat monk, Bartholomew left Michael to tend the wheezing deputy and began to run in the direction John indicated. A path wound through the undergrowth, used as a short cut between the High Street and the area of tangled alleys known as the Jewry. But by the time Bartholomew emerged in the Jewry, there was nothing to see, and John's assailant was long gone. He retraced his steps and found the Junior Proctor sitting on a tombstone, holding his stomach, while Michael stood next to him.

'You did not catch him,' said the Junior Proctor accusingly. He looked disgusted.

'I am sorry,' said Bartholomew, taken aback by the irritation in John's voice. 'What happened?'

Michael was also furious. 'Someone tried to kill my deputy. And from John's description, it sounds as though it was the same hooded man who aggravated the trouble earlier.'

'He lobbed a knife at me, but it missed – more by the grace of God than any skill on my part,' continued John. 'So he punched me instead. He was preparing to clout me over the head with that stone when you arrived.' He pointed to a rock that would have caused serious damage had it been pitted against a human skull.

'Why would anyone harm you?' asked Bartholomew. John was only the Junior Proctor, and it was Michael who carried the real power.

'Because he is my deputy, of course,' snapped Michael. 'The culprit knows I rely on him to help quell this brewing unrest. It is an attack against peace – against the very authority of the University.'

Bartholomew regarded him soberly. 'Then you

should be careful that the same thing does not happen to you. There will be a riot for certain if the Senior Proctor is not here to stop it.'

They escorted John to the proctors' office, to rest until he felt better, and resumed their walk to King's Hall. It had been founded with royal money and was the largest and most powerful college in Cambridge. It boasted more than a hundred members, and its buildings were amongst the finest in town. The grandest edifice of all was its gatehouse, designed to protect it from hostile invasion. Bartholomew surveyed its thick, crenellated walls and well-placed arrow-slits and thought it was not surprising that the scholars of King's Hall were not afraid to antagonize Peterhouse.

'I like Warden Powys,' he said while they waited for their knock to be answered. 'And I am surprised he has allowed his college to be drawn into a war.'

'Powys is away. King's Hall would never be in this situation if he were home – or if the current vice-warden were someone other than William Bardolf. Incidentally, he did not see you fighting Hugh, and, although most sane men would applaud your courage, I would advise against your mentioning it.'

Bartholomew regarded him askance. 'Do you think me a lunatic, to need to be told?'

Michael chuckled. 'I am obviously spending too much time with John, who was all for racing here and confessing. I think Beadle March overheard us, and I hope to God he does not gossip.'

The door opened before they could discuss it further, and Michael demanded an audience with the vice-warden. While a porter went to see if William was receiving visitors, Bartholomew thought about what he knew of the Bardolf family.

Its head was Lord Thomas, a baron who had fought bravely in the French wars and whose long string of mistresses had provided him with an equally long string of illegitimate children. He acknowledged them all and did his best to set them on the road to prosperity. He enrolled some at King's Hall, where he hoped they would make the connections necessary for distinguished careers at court. Unfortunately, he tended to sire louts who preferred fighting to politics. William Bardolf, his sole legitimate son, was the exception and was more intelligent than the others, although that was not to say he did not also appreciate a brawl.

When the porter conducted them to a suite of rooms in the gatehouse, Bartholomew saw that William lived in style. Thick woollen rugs covered the floor, and the furniture was of the highest quality. William was not alone. Four of his kinsmen, including Roger, lounged on benches, all swarthy individuals with bushy beards. They were also heavily armed, despite the fact that it was against University rules to carry weapons. None seemed bothered by the fact that the Senior Proctor possessed the authority to fine them for such an infraction.

'Brother,' drawled William with a lazy smile. 'What can I do for you?'

'You can make sure there is no recurrence of today's brawl,' replied Michael coolly. 'It was reprehensible. Seven men are dead, including two from King's Hall.'

'And five from Peterhouse,' one sibling murmured. 'It is a fair exchange.'

'They started it,' said Roger hotly. 'They said Michaelhouse had taken their side – a claim we now know to be false – and were gloating. Hugh was right to punish their insolence with his blade.'

William's expression was unreadable. 'Someone encouraged Hugh to do it, though – whispered in his ear that killing Peterhouse boys would be God's work. Perhaps that person should bear some of the blame for what Hugh did.'

Michael regarded him with raised eyebrows. 'From that statement, I judge that you are keen to distance yourself from Hugh's actions?'

William shrugged, silencing Roger's indignant splutter with a warning glance. 'I do not want it said that King's Hall is full of ruffians. But you know I am right about the whisperer, because you observed him yourself. I saw you watching him.'

'I did, but he kept his face concealed by his hood. Who was he?'

'Everyone was wearing his hood today, Brother,' said William, a crooked smile pulling at the corners of his mouth. 'It was raining. Perhaps it was someone from Peterhouse, aiming to see King's Hall in trouble with the Senior Proctor.'

Bartholomew regarded him closely, not sure what to think. Was he lying, and one of his own clan had goaded Hugh into launching his violent attack? Or had someone else done it, perhaps to underline the fact that King's Hall housed some very unpleasant men?

'He is almost certainly the same fellow who attacked my Junior Proctor,' said Michael in a low, dangerous voice. 'And I *will* discover his identity. Perhaps you can make that known.'

William continued to smile. 'Yes, if that is what you want.'

'Tell me about the Black Book of Brân,' said Michael, changing the subject abruptly in an effort to disconcert. 'Drayton was stabbed trying to sell it to Peterhouse, so how do you come to own it?'

'We had nothing to do with Drayton's death,' replied William, allowing his impassive mask to slip and reveal his indignation. 'And I resent the implication that you think we do.'

'Drayton was a snake,' said Roger. 'He told so many

lies about how he came by the book that no one knew what to believe in the end. However, such a fine thing did not belong in *his* tainted hands. Perhaps the saints thought so too, and they killed him for touching it.'

'Saints do not commit murder with cheap daggers bought from the Market Square,' said Michael tartly. 'Why did you decline to tell me about this book seven years ago?'

William shrugged again. 'Why? So you could include us on your list of suspects for Drayton's murder, because we tried to buy the book from him?'

'If you were innocent, then you had nothing to fear,' Michael shot back.

William laughed, genuinely amused. 'We are innocent of starting today's trouble, but you are still here, making accusations. We had nothing to do with Drayton's death, Brother. We did not even know he had elected to sell the book to Peterhouse until his body was found the next day. Until then, we believed he was going to do business with us.'

'I understand it disappeared after his murder,' said Bartholomew. 'And now, seven years later, you claim to be its rightful owners. How did that come about?'

'God arranged it,' said Roger matter-of-factly. 'We do not usually bother with morning prayers, but two weeks ago it was our college's Foundation Day, and we decided to make an exception. We use All Saints' Church as a chapel, and when we arrived there was the Black Book of Brân, lying on the altar. The Almighty put it there, you see, because He wanted us to have it.'

'And why would He want that?' asked Michael cautiously.

'Because we intend to give it to our father, Lord Bardolf,' replied Roger, as if the answer were obvious. 'He is a good man, and predictions about the future will be useful for when he goes to war.'

'But Peterhouse would give it to the Archbishop of Canterbury,' added William. 'And the Church has a habit of burning books it does not understand. God knows *we* are not narrow-minded fanatics, so He put it in a place where He knew we would find it.'

'Why else would He have chosen that particular day to lay it on the altar?' asked Roger.

Bartholomew was bemused by the tale. 'So you arrived for your morning devotions, and the book was just there?'

Roger beamed at the memory. 'Waiting for us. Ask your Junior Proctor if you do not believe us. He came in for morning prayers moments after we made our miraculous find.'

'He says he saw you admiring it but has no idea how it got there,' said Michael. 'May I see it? Given that it is causing so much trouble, I should at least know what it looks like.'

'We prefer to keep spectators away,' said William, 'for security reasons. But I think we can make an exception for you.'

All Saints' Church was on the High Street, and because it was used by King's Hall as a chapel it was one of the most lavishly decorated buildings in Cambridge. Its lectern and pulpit were studded with precious jewels, and there were gold statues in its niches. Unfortunately, this made it attractive to thieves, so the college was obliged to take precautions. Its elegant windows were fitted with heavy shutters, and its doors were nearly always locked. These made it one of the most secure buildings in the town, and it was generally acknowledged that it would prove a challenge for even the most determined of criminals. It was thus an excellent place in which to store a book that another college had vowed to steal.

In addition to the usual safety measures, the brothers had hired a full-time guardian, a studious priest named Thomas de Shirford. Shirford looked as though he needed the money. His robes were threadbare, and there were holes in his shoes. He had a reputation for solid but dull scholarship, and his colleagues tended to use words like 'reliable' and 'sensible' to describe him. He opened the door to William's knock and stood aside to let him, Roger, Michael and Bartholomew enter. The church was gloomy, the only illumination from a small lamp in the chancel.

'Has Peterhouse tried to get the book today?' asked William. 'Or has it been quiet?'

'Neuton came,' replied Shirford. 'But I declined the bribe he offered to let him inside.'

'And he would not get the book, even if he did charm his way in,' said Roger, clearly proud of himself, 'because I secured its back cover to the altar with nails. They are big ones, and I hammered them in very hard. The only way to release it would be to rip it free – and few scholars can bring themselves to damage a book.'

Michael hid a grin. 'If it is so well affixed, how are you going to take it to your father?'

Roger's face fell, indicating he had not planned that far ahead, so William stepped in to rescue him. 'We shall take book and altar together. It will make the tome more difficult to steal en route.'

'Well, there is that, I suppose,' said Michael. 'May I see it? If you have only attached the back cover to the altar, I presume it can still be read?'

'We shall leave you to it, then,' said William, beckoning Roger to follow him. 'Be sure to lock the door when they go, Shirford.'

'Obviously,' said Shirford a little testily. 'I am likely to be harmed if anyone breaks in, so I am careful for my own sake, as well as for the book's. But you are leaving,

Master Bardolf? You will not stay until they have finished?'

'I am needed at King's Hall,' replied William. 'I am afraid Peterhouse will attack, given that they lost five scholars today.'

Shirford shot Bartholomew and Michael an uneasy glance as he barred the door after the King's Hall men. 'I accepted this task on one condition: that there would be no showing of the book to spectators. Gratuitous opening of the door is a risk that does not need to be taken, and there is always a danger that viewers may decide to take the tome for themselves – dispatching *me* along the way.'

'But I am the Senior Proctor, and so exempt from such restrictions,' said Michael haughtily. 'However, no one can deny that you have accepted a dangerous commission. What made you do it?'

Shirford smiled. 'William promised me a country living when this is over. I am not a good scholar, but I might be a good parish priest. It is a chance to make something of my life.'

'What do you think about the way the Black Book of Brân came into King's Hall's hands?' asked Bartholomew curiously. 'Do you really believe it was divine intervention?'

'The Bardolfs rarely attend church, but the day they did the book happened to be on the altar. Perhaps God *did* want them to have it.'

'Why them?' asked Michael. 'They are not scholars, to study it. They are not priests, to explore it for holy wisdom. On the contrary, they plan to give it to their father as a battle aid.'

'It is not for me to judge my fellow men,' said Shirford. 'All I know is that the book was not in the church when I said my prayers at midnight, but it was there when the Bardolfs arrived the following dawn. God moves in mysterious ways, Brother, and who knows His plans?'

'Right,' said Michael, declining to comment further. He took a deep breath. 'We had better look at this text, then, to see for ourselves why it is stirring up so much trouble.'

Shirford led them to the chancel. 'Inspect it at your leisure, although you must handle it with care.'

'Why?' asked Bartholomew.

'Because it harms anyone it deems unworthy. Look what happened to Drayton. I heard he set a priory alight to get the book, killing all its occupants. Then his own life was ended by violent means.'

Michael raised his eyebrows. 'Who told you about the priory?'

'Roger. But it was common knowledge seven years ago.'

'Common knowledge to everyone except us,' grumbled Michael.

The Black Book of Brân was a shabby thing and did not seem worthy to be graced with such a grand title. Its wooden covers were crude, and it did not seem any great pity that Roger had hammered six large nails through the back of it, because there was a long cut, probably from a sword, scored across the front. There was also a dark stain that looked suspiciously like blood on the edge. Michael opened it and was pleasantly surprised to find that the writing was a work of art – the scribe had taken considerable care with his work.

The text was in Latin. He tried to resist the notion that there was something mystical about it, but the silent church and the crackle of ancient parchment as he turned the pages were having an effect. He began to lose himself in the strange poetry, and found himself linking some of the verses with events from the past, such as the early death of Richard the Lionheart and the murder of the current king's father. He was so engrossed that when Bartholomew spoke, he jumped violently.

'It is a lot of gibberish,' said the physician, who had been reading over his shoulder. 'Some verses *may* pertain to real events, but they are written so vaguely that it is impossible to be certain.'

Michael rubbed his eyes. Reading in low light was a strain, and he knew he would have a headache if he persisted. He found himself reluctant to stop, even so. 'I can see why the Church might want to suppress it, though, and why William is keen to give it to his warrior father. It contains just enough material to make one pause for thought. The lines that seem to refer to Queen Isabella and her paramour are uncanny.'

'You do not need to be a fortune-teller to predict that a queen will take a lover at some point in the future,' said Bartholomew dismissively. 'Inevitability is not the same as prophecy – most "predictions" will come true over eight hundred years.'

'Even the end of the world?' asked Michael, trying to shrug off the nagging sense that Brân's 'wisdom' should not be so summarily dismissed. 'There is mention here of cities being destroyed, and of the sinful being purged before a "Sun-bright fire of blood" appears.'

'The end of the world is the greatest inevitability of all,' Bartholomew pointed out. 'It had a beginning, so logic dictates that it will also have an end.'

Michael frowned. 'Look at this one:

"As ancient foes do burn and fight,
And foul fair fields with their woeful dead,
The Hammer of the Unruly will show his might,
The glorious sun, the golden head."

'Do you not think that sounds like the wars King Edward fought with Scotland? They caused him to be known as the Hammer of the Scots, and he had bright gold hair.'

'I suppose so, but it is hardly specific, is it. You needed to explain it to me.'

Michael tapped another quatrain with a chubby forefinger. 'Then what do you make of these lines?

"When scarce a decade since the plaguey scourge,
Far worse than northern wars have ravaged sore,
Then kings and rock will clash and purge,
And strife will visit colleges once more."

'It has been less than ten years since the pestilence was here, and we *do* have strife in our colleges.'

'I admit that rock – *petra* in Latin – may refer to Peterhouse, and kings may refer to King's Hall, but these words could just as easily have nothing to do with us.'

'What about the next verse?' asked Michael:

'*"And then, when war-blood stains the trading stones,*
Will murder spoil the rock's most sacred place.
And while the King's house mourns its shattered bones,
Will blaze the traitor's sainted face."'

'Even you cannot deny that war-blood stained the trading stones – the Market Square – today.'

Bartholomew shrugged, bored with the analysis. 'It is possible that King's Hall and Peterhouse had a spat there *because* of that verse. Someone read that it was predicted, so made it happen.'

'I hope you are right,' said Michael. 'Because if you are not, and the author of this book really did foresee what was going to happen, then we have more unnatural deaths coming – murder in Peterhouse, and shattered bones in King's Hall. What do you think about the traitor's sainted face?'

'Nothing,' said Bartholomew impatiently. 'It is gibberish. However, that said, we should visit Peterhouse and warn them against more violence with King's Hall. You do not need a prophet to tell you their mood is dangerous.'

Peterhouse was located at the southern end of the town, outside the protective gates. Although it did not have King's Hall's wealth and power, it was the University's oldest college, and its buildings were accordingly handsome. There was a large hall, used for teaching and as a refectory, and several pleasant houses provided living quarters. Daily prayers took place in the ancient Church of St Mary the Less, which stood next door and which the scholars had claimed as their collegiate chapel. Beadle March was on duty outside, his hood up to protect him from the drizzle that had begun to fall.

'Your Junior Proctor ordered me to stand here,' he said resentfully. 'He expects me to prevent any Peterhouse man from leaving to cause trouble.'

'Good,' said Michael, knocking at the door. 'Yet you do not seem happy. What is the matter?'

March's pig-like face was angry. 'I was scheduled for tavern patrol today, not standing about in the rain. I do not want to be here all night, when I could be—'

'Drinking?' finished Michael, knowing exactly why the beadle was dissatisfied with his lot. 'I am sorry your duties are interfering with your pleasures, but these things happen.'

'Will he stay at his post?' asked Bartholomew, watching March stamp off to check a back gate.

'Who knows?' said Michael. 'I have never trusted him – I think it was he who started the poisonous rumour that set the friars against each other last month, and I cannot help but wonder whether he has been doing the same with Peterhouse and King's Hall. Perhaps the tales about him are true, and he *was* a criminal before he settled in Cambridge seven years ago.'

A porter conducted the visitors to the hall, where Wittleseye was presiding over a disputation. Bartholomew did not know whether to be alarmed or amused when he learned that the topic under discussion was 'Let us enquire whether sacred books should be in the hands of warriors'. Wittleseye asked a colleague to take over the debate and took Bartholomew and Michael to a solar, where they could talk undisturbed.

'Our Master is in Ely, at a synod with the heads of the other colleges,' said Wittleseye, sitting on a bench. 'He left me in charge – naturally, given that I am the archbishop's nephew.'

'I had forgotten the Masters were away,' murmured Bartholomew to Michael. 'But it makes sense: the real heads of Peterhouse and King's Hall would have stamped out this feud the moment it began.'

'Have you arrested the Bardolfs?' asked Wittleseye, trying without success to hear what the physician was saying. 'They killed five of our students today.'

'And they will kill no more,' said Michael firmly. 'Neither will you. Hugh was mostly responsible, and he is dead himself, so let that mark the end of this unedifying business.'

'It is unedifying,' agreed Wittleseye. 'But the Bardolfs started it by gloating over the fact that they have the Black Book of Brân. They are not suitable custodians for such a dangerous tome. I urge you to take it from them and place it in the hands of priests.'

'How they come to own the book is a curious tale,'

said Michael, ignoring the demand. 'They say it was waiting for them on the altar, just as they were making one of their rare appearances in church.'

'They are liars,' replied Wittleseye bitterly. 'One of them put it there, and they only pretended to find it. How dare they expect intelligent men to believe such nonsense!'

'What do *you* think happened, then?' asked Michael.

'I think they stole it seven years ago and could not think of another way to justify it suddenly being in their possession.'

'If you think they stole the book, then you must think they killed Drayton too,' said Michael. 'Murder is a serious crime, and such allegations should not be made lightly.'

'Their guilt is obvious. They also wanted to buy the book and were furious when Drayton accepted my offer rather than theirs. Of course they killed Drayton – to get the book *and* to avenge themselves on him.'

Michael rubbed his chin thoughtfully. 'If the tome had reappeared a few weeks later, then I might be inclined to believe you. But the Bardolfs are not patient men – they would not have been able to wait so many years.'

'Especially with a book of prophecies,' added Bartholomew dryly. 'Delaying its "discovery" might mean missing a few.'

Wittleseye ignored him. 'Well, someone put that book on the altar, and if it was not the Bardolfs, then who was it?'

'Someone who wanted them to give it to their father?' suggested Bartholomew.

'And who might that be?' demanded Wittleseye. 'Lord Bardolf is *said* to be honourable – although I deplore the number of French witches he seems to have impregnated – but he is a warrior. The book should belong to the Church. I was going to give it to my uncle, the archbishop.'

'It is all nonsense anyway,' said Bartholomew. 'How can a monk writing eight hundred years ago know what is going to happen tomorrow?'

Wittleseye shot him a sour look. 'The same way you physicians use astrological charts to devise more effective courses of treatment for patients, I imagine.'

Michael raised a hand when Bartholomew started to argue. 'We did not come for a debate. We came to hear what you had to say about the Market Square incident, and to warn you against more scandalous behaviour. Where is Neuton? He did nothing to calm troubled waters, and we should speak to him too.'

'He is probably in the kitchen, filling his wineskin,' replied Wittleseye sulkily, resenting the reprimand. 'He usually is at this time of day. I will take you there.'

But the kitchen was deserted, and the door that allowed the unloading of supplies direct from the street stood ajar. Wittleseye slammed it shut with a bad-tempered kick.

'I have told the cooks a dozen times to be more careful. Do they want King's Hall to sneak in and slit our throats while we sleep? They say the latch sticks, and they leave it open for convenience, but we cannot afford to be lax—'

'Neuton is not here,' said Michael, interrupting what promised to become a tirade.

'No, but there are his wine flasks.' Wittleseye pointed to a shelf that contained several identical containers. He took one down and shook it. 'And they are full, so he *was* here not long ago. You cannot accuse me of trying to mislead you.'

'It had not entered my mind,' said Michael, forcing himself to be patient. 'But I still need to speak to him. Where else might he be?'

'In the church.' Wittleseye looked defensive. 'Not to drink without being bothered by students, naturally, but to pray at a time when the place is quiet.'

'Of course,' said Michael tiredly. 'Take us to him, then.'

Wittleseye led the way across a cobbled yard to where a tiny priests' door allowed access to the church from the college grounds. It was cool inside the chapel, and the noise of the street was muted through its thick walls. It was growing late, and the light was beginning to fade, dulling the colourful brilliance of the new stained-glass windows.

Neuton was sitting on a bench, provided for ageing scholars whose legs would not support them through the lengthy sermons preached by wordy men like Wittleseye. His eyes were closed, and one fist was wrapped around his flask. At first, Bartholomew thought he had slipped into a tipsy doze, but when his cousin tapped him on the shoulder he listed to one side. Bartholomew caught him before he fell, staggering under the weight.

'What is wrong with him?' demanded Michael. 'Is he drunk?'

'He is dead,' said Bartholomew, lowering the body to the floor. He inspected it briefly, then glanced up at the monk. 'I think he has been poisoned.'

It was a long time before Bartholomew and Michael were able to leave Peterhouse. Wittleseye was convinced that his cousin had been murdered by King's Hall, and his students were all for marching on the Bardolfs and demanding a fight that night. Michael was obliged to send for more beadles to ensure that they stayed in until tempers had cooled, aware that March could not do it single-handed. Even then, it was almost midnight before he felt it was safe for him and his

Corpse Examiner to go home. Wearily, they made their way along the High Street towards Michaelhouse.

'That wretched book has precipitated all this trouble,' said Michael bitterly. 'And I will not be able to sleep without knowing it is safe. The last thing we need is for it to be stolen – there will be a blood-bath for certain.'

Bartholomew regarded him in surprise. 'It is locked in a church with a full-time guardian. How could anyone steal it?'

'I am probably overreacting, but I cannot help it. There is too much at stake.'

It was not far out of the way, so Bartholomew went with him. All Saints' was a dark mass against the sky, although a faint light could be seen under the west door. While Michael began the protracted process of explaining to Shirford why he wanted access at such an hour, Bartholomew did a circuit of the building, checking the windows and the back door. All were locked, and he returned to the front thinking the Black Book of Brân had chosen the right place in which to make its miraculous appearance, if security was what it was after.

'It is very late,' said Shirford, opening the door a crack and peering out suspiciously. 'I was asleep. What do you want?'

'To make sure you and the book are safe,' replied Michael, pushing past him and indicating that he was to re-bar the door once they were inside. 'There was a murder tonight.'

'I know,' said Shirford. 'Junior Proctor St Philibert told King's Hall there may be trouble, and warned them to take extra precautions. Roger was all for storming Peterhouse immediately, to strike a pre-emptive blow, but your deputy said anyone who leaves the college will spend the next month in prison. He has posted beadles on all their gates to make sure no one escapes.'

'Good,' said Michael, pleased by John's initiative. 'Perhaps we shall avert trouble yet.'

'I am beginning to have second thoughts about this job,' said Shirford unhappily. 'William underplayed the dangers, and I am a priest, not a warrior. It is all very well for him to issue orders that say no one can come in, but *he* does not have to bear the consequences. Agatha the laundress was livid earlier, when I told her she could not see the book.'

'You mean Michaelhouse's Agatha?' asked Bartholomew. 'You refused her? Then you are a braver man than me! She has a long memory, so you had better hope the Bardolfs find you a parish as soon as your duties here are done. You will not be safe in Cambridge now.'

Shirford swallowed hard. Michaelhouse's laundress was one of the most formidable characters in the county, and even the sheriff was wary of her.

'We shall just ensure that the book is still nailed down, and then we will go,' said Michael tiredly. He walked to the chancel and approached the altar. The book was open, and Shirford explained that he had been studying it before he fell asleep.

'The verse about Tartarus' hordes worries me deeply,' he said. 'The current ruler of Scotland is named Alexander, and England might be one of the six Christian kingdoms to be defiled.'

Bartholomew regarded him askance. 'The current King of Scotland is called David.'

Shirford brightened. 'Really? That is a relief! I did not like the notion of being assailed by Latin traders with long spoons. I had a feeling Roger was wrong when he said that would be the next verse to come true – after the ones about Peterhouse and King's Hall.'

'You discuss the contents of the book with Roger?' asked Bartholomew, surprised. Although enrolled at a college and so technically an academic, Roger had never made any pretence at scholarship, and it was rumoured that he was barely literate.

'He is the only person I ever see,' explained Shirford. 'He brings me food each night and usually stays to chat. We have nothing in common but the book, so we invariably talk about that. He often holds forth on current affairs, so I am disappointed to learn that his grasp of world politics is dubious.'

'So is yours, apparently,' said Michael. 'But what do you know about events that took place seven years ago? We did not discuss Drayton's murder when we were here earlier, and I would be grateful for any insights you have to offer.'

Shirford frowned as he struggled with ancient memories. 'I know there was a rumour that Drayton acquired the book by burning down Hemel Hempstead's priory. I also recall that Wittleseye was expecting to buy it the night Drayton died, but Drayton had brought Aristotle's *On Dreams* to Peterhouse instead.'

'No one told us about the Black Book of Brân,' said Michael resentfully. 'We were left to assume that there was nothing odd about the presence of the Aristotle. If people had been honest with us, we might have solved that murder years ago.'

Shirford shot him a crooked smile. 'Can you blame them, when anyone admitting such knowledge would have found himself on your list of murder suspects? I met Drayton once. He was a vile creature, full of lies and craven words, and I recall thinking he was exactly the kind of fellow to burn down a priory for personal gain. No one mourned his passing, so perhaps his killer did the world a favour.'

Michael eyed him coolly. 'I have heard that argument before, but murder is murder, no matter how unpopular the victim. You are not withholding information, are you? Because you approved of what the killer did?'

'Of course not!' The priest was shocked by the notion that he might be implicated in a crime. 'I am just saying that Drayton was no innocent. Surely, you talked to witnesses who confirmed that? He was unpleasant to everyone.'

'Yes,' admitted Michael grudgingly. 'I did come away with the impression that he had not a single redeeming quality.'

They left Shirford, ensuring he barred the door behind them, and began to walk home. They passed John, who was directing the beadles to patrol the areas in which he expected most trouble. He complained that they were spread too thinly, given that so many were tied up at Peterhouse and King's Hall. Meanwhile, Beadle March grumbled that he was being forced to work too hard.

'He made me stop Agatha the laundress just now,' March whined. 'I thought she was going to tear my head off and eat it. What man would not need a drink after that experience?'

John was sheepish. 'We did not know it was Agatha until she removed her hood. To be honest, I thought she was Roger – she is the right height and build. Besides, she should not have been out at this time of night – the curfew bell sounded hours ago.'

'Agatha goes out when she feels like it,' said March. 'And we do not get paid enough to discuss curfew bells with her. When we saw who it was, we let her pass unmolested.'

'Not before you had treated her to the most grovelling apology I have ever heard,' said John, disgusted. 'She was breaking the law and you should have ordered her home.'

Michael frowned at him when March had gone. 'One of the lessons you should learn as a proctor is picking the battles you know you can win. Agatha is invincible and unassailable, so leave her alone. You are not a perfect deputy, but you will suffice, and I do not want to be looking for a replacement because you have tackled Michaelhouse's feisty laundress.'

John grimaced. 'You may not want to lose a deputy, but Joan will not want to lose a fiancé, so I suppose I had better follow your advice. Will you take a cup of wine with me before you go home? We are right outside my house.'

'So we are,' said Michael, peering at the pleasant timber-framed building that John indicated. It was one of the more exclusive residences on the High Street, and a fitting abode for a man who was destined to become kin to the Earl of Suffolk. 'Did you know Drayton rented a room here? It was long before you came, but he hired the attic on the top floor.'

'Did he?' asked John, startled. 'No one told me.'

'And that is another lesson you should learn,' said Michael grimly. 'People have a bad habit of declining to share information with proctors. Do you know any of your housemates well enough to ask them about Drayton? I questioned them when he was killed, of course, but no one was very helpful. Perhaps they will be more forthcoming with you.'

John regarded the dark house doubtfully. 'Now? But they will all be in bed.'

Michael grimaced. 'Of course not now. I need you to patrol tonight – to make sure the likes of March do not neglect their duties. Meanwhile, I shall try to devise a way to defuse this ridiculous business without further loss of blood.'

When Bartholomew reached home, he fell asleep almost immediately, although it was a fitful rest and he could hear Michael pacing in the chamber above. The creaking of floorboards continued for what remained of the night, as the monk used the silence to think about what he had learned. By morning he had assessed the murder of Neuton – and Drayton – from every conceivable angle, but had reached no firm conclusions, although he had theories aplenty. The problem, he thought irritably, was the crippling lack of evidence.

When Bartholomew awoke, the sun was up. The summer air was warm and still and stank of the river, the open drains that meandered along the town's main streets, and the sharper tang of urine from the latrines. He went to St Michael's Church for prayers and tried to keep his mind on his devotions, although images of the recent dead invaded his thoughts far too readily. He had a breakfast of pickled herrings and stale bread with his colleagues, eating the unappetizing fare in silence as they listened to the droning voice of the Bible Scholar, then waited for Michael in the yard.

The monk emerged from the kitchens a few moments later, jaws working furiously. An enraged screech from Agatha indicated that he had supplemented his paltry meal by stealing something, although his face was the picture of innocence when she demanded to know the whereabouts of a pie. Nevertheless, he headed for the gate while he was still in one piece, informing Bartholomew that he wanted to return to Peterhouse and ask questions of Neuton's friends, to see if any of them remembered anything suspicious, now they had had a night to dwell on it.

'I have been thinking about the poison,' said Bartholomew. 'And it may have come from France. When I was there last year, fashionable folk were taking a cordial made from some kind of poisonous fish and regional herbs. It is supposed to aid digestion, but only when diluted – it is quite toxic in its concentrated form. It has a distinctive smell, which I think I detected in Neuton's wineskin.'

'So our poisoner has French connections, does he?' Michael gave the matter serious thought as they walked towards the High Street. 'Most of the Bardolfs have French mothers. Perhaps they decided to avenge their brother Hugh by claiming a high-ranking victim from Peterhouse.'

'Having a French mother does not necessarily mean a supply of French cordials.'

Michael narrowed his eyes. 'But their grandmother is a witch, and it is not inconceivable that she thought such a potion might come in useful for her ambitious but not very talented grandsons.'

'It is possible, I suppose. Neuton was never without a drink, so it was an obvious way to dispatch him. The door to the kitchen, where he filled his flasks, was often left open, according to Wittleseye, which means anyone could have come in and tampered with them. But there is a flaw in the theory: how would the Bardolfs know about the poor security? I did not.'

'But you do not hate Peterhouse. You have no cause to study the weak points in their defences.'

Bartholomew acknowledged his point with a nod. 'But King's Hall are not the only ones with French connections. Wittleseye and Neuton visited the Pope in Avignon last year. Perhaps the poison belonged to them.'

Michael's eyebrows shot up in surprise. 'You think Neuton killed himself? But he was in fighting spirits yesterday, and a long way from suicide. And do not say he wanted his enemies accused of a capital crime, because he would have left more in the way of obvious clues had that been the case.'

'Actually, I was thinking of Wittleseye. He was more angry than grieved by his cousin's murder, and in the kitchen he made sure we noticed the open door. What better way to strike a blow at the Bardolf clan than have them under suspicion of poisoning a priest in a church?'

Michael rubbed his chin. 'I am still bothered by the hooded whisperer, who seems so determined to have our town awash with blood. John was lucky when he was attacked yesterday, because I suspect he would have been killed had we not arrived when we did – he is a decent organizer of patrols, but no fighter. I believe the whisperer ambushed him to eliminate a peacekeeper – to give this feud a better chance of igniting. Perhaps Neuton was killed for the same reason.'

'What reason?'

'To escalate the violence. Perhaps the culprit has a liking for fighting in the streets. Or maybe he has a grudge against Peterhouse or King's Hall and wants them in flames.'

'If you place any faith in the Black Book of Brân, and interpret "*Will murder spoil the rock's most sacred place*" to mean Neuton's death in Peterhouse's collegiate chapel, then you still have King's Hall's shattered bones to come. Your whisperer may be in luck: the feud *is* predicted to worsen.'

Michael shot him an unpleasant look. 'I thought you did not believe in this sort of thing.'

Bartholomew shrugged. 'I do not. However, it is an uncanny coincidence.'

Michael shivered suddenly, although the day was warm. 'Then we had better hurry and do our work, because I do not want more deaths in my town, no matter what that madman wrote.'

They met John on their way to Peterhouse. He tried not to be proud of the fact that the night had passed without violence, but he did not succeed. He grinned smugly when he reported that all was well, and was so pleased by his performance that he insisted he was not in the least bit tired and would accompany the

Senior Proctor and his Corpse Examiner to see what more could be learned about the death of Neuton.

'I think Joan would have been impressed with my performance,' he said, trying to keep the triumph from his voice and failing miserably. 'Lads from Peterhouse *and* King's Hall slipped past the beadles and went looking for trouble, but they did not get far. I anticipated their every move, and the proctors' gaol is bursting at the seams to prove it.'

'And no one made any more attempts on your life?' asked Michael. 'Or the beadles' lives?'

John shook his head. 'We were all careful. Did I tell you the Peterhouse contingent slipped past their guards because they intended to steal the Black Book of Brân? I heard Shirford screaming for help, and when I arrived they were trying to batter down the door. I arrested the lot of them.'

'And King's Hall?' asked Michael. 'Why did they sneak out?'

'Beadle March found them lurking behind Peterhouse making fire-arrows.'

Michael was genuinely impressed. 'You *have* done well.'

John preened, but then a shadow crossed his face. 'I do not suppose you would put that in writing and send it to the Earl of Suffolk, would you? The last time we met, he told me I was too scholarly.'

Michael smiled. 'He is not stupid; he knows wits can serve him just as well as swords, especially at court. I have heard that Joan prefers ruffians, but I am sure you will win her round.'

John looked rather daunted by the prospect, but mustered a manful smile. He cleared his throat and turned his attention to the matter in hand. 'Are you sure Neuton was poisoned? He did not die of a seizure, or some such thing?'

'There were burns in his throat,' replied Bartholomew. 'I do not think I have ever seen a more clear case of death from toxins. The killer made no attempt to conceal his handiwork.'

John shuddered. 'Then the sooner we catch him, the better. I am inclined to look to King's Hall for the culprit. They are the ones with a grudge against Neuton.'

'I agree,' said Michael. 'However, we have not a shred of evidence, so we must ask some careful questions of Neuton's colleagues first. A false accusation could start all manner of trouble, and I do not want "shattered bones" on my conscience.'

Peterhouse wanted everyone to know that King's Hall had killed five of their students. They had painted the victims' names on a sheet, which was pinned across the front of their church. For the benefit of those who could not read, drawings of the dead lads' faces had been included, each with a skull below it, to represent death. When Bartholomew, Michael and John arrived, Wittleseye was ordering the artist to add a picture of King's Hall with flames coming out of it.

'You will do no such thing,' snapped Michael. 'It would be akin to a declaration of war, and I told you last night that I want the violence to end.'

'That was before they murdered Neuton,' said Wittleseye sullenly, watching the artist slink away before the Senior Proctor could fine him for his handiwork. 'The situation has changed now.'

'We came to ask you about Neuton,' intervened John hastily, seeing Michael's temper begin to fray. The Senior Proctor did not like scholars defying him. 'Had you known him for long?'

'Of course I had,' snarled Wittleseye. 'He was my cousin, and we had known each other since childhood.

The archbishop will be furious when he hears what has happened.'

'Did Neuton have any enemies *other* than the Bardolf brothers?' asked Michael. 'And do not fob me off with nonsense about him being popular, because we both know he was anything but.'

Wittleseye glared at him but then relented. 'All right, I admit that wine made him dour on occasion. But he was not so irascible as to make someone want to kill him.'

'Sometimes the most obvious solution really is the right one,' whispered John to Michael. 'The Bardolfs lost Hugh, so they reciprocated by eliminating a Peterhouse man.'

'Will you agree to a search of Neuton's room?' asked Michael of Wittleseye. 'I must ensure that your cousin did not have a secret stash of French cordial before I tackle King's Hall.'

'I will agree to no such thing,' declared Wittleseye, incensed. '*We* are the injured party here, with Neuton and five students slaughtered. Why should we submit to such indignities?'

'Because it is part of the process of learning the truth,' replied John soothingly. 'Please let us do our duty, sir. It will be better for everyone in the end.'

Wittleseye was mollified by the polite plea. 'Very well, John de St Philibert. But only *Neuton's* chamber. If you set so much as a toe in anyone else's, I shall have you removed by force.'

Michael narrowed his eyes, suspicious of the caveat, and immediately launched into an interrogation of Wittleseye that was only just short of offensive. Bartholomew left them bickering and accompanied John to Neuton's quarters, afraid the Junior Proctor might not recognize the French cordial if he found it. It did not take long to root through Neuton's worldly goods, but Bartholomew had the distinct impression that someone had been there before them, although whether to hide poison or just to see what there was to inherit was impossible to say.

'I did not like the way Wittleseye ordered us not to search anywhere else,' John whispered when they had finished. 'I am going to have a quick look around. You keep watch.'

Bartholomew was acutely uneasy with that. 'We have no authority—'

John gripped his arm, his voice urgent. 'Wittleseye wants us to accuse King's Hall of the crime, but his own behaviour is deeply suspect. This will not take a moment, and I have a bad feeling about Peterhouse's vengeful priests.'

He had disappeared before Bartholomew could object further, then took far longer than 'a moment'. When footsteps warned that someone was coming, and John still declined to break off his hunt, the physician braced himself for the embarrassment of discovery. But with impeccable timing, the Junior Proctor appeared an instant before Wittleseye came to see what was taking so long.

'There you are,' said Wittleseye. He glanced at the door to his chamber, which now stood ajar. 'I hope you confined your activities to my cousin's room and have not trespassed elsewhere.'

'Of course not,' said John, although the uncomfortable expression on his face screamed that he was lying. He turned to Michael and began to gabble. 'Have you finished, Brother? If so, then we should let Wittleseye go about his business. I am sure he is very busy.'

Michael raised his eyebrows when they were outside. 'You need to learn how to dissemble, man! Wittleseye would have to be a drooling idiot not to guess that you had extended your search.'

John raised his hands defensively. 'I am sorry, Brother, but he was so vehement about keeping us out of his room that it made me suspicious.'

Michael nodded slowly. 'Me too – and I am delighted that you had the nerve to act on it. Well? What has unsettled you so? Did you find evidence that he poisoned his own cousin in order to see King's Hall blamed for the crime?'

In reply, John shook his arm, causing an object to slide from his wide sleeve and fall to the ground. It was a mallet, the kind that was used to smash stones into gravel. It had a metal head, and something red adhered to it. Bartholomew bent to inspect it, then rose slowly and met John's eyes.

'I found it hidden under Wittleseye's bed,' explained John quietly. 'Wrapped in some old linen. Is it blood?'

Bartholomew nodded. 'I think so.'

'So what?' asked Michael, looking from one to the other. 'Neuton was poisoned, not bludgeoned. And it cannot be connected to yesterday's slaughter, because all those victims died from wounds inflicted by swords or daggers.'

'Perhaps we just have not found the body yet,' said John. He scowled, as if this was a personal affront. 'I thought I had prevented mischief last night, but maybe I gloated too soon.'

'The beadles claim a mouse could not have wandered about unseen last night,' said Michael. 'March was complaining bitterly about it, because he was obliged to work for once.'

John looked angry. 'But we were looking for *groups*, not lone men. It is possible for a stealthy fellow to have slipped through my net. Damn! I thought I had done a decent job. I hope the earl does not hear about this – or Joan. She told me *she* is rather good at organizing military-style manoeuvres.'

'She does have something of a reputation in that respect,' agreed Michael. 'But you are jumping to conclusions, man. There is nothing to say Wittleseye harmed anyone with that mallet.'

'Then why was he so determined to keep us from searching his room?' demanded John. 'And why wrap the thing in rags and hide it under his bed?'

'If you are so convinced of his guilt, then why did you not confront him with it?' asked Michael. 'Why wait until you were out here before showing us what you found?'

John sighed. 'Because I wanted to *think* about it first. If I had launched into an interrogation ill-prepared, he would have fobbed me off with lies. I needed to gather my thoughts first. Was I wrong?'

'No,' said Michael, although the expression on his face said otherwise. 'Take the mallet to the proctors' office and put it somewhere safe. We may need it to challenge him later. Meanwhile, Matt and I will go to King's Hall to ensure that everyone there is hale and hearty.'

The town was wary after the trouble of the previous day, and the streets were quieter than normal. Carts still clattered to and from the Market Square, and merchants still opened their shops for business, but the atmosphere was subdued and cautious, and there was none of the customary banter as folk went about their affairs. Some churches remained closed too, while all the colleges and hostels retained the extra guards on their gates. Without the usual crowds to hinder their progress along the High Street, it did not take Bartholomew and Michael long to reach King's Hall.

They found it in a state of turmoil. Even from outside, they could hear folk running this way and that, and voices raised in anger and alarm. Michael's first knock went unanswered, so he pounded the metal-studded gate until he was able to attract someone's attention. He was astonished when it was Beadle March who opened the door.

'What are you doing here?' the monk demanded. 'You are supposed to be at All Saints'.'

'I have resigned,' said March smugly. 'I am tired of being treated like an ordinary beadle, when I am more intelligent than the rest of them put together. Besides, I overheard John de St Philibert tell you that *he* killed Hugh, and I do not want to work for proctors who condone murder.'

Michael glowered at him. 'If you have aggravated the situation by telling tales, you will spend the next four weeks in gaol. But you have not answered my question: what are you doing *here*?'

March glowered back. 'Vice-Warden Bardolf hired me, because he says I might prove useful.'

'Then he is a fool,' said Michael, regarding the ex-beadle with rank disdain. 'However, there are more important issues than you at the moment, such as why is everyone in such a panic?'

'Murder,' replied William coldly, coming to greet them. He was wearing a military-style jerkin in place of his academic tabard and boiled-leather leggings. He carried a sword, and there was a mace tucked in his belt. His brothers were similarly armed, and so were many students.

Michael was alarmed. 'I know you grieve for Hugh, but—'

'Not Hugh,' snapped William, rounding on him so furiously that the monk took an involuntary step backwards. 'Although that was outrage enough. It is Roger.'

'Roger is dead?' asked Michael, shocked.

'March found him at dawn,' replied William angrily.

'His body lies in our hall, although you will not need your Corpse Examiner to tell you he was unlawfully slain.'

'Show me,' ordered Michael, intending to keep him occupied until his temper had cooled, in the hope that he would have second thoughts about leading his troops in a frenzy of revenge.

'With pleasure,' snarled William. 'We *want* the Senior Proctor to see what Peterhouse did.'

'Follow me,' said March, clearly enjoying himself. 'I will lead the way.'

Roger's body had been placed on a table behind the servants' screen. He was covered by a blanket, which Bartholomew peeled away at a nod from William. Roger's unattractive face was pale and waxy in death, the eyes half-open. There was a dark stain behind his head, and when March helped him turn the body Bartholomew saw that the back of Roger's skull had been stoved in.

'Where did you find him, March?' asked Michael, watching the physician assess the body for other wounds.

'All Saints' churchyard.' March tried to keep his face sombre, but he was too pleased with all the attention to succeed. 'John de St Philibert made me patrol the High Street, and I discovered Roger when I went to rest on a tombstone for a while. I immediately came here, to bring the news to—'

'It did not occur to you to report the incident to *me* first?' asked Michael, fighting down his anger. The news could have been broken more gently by a proctor, and the potential for violent revenge considerably reduced.

'No,' replied March insolently. 'I thought his kin had a right to know before you.'

Michael shot him a disgusted look, then addressed

William. 'Why was Roger out in the first place? I asked you all to stay in.'

'He wanted to be near the book,' replied William. His temper was only just under control. 'He was afraid it might be stolen, and was eager to help Shirford protect it.'

'Did he go alone?' asked Michael.

'Yes. I offered to accompany him, but he said he could look after himself. I thought he was right.' William sounded bitter as well as angry.

'Well?' asked Michael, as Bartholomew completed his examination. 'What can you tell me?'

'He died from a blow to the back of the head, delivered by something heavy and blunt. The wound is too well defined to have been made by a stone, and not well defined enough to have been made by a sword. It was caused by some other implement.'

'Such as a mallet,' said Michael flatly, seeing where the physician was going.

'A mallet would be a likely contender,' agreed Bartholomew. 'And there is something else.'

'Yes,' said William tightly. 'The killer was not content with just bludgeoning poor Roger. He insisted on mocking us too.'

Bartholomew turned Roger's face to one side so it caught the light. The left cheek was untouched, but the right one had a bloody mark carved into it. It was the letter P.

'What does that mean?' asked Michael, gazing at it in bewilderment.

'It stands for Peterhouse, of course,' replied March. 'What else could it be?'

Michael was deeply uneasy as he left King's Hall and followed William to All Saints', Bartholomew in tow. He had managed to persuade the vice-warden to refrain from tackling Peterhouse until the proctors had inspected the scene of the crime and spoken to witnesses, although agreement was given reluctantly, and he was not sure William could be trusted to keep his word. The man was mad with grief and fury, and it would take very little for him to gather his troops and head off for a confrontation with the foundation he had grown to hate.

'It seems so unlikely,' said Michael to Bartholomew as they walked. He spoke in a low voice, so William would not hear. 'Why would Peterhouse advertise what they had done?'

'Peterhouse?' asked Bartholomew. 'You mean Wittleseye. He is the one with the bloody mallet under his bed.'

'Not necessarily. Perhaps one of his students did it – killed Roger, cut the mark into his victim's face, then realized it was stupid, so hid the hammer in Wittleseye's room because he did not know how else to extricate himself from his predicament.'

'It is possible, I suppose,' conceded Bartholomew, although with scant conviction. 'Do you think Roger killed Neuton and was dispatched in revenge? I would not have thought Roger was the type to poison someone, but then I would not have said he was the type to discuss prophecies with Shirford either.'

'I am not comfortable with March's abrupt defection to King's Hall,' said Michael, voicing another concern. 'I would not put any low deed past him – poisoning, bludgeoning, planting murder weapons on innocent parties, assaulting proctors. And not carving letters on a dead man's face either.'

'Can he write?'

'Yes, unusually for a beadle. But speculation is taking us nowhere: we need solid proof.' Michael called out to William, who was walking a few steps ahead of them.

'After yesterday's brawl, everyone from King's Hall went home. Did Roger leave the college at any point, other than to go to All Saints' and guard the book?'

William turned to face him. 'No. Some of our lads escaped in the night, to be caught by John de St Philibert. But my brothers and I held a wake for Hugh. It started immediately after you left and did not finish until morning Mass. Roger was the only one to leave, which he did about an hour before dawn – to watch over the book, as I said.'

'And when did March come to tell you what he had found?'

'Shortly after sunrise. Roger must have been killed not long after he left us, because his corpse was cooling. I have been in enough battles to know about that sort of thing.'

They arrived at All Saints', but Shirford had heard what had happened to Roger and was loath to answer the door. He yielded only when Michael threatened to set fire to it. The priest's face was pale, and he looked as though he had been crying. Whether the tears were for Roger or for his own unenviable predicament was impossible to say.

'The book has precipitated some evil deeds,' he said miserably. 'Poor Roger! He was a sullen devil at times, but he had a good heart. He brought me food every evening.'

'Even yesterday?' asked Michael. He glared at William when Shirford nodded. 'You said Roger did not leave Hugh's wake until an hour before dawn.'

William shrugged. 'I forgot about the earlier excursion. But he was gone less than an hour.'

'An hour?' Michael was not amused. 'That is a long time for delivering victuals.'

'He was not with me that long,' said Shirford, before catching William's eye and falling silent.

'Perhaps I misremembered the length of his absence,' hedged William. But he saw he was not going to fool the Senior Proctor and gave an impatient sigh. 'All right. Roger left the wake before sunset to take Shirford his supper. But I decided not to tell you about it, because I knew what you would think – that he used the time to go and kill Neuton.'

'He had a motive,' said Michael coldly. 'And now we learn he had an opportunity.'

'If you think that, then you are a greater fool than you look,' snapped William. 'Roger would never stoop to poison, not when he had a dagger in his belt.'

'He might follow orders, though,' argued Michael. 'Such as to deliver something to a kitchen while cooks were out. I imagine he was excellent at fulfilling that sort of duty.'

Shirford smiled, keen to say something positive about the man who had been kind to him. 'Oh, he was very good at errands. He ran them for me all the time – fetching books from the library, ensuring I had clean clothes, buying fuel for my lamp . . .' He trailed off when he became aware that he was the subject of another furious glare from William.

Bartholomew stepped forward when he saw the vice-warden beginning to lose his temper. 'Michael will find out what happened to Roger,' he said soothingly. 'He knows what he is doing.'

'But I will not succeed unless people are honest with me,' added Michael. 'How can I solve any murder when no one tells me the truth?'

'I have not lied,' snapped William. 'I just neglected to mention something.'

Michael grimaced but declined to argue. He turned to Shirford. 'Roger's body was found in the church-yard, right outside. You must have heard something.'

Shirford's expression was apologetic. 'Unfortunately,

I did not. After you left, all was calm until your Junior Proctor caught those Peterhouse lads trying to break in. And then all was quiet again until March found Roger's corpse.'

'So,' summarized Michael, 'Roger brought you your supper around the time when Neuton was poisoned. Then he returned to King's Hall and joined the wake with his brothers. Shortly before dawn, he left the party because he was worried about the book.'

'Why are you wasting time here?' barked William, his patience finally breaking. 'Peterhouse killed Roger. The culprit might even be Wittleseye himself. He claims he is no warrior, but warriors do not sneak up behind someone and batter out his brains.'

'Shattered bones,' murmured Michael, so only Bartholomew could hear. 'Roger's bones are shattered, and the King's house is certainly mourning – far more so than the occupants of the rock, when murder spoiled their most sacred place. Now all we need do is wait for the traitor's face to blaze. Whatever that means.'

'Judging by the speed at which these events are coming true, I do not think we need wait for long,' whispered Bartholomew. 'Indeed, I think the traitor might be standing right here in front of us.'

'William? Yes, I see why you settled on him as your prime suspect. He is mine too.'

'Not William,' said Bartholomew. 'Shirford.'

Michael was startled by the physician's choice but knew better than to dismiss his opinion out of hand, no matter how outlandish it sounded when phrased so tersely. They escorted William home to King's Hall, where they left a whole pack of beadles to ensure that he could not escape to wreak havoc. William was furious to find himself effectively imprisoned in his own college, but the monk tartly informed him that he could spend the day in the proctors' gaol if he would prefer. March came to stand next to the seething vice-warden and began whispering in his ear.

'He will not stay in long, Brother,' warned Bartholomew as they left. 'He wants revenge, and if you do not present him with Roger's killer soon he will go out and find himself a culprit.'

'Bartholomew is right,' said John. He was waiting for them outside the gate, having delivered the mallet to the proctors' office. 'William Bardolf is out for blood, and I suspect yesterday's riot will be nothing if he is allowed to do as he pleases today.'

'If anyone dies as a result of his agitating, he will stand trial for murder,' vowed Michael. 'His father may be the king's favourite, but that will not save him from the full rigours of the law if he disregards my orders. I will see to that.'

'He is on the verge of presenting "the king's favourite" with a powerful book of prophecies,' Bartholomew pointed out. 'I imagine all manner of blind eyes might be turned in repayment for that sort of service. The only way to prevent further bloodshed is to solve these murders fast.'

John pulled the Senior Proctor and his Corpse Examiner into the churchyard surrounding All Saints', near the spot where March had found Roger's body. It was peaceful, and they were shielded from view by a row of trees, so it was a good place in which to talk without distractions.

'Then you two had better start analysing,' he said practically. 'You need to review all you have learned, to put the clues together and see if you can come up with a viable suspect.'

Michael was loath to chat when time was so critical, but he saw the sense in his deputy's suggestion. He took a deep breath to calm himself. 'Then tell us why you think Shirford is the culprit, Matt.'

Bartholomew marshalled his thoughts. 'Shirford insists that Drayton was unpleasant, as if that justified his murder. And I am suspicious of why he agreed to become the book's guardian, when it is obvious the task would transpire to be dangerous.'

'Is that it?' demanded Michael in disbelief. 'I thought you had something sensible to suggest! You only have to look at Shirford to see why he accepted the Bardolfs' offer: he is desperately poor and wants a parish of his own. This task represents a few weeks of risk in return for a lifetime of comparative ease and security.'

John nodded his agreement. 'Furthermore, your theory does not explain who killed Neuton and Roger. Shirford cannot be the culprit, because he was locked inside All Saints' when they died.'

'We have only his word for that,' countered Bartholomew. 'Perhaps he slipped out.'

'But why would he kill them?' asked John. 'What could he gain?'

'He obviously does not want Peterhouse to have the book,' replied Bartholomew, thinking fast, 'or he would not have agreed to protect it for King's Hall. So he poisoned Neuton in order to frighten Peterhouse into dropping their claim.'

'And Roger?' demanded Michael, deeply unimpressed by his reasoning. 'Roger was kind to him, bringing him supper and conversation. Why would Shirford kill him?'

Bartholomew was struggling for answers. 'Perhaps he did not like the fact that Roger was of no use in interpreting the prophecies. He gave false information about the King of Scotland.'

'Men do not kill for such paltry reasons,' declared John disdainfully.

'Actually, they do,' countered Michael, who had a lot more experience of murder than his deputy.

John sniffed. 'Well, I refuse to believe Shirford is such a ruthless villain. As far as I am concerned, Bartholomew's theory is seriously flawed – and accusing the wrong man may lead to even worse trouble than we have already. I sincerely hope *you* have a more convincing suspect, Brother.'

'I do: William. Why else would he be so determined to go on the rampage? He is trying to cause so much chaos that we will be overwhelmed, and the murders he committed will be forgotten amid a wider slaughter. The only way to stop him is to arrest him.'

'But if you are wrong, the consequences will be catastrophic,' argued John. 'One of his kinsmen will assume command, and they are far more brutal than he. And if William is innocent, then his father will have your head – and mine – on a platter. And my prospective father-in-law, the earl—'

'This is not the time to think about ourselves,' snapped Michael, beginning to aim for the road.

John put out a hand to stop him. 'I know you are keen to discharge your duty, but we *must* take time to review the situation – to use wits and logic, and ensure we take the course of action that will bring this vile business to a swift and bloodless conclusion.'

Michael knew he was right, and that relations between the two colleges had reached a critical point. A wrongful accusation might well precipitate more strife. He took another calming breath. 'We have three murders,' he began, 'all connected to this damned book. At least two – Neuton and Roger – seem to have been predicted by it. Drayton's death was seven years ago, but his killer still walks free, and I cannot help but wonder whether William has turned to slaughter again.'

'You think all were murdered by the same hand?'

asked John in surprise. 'I suppose it makes sense, although it does not explain why William waited so long before claiming a second victim.'

'He is not killing for killing's sake,' snapped Michael impatiently. 'He is killing for a purpose – a purpose clearly connected to the book. I imagine he stabbed Drayton to lay hands on it, then arranged for its miraculous reappearance after the passing of what he thought was a suitable amount of time. But his plans went awry, and he was obliged to kill again.'

'Your argument does not make sense,' said Bartholomew dismissively. 'It leaves too many unanswered questions.'

Michael made an exasperated gesture. 'Then that is too bad, because we do not have time for lengthy explanations. William will transpire to be the culprit. Or rather, William and Roger together. I imagine they killed Drayton because they did not want Peterhouse to have the book. Then they poisoned Neuton in revenge for Hugh.'

Bartholomew was not convinced. 'William and Roger are not the kind of men to wait years before capitalizing on the proceeds of a crime. You said so yourself. They are crude and impetuous.'

'William can be patient when he wants – he must have managed patience when he was elected vice-warden, because his colleagues do not bestow that sort of honour on hotheads.'

'I took the opportunity to gossip with some King's Hall students last night.' John spoke hesitantly, unsure whether he should share what he had learned. He hurried on when Michael glared at him. 'When Roger was sick of the flux last term, William doctored him with a remedy sent by their grandmother, the French witch.'

'Hah!' exclaimed Michael in triumph. 'Perhaps she sent other potions too. Such as cordial.'

'All right,' acknowledged Bartholomew. 'So Roger put the poison in Neuton's flask after he took Shirford his supper – and it *is* suspicious that William "forgot" to mention him going out at the pertinent time – but then what? Who killed Roger?'

'William.' Michael held up his hand when the others started to voice their objections. 'He was not overly distressed when Hugh died, so why should Roger be any different? His so-called grief is a ruse, so we will not think he killed his own kinsman.'

'And what has he gained by dispatching Roger?' asked Bartholomew sceptically.

'Safety – no one to let slip that *he* ordered Neuton's death. And he is right to take precautions, because Roger was indiscreet and stupid, and might well have blurted out something by mistake. However, all this would make a lot more sense if we knew where this wretched book has been for the last seven years. And do not say God was looking after it, because it is not the kind of tome that warrants divine attention.'

'Why not?' asked John, startled by the assertion.

'Because I do not see Him protecting a text that describes a queen's dalliance with a lover or a spat between colleges. These events are important to people, not to the Almighty. Ergo it is a person who has had this book for the last seven years, and the obvious suspect is William.'

'Or Shirford,' countered Bartholomew. 'And we have overlooked the whisperer in our analysis too. Shirford claims he was locked in the church during the riot, but perhaps he was out with his hood hiding his face. *He* goaded Hugh and later tried to kill John.'

Michael looked dubious. 'Shirford will desire peace, Matt. He will not want Peterhouse trying to take the book by force, because he is the one obliged to protect it.'

'Wittleseye!' exclaimed John suddenly. '*He* killed Drayton and hid the book for seven years. But somehow he lost it, and it appeared in All Saints' to be claimed by the Bardolf brothers. That is why he maintains King's Hall has no legal right to it. And it is obvious that Wittleseye killed Roger, because the murder weapon was in his room.'

'All right,' acknowledged Bartholomew cautiously. 'Then why did he poison Neuton?'

'Perhaps Neuton found out that he killed Drayton,' suggested John, 'and threatened to blackmail him over it. So Wittleseye poisoned Neuton, but was careful to ensure you noticed the lax security at the back door, so you would assume he was killed by an outsider.'

Michael frowned unhappily. 'You are right: the evidence *does* make sense when we have Wittleseye as the killer.'

'There is another suspect too,' said Bartholomew, deep in thought. 'March enjoyed yesterday's brawl and is clearly eager for another. He encourages William, whose side he has joined, to defy the proctors, and he had access to Peterhouse *and* All Saints' last night. Moreover, he was muttering to William today, so perhaps he whispered to Hugh yesterday.'

John nodded slowly. 'And he was in Cambridge when Drayton was killed, because he told me some tale about Drayton pilfering library books. Plus there is his criminal past to consider.'

Michael began to stride towards the street. 'We have talked enough. It is time to act.'

'And do what?' asked John, hurrying after him. 'We cannot agree on a suspect.'

'Extreme situations call for extreme measures. Our first priority is to prevent further bloodshed, so that is what we shall do. We shall arrest the whole Bardolf clan, Wittleseye, March *and* Shirford. Perhaps it will mean trouble with Lord Bardolf and the Archbishop of Canterbury, but we shall just have to weather that storm when it comes.'

There was a sudden crash, followed by furious yelling.

'It is too late,' said Bartholomew, breaking into a run. 'William must have overpowered your beadles and made a bid for escape.'

'Not William,' said Michael, skidding to a halt and staring at the crowd that was massing outside King's Hall. 'Peterhouse. They are laying siege to their enemy's camp.'

The High Street was full of noise. The Peterhouse men were armed mostly with sticks, but they had also brought pitch torches and an ancient bow, and it was clear that they intended to shoot burning missiles over the walls. Because it was not just King's Hall that had thatched roofs and timber-framed halls, residents from the surrounding houses were trying to stop them. The result was pandemonium, and a number of skirmishes were in progress. Meanwhile, the scholars of King's Hall leaned out of their windows and jeered at the besiegers.

'Fetch the Black Book of Brân,' said Michael urgently to John. A plan was forming in his mind.

John demurred. 'That would be unwise, Brother. Peterhouse will grab it, King's Hall will rush to grab it back, and we shall have a riot for certain. Besides, it is nailed to the altar.'

'Only the back cover,' argued Michael. 'Tell Shirford to rip it free and bring it to me. Hurry, man!' He gave his bewildered deputy a push to send him on his way.

'I hope you know what you are doing,' said Bartholomew uneasily. 'The book *is* more likely to inflame the situation than calm it. And look over there: March is organizing bowmen in King's Hall's gatehouse, while

Peterhouse has requisitioned three carts and intends to use them as battering rams. The situation is already precarious.'

Michael's beadles began to arrive, some gasping apologies that they had been unable to keep Peterhouse from breaking out. The monk directed them to stand between the two factions. They were alarmed at having arrows pointed at them from both directions at once, and only their devotion to Michael kept them from running away. Their unquestioning obedience, when compared with the defiance of Peterhouse and King's Hall, was the last straw for Michael.

'This has gone far enough,' he roared. The volume of his yell, and the anger in it, stilled the babble of excited voices. 'Peterhouse will go home, and King's Hall will put up their weapons. Anyone who disobeys can consider himself no longer a member of the University.'

'We will disarm when Peterhouse leaves,' yelled William. March was at his side, leading cheers of encouragement. 'Not a moment sooner.'

'Killers!' howled Wittleseye. 'Poisoners! Thieves! You deserve to be roasted alive.'

'Where is John?' demanded Michael of Bartholomew. 'If he does not bring the book soon, nothing will stop these turbulent scholars from attacking each other. Shirford must be refusing to let him have it. Go and hurry them up.'

Although Michael had considerable experience at quelling riots, Bartholomew still did not like the notion of leaving him. 'I should stay and—'

'Go! I have a plan, but it hinges on the tome. Do not just stand there! Hurry!'

Hoping Michael knew what he was doing, Bartholomew left the brewing riot and raced towards All Saints'. He ran hard, and it took but a moment to reach the church. He found John outside, perched negligently on a tombstone, humming to himself. When he saw the physician, the Junior Proctor leaped to his feet and began to hammer on the door.

'Who is it?' called Shirford from inside. His voice was uneasy. 'One of the Bardolf brothers?'

Bartholomew frowned, trying to understand why John had dallied before doing as Michael had ordered – he could tell from Shirford's response that it was the first time John had attempted to rouse him with a knock.

'Shirford must have been asleep,' explained John. 'I rapped several times, but there was no reply. He has obviously just woken up.'

Bartholomew was sure that could not be true. 'He knows there is trouble afoot today, and will be alert to any kind of disturbance. He would have heard even the slightest tap.'

'No one has knocked since you left earlier,' called Shirford, overhearing the discussion. 'And I never sleep during the day. What do you want? I am not opening the door, regardless.'

'I do not blame you,' replied John. He turned to Bartholomew. 'The pressure of the situation has addled Michael's wits, because only a madman would take the book from its sanctuary when a riot is brewing. You must see—'

'Oh, God!' gulped Bartholomew suddenly, as all became clear. 'It is you! You are the killer.'

John gaped at him. 'What?'

'The prophecy! After the murder in Peterhouse's sacred place and King's Hall's shattered bones comes the traitor with his *saintly* face. You are John de *St* Philibert!'

John's eyebrows shot up. 'I thought you did not believe in fortune-telling. Besides, accusing me of treachery on the basis of a single word is—'

'It is not the book's garbled verses that tell me you are guilty; it is logic and hard evidence. Although the use of the word "saintly" is a curious coincidence . . .'

John made a moue of impatience. 'How can I be the killer? I was almost one of his victims.'

'We have only your word that the attack even happened. There are no witnesses and—'

Bartholomew only just managed to duck away from the dagger that came slicing towards him. John followed his swipe with a kick that caught the physician on the knee. Pain blazed down Bartholomew's leg, and he knew the injury would slow him down, doubtless exactly as the Junior Proctor had intended. He had no weapon, and all he could do to defend himself was to back away, acutely aware that while he dallied, Michael was in ever-increasing danger.

'You will not survive this encounter,' said John softly, so Shirford would not hear. 'I may not be a warrior, but I can best an unarmed man. Give up, and you will have an easy death.'

Bartholomew's thoughts were a chaotic jumble, solutions and answers coming to him so fast that he barely knew where to begin. 'You engineered today's trouble,' he said, scrambling behind a tombstone. 'And yesterday's too. I thought it was March, who is goading William to violence even as we speak, but it was you.'

John sneered at him. 'But you would never have guessed it, had I not shown my hand by deciding to kill you.'

Bartholomew felt sick. 'The discussion you insisted on having just now was not to stop Michael from accusing the wrong culprit, but to give Peterhouse time to mass outside King's Hall. You started the rumour about my college siding with Peterhouse for the same reason, and it was you, disguised by a hood, who whispered poisonous thoughts at Hugh until he drew his sword.'

John's expression was dangerous, and he hurled himself across the tombstone in a determined effort to reach his quarry. Bartholomew jerked away and managed to score a punch before limping to safety. John gasped when the physician's fist connected with his ribs.

'The dispute between King's Hall and Peterhouse could never have reached this pitch on its own,' the physician went on. While John climbed to his feet, hand to his side, Bartholomew seized a piece of fallen timber. It was slimy with rot, but better than nothing. 'Someone has coaxed it and nurtured it every step of the way.'

'I killed Hugh to stop him from slaughtering you,' John snarled. 'I should not have bothered.'

'You killed Hugh because you wanted his death to fuel the quarrel,' countered Bartholomew. 'It did not work, because King's Hall were content to lose two scholars to Peterhouse's five, so you saw you would have to try again. You poisoned Neuton, knowing from your duties as proctor that he filled his wineskins in a kitchen that was often left unlocked.'

John's face creased into a smug grin. Like many killers, he could not resist the urge to brag about his cleverness – or his protagonists' stupidity. 'It never occurred to you that I had the run of the town last night and could do what I liked – visit Peterhouse or All Saints'. You probably have not realized that I am from St Philibert either, and that my French father sends me a certain cordial . . .'

Bartholomew blocked a blow with his piece of wood. It flew into pieces, showering them both with rotten splinters. He ignored the jibe about the cordial, because John was right: the Junior Proctor's Gallic connections had not crossed his mind.

'And then, to make sure there would be trouble today, you killed Roger,' he said, continuing to back away. He was running out of space, and furious yells from the High Street told him that Michael's situation was not much better. 'You may even have told March where the body lay, knowing he would respond by charging to King's Hall and urging them to retaliate. And it was you who "found" the bloody mallet in Wittleseye's room.'

John shook his head incredulously. 'I could not believe it when you and the monk refused to accept that Wittleseye had bludgeoned Roger. The mallet and the P carved into Roger's face were as brazen a set of clues as I could concoct, and yet you still declined to arrest him.'

Bartholomew staggered when John came close to spearing him by feinting one way and striking hard the other. John was tiring of the game, and the physician knew it would not be long before he made a concerted effort to finish him so he could be back in the affray, coaxing the trouble until it erupted. He tried to distract him with more conclusions.

'You did not kill Drayton, though, because you were not in Cambridge at the time. Of course, that was why you were willing to accept Michael's contention that there was only one killer – you are innocent of Drayton's death, so logic dictates that you cannot have killed Roger and Neuton either. The only question I cannot answer is *why* did you do it? To impress your future family? I know that is why you became a proctor.'

'Joan will adore me when she hears it was I who saved the town from certain destruction.'

Bartholomew hurled the remnants of the branch at him in a futile attempt to stall the relentless advance. 'And how do you plan to do that?'

John ducked. 'It is all explained in the book. The verse about the Hammer of the Unruly refers to me. *I* am the glorious sun with the golden head, using my might to quell unrest.'

Bartholomew gazed at him in disbelief. 'Are you sure it does not refer to King Edward, nicknamed Hammer of the Scots?'

John did not think the issue worth debating. He resumed his advance, waving the dagger in front of him. 'You can think what you will, but everything predicted in the book has come to pass.'

'Only because you made it so,' objected Bartholomew. Something else became clear too. 'You live in the house that Drayton once rented. He must have hidden the book before he went to do business with Peterhouse. You found it.'

'Plastered inside a hole in the wall,' acknowledged John. 'I discovered it when I was replacing some rotten floorboards. I knew Peterhouse would try to claim it, so I devised a plan to prevent that: I left it in All Saints', intending to be the person who discovered it lying on the altar.'

'But you bargained without the Bardolfs attending church, and they got it first.'

John gave a beatific smile. 'I was appalled to start with, but then I realized it did not matter. What is important is the prophecy – and that is going to come true regardless.'

Without warning, he came at Bartholomew with a series of vicious swipes that drove the physician backwards so fast that his bruised knee could not support him. He fell, crashing against a buttress. John moved in for the kill. The dagger began to descend. Then the church door was hauled open, there was a loud thud and John collapsed to the ground in a heap.

*

For a few confused moments Bartholomew did not understand what had happened. Then he saw Shirford standing over the insensible Junior Proctor with the Black Book of Brân in his shaking hands. Hoping the priest would not hit him too, Bartholomew crawled forward to examine John. He was still breathing, but a darkening mark on the back of his head said he would not feel well when he regained his wits.

'I heard everything,' whispered Shirford, white with shock. 'John spoke softly to start with, but then he forgot himself and began to gloat. It is only right that this self-proclaimed Hammer of the Unruly should be hammered by the book he was trying to abuse. I am not sorry.'

There was a sudden roar of voices from the direction of King's Hall. 'Michael!' exclaimed Bartholomew, snatching the tome from Shirford and beginning to hobble towards the High Street. He would see to John later.

The scene outside King's Hall had degenerated badly. The Peterhouse students were hurling themselves at Michael and his beadles, furiously trying to get past them and attack King's Hall with their makeshift battering rams. Arrows rained down on them all, hitting the peacekeepers as well as the enemy, and the cries of the wounded added to the cacophony. March was screaming at the Bardolfs to aim true, and Wittleseye was encouraging his lads with fiery prayers. The ex-beadle's tirade stopped abruptly when a well-aimed stone struck him in the throat. He staggered back, hands to his neck, and did not appear again.

'At last!' snapped Michael, ripping the book from Bartholomew's hands. 'Where in God's name have you been? And where is John?'

'Later,' gasped Bartholomew. He ducked as a

fire-arrow sailed over his head. 'If you have a plan, Brother, now is the time to implement it.'

'Behold the Black Book of Brân!' yelled Michael at the top of his voice. He climbed on to a horse trough to wave it aloft, ensuring it could be seen by everyone present. Bartholomew itched to drag him down, aware that he made a tempting target for both sides. There was, however, an immediate hush as the combatants saw what he held.

'It has been damaged,' cried Wittleseye in horror. 'There are holes in its back cover.'

'It is not the cover that is important,' declared Michael. 'It is the poetry. And I want you to hear some of it before you go any further with this feud. Can everyone hear me?'

'We can,' called William from a window in King's Hall. 'But this had better be important, Brother. If you are wasting our time, the next arrow will be for you.'

'Christ!' muttered Bartholomew.

'Right,' said the monk, riffling through the pages. 'Then take heed of this:

"When rocks and kings a brawl incite,
God's anger doth begin to boil.
And when arrows fly and scholars fight,
God kills them all with a thunderbolt."'

There was absolute silence amongst the assembled horde, followed by some urgent whispering. William ducked back inside his window to confer with his brothers, while Wittleseye gestured that his own scholars were to gather around him.

'That was terrible!' hissed Bartholomew in alarm, certain that no one was going to be deceived by such a transparent ploy. 'Your poem has a different rhythm from the rest of the verses, and it does not rhyme properly. Was that your grand idea? You are insane!'

'No,' whispered Michael furiously. 'My grand idea was to invite the ringleaders to my office – with the book – to discuss the dispute like civilized men. But you took so long to bring it that the time for such gestures had passed. I was obliged to improvise.'

'Let me see that,' demanded Shirford loudly, snatching the book back before the monk could stop him. 'I have been studying the text for the last two weeks, and I do not recall this quatrain.'

'Lord!' groaned Bartholomew, sure Michael was about to pay dearly for his bravado.

'Ah. Here it is,' announced Shirford loudly. 'Near the end. You are lucky the good Brother remembered this particular verse, because it would be a pity to lose you all to divine fury.'

'We had better go home, then,' said Wittleseye in alarm. There was a rumble of assent from his students, and the bowmen in King's Hall began to lower their weapons. 'Nephews of the Archbishop of Canterbury do not defy God. Other prophecies in that book have come true, so there is no reason why this one should not, and I am a priest – it would be embarrassing to be struck by a thunderbolt.'

'Thank you!' breathed Michael to Shirford. 'I was not sure they were going to fall for it.'

'I would have been astonished if they had,' replied Shirford dryly. 'You should have asked me to compose something; I would have made a more convincing job of it. But I could not stand by and see you shot, not when you took the trouble to ensure I was safe last night. You were bone-weary, but you came anyway, and I appreciated your concern. No one else bothered.'

'The dispute is not over, though,' called Wittleseye to King's Hall as he left, students in tow. 'The book belongs to Peterhouse, and—'

'Actually, it does not,' interrupted Michael, moving away from Shirford to brandish a piece of parchment. 'I had a message from the king this morning, and *he* wants it. If anyone feels we should not do as His Majesty desires and make him a gift of it, he can leave his name at the proctors' office and I will be sure to mention him in the missive I write.'

'You are a clever man, Brother,' said Shirford admiringly, watching the scholars disperse. Wittleseye was white-faced with anger, and William bitterly disappointed, but neither were about to argue with a 'request' from the king. 'You left them with no choice but to let you send the book to Westminster. But how timely that you should happen to receive His Majesty's letter today.'

'How timely indeed,' muttered Bartholomew.

III

Although Michael had prevented the trouble from going too far, there were still casualties, and Bartholomew was overwhelmed by demands for his services. Meanwhile, the monk was busy ensuring that the embers of the quarrel were well and truly dead, so it was more than a week before they were able to discuss what had happened. They went to sit in Michaelhouse's orchard, where a fallen apple tree provided a comfortable bench.

'Any word about John?' asked Bartholomew. The Junior Proctor had vanished by the time the beadles had been free to go to All Saints' and arrest him, and he had not been seen since. Michael believed he had fled to the Earl of Suffolk, hoping to convince his future kinsman that there had been a misunderstanding.

'No,' replied Michael. 'But Shirford told me everything John said – that *he* found the book Drayton had hidden, engineered a dispute between King's Hall and Peterhouse, poisoned Neuton, bludgeoned Roger and pretended that he had been attacked. He did it because he read the verses about kings and rocks and thought it was all foretold.'

'He also decided he was the Hammer of the Unruly. It was all to impress the earl.'

'But unfortunately for him, the wedding is off,' said Michael with gleeful malice. 'The earl sent word to say that he has other plans for his daughter now. I wonder what will become of John – I cannot imagine the earl wanting that sort of embarrassment roaming about freely.'

Bartholomew did not want to think about it. He had liked John and thought it a pity that two months of able proctoring had ended in two weeks of needless havoc. He also thought it rather pathetic that John had had such a low opinion of his own abilities that he had felt compelled to manufacture a situation in which he could be a hero.

'*He* could not have stopped the fighting outside King's Hall,' he said, more to himself than to Michael. 'It would never have occurred to him to compose bad poetry and tell lies about letters from the king. And even if it had, he would not have had the audacity to try it.'

Michael grinned. 'I admit it was reckless, but I could see no other way to end the confrontation. Did I tell you the book is currently on its way to Westminster?'

Bartholomew stared at him. 'Is it? I thought the king's request was something you invented.'

'It was, but then it occurred to me that it was a good way to get rid of the thing. The king is away, but the Prince of Wales has agreed to accept it in his stead.'

'I hope he is not expecting a real book of prophecies,' said Bartholomew uneasily. 'Because if he is, he is going to be disappointed. It is just not possible to predict the future.' He hesitated. 'Except that I still cannot explain the reference to the traitor's "sainted face", which prompted me to consider John de St Philibert as the killer.'

'Coincidence,' said Michael with a shrug. 'It is bound to happen over eight hundred years.'

'It is a pity we did not solve Drayton's murder, though. As long as his killer remains free, King's Hall and Peterhouse will be suspicious of each other.'

'But I have solved it,' said Michael. 'Did I not tell you? It was Shirford.'

Bartholomew was not sure whether to believe him. 'Prove it.'

Michael began to count off points on fat fingers. 'First, he knew that the book Drayton took with him to Peterhouse the night he was murdered was Aristotle's *On Dreams*; we never made that detail public, so it was something only the killer could have known. Second, he made sure we knew Drayton was a reprehensible character whom no one mourned. Third, I do not believe he took the post as guardian in order to get a parish; I think he did it because he wanted to grab the book as soon as he could safely do so.'

Bartholomew remained sceptical. 'Why? He is not ambitious.'

Michael smiled and handed him a piece of parchment. 'And fourth, this arrived yesterday.'

Bartholomew read it quickly. 'It is a royal writ, issuing a pardon for Shirford's killing of Drayton. It is signed by the Prince of Wales.' He regarded Michael with troubled eyes. 'Who took the book to the prince in Westminster?'

'Shirford, its faithful guardian. Who else? It seems

to me that orders were issued from high places long before we knew of the existence of the Black Book of Brân. And these orders have allowed Shirford to get away with murder.'

HISTORICAL NOTE

Thomas de Shirford, priest and scholar at the University of Cambridge, really did kill William de Drayton in 1350 and was later pardoned for the crime at the behest of the Prince of Wales (the 'Black Prince'). Shirford lived until at least 1387 and did well for himself, rising to the rank of archdeacon and Keeper of the Spiritualities at Norwich. We will never know why he killed Drayton, or why the prince should have ordered him pardoned.

William Bardolf, kin to Lord Thomas Bardolf, was admitted to King's Hall in the 1380s, where he studied civil law. He went on to become a canon and prebend at York. Meanwhile, the Archbishop of Canterbury's nephew was enrolled at Peterhouse. Wittleseye became an archbishop himself, and his will mentions a kinsman called Roger Neuton. Adam de la March was a University beadle in the mid-fourteenth century. Finally, John de St Philibert was indeed betrothed to Joan, daughter of the Earl of Suffolk. But the marriage never took place, and John disappears into the mists of history without further mention.

ACT FIVE

Ruler of two kingdoms, parleyment not humble,
Against great Rome do faithless spark.
He guides the means whereby their house doth crumble,
And fires the date henceforth will mark.

I

'I don't understand,' I said to my friend Abel Glaze. 'I didn't even know he was alive.'

'He's not, it seems,' said Abel, indicating the letter that lay open upon the table between us. 'At least, he is not alive *and* well. Dying, rather.'

'What I mean,' I said, 'is that I had no idea of my uncle's existence until I got this letter. My father never mentioned he had a brother.'

'You sound aggrieved, Nick.'

'I don't mean to. It's come as rather a shock. How would you like it if you discovered you had uncles and aunts hidden away by a father who hadn't bothered to—'

I stopped, noticing the look on Abel's face and remembering that, quite apart from a lack of uncles and aunts, he possessed no memory at all of his mother and not much of his father. Abel Glaze had gone off to fight in the Dutch wars in the '80s of the last century when he was scarcely out of boy's clothing.

'Anyway,' said my friend, 'what are you going to do about it?'

'I'll have to go, I suppose.'

'Well, I don't know about you, but I am going for a piss, Nick. Get us another while I'm gone.'

He stood up and threaded his way through the crowd of drinkers in the Knight of the Carpet. It wasn't a particularly salubrious tavern but it was close to our workplace. Or our play-place, I should say perhaps, since both Abel and I were actors in the King's Men. Our company was based at the Globe Theatre on the Southwark shore of the river.

I drained my tankard and beckoned to the potboy to bring me a couple more. While Abel was outside relieving himself in the stinking alley that ran between the Knight and the brothel next door, I picked up the letter from the tavern table, although I'd read it a dozen times. Once more I scanned the outside of the letter and its simple direction to 'Nicholas Revill' at 'the Theatre, London'. And the mysteries started right here. For the person who had written it knew enough to be familiar with my name and the fact that I was employed in one of the London companies. What they didn't know was that the Shoreditch playhouse which went by the name of the Theatre had been demolished a few years ago. Some of its timbers had actually been used to build the Globe. It's possible, of course, that the letter-writer had assumed there was only one playhouse in London and simply called it the Theatre – but, if so, that showed the writer to be very ignorant indeed.

The letter reached me by chance after being delivered by the post rider to the Swan, a rivals' house which lies a bit further along the river bank. Someone

I knew there had been kind enough to walk the few hundred yards from his play-place to mine and give it to me in person. I'd received the letter that very morning and spent the rest of the day puzzling over it. Naturally, I wanted to share my puzzlement with my good friend Abel Glaze.

When I'd exhausted what I could learn from the outside of the letter – which wasn't much – I turned again to its contents. Although apparently from an unknown uncle, it was written not by him but by his wife. The letter had come from a house in Shipston on Stour. My uncle, who was also called Nicholas Revill, was too ill to write but capable of dictating words to his wife, acting as a secretary. These facts were stated at the beginning.

In brief, the letter claimed that the sender was brother to John Revill, my father and the late priest of the parish of Miching in Somerset. The sender was aware that my father had perished with my mother in an outbreak of plague that struck the country around Miching some time in the final years of Queen Elizabeth's reign. Now Nicholas Revill too was dying and wished to see the nephew who was named after him. That's what he claimed: that I was named after him.

I say the sender of the letter 'claimed' all this because the news of an uncle – to say nothing of a *dying* uncle – had come out of the blue. As I'd said to Abel Glaze, my father never once talked of a brother called Nicholas or any other member of the family living near Shipston on Stour or anywhere else. Nor could I remember my mother ever mentioning a brother-in-law.

But then my father wasn't very forthcoming. In truth, he could be a fearsome man. He disapproved most strongly of the stage and all the players on it. If he was still alive, my choice of profession would probably have driven him to his grave all over again. As for my mother, she tended to follow her husband's lead. When a topic displeased him, neither of them referred to it. And if my reverend father had never mentioned his brother, that might be explained by some falling-out in the family. A falling-out lasting several decades. That there could have been some ill feeling between the brothers was suggested by a reference in the letter to an 'old estrangement'. The writer, Nicholas Revill's wife, had some difficulty with the long word. She'd crossed it through and then written it exactly the same above.

There was no indication in the letter why I should visit my dying kinsman, but then the dying do not have to give reasons. I could sense my uncle's frailty in the very shaky signature that was appended to this letter. More pressing than *his* dictated request, though, were two words scrawled beneath the signature. 'Please come.' She'd signed it with her own name: Margaret Revill. I visualized my aunt adding that last plea once she'd sanded the letter and taken it out of the sickroom.

At that moment Abel Glaze returned to the table. He wasn't alone but accompanied by a new associate of ours, or an associate of Abel's, I ought to say. Thomas Cloke was a fellow around our age or a little older. He was tall, with a large nose and dark hair that poked out from under his cap. My friend Abel was short, but he also had a prominent beak, and there was something about the way he walked, with a bit of a bounce, which was similar to Cloke's confident stride. So seeing them together making their way across the Knight of the Carpet, you might have thought that one man was imitating the other. If you'd been asked, you would have said that Abel was copying Cloke.

When he caught sight of me at the corner table,

Thomas Cloke did a mock bow. 'Why, if it isn't Master Revill, the master player.'

Straightening up, he snapped his fingers at the potboy who'd just delivered our refilled tankards to indicate that he'd like one of his own, and best be quick about it. Cloke had this peremptory manner. I knew little about him except that he came from a well-to-do family and that he didn't seem to do much apart from being a keen attender at the Globe. He was one of those who hang around the taverns frequented by players in the hope that a bit of our magic will rub off on him.

Don't laugh. There are more than a few individuals like Master Cloke, both male and female. Some of the males want to take up playing themselves. Indeed, I'd spent my first few months in London haunting inns like the Knight in the hope that some playhouse shareholder would discern my talent and offer me a job without my having to ask for one. (It didn't work for me but you might be luckier.) Then there are other people who may not want to act on stage but whose tastes are so odd that they enjoy the company of actors. We don't object to them. Especially we don't object to the women who feel like that.

So now Thomas Cloke eased his gangling frame on to the bench next to me. He mimed a man gasping for breath, he uttered strange noises, and then let his face fall forward until it was grazing the dirty surface of the table. He squinted sideways at me.

'You were very good, Nicholas.'

I managed to smile for an instant.

'Tom is praising your death scene,' said Abel helpfully. He settled himself on the opposite side of the table.

'Not so sure about the living scenes, mind you,' said Cloke. 'But there was plenty of blood when you went.'

'Only a sheep's,' I said, patting the spot on my chest where, on stage, I'd burst the little bladder of sheep's blood which simulated violent death. I'd just done a turn as an assassin in a piece called *The Melancholy Man*. And as an assassin I'd naturally come to a gory end, giving off the kind of strangulated sounds that Cloke tried to imitate. Dying on stage is not as easy as one might think. Cloke did not do a convincing impression of a dying man.

Abel too had a part in *The Melancholy Man*. He played a corrupt cardinal. We'd finished the afternoon performance and changed in the tire-house, Abel taking off his cardinal's red while I divested myself of the assassin's black. We wiped most of the paint off our faces and repaired to the Knight for a tipple. Evidently, Tom Cloke had attended the performance as well.

'What about me, then, Tom?' said Abel. 'No words of praise for me?'

'Remind me who you were again, Mr Glaze,' said Tom Cloke in his lordly fashion, taking a fresh tankard of ale from the returning potboy.

'I played Cardinal Carnale,' said Abel. 'You know, the one who smears poison on to the Bible which he gives to his mistress to kiss – oh, I see—'

Tom Cloke was nodding at Abel to show that he knew perfectly well which part my friend had taken. He'd been joking. Or had he? I was surprised at the level stare that Cloke now directed at Abel, level enough to cause him to pause with his tankard halfway to his mouth.

'I have no praise for your cardinal, no,' said Cloke.

'Ah, well, you can't please 'em all.'

But I sensed that Abel was disappointed. Perhaps it was because Thomas Cloke was really his friend, not mine, and he valued the other's good opinion. A few weeks ago they'd got chatting in another players' tavern, the Goat & Monkey, and, for reasons I couldn't fathom, fallen into a sort of companionship.

There was a pause. Cloke noticed the letter, which was still lying open on the table. The letter from my supposed uncle, Nicholas Revill. Maybe he made out the urgent words scrawled at the end, 'Please come', and the added name of Margaret Revill. Maybe his curiosity was pricked. I wished I'd folded up the letter and put it away in my pocket before Cloke clapped eyes on it. Too late now, as he said: 'What's this?'

I was already reaching for the letter when Abel, perhaps eager to placate the other man, said: 'Nick here has discovered he has an uncle living near Shipston. The strange thing is, he never knew of the man's existence until this very morning. And now his uncle is dying.'

'Is that so?' said Thomas Cloke.

He turned to look at me. I shrugged. I was irritated with Abel for giving away so much. This wasn't really any of his business and it certainly wasn't Cloke's. I shoved the letter into my doublet and launched into a few words of explanation, hoping to kill the subject.

'Interesting,' was the only remark that Cloke made.

'We are thinking of journeying to Shipston,' said Abel, 'to visit this unknown branch of the Revill family. But we shall have to be quick about it since Nicholas's uncle is on his deathbed.'

'*We*?' I said.

'Have you finished playing at the Globe, then?' said Cloke.

'The King's Men are preparing to go on the road for the summer,' said Abel. 'There's a final performance tomorrow afternoon and then we are packing up for our summer tour.'

'Just a moment, Abel,' I said. 'What's all this about *we* going to Shipston?'

'I thought you'd like me to come along with you, Nick. I don't mean to intrude on your family concerns, but I thought you might value my company on the road. Maybe I'm wrong.'

'Naturally, I'd be pleased to have you with me.'

'It's not as if we have to travel much out of our way because, you know, we are due to play in Warwick in – what is it? – ten days' time.'

This was true. Like the other London companies during the later part of the summer, the King's Men loaded their costumes and a handful of props on to a couple of carts and trundled into the provinces to give the bigger towns a taste of what the capital of England enjoyed for the rest of the year. We favoured a different part of the country each summer and now, in the August of 1605, it was the turn of Warwick and Coventry. By chance this was also the region where our principal author and shareholder, William Shakespeare, had grown up. There'd been talk that we might be playing in Stratford itself.

I noticed that Tom Cloke, who'd been silent for a few moments, was looking from Abel to me and back again. When he spoke it was with an unusual tentativeness.

'Here is a fortunate coincidence, gentlemen,' he said. 'Abel, you know that I have cousins who live on the way to Warwick. It has been in my mind to visit them for some time. What would you say if I joined you on the journey? Safety in numbers, eh?'

'That's a good idea,' said Abel.

'Of course,' I said.

'Let us drink to it,' said Cloke, snapping his fingers at the potboy once more for our cups to be refilled. 'Drinks on my slate, of course.'

And so it was settled that the three of us would set off the day after tomorrow, once we'd given a final performance of *The Melancholy Man* at the Globe.

I didn't greatly relish the idea of Thomas Cloke keeping us company, but I could think of no plausible objection, even if he had muscled his way into our trip.

I had the obligation to visit my dying uncle and doing so as soon as possible. Abel Glaze was offering to accompany me out of friendship, and, as he'd pointed out, we were due to travel in that direction anyway. We'd simply be getting a head start on others in the company and, once I had called in at my uncle's house, I could join Abel and the rest of the fellows in Warwick. And if Cloke also had family to visit in the area, then it made sense for him to ride with us. The roads were more secure and easier to travel in high summer, but there was something in his comment about safety in numbers. Three men on the road made a more forbidding prospect for thieves and highway robbers.

Nevertheless, I wasn't altogether at ease. There was an element in Thomas Cloke I didn't trust even if I couldn't put my finger on it.

II

It was the third day after the three of us had set off when I started to feel real suspicions that everything wasn't as it should be. There was nothing amiss in the sunny weather or the state of the roads. They were dry and the hooves of our hired horses threw up plenty of dust, but all that was preferable to the mires of winter and spring. The travellers we passed going towards London or the ones we overtook waved cheerful greetings or at least regarded us with the minimum of suspicion.

There was nothing wrong with my companions either, or with me, I hope. We got on well enough. Abel

Glaze and I were old friends dating back to the days when the King's Men went under no more ambitious a title than the Chamberlain's. The two of us talked quite a bit of players' shop, which Tom Cloke was happy enough to listen to, occasionally chipping in with some comment of his own. I had to admit that Cloke was fair company. He was generous with his purse, buying us our supper on the first two nights because, as he said, he'd wished himself on us and we were entitled to some compensation. Overall, I was enjoying the journey, not thinking much about the deathbed that awaited me at the end. I'm no great rider, but my horse was biddable enough and we proceeded at a gentle jog.

We were following the usual road out of London on the way to the Midlands – the one through Slough and on to Oxford via Wallingford before heading further north. It was the route that William Shakespeare took on his journeys home. I'd mentioned to WS that Abel and I were leaving London early, explaining about my dying uncle and adding that I'd first heard of this man's existence scarcely more than twenty-four hours earlier. WS was all quick feeling whenever he heard such news affecting one of his company, and he grasped my hand in farewell.

'It is hard to gain and lose a member of one's family in the same instant, Nick. But you are doing the right thing by going. One should not neglect family.'

A shadow passed across his face, and I recalled the company talk about WS: that he did not often go home to Stratford despite acquiring a large house in the town some years ago and – although he would not have said so himself – despite being one of its most notable citizens.

From the moment when Abel Glaze, Tom Cloke and I gained the open country beyond the fringes of London, I observed that Cloke was watchful. Not just on the more deserted or heavily wooded stretches of the road but when we arrived at the hostelries where we put up each night. These places were nothing special, and we chose them at random. But before we sat down to supper our companion would survey the other guests and travellers almost as if he was searching for someone whom he knew – and feared to see. Only when he'd established that there was no such individual amongst the itinerant merchants and the locals in the room would he breathe more easily and go about ordering food and drink. If someone came in, he stopped eating or drinking for an instant to glance at them. But it was more than a casual glance, if you know what I mean.

On our first night we shared a room with several other travellers, and Cloke gave them the same scrutiny. The same on the second. On the third night the three of us had a tight little chamber to ourselves, mostly occupied by the large bed. This time, with no one to be suspicious of inside the room, Cloke spent some minutes gazing out of the window after supper. It was growing dark. He beckoned to me. I was just taking off my boots and outer garments before lying down. Abel Glaze was already asleep and snoring his head off. I went to the window.

In a conspiratorial whisper Cloke said: 'Do you see those men over there, Nicholas? Under the trees.'

I squinted through the leaded panes. The inn, which was called the Night Owl, was on the outskirts of Wallingford. The town and its castle were to one side and to the west was the river, while wooded countryside crept up near the inn. The dust of the road seemed to glow with a light of its own. There was a stand of trees opposite the Night Owl. Tom Cloke said: 'There! Do you see?'

The glass in the window was old and lumpy, and the

light outside was fading. If it hadn't been for a sudden spark as someone in the group struck a tinderbox, I don't think I would have noticed the little knot of men standing in the shadows of the trees. Then I made out the pale blur of faces, the movement of hands.

'Yes, I see them,' I said.

'They were at supper downstairs.'

'I don't know, I can't see clearly enough from here. Anyway, so what if they were?'

'They are looking up at our room,' said Cloke.

I could feel his breath on my cheek as we crowded at the little window. His agitation was plain. Such is the power of suggestion that I became convinced for a moment that the group outside was indeed looking up in the direction of our chamber. Like my companion, I grew uncomfortable. An owl hooted in the trees. But then one of the men in the group laughed – the sound carried quite clearly on the still evening air – and common sense returned, to me at least. It was a natural laugh, not a thief's, not a conspirator's.

'They're having a quiet smoke before turning in for the night, that's all.'

The little red embers of their pipes pulsated in the dark. I counted four embers. I clapped Tom Cloke on the shoulder and went back to undressing for bed. I lay down next to Abel, who was still snoring. Cloke stayed at the window until it grew completely dark outside. Before he joined us in the bed, I heard him go to the door and softly rattle the latch as well as sliding the bolt back and forth a couple of times. I thought he was going outside but he was only checking that we were secure. Eventually, the bed creaked as Cloke got in. I feigned sleep even as I sensed him lying wakeful beside me. The owl hooted again. I wondered why our travelling companion was so alert, so nervous.

*

The morning after we left Wallingford, Cloke seemed to relax. I made some reference to the pipe smokers we'd glimpsed from the window of the Night Owl and he shrugged it off. Abel looked curiously not at him but at me. We paused in Oxford to hire fresh horses and rode a few miles further from the city walls as far as Woodstock to take advantage of the fair weather and the longer hours of summer light.

We were getting close to the dwelling of Tom Cloke's cousins, whose family name was Shaw and who lived beyond the small town of Bloxham in a place called Combe House. The three of us had one more shared night in an inn, and then the next day we'd be parting company as I went on to Shipston on Stour and Abel made his way to Warwick to wait for the rest of the King's Men. Occasionally, I thought of the dying uncle whose name I shared. But since I had never met him or his wife Margaret, my thoughts did not go very far. I hoped to arrive in time, but it was all out of my hands.

The Green Dragon at Woodstock was comfortable, as befits a hostelry in a town where there is also a royal palace, and we drank and ate heartily. Cloke thanked us for sharing our journey. He bought us supper and I felt well disposed towards him, and not merely because I knew I wouldn't be seeing him beyond the following day. He wasn't such a bad fellow after all.

The next morning, however, his nerves seemed once again to have got the better of him. We were leaving the Dragon early, impatient to get to our various destinations. It was crisp, bright August weather, with a hint of autumn already in the air. Cloke was in the stableyard of the inn when Abel and I got there. He'd already taken down Abel's bag in addition to his own and had offered to take mine too. A man in a hurry. Now he was talking to the ostler, who was bringing out our horses. Tom started when he saw us, his friends and fellow travellers, draw near. The sun was at our backs, streaming over the wall of the yard. Perhaps he hadn't recognized us at first. Who was he expecting? Yet, close to, he looked more guilty than alarmed.

'Something wrong, Tom?' said Abel.

'Nothing,' said Cloke. 'I am anxious to be going, that's all.'

We passed through Bloxham, with Tom Cloke telling us that the spire of St Mary's was the highest in Oxfordshire, although these were almost the only words he uttered during the morning.

The country grew more hilly and the roads emptier. Tucked away down in a side valley I noticed a splendid house, standing alone. I was wondering whose it might be when, to my and Abel's surprise, Tom Cloke suddenly straightened in his saddle and pointed.

'There's Combe,' he said. 'It is the home of the Shaws, my kinsmen.'

We reined in for a moment to examine the prospect. I knew that Tom Cloke came from a well-to-do family but, if this place was anything to go by, he'd been reticent on the subject of his cousins' wealth.

In the noonday sun that hung over the west-facing valley, Combe House was set like a jewel against a backdrop of trees and water. The warm stone glowed and the windows sparkled. There was a moat, and a gatehouse approached across a bridge. I guessed Combe House dated from the reign of Queen Elizabeth's father, a time when prosperous families began to move away from the safety of towns and to construct country dwellings with the appearance of mansions rather than castles.

'You will stop for some refreshment before you go on your way,' said our companion. It was more of a command than a request. 'The horses will need watering.'

There was no disagreeing with that, and I for one would be glad to dismount for an hour or so and stretch my legs, as well as having a bite to eat. We turned our horses off the main road and started down the winding path that led into the valley. The path was wide and rutted with the tracks of wagons and carriages. We made a gradual, sinuous descent through copses of trees.

'This is a fine place,' said Abel, half-turning and calling over his shoulder. 'I shall have to speak with more respect to you in future, Tom.'

By now we were almost on the flat and moving in single file, passing through dense ranks of trees that overhung either side of the path, which was slightly sunken. Combe House was out of sight. When we'd been high up above the valley and looking down I'd been in good spirits, but now something was making me uneasy. There was no sound of birdsong, no sound but the breeze rustling in the leaves and the plodding of our horses. My horse seemed to share the unease I felt. I was in the middle, with Abel to the front and Tom to our rear. A dozen or so yards separated each of us from the other.

As I glanced back to see whether Cloke was going to respond to Abel's comment, I heard the whinny of a horse and was puzzled, for it was not one of ours. Then there was a flash and a loud bang from the trees to our rear. Tom was leaning forward but his head was up and his mouth wide open. Even amongst the shadows cast by the trees I could see him gaping ferociously as if trying to force words out.

With a great effort, Tom Cloke straightened in his saddle and looked down at his chest. Almost in curiosity. There was a bloom of red spreading across his shirt, clearly visible beneath his unfastened doublet. And then several things happened at once. Behind us, from further down the track and between the trees, several men appeared on foot in a jostling mass. They started to run towards us.

Tom's horse panicked and cantered ahead. Cloke was bent forward once more, clinging to the reins. My own horse was putting on speed too. I didn't have to urge him; he was doing so by instinct. I called out a warning to Abel Glaze – in my terror, I don't know what I said and words were unnecessary anyway since Abel was already twisted around on his mount and staring past me in amazement – and then the three of us were thudding along the narrow path and out into a wide grassy space that fronted Combe House and its encircling moat.

Either the occupants of the house were on the lookout for us or they had some guardian permanently on duty at the main entrance, for, by the time we'd covered half of the few hundred yards of sunlit grass that separated the trees from the moat, the alarm had been raised and people were gathering under the gatehouse arch at the far end of the bridge, with more arriving at every instant.

I risked a glance behind me. Tom Cloke was still with us, but he was all huddled up on horseback. I sensed rather than saw a group of men emerging from the shelter of the trees. They halted, no doubt seeing the party waiting on the far side of the moat and realizing that we'd reach the safety of the house before they could catch us. Abel and I managed to rein in our horses when we were almost at the bridge. The band of men by the wood – there were four of them – moved a little out of its shelter. At least two of them were carrying muskets. One of them raised his weapon and sighted down it. I understood now what had happened to Tom Cloke. The meaning of the red stain across his chest. But the man lowered his weapon. We were either out of range altogether or too far away for accurate shooting.

These men were no common footpads or chance thieves. They must have tethered their own horses in the woodland near Combe House and waited for us to arrive. They had chosen their moment carefully, when we were away from the main road and off our guard near the moated house.

I realized all this later. Now my attention was caught by the sight of poor Tom Cloke vainly trying to hold on to his horse. He must have pulled on the reins, for the animal veered around, away from the house, and began to bolt towards our ambushers.

A handful of men started out from the gatehouse on the far side of the bridge. Some were carrying staves, one of them a musket of his own. Abel crossed the narrow bridge; I was close behind him. Several men grabbed at the reins of our horses. Abel and I jumped down. All was confusion, with the horses jinking about, men shouting and dogs barking. No one could decide whether to take shelter in the courtyard, which lay beyond the gatehouse, or to venture to the far side of the moat and confront the ambushers.

The individual with the musket ran to the far end of the bridge and raised his gun in the direction of the trees, but he did not fire either. Our companion's horse, with Tom slumped across it, had almost reached the woods. Then it slowed as if uncertain where to go next, and one of our assailants walked forward quite nonchalantly, like a man strolling in a meadow, hand outstretched. He seized Tom's horse by the bridle. At the same time Tom's body fell from the horse. The ambusher, who was clad in black, at first seemed inclined to leave him lying there. Then he beckoned to one of his fellows. The two of them unceremoniously hoisted up our friend and tossed him over the saddle as though he were a hunter's quarry. From their handling of the body, Tom was dead. Dead or dying. The horse and its burden were led off into the woods.

I was surprised the men made no attempt to approach closer to Combe House. Although they were outnumbered, they were obviously determined individuals. Perhaps they'd got what they had come for.

So far, no one had spoken directly to us. But now a tall, handsome young woman came forward. 'What trouble have you brought to our house?' she said.

III

'You think it was the same men you saw at Wallingford?' said Abel Glaze.

'I'm not sure,' I said. 'All I know is that Tom was worried about something and he called me to the window of our room as it was getting dark. You were fast asleep. There were four men standing outside. They were smoking pipes and laughing amongst themselves. I thought nothing of it at the time, but it seems as though they must have been stalking us all the while and waiting for their opportunity.'

'Why wait until we'd almost arrived here?'

'Perhaps they needed to be certain of our destination before they attacked.'

'It doesn't make sense, Nick. What did they want?'

'They are not common thieves, that's certain.'

'I noticed that Tom was anxious through the whole journey.'

'I did too,' I said, wondering why Abel hadn't mentioned this earlier.

'So it must have been Tom Cloke they were after,' said Abel. 'Why would anyone bother to follow a couple of poor players?' There was almost relief in his voice.

Nothing to be ashamed of. He was expressing my own thoughts.

'Poor Tom,' said Abel. He sunk his head in his hands.

Abel and I were sitting in an upper bedchamber of Combe House. The interior of the place was as fine and spacious as the outside promised. After the striking young woman by the gatehouse had asked us that question about the trouble we'd brought them, we spent some moments identifying ourselves to her, since she seemed to speak with authority.

While we were busy explaining our connection to Tom Cloke and the reason why we'd pitched up at the moated house, a young man appeared in the courtyard, closely followed by an older couple. There was such a strong likeness amongst these handsome people that it was evident they were father and mother, son and daughter. These were indeed the Shaw family, and I'll say more about them later.

The older man gave orders that an armed party from the house was to scour the woods and valley in search of our assailants and, although he did not say this in our hearing, most probably of Tom's body. Meanwhile we were taken inside and given refreshment, while our horses were stabled. Neither Abel nor I had much appetite for food, but we drank several draughts of some fiery spirit which helped steady our nerves. We sat in the hall of the house. The two women of the household, Elizabeth and Mary Shaw, mother and daughter respectively, attended to us in person, dismissing the servants once they'd brought the refreshments. There were younger children peering at us curiously, but they too were ushered away. A couple of spaniels that were too idle and pampered to go on the hunt for our assailants hung around the table. Abel fed them scraps.

All around was bustle and activity, but we were a still

centre. Now we were able to tell our story in a more ordered style, up to the moment of the ambush.

I was glad to discover that the Shaws were actual kinsmen to Tom Cloke. I think part of me hadn't quite believed the claim he'd made as we gazed down on Combe House. For their part, the women accepted us for who we were, members of the King's Men and travelling companions to Tom, by chance more than by design. Abel described how Tom had attached himself to us when he found we were journeying to the Midlands in our profession as players. He added that I was visiting a dying uncle. Mary Shaw made some commiserating remark to me about this and I simply nodded, too embarrassed to say that I had been unaware of my uncle's existence until a few days before.

I noticed that neither Elizabeth nor Mary showed much grief about Cloke's death. Perhaps they were still too shocked by the suddenness of it all to respond or perhaps he had been a distant kinsman whom they'd scarcely known. Towards the end of our recital, however, Mrs Shaw abruptly said: 'Did our cousin Thomas have anything with him?'

'What sort of thing?' said Abel.

The lady of the house, tall and good-looking like her daughter, appeared slightly uncomfortable at her own question.

'I mean, did you notice whether he was carrying anything . . . unusual? Large enough to be in his bag or cap case?'

'If he was, then it will be in the hands of our attackers,' I said. 'They made off with Tom and his horse. All his possessions were in the saddlebag.'

'That is so, Mother,' said Mary Shaw. 'We saw one of the thieves snatch at the horse's bridle and lead the beast and the body of our kinsman into the woods.'

Mother and daughter exchanged quick glances. And

when the father and son reappeared – they had gone out at the head of the party searching for our attackers – I thought I saw an odd exchange between William Shaw, the owner of Combe House, and his wife. Mr Shaw came striding through the door of the hall, his son Robert close behind him and a gaggle of armed servants in their wake. Abel and I were still seated at the great dining table with Elizabeth and Mary. William Shaw announced to all of us what was already apparent from the expression on his face: 'They are nowhere to be found, I fear.' Then he gave a slight and separate shake of his head to his wife as if in confirmation of his words. But I sensed he was sending a different message to her. I cast a glance at Abel. He too had noticed.

This was a further small mystery for Abel and me to puzzle over after we'd been ushered upstairs to our chamber. We were to stay at Combe at least for the rest of the day and the night to come. The attack on us and the murder of Thomas Cloke would be reported to the justices in Banbury (the nearest town of any size), although this would have to wait since no one was going to venture far from the house that day. Realistically, any chance of tracking down and apprehending the culprits lay with the occupants of Combe, and that seemed to have failed.

'Ah, well,' said Abel, lifting his head from his hands. 'Poor Tom.' He sighed and lay back on the bed. I was sitting in a chair by the open casement window. Below was a sheer wall, at the base of which stirred the waters of the moat. This was not as wide or deep as a castle's, but it was enough to make access to the house almost impossible except via the bridge in front of the gatehouse. At that moment I was glad of the security. I gazed over the water at the sunlit trees fringing the cleared area around Combe. On our ride up here this morning the countryside had looked peaceful, innocent. Now the shadows under the trees might conceal a band of murderers.

I was vaguely aware of Abel rising from the bed and going to the corner of the chamber where our bags had been stowed, brought to us from the stables by a boy servant. I travelled light, as did Abel. The costumes and everything else we required for our work were being conveyed direct to Warwick in the company wagons.

Now I heard Abel give a grunt of surprise.

'What is it?'

He didn't answer but swung his bag on to the bed. It was a battered old thing, going back to the time when Abel had made his living in an even more disreputable way than as a player. My friend was a reformed character these days, but he'd once tricked money and alms out of travellers by pretending to suffer from distressing ailments like the falling sickness. He used the cloth bag to carry the various items he needed (mostly cosmetic, like a player's). But as he looked inside the cap case now it was evident that he wasn't finding what he expected. He lifted out a square-shaped item that was wrapped in drab cloth and secured with cord.

'I thought my bag was heavier than it should be,' he said.

'What is it?'

'I don't know. I didn't put it in here.'

Abel placed the item on the bed. He ran his fingers along its edges. 'Feels like wood. Or a book of some sort.'

The same thought crossed our minds at the same moment. Abel looked at me.

'It must be Tom's,' he said.

I recalled that very morning in the stableyard of the Green Dragon at Woodstock. How Tom Cloke had been in the yard before us, chatting to the ostler. How he appeared startled or guilty when he saw us approaching. Had he slipped this . . . this item . . . into Abel's bag beforehand? He'd taken the bag down to the yard early, as if he was doing Abel a favour. He had offered to take mine too, but I refused.

'Put in here by accident?' said Abel, then, seeing my expression, added: 'No, I don't think so either.'

'He placed that – whatever it is – inside your bag when he was carrying it to the stableyard. He did it because he feared what might happen. Feared he might be attacked and his goods stolen.'

'Not just him. *We* were attacked, remember.'

I could see Abel was angry and upset because Tom Cloke's actions had placed all three of us in danger. I felt angry too, but Cloke had been Abel's friend more than mine.

'I am going to see what's inside this piece of cloth,' said Abel defiantly. 'It may be a dead man's property, but he has forfeited the right to it by his behaviour.'

Nevertheless, Abel Glaze continued to stare at the item in its drab covering where it lay on the bed. His reluctance to open it seemed to be based on more than some simple scruple about tampering with Tom's possessions. But after a few moments he took a small knife from out of his cap case and, slitting the knotted cord that was bound about the parcel, unfolded the cloth. By this time I was standing beside him, looking down.

I don't know what I expected to see. Something valuable for sure, valuable enough to cause four mysterious men to tail us over several days before launching an attack and murdering Tom. Something valuable, but not this. Abel had been right when he said that the object felt like a piece of wood or a book. It was both of those, an old volume with primitive wooden covers to which shreds of leather still clung. Crude stitching bound the covers together.

Abel lifted the book up without opening it. He handled it warily, as if it might bite. The back cover was pierced by several holes, suggesting it had once been nailed down somewhere. Altogether, the nail holes did not add to the attraction of the volume. Perhaps it had been used to stop up a hole in a wall. It was definitely ancient. The surprise was that it had survived at all and not been put to kindle a fire.

Only now did Abel open the book. I was peering over his shoulder. The leaves were of parchment and crackled to the touch. One of them was discoloured, as if a careless reader had spilled wine on it. Abel drew in his breath sharply, for the contents were in complete contrast to the unpromising exterior: a series of short handwritten texts positioned in the centre of each page, and with the lettering immaculately formed. The scribe, whoever he was, had taken pains to produce something imposing. Which argued that the contents must have been important – at least to him. Unfortunately, they didn't make any sense.

'It's rubbish,' said Abel. There was a mixture of regret and relief in his voice.

'Let me see.'

I cradled the volume in my hands. I was conscious of the stillness inside the chamber, of a fly buzzing at the casement window, of the sunlight outside.

'It's in Latin, I think,' I said.

'Of course, Nick. I forget you are an educated man.'

'My father saw to that – with his rod if he had to.'

I was only half-aware of my own words, too absorbed in the writings of someone from centuries ago. For the volume seemed to stretch further into the past even as I was holding it. I went back to the seat by the window, where the light was better.

'I can spell out some of it. Here's a phrase about the house of a king and broken bones, and another one about the sacred face of a traitor. Set out like the lines of a poem.'

'Rubbish, like I said.'

'I'm not so sure. Have you got anything to write with? Anything to write on?'

Abel sighed and fumbled in his case. He produced a thin stick of charcoal. I don't know why he had it but guessed it was part of the gear from his counterfeit crank days, when he'd conned money out of people. He hung on to the stuff for sentimental reasons. He gave me a roll of paper as well, saying it was the lines of some part he'd played recently and forgotten to return to the book-keeper at the end of the performance.

But I wasn't interested in Abel's part. I was too caught up by now in attempting to puzzle out a block of lines which occurred near the end of this slim volume. I tore off a fragment of the paper. Resting the book on my knees and using the smudgy charcoal, I copied the words on to the back of the paper scrap. It didn't take long. Then I attempted to turn them into English. That took a lot longer. And then I sat staring at the whole thing until Abel grew exasperated and said: 'Well?'

'It's not rubbish,' I said, 'even if the lines don't appear to make much sense. It seems to rhyme in the Latin so it would go like this in English.' I paused in the way that I would have done in delivering an important speech on stage.

'"Ruler of two kingdoms, parleyment not humble,
Against great Rome do faithless spark.
He guides the means whereby their house does fall,
And fires the date henceforth will mark."

'But if I change "fall" to "crumble" I can get a rhyme with "humble".'

I made the alteration in what I'd written and sat back, rather pleased with myself.

Abel was staring at me, though not in admiration. 'I think you'd better leave the poetry to Master Shakespeare, Nicholas.'

'You must admit it has some meaning even if it's obscure.'

'Possibly. It could be a prophecy or a prediction. I remember a fortune-teller near Paul's Wharf who used to go in for that sort of thing. Rhyming lines and all.'

'This must have been what they were after, those men,' I said. 'It's the only thing that Tom transferred to your bag.'

'If so, they were ready to murder for it.'

I closed the book. It suddenly weighed heavily in my lap. I felt slightly dizzy, the effect of the drink we'd taken downstairs, perhaps. We were silent for a moment. When Abel next spoke it was to echo my own thoughts.

'Nick, when those men search inside Tom's saddle-bag—'

'—which they will have done already—'

'—they'll see straight away that the book isn't there—'

'—they'll assume we have it—'

'—we do—'

'—and come in search of it here—'

'—come in search of *us*.'

As Abel concluded with this alarming prediction, I glanced out of the open window once more. The shadows under the distant trees grew darker.

'We're safe as long as we stay here,' said Abel. 'This is a well-defended house.'

'We can't stay here for ever. Some of us have got a

living to make. I've got a dying uncle to see. Besides, we may be in as much danger within Combe House as outside it. I reckon that the Shaws were waiting for cousin Cloke to arrive. Mrs Shaw asked us whether Tom was carrying anything unusual on the journey. And you saw the look that passed between husband and wife when he returned from his hunt for the attackers. It wasn't about not finding those men; it was about not finding . . . something else.'

'So why don't we just give them the book? Explain how Tom must have put it in my bag by chance?'

'What's to stop them kicking us out of here if we do? Kicking us out or something worse . . .?'

'This is a respectable family, Nick. The danger lies outside.'

'Maybe,' I said. 'But we should keep hold of this book for the time being. Let's sleep on it. Tomorrow we can hand it over as we leave.'

'All right,' said my friend. 'But in the meantime we'd better find a place in which to conceal it. I don't want to put it back with my own things.'

In the end we tucked the book under a mattress on the bed. One of several mattresses on the bed, for this was a wealthy house. We had carpets on the floor too. We hid the book only just in time, for there was a knock at the door. It was Mary Shaw, the daughter of the house.

'Gentlemen,' she said, 'I fear that we are not treating you as guests deserve to be treated. Please come with me.'

IV

It seemed that Mary had summoned us for no other purpose than to show off something of the house, or rather its immediate surroundings, before the evening meal. As we went downstairs into the hall, we saw the children again, a boy and a girl. They were attended by a clean-shaven, jowly man who inclined his head slightly to our guide. Mary Shaw explained that the children were also her cousins. Her mother's sister, whom we hadn't yet met, was a widow and a permanent resident in Combe. The clean-shaven individual acted as the children's tutor.

We walked over the bridge across which we'd galloped on our arrival. We were not alone. A couple of the household servants, strapping fellows in livery and armed with staves, kept a discreet distance behind us. Their presence should have made me feel easier, but it did not. Also trailing behind us were the spaniels that had been in the hall. They were the particular pets of Mary Shaw. She called them Finder and Keeper.

Abel and I couldn't help glancing towards the place under the fringe of trees where we'd last seen Tom Cloke, dead or dying, draped across his horse.

'You knew your cousin Tom Cloke well?' I said.

'Not really, Master Revill,' she said, 'although the Clokes and the Shaws have long been linked through marriage.'

'Have you any idea why he should have been attacked?' said Abel.

'It was an attempted robbery, was it not?' she said as casually as she could manage. 'Besides, I thought that all of you were attacked, not only Tom.'

She was a good liar but not good enough. I wondered why her mother Elizabeth wasn't showing us around and answering our inevitable questions. The older lady might have been more convincing.

Combe House and its environs were delightful. Or they would have been under normal circumstances. The late-afternoon sun glittered off the dark moat.

Ducks paddled in the water or preened themselves on the banks. Wagtails darted around. Mary pointed out the stews, or fish ponds, that were fed by the overflow from the moat, and the way in which the water was eventually channelled into a stream that ran at the lower end of a meadow beside the house. There was a certain pride in her voice, but Abel and I were uneasy and looked around as if our ambushers might at any moment emerge from the surrounding woodland. The two servants loitered just out of earshot, while Finder and Keeper went about their own affairs.

After half an hour or so we returned to the house and the hall, where the table had been prepared for supper. Abel made himself absent for a moment while Mary made small talk with me. Had I visited this part of the country before? Did I enjoy the player's life? Usually, I would have welcomed her attention. She was a good-looking young woman, if somewhat serious, but her interest was for form's sake only, and when her mother entered the chamber she at once turned away and began a private conversation with her.

Mary's place was taken by the steward of Combe House, a man called Gully. He was as sober as stewards tend to be, but he fitted well into this household of grave individuals.

'This is a sad business, Master Revill,' he said.

'Yes,' I said. 'The death of a kinsman and all.'

'He has brought trouble to Combe,' said Gully, echoing Mary Shaw, although at least he did not blame Abel and me. 'This is a peaceful spot, out of the world. Some of us do our best to ensure it remains that way.'

'Sometimes the world comes to you, willy-nilly,' I said.

'You look as though you might enjoy the world coming to you, Master Revill.'

'You can't be otherwise and be a player. The world is our business, you might say.'

Before I could embark on any more high-sounding guff, Gully was summoned by his mistress.

Now Abel returned and tugged at my sleeve. He whispered in my ear: 'Our room's been searched.'

'What!'

'It's been done quite carefully, but my things aren't exactly as I left them.'

'Is the book still there?'

'Under the mattress, yes.'

'Maybe we should have put it somewhere more obvious so they could find it.'

I was starting to regret hanging on to the damned thing. Our enemies seemed to be inside Combe House as well as beyond the place. I believed that Mary Shaw had been instructed to lure us out of our room so that our luggage could be examined.

After grace, we sat down to a plain but ample meal of fish and pigeon pie, with salads and sweetmeats. It was a subdued affair – not surprisingly, given that a kinsman had lost his life a few dozen yards from where we were sitting in the hall – and I had the chance to study our hosts.

William Shaw was a tall bearded man with prominent eyes, a feature inherited by his son Robert. The father had a quiet manner, apart from what was produced by the circumstances, I think. I noticed that he frequently glanced at the children's tutor, Henry Gifford, who had joined us at table. The widowed sister to Elizabeth was called Muriel, but I did not catch her last name. She was not from the same mould as the rest of the family, being rather short and red-faced. More cheerful too. She seemed to be the only one familiar with the stage-play world and had once seen a performance of Master Shakespeare's at the Globe. It was before my and Abel's time in the company, however, and she could not have been very struck by the piece, for she remembered little about it apart from the violent killing of 'that Roman'.

'It is called *Julius Caesar*,' said Abel.

'That is the very one,' said Muriel. 'He was struck down as he was speaking before their parleyment. There was much blood spilled, and the assassins washed their hands in it afterwards.'

The word 'parleyment' reminded me of the obscure verse in the book hidden beneath our mattress.

'The killing of a tyrant is permissible,' mused Robert Shaw. 'I refer to Julius Caesar, of course. Do you think—?'

'Does play-acting please you, Master Revill?' said Henry Gifford the tutor, interrupting the young man. These were the first words he'd uttered.

'Why, yes, it does.'

'It has not always been seen as a respectable way of making a living,' said Elizabeth Shaw.

'What is respectable these days?' I said. 'Some of the noblest people in the land have been our patrons, and even the late queen was fond of attending our performances.'

'And now we are become the King's Men,' added Abel.

'It makes no difference how many kings and queens attend your performances when a greater King than all of them looks down on us,' said Gifford firmly. 'Properly considered, playing is a form of lying. A player pretends to be what he is not.'

'But it's a pretence which is shared amongst the audience,' I said, ignoring his opinion of what God thought of it all. 'An agreed pretence which does no harm.'

These were familiar arguments, both for and against plays and players. Maybe I spoke more strenuously than I should have done, because I felt both aggrieved and on the defensive. Maybe that accounted for what I said next.

'You should know that your late kinsman Thomas frequented the playhouse.'

Raised eyebrows and expressions of disbelief around the table showed that my point had not been well received. Doubtless the Shaws considered that attending playhouses was exactly the kind of loose behaviour that infected young men when they were unwise enough to visit London.

'We must not be too harsh,' said Elizabeth Shaw in a conciliatory way. 'The players are not beyond the pale. They even have their own saint.'

'His feast day is next week,' added Robert Shaw.

'I should thank you two gentlemen for accompanying Thomas to Combe despite the sad outcome of your journey,' said William.

Conversation was desultory after that. It was arranged that we should leave Combe House the next morning. Mr Shaw offered us an escort for a few miles, although, he said, in his view the fellows who attacked us were long gone.

Abel and I returned to our chamber while the rest of the family went about their business. Abel examined his possessions yet again. He did not think they had been disturbed for a second time.

'The room hasn't been searched because the Shaws no longer think we've got what they are looking for, Abel. They believe our attackers already have it, which is the reason Mr Shaw does not expect us to be attacked again.'

'But *we* know they haven't got the book, which is the reason *we* may be attacked again. So let's give it up to the Shaw family before we depart, Nick. Let them deal with the problem. Or we can simply leave it where it is.'

We checked to see that the book was still tucked

amongst the mattresses. It was. I drew it out once more and looked at its ancient pages with their obscure verses. Were they predictions? Forecasts of events that had already occurred or were still to happen? I took out from my pocket the paper on which I'd scrawled my makeshift translation.

Some words leaped out at me – 'Ruler of two kingdoms', 'parleyment', 'great Rome'. If they applied to the present time, it was not difficult to understand the references. Our new ruler, James, had also been King of Scotland before he journeyed southwards to take the throne left vacant by Elizabeth. 'Rome' could only refer to the papal seat. The Popes sometimes found it expedient to regard the English kings as usurpers and tyrants.

But if individual words and phrases were clear, the general sense of the verse was cloudy. Or perhaps it was that I was reluctant to look too closely into its meaning for fear of what I might find.

'Who is the patron saint of players?' said Abel, breaking into these alarming thoughts.

'St Genesius. He was a Roman, like Julius Caesar the tyrant. Except he was an actor, I think.'

'Did you know that the feast day of Genesius was next week?'

'I didn't.'

'Yet the son of this household did. Odd, eh? Do you know what I think, Nick? That we have stumbled into a nest of recusants.'

The same thought had been on the edge of my own mind, but I'd been reluctant to admit it. This region of the country, spreading out from Warwickshire into the neighbouring counties, was known to be fertile soil for adherents of the old religion. There was a guarded quality to all the Shaws that fitted a family that must always be looking out for trouble from the authorities.

Then there was an unexpected familiarity with the feast days of obscure saints, and some out-of-the-way reference to the permissible killing of tyrants. Above all, there was the figure of Henry Gifford, the supposed tutor to Muriel's children. Tutor he might be in his spare moments, but I would have wagered a month's worth of my meagre wages against a bead rosary that he was the priest who ministered to the souls in Combe.

Households like Combe might be tolerated by the authorities, but they could expect visits from pursuivants or priest-catchers, who would interrogate the occupants. If they didn't receive satisfactory answers, they would take measurements of room dimensions, then tap on walls and ceilings in their search for hidden compartments. If necessary, they would simply wait for the hidden priests to exhaust their supplies of food and water. I thought of the men who'd lain in ambush for us. Pursuivants? No, there would be no need for *them* to hide in the woods or launch a murderous attack. They acted with the full power and approval of the state. The four men weren't pursuivants but something different – and worse.

'Yes, I think we are in a Catholic house,' I said to Abel.

'Thomas Cloke must have been a follower of the old religion too,' he said. 'Remember that he did not like my portrayal of a cardinal on stage.'

I did recall that odd moment in the Knight of the Carpet when Cloke had seemed displeased with Abel.

'Whether that's so or not,' I said, 'the Shaws are surely followers of the old religion, and Henry Gifford is the guardian of their immortal souls.'

I returned the book to its hiding-place beneath the mattress. I screwed up the piece of paper on which I'd written in smudgy charcoal the English version of the Latin and went over to the window. I opened it, leaned out and dropped the paper into the moat, where it floated, its whiteness clearly visible in the fading light, before it became clogged with water and sank into the depths. The moon, nearly full, had risen above the edge of the valley and cast a ghostly glow across the fields and woodlands beyond Combe. I shut the window against all that.

There was no key or bolt on the door, but Abel fastened a piece of cord around the latch. It wouldn't prevent anyone getting in for long, but at least it would give us warning of the attempt. Then we retired to the single but spacious bed. It was more comfortable than any we'd been accommodated in at the various hostelries where we'd stayed, but I don't think either of us slept soundly. I certainly didn't. And that was before we were disturbed in the middle of the night and had no more sleep at all.

I was awoken by a thump from the far side of the room and the sound of scuffling and panting. Abel was out of the bed and at first I thought he had been taken sick, but within moments I saw two shapes writhing on the carpet in a patch of moonlight. Even as I scrambled from the bed, one of the figures leaped away from the other, who remained moaning on the floor by the door.

'Help me, Nick.'

It was Abel, standing at a crouch between the bed and the crumpled shape. He was holding something. I recognized the book which had been stowed beneath our mattress.

'He was trying to steal it,' said Abel, his breath coming short.

I didn't have to ask who *he* was, for the moon shone full on the other man – Henry Gifford, the 'tutor' to widow Muriel's children. The light gave the man's jowls a bluer tinge. He was not so much injured as winded. I wasn't surprised he'd come off worse in a tussle with Abel Glaze, who was tough and wiry for all his slightness.

Now Gifford sat up. He said: 'It is you who are the true thieves. Give me that.'

He spoke with the same kind of certainty as when he condemned us players during the meal.

Abel shook his head and moved until he was next to me. We perched on the edge of the bed, gazing down at the man on the floor. Incongruously, the tutor-priest propped his back against the wall and stretched his legs out, a man at ease.

'If you do not surrender the book I will summon the household,' he said.

'And if you do,' said Abel, 'I will open the window and fling this . . . this item into the moat below before anyone can get here. I wonder how long your precious book would last in the water.'

'It has survived worse than that,' said Gifford. He sounded both defiant and doubtful. For my part, I was struck by Abel's firmness. But, of course, he was angrier than I was.

He said to me: 'So much for hospitality towards guests, eh, Nick? I felt a draught of air and saw this fellow crawling towards our bed on all fours like a beast, then I felt him fumbling beneath the side where I was lying. Aha, I thought, I know what you're after. So I fell out of bed on top of him.'

Felt a draught of air? I'd been too preoccupied before to notice a chill together with a damp, musty odour which had crept into our chamber. Nor had I seen what Abel now directed my attention towards: a darker square at floor level in the linenfold panelling of the wall beside the bed. A space just large enough for a man to wriggle in and out of. Next to it, leaning against the wall, was the square of wood that usually concealed the opening. In a rush I realized that here was an authentic priest-hole, the kind of hiding-place that the pursuivants would search for with their measures and probes. At that moment I would have welcomed a band of pursuivants bursting into the room and taking up Master Gifford. The trouble was that we'd probably have been taken up with him.

'He must have been spying on us,' said Abel, the anger still in his voice. 'He saw where we'd put this book. Admit it, Master Gifford, you were watching through some spyhole behind the wall.'

From where he'd also heard our speculations about the Catholic household, I thought.

'Yes, I have been observing you,' said the other calmly. 'I know that you know who – or rather what – I am.'

'We have no quarrel with any priest or with the Shaw family,' I said. 'In fact, we want nothing more to do with anyone at Combe House. We came here by chance, not choice, and we leave here of our own free will tomorrow morning. Neither my friend Abel nor I have any desire to cause you or the Shaws . . . difficulty.'

This was my way of hinting that we would not report them to the authorities. If I'd expected Gifford to be grateful I was to be disappointed. He gave a kind of snort and said: 'Very well. But in return for a safe passage from Combe you should return the book which was brought here by Thomas Cloke.'

I looked at Abel, still sitting beside me on the bed. The moonlight streamed over our shoulders and fell on the priest's extended limbs. Abel nodded almost imperceptibly.

'We'll give you back the book,' he said, 'but on one condition. Tell us what is so important about it.'

Henry Gifford was silent for a moment. I wondered whether he was going to claim that the book was unimportant, which would have been absurd. Instead, he decided to tell the truth or part of it.

'Master Glaze, you are holding in your hands a very old volume, a piece of antiquity. It was composed by a monk in Ireland many hundreds of years ago. Some say he was divinely inspired, others that he was mad and wrote in a delirium. There are at least two names for the book: the Armageddon Text and the Black Book of Brân. It contains verses that some think predict the future. There has long been talk of such a volume, but it has not been seen for centuries.'

'Armageddon is the final battle between the nations,' said Abel. 'The end of things.'

I felt a chill that was unrelated to the cold in our chamber.

'I have translated one of the verses,' I said.

Gifford snorted again, this time with amusement. No doubt he was surprised that a lowly player could understand Latin.

'The lines referred to a ruler of two kingdoms and to Rome and a house crumbling to ruin.'

It was gratifying to see the effect this had on the priest. No more snorting with amusement. He sat straight up and thought for a moment.

'Yes, that is a description of the end of things, as your friend says. The ruler of two kingdoms is the devil himself, who lives in hell and has a mere leasehold upon the earth. But the day will come when he shall be vanquished and the house of earthly vanity shall crumble. Rome will play its part in this as the source of true religion. You see, gentlemen, how honest I am being. I do not conceal my faith or my allegiance. I am at your mercy.'

I didn't altogether believe him and his explanation.

But what business was it of mine or of Abel's? I could understand how a household such as the Shaws' would value an ancient book of prophecies which apparently predicted the part played by the Catholic Church in the end of things.

Abel said: 'How did Tom Cloke come by this book?'

'I don't know precisely,' said the priest. 'I believe it was acquired by chance in the area around Westminster. Recognizing that it would be . . . of interest . . . to his Shaw kinsmen, Thomas decided he would bring it with him on his visit to Combe.'

'Then it is unfortunate that Thomas was murdered for his pains.'

'That was coincidence, Master Glaze. The three of you had the bad fortune to encounter a band of robbers on the road. But you and Master Revill had the good fortune to be close to Combe and to find refuge here.'

I reckoned that Gifford had started accurately enough when he was describing the origins of the Black Book of Brân but that he was now leaving the truth further and further behind. If the book was no more than an odd piece of antiquity, why had Tom Cloke secretly slipped it into Abel's luggage, why had we been attacked on the road (which was no coincidence whatever Gifford said), and why was the priest prepared to sneak into our chamber in the middle of the night to snaffle the item?

'Have I satisfied your curiosity?' said Gifford, standing up for the first time.

'No,' said Abel. 'But, speaking for myself, I do not wish to pry into these matters any further. Here's your Black Book and be done with it.'

Gifford's hands closed around the volume. He thanked Abel and inclined his head slightly. He replaced the wooden panel that he had removed to sneak into our chamber and left the room in more conventional fashion, although he was hampered for an instant by the cord that Abel had wound about the door latch. The end of this scene, like the rest of the encounter, was played out by moonlight. Its eerie glow gave an edge to our discussion of the end of things.

I tried to sleep but was too shaken by the encounter to succeed. There were distant noises elsewhere in the house, the sound of whispers, feet shuffling. I wondered what Gifford was up to. Was there a whole clutch of priests at Combe, creeping about in the woodwork? For all that, I did fall asleep eventually as the sky was beginning to lighten.

V

If we thought or hoped we'd seen the last of the tutor-priest, we were wrong. Abel and I rose early the next morning and went downstairs, carrying our baggage, bleary-eyed and yawning all the way.

I'd assumed it was too early for the majority of the household, or at least for the family, to be up, so was surprised by the buzz of noise coming from the area of the kitchen. Instead of the to and fro of servants on their way to the dining hall, however, most of them were crowding towards the kitchen as if there were some attraction inside.

'What is it?' said Abel to a knot of servants standing in close conference by the door.

'Body,' said one.

'Whose?'

'Dunno,' said the same person. He'd obviously got our measure the previous day (we weren't important).

We might have got no nearer than that except for the appearance of Mr and Mrs Shaw. They were still in their night attire. The crowd around the door parted to admit the householders, so Abel and I squeezed through after them.

The kitchen was large, with brick arches containing the hearths and a separate oven for baking. The place was heavy with the smell of last night's cooking and the press of people. There were a couple of sinks set into the outer wall, and it was in this area that everyone's attention was concentrated. One of the flagstones in the floor had been lifted and placed to one side.

Rather than earth or rubble, what lay beneath must have been a conduit of some kind, usual enough in a large kitchen like this. Gully the steward, the most important man there apart from the family, was standing by the hole. He alone out of the household looked spruce and trim. He caught his master's eye and gestured downwards. He did not speak. I saw Shaw peer over the edge and flinch away. His wife stepped forward and also looked down before drawing back sharply. She clutched at his arm.

Naturally, my curiosity was stirred. Abel and I edged our way towards the cavity in the floor. By now, most of the people in the kitchen had had their fill of the sight and all eyes were on the Shaws to see what they were going to do or say next. I glanced down. I'd been right. About five feet below was a brick-lined drainage channel. Its function was to carry the waste from the kitchen sinks and, judging by the smell, probably the waste from the garderobes in the house as well. It was wide and deep. But that wasn't what caught my attention.

Clearly visible at the bottom was the bare head, exposed neck and clothed back of a man. He was wedged along the line of the drain, his face hidden, submerged in a couple of inches of water. I knew, by instinct more than direct recognition, that the body was that of the recent visitor to our chamber. It was Henry Gifford, the tutor-priest.

For some reason I experienced a pang of guilt. I exchanged glances with Abel. He too had recognized Gifford and looked as uncomfortable as I felt.

'Who found him?' said Mr Shaw, breaking the silence.

'I did, sir.'

It was one of the cooks, a large white-faced woman. (But her pallor might have been caused by shock.) She stepped forward.

'Well, Anne?' said Shaw.

'When I came in this morning I noticed that the flagstone was out of place, sir. It was pushed to one side a bit. I couldn't put it back by myself and I called to Adam to help.'

A servant, presumably Adam, now stepped up beside the woman. Words tumbled out of him.

'She called and I came and we was trying to shove the flagstone back and I saw something wasn't right and I said to Anne, "Something is wrong", and we shifted the flag right away from the hole and looked down and saw . . . what anyone can see lying down in the bottom there. A person, sir. Now the steward comes in—'

'I heard the stir, Mr Shaw,' said Gully, stepping forward to join the line of witnesses. There was a pause as if he was going to say more, but he stopped short.

'How did he die?' said Shaw. Even at the time, it seemed an odd question or, rather, an odd moment to ask it.

'Drowned, sir?' said Gully.

'Choked by the foul vapours?' said someone else. Whether the speaker had intended it or not, there was something almost humorous in the remark, and one or two titters broke the tension. Then, as if a dam had been breached, the room was filled with talking.

Abel nudged me. He indicated the flagstone propped against the wall. He whispered in my ear: 'Do you see, Nick, there are handholds on either side of that thing?'

Abel was right. The sides of the piece of paving stone were fairly regular except for two ragged indentations at opposing points. You wouldn't have noticed them if the stone was in its place amongst the other rough-hewn flags on the floor. But a strong man, preferably a couple of strong men, would have been able to prise the slab from where it was set in the kitchen floor, using these handholds. This would have been useful if you'd wanted access to the drain to inspect it or to clear a blockage. What was odd was that, if the flagstone was intended to be raised, then the simplest thing would have been to set an iron ring in its upper surface. Much simpler than providing a couple of makeshift grips that looked as though they'd scrape your fingers when you grasped them. Unless, of course, one wanted to conceal the fact that this was a secret method of raising the stone and getting into – or out of – the drainage channel.

It was probably because we'd seen the priest-hole in our bedroom that Abel and I simultaneously realized the significance of the flagstone. Combe House had been adapted to conceal the followers of the old religion, or rather of its priests and ministers. There was most likely a secret network of tunnels, channels and hidey-holes throughout the house. Secret, but, of course, known to everybody at Combe. It could hardly be otherwise. No doubt all of its occupants were adherents to the old religion or sympathizers, at least. I remembered that the steward Gully had talked about the house being 'out of the world'. It wasn't only peace and quiet they were looking for but the freedom to persist with the old forms of worship.

William Shaw noticed the direction of my and Abel's

glances. He too looked at the flagstone. He was no fool. He realized what we'd understood.

'We must get him out,' said Mr Shaw, raising his voice to quell the babble.

Silence fell, but no one moved. Perhaps they were reluctant to descend into the drain and grapple with the body. Perhaps each person in the kitchen was waiting for someone else to step forward.

'I'll do it,' said Abel. 'It's a small entrance and I am slight enough. I was familiar with bodies once. I served in the Dutch wars.'

I was proud of my friend. He was showing the stuff that we players are made of. He wasn't far wrong either in drawing attention to his convenient slightness and the narrowness of the entrance to the conduit. Maybe at the same time, by volunteering himself, Abel was drawing attention away from the fact that he and I were the outsiders in the place, that we had our suspicions about Combe and because of that were ourselves objects of suspicion.

Scarcely waiting for Shaw's assent, Abel perched on the edge of the hole and lowered himself into the drain. I went nearer to help. Several of us crowded around the aperture. I became more convinced than ever that this odd means of access to the kitchen conduit was part of the hidden realm of Combe.

Abel found it difficult to manoeuvre himself around the form of the prone man. He leaned forward in the confines of the channel but could not get sufficient purchase on the body to move it more than a few inches. His feet squelched in the mixture of water and detritus at the bottom of the drain.

'A rope,' he called up.

A rope was produced and, after a deal of grunting and muffled cursing, Abel secured it under the arms and around the chest of the dead man. Then, with the help of three of us pulling from the surface, the body was tugged to a position immediately below the hole, raised to a curious bent-backed position, then a standing one, and finally hauled out in a fashion that was inevitably unceremonious and undignified.

Abel Glaze scrambled out, unassisted. He was filthy, his hands and front smeared with slime, mingled with blood and water. He smelled rank. Meantime, the mortal remains of Henry Gifford were laid out on the kitchen flagstones for all to see. And what I could see was that this man had not been drowned or choked by foul vapours but murdered. Now that he was rolled on his back, eyes glassy and mouth gaping in the centre of his blue jowls, there was visible a great gash on his forehead. If there was not more blood on his countenance, it was because it had been washed away in the slop of the drain. I noticed that the members of the family – by this stage the son and daughter had arrived on the scene together with the widow Muriel – as well as the servants reacted with gasps or groans at the sight of Gifford's corpse. But there were no tears, no cries of grief.

Such a fatal wound might have been an accident. Gifford might have slipped and struck his head on a stone ledge while creeping about underneath the house, but my mind straight away leaped to murder. Not the mind of William Shaw, however. He bent over the body, with his wife keeping at a slight distance. After a short scrutiny, Shaw pronounced: 'An accident, a tragic accident.'

He was looking at Abel and me while he said this, as if daring us to question his judgement. He didn't speculate or explain what Gifford had been doing down beneath the kitchen floor, but then, perhaps, in this house of secrets he didn't have to. He gave orders that the body should be removed.

It was evident that we wouldn't be able to leave Combe House just yet. Abel required a wash and a change of clothes, and Mr Shaw was too distracted to arrange for the escort he'd promised us. While Abel went outside to the yard, where there was a well and a hand-pump, I made myself scarce on the upper floor. In truth, I wanted to keep well away from the whole business of the dead tutor-priest, especially if his end had been deliberate, not accidental. I wondered what had happened to the so-called Armageddon Text. I wondered if Henry Gifford's abrupt death was connected to the mysterious black book.

As I was standing in the passageway by our bed-chamber, my musings were interrupted by a whimpering sound. I paused with my hand on the latch. The whimpering was now augmented by the noise of scratching. Further along the passage stood one of Mary Shaw's spaniels, the source of the scratching and whining. Whichever name it went by, whether it was Finder or Keeper, the dog was pawing at the entrance to a room two or three doors along from mine and Abel's.

I walked along to open the door of the room. As I neared the chamber I realized that the dog was anxious to join its mate, since an equivalent whining and scrabbling was coming from the other side. There was a hefty lock on the door, but it wasn't secured. The instant the door widened sufficiently, Finder (or Keeper) slipped out to join his fellow, and the two of them scuttled down the passage without any acknowledgement to their rescuer.

I peered into the room. Though quite small, it was well lit, with a cluster of windows set irregularly in the east-facing wall. The sunlight pouring through was enough to dazzle my eyes. There was a pleasant smell from the herbs strewn on the floor. The room was seemingly a house of office, since there was a close-stool positioned beneath the windows. I looked at the view. In a spirit of curiosity I lifted the lid of the stool. The pierced seat was padded to make it more comfortable for the sitter. It must be for the benefit of the family, since only the Shaws would require privacy and padded seats for their private functions. In fact, they would most likely have a couple of such rooms in a property the size of Combe House. The servants enjoyed a communal privy on the ground floor, to which Abel and I had been directed after our arrival.

Yet there was something odd about this room. Privies, even refined ones for family use, are usually blind and airless places, not equipped with windows that give a fine view over the countryside as this one did. In the other wall was a door, also unlocked. It gave on to a bedroom. This was a large apartment, unusually so for a guest chamber (if that's what it was, rather than a member of the family's, since there appeared to be no personal possessions here). I looked around. There was a wardrobe against one wall. The wardrobe was unlocked and empty. I went to the main door, which led into the passage, and came to one or two conclusions. I returned to the first room and gazed around, particularly at the floor covered with rushes and clippings of rosemary and lavender.

I was on the point of leaving the room when I heard steps coming along the passage. I shrank back, reluctant to emerge. Then I recognized the steps as Abel's. I stepped outside to meet him. He started when he saw me.

'Nick, is that you? I have something to tell you.'

'And I have something to show you,' I said. 'Where is everyone?'

'Safe downstairs. I have been washing myself. And changing my shirt.'

I almost pulled him into the room I'd just emerged from. I shoved the door to. I pointed out the disordered state of the floor coverings, with the rushes and sprigs of rosemary and lavender not neatly spread about but lying in heaps and swirls. Near the close-stool was the outline of a trapdoor. It was difficult to see it straight away because of the light streaming through the windows.

'So?' said Abel. 'It is for emptying the contents of *that* out of the pan beneath the seat and into the house drains.'

By *that* he meant the close-stool.

'It's a large trapdoor for emptying a pan of shit,' I said, bending down and grasping the iron ring set into the floor. The trapdoor swung smoothly open. No sound, no creaks or squeaks. A slanting shaft of stone led down into darkness. A waft of colder air emanated from it, together with a less pleasant odour than that which had filled the room.

'Big enough to take a man . . .,' I said, closing the trapdoor.

'. . . and probably linking to the drain running beneath the kitchen where Gifford was discovered,' said Abel. 'Though I'm not sure I'd care to slide down it.'

'You would if you had to. I think the close-stool normally sits over this trapdoor. It's not deliberate concealment but it draws the eye away from a careful examination of the floor. And when I first came in here I was struck by the number of windows. They're at eyelevel too. The first thing you do when you come in here is to look outside. Your eyes would be filled with the daylight. You wouldn't be likely to bother with the floor.'

'And if you did,' said Abel, 'you would find only a channel going down to the main drain.'

'There's more,' I said. 'Next door is a bedroom, but it is large and somehow empty – apart from the bed. Anonymous too. We're in a recusants' house, Abel. They need somewhere to worship. Their priest needs somewhere to robe himself, and to live and sleep. I think this is where Gifford prepares for Mass – where he prepared for Mass, I should say – and next door is where the family assembles for it.'

'I heard voices last night,' said Abel. 'The Mass would be said at a secret time, the middle of the night.'

'Probably it's also where Henry Gifford slept. We're a long way from the main entrance to the house, and the doors are especially thick here and the locks are solid. If the priest needed to make a quick escape he only had to open the trapdoor and hide in the drains until the pursuivants left.'

'And the bedchamber next door abuts on our room of last night,' said Abel.

'There's probably a space between the walls. That's how Gifford was able to spy on us last night. This place is a honeycomb of false walls and secret places.'

'I haven't told you of my own discoveries yet,' said Abel.

Standing in the room with the close-stool, we leaned towards each other like conspirators.

'I went to wash myself in the yard and then I asked the laundrywoman for a fresh shirt, since mine had got all dirty and bloody while I was down in that kitchen drain. I thought it was the least that Combe House owed me, a clean shirt, since I'd recovered a body for them.'

'Wasn't the laundrywoman willing to give you a shirt?'

'Very willing. She handed me this,' he said, indicating the shirt beneath his doublet. It looked too large for him. 'But when I was in the washroom I noticed a pile of clothes that were due for washing. Some of them had spatters of blood on them.'

'Difficult to get out, bloodstains,' I said.

'You can use salt and water, or milk or even human spit,' said Abel. 'I remember the tire-house man in the Globe telling us so. It may take a couple of washings, but the stains will fade eventually. But that's not the point, Nick. Those items of clothing with the stains were good pieces, doublets and hose and women's bodices. Fine pieces made of brocade, taffeta. They weren't servants' garments. They belong to the Shaws.'

'Perhaps they got their clothes marked when they were attending to Gifford's body.'

'No, these things were already in the washroom. They must have been there before the body was found.'

'So you've made a jump between the bloodstained clothes and a dead man.'

'Wouldn't you?'

'You think the Shaws had a hand in Gifford's death?'

'Don't you?'

'Yes,' I said. 'William Shaw was very quick to declare it was an accident in front of the whole household. Too quick. In fact, I had the impression he was saying it for our benefit.'

'The servants are loyal to the Shaws. They would accept whatever their master or mistress told them. They might even accept a violent death. They would not ask questions about blood-spattered clothes.'

'The sooner we leave this house of murderers the better,' I said.

'There's more,' said Abel. 'I said I'd made discoveries. The bloody clothes weren't all.'

He paused. I thought he was doing it for effect. But he'd heard something in the passageway outside. The scrabbling of claws on the wooden floor. The sound of the spaniels. Then a shushing noise. A woman trying to silence the dogs. Abel and I had been so absorbed in our speculations that we hadn't been conscious of anything beyond the close-stool room. The door was slightly ajar. I'd pushed it to, not latched it.

As one we made for the exit. Too late. In the passage outside was assembled the whole family. Mother and father, son and daughter, the sister-in-law, the steward Gully. How long had they been there? What had they overheard?

Curiously, they had the air of suppliants, as though they'd come not to surprise us but to make a request.

'We must speak to you,' said William Shaw.

VI

We were ushered into the large empty bedchamber, the one that I'd speculated might have been used by the family for hearing Mass. Abel and I stood awkwardly in the middle of the room while the Shaws and Gully clustered about us in a half-circle. Incongruously, the spaniels Finder and Keeper scampered about their heels. I didn't fear the family exactly – the three men surely would not attempt anything against Abel and me in the presence of three women – but it was a very uncomfortable moment. I felt my palms go clammy. Sweat ran down my sides. I cursed Tom Cloke, dead as he was, for ever having introduced us to this house.

'Gentlemen,' said William Shaw. 'We have been listening to your conversation. I heard you, Master Revill, suggest that this was a house of murderers.'

I blushed, as if I was the one guilty of some offence. I opened my mouth to apologize, to justify myself, but Shaw gave an impatient wave of his hand.

'You are wrong. The Shaws are not murderers. Hear

me out. Say nothing until I have finished. Then you may decide on your next step. You have correctly understood the nature of Combe and of my family. We are followers of the old religion. We wish harm to no man or woman, we wish no injury to our country or its rulers. We are not plotters or conspirators, although some would like us to be. Such are the present times that we live under the shadow of suspicion and in constant fear of persecution like other houses in this part of the world.

'Henry Gifford was here as a tutor to sister Muriel's children. But he was principally at Combe to minister to our souls, in this very chamber where we are standing. He is – he was – a recent arrival in Combe, here only a matter of months. He replaced another . . . individual . . . who was a truly good man but who has been called to serve elsewhere. I will not conceal from you the fact that we did not care for Gifford. We felt obliged to give him shelter, however, because of what he was and who he represented.'

Shaw hesitated and glanced at his wife. She took up the story.

'It is true that we have been harbouring a priest,' said Elizabeth Shaw, speaking with more directness than her husband. 'However, we came to believe that Henry Gifford had more worldly aims than the salvation of souls and the cause of the true religion. He talked easily about the death of tyrants and the ousting of lawful kings and encouraged us to talk of such things too.'

She glanced towards her son Robert. I remembered that he'd touched on the subject at yesterday evening's meal. And that Gifford had quickly changed the subject.

'Such talk is dangerous,' said Elizabeth. 'But it was not just talk. Gifford seemed to be in communication with other forces, external forces, who might prefer action to mere words. He received messages, visitors sometimes, that he would not tell us about. This is a quiet and godly house. We live secluded from the world.'

Gully was nodding vigorously. Elizabeth's words were more or less what he'd said to me the previous day. Now William Shaw resumed.

'We heard from a distant kinsman, Thomas Cloke, that he had an ... object ... of great value to deliver to us, or rather not to us but to Henry Gifford. That this was a secret affair was shown by the way the message was conveyed. Nothing was committed to paper, but all was done through hints and whispers. Then in due course you two gentlemen arrived here with Thomas. Alas, our fears were shown to be all too real by the attack on our very doorstep and the violent fate of our kinsman. Gifford seemed not at all concerned by the death but only troubled by the whereabouts of the ... object.'

'It was a book,' said Abel. 'We know about it. A book with covers made of wood and containing verses.'

'Complete gibberish,' I said before Abel could reveal more. 'Couldn't make head or tail of it. Meant nothing to us.'

But William Shaw and the others didn't seem interested in our opinion of the Black Book of Brân or the implication of Abel's words that we'd caught sight of it.

'It brought matters to a head, the death on our doorstep,' said the master of the house. 'We held a family council, for we are, all of us, concerned in this matter. Gully joined us. There are no secrets between the Shaws and their steward.'

Gully looked resolute but also gratified at this

compliment. He would surely have died to preserve this house and its occupants.

'We talked long into the night,' said Mary Shaw, the daughter. 'We came to a fateful decision.'

I drew my breath in, sharp. Was she about to say that they had decided to do away with the priest?

'We determined that he should leave Combe and leave straight away, on this very morning,' said the son, Robert Shaw. 'We came here to tell him so. We made a reasonable request.'

'Merely that he should quit Combe,' said Mary.

'Quit our house today,' said Robert.

I imagined the family arriving as a delegation at Gifford's door. I would not have wanted to face them, so firm, so united.

'Words followed,' said the widow Muriel. It was the first time she had spoken. 'Words followed and then blows.'

'It was my fault, Master Revill, Master Glaze,' said Gully now. 'You should blame me and no member of the family.'

William Shaw put a hand on Gully's arm, but the steward shrugged it off and continued.

'I could not bear to hear Gifford say things against the family that was harbouring him. He called us traitors and apostates. He was holding the black book in one hand and the cross in the other.'

Gully raised both arms, clutching an imaginary cross and book in imitation of the priest. I noticed he referred to 'us traitors'.

'He was holding a large cross made of brass,' said William Shaw. 'It was stored in that cupboard over there. Henry Gifford was brandishing the sign of our salvation. He was speaking low and soft, but his voice was as full of venom as the sting of a snake. He kept on saying, "You shall not have it, you shall not have it".'

'The cross?' said Abel.

'Not the cross, but the book brought here by Cloke,' said Elizabeth. 'My husband asked him how he had laid hands on the thing, since Thomas had been shot and his goods and horse stolen before arriving at Combe. Henry Gifford claimed that the book was already in *your* grasp and that he had taken it from your bedchamber yesterday.'

'That part is true enough,' I said. 'But the book was hardly in our grasp. Abel and I brought it to Combe without knowing it. Thomas Cloke had slipped it into one of our bags earlier in the journey – perhaps because he expected to be attacked.'

It was easy to be honest. I no longer felt in any danger from the Shaws and their steward. They were too busy accounting for their actions, as if we were justices. It was William who continued.

'I approached Henry Gifford. Perhaps he thought I was about to take the wretched book from him. He became like a man possessed. He raised the cross higher in the air and made to bring it down on my head. I moved back in time and he missed but it was a wicked stroke. Then he held out the cross, half in threat, half in supplication.'

'I came forward,' said Gully. 'I thought I could reason with Gifford. But as Mr Shaw says, he was possessed. The priest must have believed that I too was attempting to take the book from him, for he lunged at me and I stumbled and fell back on the floor. Then Mistress Mary here stepped forward to help me, and Gifford lashed out at her too.'

'It is true,' said the daughter of the house. 'I tremble to remember it.'

'I was angry now,' said William. He was stroking his beard. His eyes were prominent. 'There was a tussle and one of us wrested the cross away from Gifford and struck *him* a great blow across the forehead.'

'It was I who struck him,' said Gully, 'and although I am ashamed that I should have put the instrument of our salvation to such an impious use, I trust that He who sits above and judges all our actions will absolve me of any murderous intent. I acted in defence of this family – and in defence of myself, of course.'

There was no defiance in the steward's tone. Merely a plain statement of what had occurred in this chamber, the place where the family was accustomed to make its religious observances. Abel and I heard how Henry Gifford had staggered back, hardly able to see on account of the blood gushing from the wound in his forehead. It seemed that he was not so badly injured for, under the gaze of the distressed and distracted Shaws, he made a stumbling escape from the close-stool chamber, using the trapdoor and sliding down the stone chute that led to the drains and sewers of Combe.

He was still clutching the book as if his life depended on it. William Shaw likened Gifford's disappearance to that of a rat creeping back into its hole, as if he would naturally retreat down the shaft rather than try a more orthodox exit. Perhaps he thought in his panic that the Shaws would try to stop him getting away from Combe.

Did they in fact try to stop him? No, said Elizabeth, they were horror-struck at the scene. Did they think they'd seen the last of him? Yes, explained William, since he had got his hands on the black book and no longer cared a fig for the spiritual welfare of the house, if he ever had. There were various secret exits from Combe, including a grille which covered the outlet from the drain under the kitchen and which might be removed to give access to the moat. From there a determined or desperate man could swim or wade his way to safety.

That was what they thought – and hoped! – had happened to Henry Gifford. He wasn't so grievously wounded after all. He'd escaped from Combe House, clutching his precious book. They'd never see him again. They'd be left to the peace and quiet of their estate. At this time the family were still in their day clothes – they had debated into the night whether and how they should confront Gifford – and they now discovered that their garments were spattered with the priest's blood. They discarded their clothes and put on their night attire.

But Gifford had not got away. Whether he was more badly wounded than they assumed, whether he'd harmed himself in his descent down through the drains, he had evidently tried to emerge inside the kitchen, via the flagstone. His life fading, he had managed to dislodge the stone but did not have the strength to push it away and climb out. So Gifford expired face down in the muck and slop of the kitchen drains.

His discovery was almost as much a shock to the Shaws as it was to the servants of Combe. But not quite as much. William had pronounced the death an accident, knowing that his people would not question his opinion, but he observed the suspicion on Abel's face and my own. So they had decided to give this full account of the previous night, a resolution that was strengthened when they overheard my reference to a 'house of murderers'.

Later, I asked myself why it meant so much to the Shaws (and to Gully) that a pair of wandering players should listen to their story of how a corrupt priest had tried to steal a black-bound volume and then resorted to violence to keep it in his hands. It was as if we were justices and jury. And then I realized that the Shaws were appearing not in front of Abel Glaze and Nick Revill but before the bar of their own consciences. It wasn't we who had to acquit them. Only they could acquit themselves. Their extended confession took place while Finder and Keeper skittered about the room until, growing tired, they fell in heaps in a corner.

There were a couple more questions.

What had happened to the cross, the one that had inflicted the head-wound on Henry Gifford?

No longer sanctified, it had been thrown into the moat, where it promptly sank.

And the book, the black book?

The Shaws did not want to know what had happened to it. The book, whose contents were unknown to them, had brought trouble to Combe. It had, presumably, led to the murder of their kinsman Cloke and to the frantic avarice of Gifford to possess it. Whatever the book was, it was not a sacred thing to be consulted and revered. Good riddance if it was down in the mud and muck of the house drains. Not that they were even aware of its title, but the Armageddon Text could stay in the mire until doomsday. It was I who had asked the question about the book's whereabouts and I reflected that, because of Gifford's explanation, we two players probably knew more about it than anyone else in the room.

And that was that. William Shaw directed half a dozen of his burliest serving men to accompany us a few miles along the road. The parting that we had with the Shaws was a formal one, neither warm nor cold. We were privy to their secrets but, even had we been inclined to, there would be little purpose in alerting the authorities to the demise of the priest. In fact, by helping him to his death, the Shaws had shown themselves loyal Englishmen and Englishwomen. They wanted no part in the seditious talk and rumours of plots which were swilling around this part of the country. The body of the priest, which was presently being washed and laid out, would be decently buried with the appropriate obsequies.

'Decently.' That was William Shaw's word, and I think it applied to the whole household. They were decent people, well-to-do, God-fearing, honest and honourable and law-abiding, except insofar as they observed the older religious practices.

Shaw gave Abel a couple of sovereigns not so much as a way of buying his silence as in gratitude to my friend for helping to fish Gifford out of the kitchen drain. Mary Shaw expressed the hope that my uncle would still be alive by the time I got to Shipston on Stour. (I confess I'd forgotten my uncle and namesake in all the excitement.)

We rode out of the valley scarcely twenty-four hours after we'd arrived at Combe House. We had our escort of liveried servants, who rode fore and aft of us. I was glad of this as we retraced our passage through the belt of trees where we'd been ambushed the day before. There was no sign of the black-garbed men nor any trace of our companion Thomas Cloke, though I'd been half-expecting to see his body tossed casually into the undergrowth by the wayside. Surely, when they discovered that he wasn't carrying what they were searching for, they would have no further use for his corpse?

As we reached the rim of the valley, Abel and I turned to look back at Combe. The house lay, jewel-like, in its moat. The birds were singing while a breeze was combing the trees. The day was clear. You would not have thought that a murder had taken place so recently in the precincts of Combe nor that another man had met a violent end inside the house.

The main road was in sight. A band of travellers was trotting along, their passage raising swirls of dust. There were a dozen or more of them – all classes, to judge from their clothes – enough to deter all but the most violent robbers. This was probably the reason why they were travelling together in the first place. Anyway, Abel and I decided to take our chances by following in their wake. In truth, since no danger was in prospect, we wanted to part company from the liveried escorts and be about our own business.

So we cantered on, thinking we'd left the whole raft of priests, agents and recusants well behind us. At least I did. After a couple of hours our stomachs told us it was time for refreshment, and we reined in on a patch of ground, which, though surrounded by woodland, was not far from a scatter of cottages. We had bread and cheese and ale from Combe, so we tethered our horses while we sat on the grass and talked about everything that had happened over the last day and night.

It was then that Abel Glaze revealed his final surprise, the second of the discoveries he'd been about to broach to me in the chamber when we were interrupted by the Shaws.

He had the book with him, the Armageddon Text, the bloody Black Book of Brân.

VII

'Jesus, Abel, what are you doing with that?'

Abel had retrieved the book from his bag. It sat between us on the grass, a tainted thing. Abel's pride in pulling off a neat trick had turned to unease when he saw my reaction.

'I took it from the kitchen drain. When I was down

there with that Gifford, what should I see lying next to his body but this what do you call it? This Armageddon Text? While everyone was busy getting the body laid out on the kitchen flags, I tucked the book under my doublet so's no one should see it and climbed out.'

'In God's name, why didn't you leave it where it was? That's what the Shaws wanted. Or rather, they never wanted to see the bloody thing again. I don't want to see it either.'

Abel looked so crestfallen that his long nose actually seemed to quiver.

'I thought it was valuable.'

'I don't know about valuable, but it's certainly dangerous.'

I looked around as if we might be being spied on at that very instant. We were in sight of the road, but there were no riders close. The party of travellers had passed into the distance. I started because I thought I detected a movement in a nearby clump of trees and bushes, but it was nothing, only a pigeon taking flight.

'All right,' said Abel. 'I'll leave it here. Throw it into those bushes.'

'You can't do that.'

'But you just said—'

'I know what I said. But you can't discard the book now. We're lumbered with it.'

'Perhaps it's fate, Nick.'

I was about to say what I thought of fate, and in a particularly pithy way too, when I was distracted again by a stir in the nearby trees. More pigeons taking flight.

But not only pigeons. From the shelter of the trees there emerged, with much rustling and crashing, a band of men. Black-clad men. And not four this time, but five. One of them went to stand sentry at the roadside, while the others approached us.

Abel and I had already jumped to our feet. We had no weapons. Our horses were tethered several yards away. As I said, there were a handful of houses in view but no sign of any of the occupants. In any case, I don't think these tough and resolute-looking men would have been distracted from their purpose by the presence of a few locals. We were trapped.

All this flashed through my head, and probably Abel's as well. But it wasn't the principal thought in my mind. Instead, I stood there, mouth hanging open like an idiot, heart hammering away in my chest, the blood roaring in my ears. For striding towards us was the figure of Thomas Cloke. The dead man, whom I'd seen the previous day shot off his horseback perch and tumbling to the ground. The late Thomas Cloke who, out of cowardice or prudence, had slipped the Armageddon Text into Abel's case. Not a ghost but a living, breathing, grinning piece of flesh.

Cloke walked with that familiar bounce. He was enjoying the looks of disbelief on our faces. He was wearing the same gear as on the previous day except for a clean shirt replacing the one that had been soaked in his own blood.

'Yes,' he said. 'It is I, Thomas Cloke.'

The other three men stood slightly to his rear, suggesting that Cloke was their leader. Two of them were carrying muskets. At the edge of the road, the fourth man kept watch against passers-by. I glanced sideways at Abel. He looked too dumbstruck to speak. So I felt it was incumbent on me to make some remark, to say something halfway intelligent.

'You've been planning this a long time, Master Cloke?' I said, even managing to strike a casual note.

'A combination of planning and the willingness to seize an opportunity,' he said. 'When I heard that you and Abel Glaze were to visit the Midlands, we thought it would be a good moment to put a particular . . . plan into effect.'

Cloke glanced down at the black-bound book where it lay neglected on the grass. The book that he'd secreted in Abel's bag. The book that was surely part of the mysterious plan he referred to.

'We?' said Abel, finding his voice. 'Who's *we*?'

'A certain group connected with the Council,' said Cloke. 'A private group.'

He meant the Privy Council. More specifically, he meant those agents of the Council under the direct control of Robert Cecil. Little Cecil, recently ennobled (again) and now the Earl of Salisbury. Wrynecked Cecil who had his fingers in more pies than you could count. Crookback Cecil, who ran a network of spies and intelligencers in the name of national security. I had encountered Robert Cecil once at the time of the Essex uprising in Queen Elizabeth's dying days. The thought of those days – and of Cecil in particular – was enough to make my guts do a little dance. I tried to keep this from showing on my face, but no doubt Cloke was accustomed to the reaction prompted by any mention of the Council.

'I thought you were our friend, Thomas,' said Abel. 'I thought you enjoyed being in our company and attending our plays.'

'I did not object to your company and I am a devotee of the playhouse. But some things are more important than friendship, Master Glaze.'

'You are not even Thomas Cloke,' I said. 'Tell the truth – your name is not Cloke.' Abel turned to look at me. The other man said nothing so I ploughed on, more confident in my theory. 'The Shaws were surprised when I told them that their kinsman was a playgoer. He is not, but *you* are. So who are you, Master . . . ?'

'Never mind,' said the man we'd thought of as Thomas Cloke.

'Is there really a Thomas Cloke?' said Abel, and then, realizing the question was foolish (since the Shaws had willingly acknowledged Cloke as their kinsman), he asked instead: 'What has happened to the real Cloke? Is he dead?'

'Alive and well, as far as I know,' said the man who wasn't Cloke. 'I took on his name as a means of getting close to Combe House. Cloke is indeed a cousin to that nest of recusants.'

'But you could not get too near the house or the family, could you?' I said. It was all becoming clear to me. I had to struggle to keep the admiration out of my voice, admiration at the neatness of the scheme concocted by the 'private group' of the Council. 'For some reason you wanted to convey that item to Combe, but you had to make yourself scarce before you got there. Otherwise they would have recognized you – or *not* recognized you as Cloke.'

'Very good, Nicholas.'

'You pretended that your companions now, these gentlemen, were actually your pursuers. You put on a good act of being fearful so that when we were ambushed – and you were apparently killed – we'd accept it without question.'

'Good again, Master Revill.'

'So what did you use for your imaginary wound? The fatal wound?'

'You recall our chat in the Knight of the Carpet? The two of you had just come offstage from playing in *The Melancholy Man.* You did a good death scene, Nicholas, you with your bladder of sheep's blood and all that writhing about. Well, what did you think of *my* death scene, eh? The shot that rings out in the woods, the pool of blood that spreads across the chest of the victim, the way he huddles over his horse's neck, the manner in which he falls helplessly to the ground. I used sheep's blood too. Convincing, eh? Do you think Master Shakespeare and the other shareholders would give me a place with the King's Men?'

'No,' said Abel. 'There's more to being a player than dying well.'

'Sir!'

It was the man stationed by the road. He gestured in the direction we'd come from, to the south-east. I noticed the way he addressed Cloke as 'sir'. The other three stiffened and one of the musket-holders took a sudden interest in his weapon.

'Why did you go to such lengths? What was it all about? Was it on account of that book there?'

I asked partly out of genuine curiosity but also to distract 'Thomas Cloke' from whatever he planned to do with us. He spoke with great certainty and command. He was quite different from the man I'd encountered in a couple of taverns, quite different from the idle follower of the players. But he was human enough to be proud of his trickery. And the longer he talked, the greater the chance of some travellers passing.

'On account of that book? No, not directly. The Armageddon Text – as they are pleased to call it – is useful to smoke out renegades and traitors. There was one such in Combe House.'

'Henry Gifford?' said Abel.

'That was one of his names, but he was no more a Gifford than I am a Cloke.'

'You know the priest is dead, then,' I said.

'We have heard. We did not stir far from Combe last night or this morning. We became . . . aware . . . that a man had died in the house. But he was no priest. Or if he was, it was merely a cover for worse work. Gifford was an agent for our old enemies.'

'Old enemies? The Spanish? I thought we were at peace with them. A treaty was signed last year.'

The Council man smiled slightly as if in pity at my ignorance or naivety. 'Oh, we are at a formal peace, Nicholas. But there are elements on their side who are conspiring with sects over here . . .'

'So the whole business was a means of smoking out this Gifford?'

'You have hit on it. We knew that the Armageddon Text would be irresistible to Gifford . . . for reasons I do not wish to enlarge on. It smoked him out, as you said. What we could not have counted on was such a happy result after the smoking-out. That Gifford would perish in Combe House. One less of them!'

'Cloke' snapped his fingers to reinforce his last words. The man at the roadside called out in greater alarm. He unclasped his raised hand twice to show that a substantial number of travellers was moving up the road.

'Now if you'll just surrender the Armageddon Text, Abel,' he said. 'It is a dangerous volume, ripe for sects and factions.'

Abel bent down to pick up the black book. It had grass stains on the wooden cover, to join the other marks of use. My friend handed it to our erstwhile companion, who said: 'We will leave you now. You have played your part as true Englishmen, whether you meant to or not. But, Nicholas and Abel, do not enquire into this matter any further. There is a very serious threat to our land, but with the help of this black volume we shall smoke out more of the traitors.'

The individual we'd known as Thomas Cloke vanished into the trees together with his retinue. A couple of minutes later, another large party rode past the clearing, and Abel and I remounted and trotted off in their wake. I can't speak for Abel, but it took many miles before I stopped looking over my shoulder and grasping my reins tight. Had we seen the last of the Armageddon Text? I devoutly hoped so.

There were a couple of sequels to our excursion at Combe House, one private and sad, the other public and terrifying.

After Abel and I parted company, I reached Shipston on Stour in time to see my dying uncle and his wife Margaret. She was profuse in her thanks for my arrival. He, poor fellow, was scarcely in a condition to recognize me or anyone else. But he was a Revill, and a Nicholas to boot, and he was my father's true brother. With a moist eye, I saw the likeness in his drawn face. He clutched my hand and mumbled some words before I was shooed out of the room so that a priest could administer the final rites.

Yes, my uncle also was an adherent of the old religion. It was on account of his faith that he had fallen out with my father or vice versa. All this I had from Margaret. My father, an unforgiving man in some ways, had cut himself off from his only sibling, had never spoken to him, had never attempted to communicate with him.

Margaret had seen my name on a playbill she had picked up in Oxford a couple of years previously. The Chamberlain's Men, as we then were, had played Oxford at a period when plague closed the London theatres. Margaret Revill had been struck by the coincidence of names. When she showed the bill to her husband, he remarked that John, my father, had himself been drawn towards the stage-play world in his young days. (This was amazing to me. My father was stout in his abhorrence of the stage. But then I reflected on the way in which people's passions can change violently to their contrary and it became less amazing.) Anyway, the coincidence of names and my father's one-time ardour for acting had been enough for Margaret to write at her husband's dictation a letter addressed to me at the Theatre, London. Nicholas was on his deathbed and he was eager to see his nephew, having no surviving children of his own. So even if he was not absolutely sure who I was, I hope I brought some comfort to his dying moments.

The other event was more momentous. The cryptic lines in the Armageddon Text about parleyment and sparks and fires were a prediction of the powder-treason which caused such a stir in the land later that year. When the attempt was made to destroy parleyment, Abel and I at once remembered that verse which I had laboriously copied out and translated. We could scarcely look each other in the eye for a time, as if we were the guilty ones!

It was said that the plot and plotters, both lay and priest, were nurtured in houses very similar to Combe. I am sure that was true. But we two humble players were less certain about the part played by the Black Book of Brân. When Abel and I did eventually talk together after the powder-treason was revealed in the November of 1605, we conversed in low tones and whispers. Like everyone else, we were outraged by the attempt to destroy our king and the members of parleyment (to say nothing of those innocents who would have been caught up in the slaughter).

As you know, the plot was thwarted and no lives were forfeit except those of the plotters. But in our hints and whispers Abel and I couldn't help wondering how long beforehand the authorities had been aware of the conspiracy, whether, in fact, they might have been instrumental in bringing it to a head so that it could be lanced like a boil.

In this counter-plot against the powder-plot, it was useful to both sides to have possession of the black-bound volume, the Armageddon Text. For the plotters, the prediction of the ruin of parleyment gave validity to what they were trying to do. See, they could say, this event was foreseen hundreds of years ago by an Irish monk, divinely inspired. While for men like Robert Cecil and his agent 'Thomas Cloke', the existence of the book and the 'parleyment' verse in particular was proof of the other side's wicked purposes and a useful means of smoking out traitors. Those who suffered were people like the Shaws, decent and honourable families who simply wanted to live and worship as they had always done. No doubt they were under special scrutiny now. My uncle too, had he survived, might have been added to the catalogue of suspects.

But I kept this line of thinking to myself. It was not a good time to voice doubts about the activities of the Privy Council nor to express fellow feeling with adherents of the old religion. The world slipped back to black and white, as it does from time to time.

I wondered what had happened to the Black Book of Brân. The man who wasn't Cloke had carted it off, no doubt taking it back to London, where it might cause further mischief. I wondered too what was contained in the rest of the volume, what other disasters and catastrophes it predicted. Best not to know, I thought. If the disasters were in the past, they had already happened and the world had survived. And if Armageddon was still to come – and we are promised it will come – well, then, it would come despite anything that Nicholas Revill might do. With luck, he would not be around to see it. I shouldn't think you would feel any different.

ACT SIX

March 2135

Five hundred thirty years, then God returns to save
His chosen, once the sinful have been purged.
Their wicked cities flayed by burning sun and
drowned in purging flood,
And at the end a sun-bright fire of blood.

I

The news on the radio that morning was bad. Shiva listened to it as he dressed. The giant rivers carrying meltwater from the remnant Antarctic ice sheet had risen again; another metre rise in sea levels was predicted for the decade. Locally, the newscaster reported that changes in seabed currents around the drowned Sizewell B power station had brought increased radioactivity in the sea around the eastern English islands. Shiva thought ruefully that in coming to Yorkshire for his holiday he had only placed himself in a different kind of danger from that which he faced in his work. Like most English people, Shiva wore a radiation ring; Alice had given it to him, a heavy gold ring with a circle in the middle. The circle turned red if the radiation in the atmosphere approached dangerous levels. It was the usual safe dark green this morning, but he would avoid the fish tonight.

On the windowsill he had set his foot-high copper statue of Shiva, the Indian god after whom he was named, a young man dancing inside a circle of fire, keeping the world in existence, in balance. It was a thing of beautiful symmetry, brought by an ancestor from India. Although Shiva had no religion, he liked to sit contemplating it. The face of the four-armed god was enigmatic, with a secret smile.

There was a beeping sound from the computer on the table. Shiva frowned. The POWER OFF switch could be overridden only by an urgent official message. Hastily buttoning his kaftan, he crossed to his machine and opened it up. A single, short message in his receive-box, unsigned:

> Please attend EU Commissioner Williams at Commission HQ, Victoria Square, Birmingham, today 21.3.35 at 9 p.m. Fast motorboat arriving to collect 10 a.m. Please confirm receipt.

Shiva hesitated, then pressed the ACKNOWLEDGE button. Ten a.m. – he had only an hour. He looked thoughtfully at the blank screen. A commissioner rather than his superintendent? And a motorboat, eating into the Commission's petrol ration? This was something urgent.

He walked outside. A pair of canaries took off from the bush beside the chalet. The air was crisp and clear, the heat of the day hours off. A palm-shaded walkway led past the other chalets, the rising sun glinting at an angle on their solar panels. Nearby, dwarfing the young coconut palms with its steeple, stood a square-towered Norman church. There had been a village here for a thousand years and there still was, a cluster of low earthhouses, the blades of their little windmills clacking gently in the morning breeze, chickens and skinny goats poking for food in the dusty street. The space between the chalets was closely planted with vegetable gardens; every patch of fertile ground on earth was planted now.

A tall red-haired man, an inspector from Wales, stood in the doorway of the next chalet, cup in hand, enjoying the early cool. Shiva nodded and walked past him, down to the sea. He had spoken little to his fellow vacationers since his arrival a week ago. The hurt look Marwood gave him as he was led down from the dock kept coming back to him in the middle of conversations.

The sea was nearby; the island was small, only a few miles across. Warm surf splashed on the rocky shore, and the water, deep and blue, stretched westwards to the Pennines. A clipper passed in the distance, tall and stately. In the far distance was a vague white blob. Shiva fixed his eyes on it. A couple of days before, he had seen, through binoculars, the twin towers of York Minster rising sixty feet from the water. Most of the high twentieth-century buildings of London had collapsed as the sea rose around them; he had seen films of the toppled steel skeletons leaning against each other, a crazy giant latticework in the water. Yet the medieval minster still stood, resisting monsoons and hurricanes.

The Great Catastrophe of the Twenty-First Century. On the computer, the documentaries and discussion programmes were endless. Shaky footage of huge refugee boats being bombed out of the water as they crossed into European territorial waters; the migrant wars in the Alpine foothills; the mushroom clouds as Chinese missiles rained on Moscow, China's reply to the Russian nuclear attack on the millions marching into Siberia from the flooded northern provinces.

Watching these programmes, the human race endlessly scratched its great wound, assuaging guilt, perhaps, or simply seeking contact with the dead billions.

Many cursed the people of earlier generations for their refusal to act before the changes spiralled out of all control, and the worst, the very worst predictions of climate change came true. Scientists had warned that the great stores of methane hydrates on the seabed could erupt to the surface as the seas warmed, and in the 2040s they did, the oceans boiling, throwing millions of tons of methane into the air. Runaway chaos followed, worsened when the Antarctic icecap started to melt, destabilizing the tectonic plate on which the continent rested and causing huge earthquakes that sent hundred-mile sheets of ice sliding into the sea.

Humanity almost died. In the catastrophe that followed, whole regions disappeared as the seas rose nearly two hundred feet. The equatorial regions grew too hot for human life, while in most of the temperate zones the unstable rains finally stopped for ever and desert took over. Great waves of people moved north; the USA invaded Canada; China invaded Siberia; southern Europe invaded northern Europe. Populations ravaged by disease and hunger sought to make lake-strewn peat bogs of melted permafrost habitable. The world's population shrank to a hundred million, less than in biblical times.

Now, after fifty years of stability, it was starting to rise again. In Canada and China there were advances every year in creating artificial soils for the Arctic regions; there were even experiments in laying artificial soil on the bare rock of ice-free Greenland. After years of chaos and authoritarian rule, the European Union and America had returned to democracy; even China had an elected government now, millennia of authoritarian tradition shaken out in the great flight north. Other than the three major states, a few small countries dotted the habitable regions of the earth; a residual Canada proudly maintaining its independence in Newfoundland; a relict Japan withdrawn into medieval obscurantism on Sakhalin Island. South of the equator, connected to the north by the internet but physically almost unreachable because of the unendurable heat in the tropics that made travel by boat impossible, were Patagonia and the Tasman Islands – Tasmania and New Zealand, where the surviving population of Australia had taken refuge. Everywhere, even in the refugee camps, disease was declining, and harvest failures were fewer as the climate stabilized. The seas still rose, but very slowly now; near the drowned nuclear power stations they were irradiated, but in most places to less than fatal levels. Fish stocks too were rising again in the traumatized oceans. Order had returned, as had police forces like the European Fraud Investigation Office for which Shiva worked.

In the distance he saw another smudge on the horizon. It grew bigger, and an unfamiliar buzzing sound became audible in the distance. The petrol boat, coming for him.

It was a small boat with a single boatman. It was not a true petrol boat; it had a fuel-cell engine and sails but also an old outboard motor, still allowed under licence when a trip required speed. It was a government boat, the burly middle-aged man in the stern wearing the blue badge with yellow stars of the European Union on his dirty cotton smock. He was surly; when Shiva passed him his suitcase he asked if he had bricks in it. No, Shiva wanted to reply, only a copper god. The man started the engine, and Shiva grasped the rail as the boat sped out to sea, the little island fading away to a green dot and vanishing.

It grew hot on the water. Shiva went into the little cabin to escape the heat, though the unfamiliar stink of petrol was nauseating. He lay down on a bench and presently slept.

He awoke to the sound of angry cries and something hitting the side of the boat. He jumped up and looked out of the cabin window. A large sailing boat was passing nearby, and a group of teenagers was hurling the contents of a compost-pail at the petrol boat. A rotten potato hit the window frame, its smelly inside spattering Shiva's kaftan.

He went outside. Already they had passed the sailing-boat, but the cries of the youngsters followed them. 'Stinking polluters! Petrol kills!' The boatman, sitting at the tiller, stared back impassively, then suddenly shouted: 'What about keeping compost? Think what they'd give for that in Siberia!'

'They're protesting a hundred years too late,' Shiva said.

'Kids always protest. You should see the hoops I have to go through to get my little drop of fuel. And I'm government.' The boatman looked at him. 'They must want you urgently in Brum. I've got a railway pass to give you at the other end. You police?'

'Yes.'

'Wish boatmen had their own holiday island.'

'It's for other officials too. I wasn't enjoying it. I don't mind getting back to work.'

The answer seemed to please the man. He reached beneath his seat and pulled out a basket. Shiva saw fruit and dried fish. 'Want some lunch?' he asked.

'I'll have some fruit.'

They sailed on, over drowned Lincolnshire, thirty fathoms below.

*

An hour later they passed Nottingham, with its crowded wharves, and entered West Midlands Bay, sailing past the towering Pennine hills and down the narrowing bay to the new port below Lichfield. The boatman steered the little craft expertly between the passenger and cargo boats and tied up at the big wooden wharf. He helped Shiva out on to the land. He handed Shiva his railway pass, then shook his hand warmly in farewell – to Shiva's surprise, for they had scarcely spoken since their shared meal.

Shiva followed a sign to the railway station. Passengers were already boarding the train to Birmingham. He heaved his suitcase on board and glanced at his watch. Quarter to seven. He would be early.

On the journey he shared a first-class carriage with two young women wearing well-cut linen jackets who looked like officials. He took his suitcase to the lavatory and changed into his somewhat crumpled suit. When he returned, the women were studying a scientific report and looked up at him irritably. He sat and looked out of the window as they continued discussing drainage problems on Scottish mountain soils. The train clattered along the tracks, the electric motor humming softly. Outside the open windows, immaculately tended fields of rice and cotton, bananas and the new tropical wheat passed by; palm groves sheltered the villages of single-storey earth-walled houses, with solar panels, interspersed with little clusters of old brick buildings, windmills turning everywhere. Everything was suffused with red from the setting sun. The rusting hulk of one of the old combine harvesters stood in a field where it had been abandoned ninety years before, a relic of the Age of Extravagance.

Shiva remembered his last visit to the capital, for Marwood's trial. He had not given evidence, because if his face appeared in the newspapers he could never do undercover work again, but he sat in the public gallery on the day of the verdict. It was the rainy season, and the courtroom was muggy and sticky. Rain lashed down outside, spattering the windows. The evidence of fraud was overwhelming, and though the trial had lasted for four weeks the jury took only half an hour to reach a verdict. Sentenced to ten years, Marwood had shouted from the dock that he was innocent, this was not justice. Staring around wildly, he saw Shiva and from his look Shiva saw that, despite all Marwood had done, all the evidence of lies and deceit, he somehow believed he was innocent and that Shiva, the employee who had become a friend, had betrayed him from some unfathomable, base motive.

The train slowed as they approached the city. More old houses now, though still interspersed with modern earthhouses, and fields and vegetable gardens where once industrial sites had stood. Then they were in the warren of the old city centre. Shiva hauled his heavy suitcase out into New Street, loud with voices and bicycle bells, the buzz of electric cars and the clip-clop of horses' hooves. Huge nineteenth-century buildings loomed over him.

Dusk was deepening into darkness, and behind the streets generators hummed as the dim streetlights came on. The passers-by were mostly white but with a heavy sprinkling of other colours, the English racial mix frozen when immigration ended in 2020. People looked hot and tired, waiting for the monsoon.

Shiva entered Victoria Square. Great pillared and porticoed edifices, monuments to nineteenth-century civic pride, still stood. The old Council House was now the administrative centre for the European Union.

One of the guards standing outside the Council

House let him in. Inside, the building was crowded, cavernous old rooms partitioned into hundreds of small offices. A receptionist at the front desk made a telephone call, and an elderly clerk came and led him into the great warren.

Shiva was taken up a flight of stairs, blue-uniformed guards at the top and bottom, to one of the original offices where long-dead councillors once held sway. Behind a large battered desk strewn with papers, a white-haired man in a yellow cotton suit and black, wing-collared shirt sat reading papers by the light of an antique standard lamp. He was thin, his cheekbones prominent under sallow skin. He rose and shook Shiva's hand with a cold, dry clasp. His eyes were blue-grey, piercing. Behind him on the wall was a map of Europe, a thin band of habitable land coloured green between the blue of the seas and the yellow of the deserts, the irradiated zone at the eastern border coloured dull grey.

'Inspector Moorthy. You made good time. I am Commissioner Williams.' He spoke in the clipped, military tones that officials had adopted to deal with the endless crises of the Catastrophe and which had now become an affectation.

'Caught a train as soon as we landed.' Shiva responded in the same manner.

'Good, good.' Williams waved him to a chair before the desk. 'Moorthy, that's a southern Indian name, I think?'

'Some of my forebears came to England after Indian independence.'

Williams nodded, then glanced at his watch. 'I'd like to talk now, got a meeting at 22.30. Afterwards you can rest; there's accommodation for you here. Sorry to have interrupted your holiday,'

'I was getting bored.'

The commissioner looked at him with interest. 'I would have thought after the Green World trial you'd need a rest. Good to see Marwood go down, by the way. These people who say they've found magic solutions to all our problems waste a lot of time and money. Formula for a new type of artificial soil, wasn't it? For greening the Norwegian mountains?'

Shiva was sure the commissioner knew the story, but Williams listened attentively as he told it again, the lamp making deep shadows in the lines of the old man's face.

'Green World said they'd made a breakthrough. A soil with a high ratio of sand to organic components, easy to produce in large quantities. They had apparent good results with experiments in Canada, and the Norwegian government gave them a contract. Science Office had doubts, but the Commission didn't back them.' He was criticizing the Commission, but there was no point in gilding the lily; it had all been in the press.

When he was finished, Williams's face looked sad and tired. 'So eager to solve our problems,' he said. 'Makes us vulnerable to tricks. Snake-oil salesman. The Norwegians want their mountains farmed, the Commission wants a Europe independent of Chinese soil technology. I argued against giving Green World a licence. Overruled.' He raised an eyebrow. 'Mr Marwood addressed the commissioners; he was very plausible.'

'He had the greatest skill a confidence trickster can have.'

'Which is?'

'He believed that what he was saying was true when he said it, and that somehow it became true *because* he said it.' Again he remembered Marwood's face at the trial, frantic and accusing.

'How did your people get you into Green World?'

'Marwood was looking for a head of public relations and I applied. He had an interest in nineteenth-century furniture – his house was full of the stuff – so I read up on it. He liked educated people working for him, giving him admiration. It took a year, but I managed to get papers out showing the Canadian results were doctored.'

The commissioner studied him closely. 'What was it like? Working closely with him, when you knew what he was?'

Shiva smiled sadly. 'I came to like him. He had a sort of infectious optimism. He came up from nothing, you know; he was brought up in an orphanage.'

'So were many of us. But it must have made it hard, if you liked him.'

'You always have to remember that the people you're spying on are telling lies for themselves, while you're telling yours for higher ends.' He met the commissioner's appraising gaze.

'And fear? You must worry about what might happen if you are ever found out.'

'You have to live with that. Some agents even enjoy it.'

'But not you.'

'No.'

There was silence for a moment. The sound of voices came faintly from the crowded street, the neigh of a horse.

'Your ancestry is mixed Indian and English, I believe?' the commissioner asked abruptly.

'My father's forebears were Indian. My mother's were English. With a dash of something else.'

'Most of us have a dash of something else, I guess. In you the Indian genes look predominant. Your parents are dead, I think.'

'In the Guildford smallpox outbreak five years ago.'

'Yes. We thought we had the disease under control; that outbreak was a shock. No other relatives?'

'No.' You must know this, Shiva thought. You've obviously seen my file.

'Ever searched for ancestors on the internet?' Williams asked. 'So many do.'

'No. You can end up building a bond with some distant relative you don't like.' Shiva paused. 'And I don't like looking at the records. Seeing how many billions died.'

The commissioner nodded. 'That must be especially hard if you have ancestors from the destroyed nations. Like India. Though some people spend all their time researching their past these days. Becomes an obsession. Didn't have time for that when I was young. Too busy trying to rebuild.'

'Yes.'

'In the last fifty years we've come very far. The main diseases are coming under control, and we no longer face a crisis after a bad harvest – in Europe, anyway. Relations with America and China tolerable if not close. The refugee camps are emptying, most going to Norway and Iceland. But there are still threats. The continued warming, the irradiated waters, the nuclear arsenals the three powers took north with them.' He looked at Shiva. 'And now another old danger is coming back. Religious fundamentalism.'

'That hasn't been a threat for a long time,' Shiva said. He remembered his mother talking about the sectarian violence after the British left India; Hindus and Sikhs against Muslims.

Commissioner Williams raised his eyebrows. 'So we thought. Religion's mostly gone contemplative since the Catastrophe, Muslims turning to Sufism and Christianity with its little utopian communities contemplating God in the desert fringes. But something different is on the rise down south.'

'The Black Book people?' Shiva asked. 'I thought they were a bit of a joke.'

'In Europe they are, and in North America. But in the Tasman Islands their party's the third largest in Parliament. The Shining Light Movement.'

'I've heard a little about them. They sound mad.'

'They are. They think the calamities last century were caused by God, fulfilling the disasters prophesied in the Book of Revelation. They see the survivors as God's elect, waiting for His Second Coming. But they're very disappointed that the elect aren't living pure Christian lives, as the Bible prescribes.' He smiled bitterly. 'Fornicating and sodomizing and denying God, and so on and so on.' He sighed wearily. 'It's all happened before, of course, in America before the Catastrophe. They even got into government there at the turn of the last century. Some say that was the tipping point. If Bush hadn't won those elections, the world might have been able to take real steps to avoid what was coming. Who knows, now? Some Christians in America then thought the End of the World was coming, God's will revealed in the Book of Revelation. But there were people who thought that in the sixteenth century.'

'Don't the Black Book people believe there's a second Book of Revelation?'

'Yes. Prophecies by an Irish monk from the sixth century. What happened to humanity in the last century isn't enough for our Black Book friends. They say the monk foretold that today's remnant of humanity will be visited by another, final catastrophe, a last winnowing of the irremediably sinful, leaving – surprise – only the Black Book followers to be taken up to heaven.'

Shiva thought, What has this to do with me?

'The wretched book was lost for centuries,' Williams went on. 'Then thirty years ago, when people began sorting the evacuated London archives in Derby, some bright spark found it in a seventeenth-century chest and put the wretched thing on the internet. Seems to have come from the private archives of the British secret service, which go back to Stuart times. Then the fuss started. Because the book's supposed to have predicted various events that did happen, like the Black Death and the Gunpowder Plot.'

'Why is the movement so big in the Tasman Islands?'

'Who knows? Some say it's to do with guilt; the Aussies and Kiwis were quicker than anyone to blow refugee boats from Asia out of the water. The man who uncovered the supposed truth of those prophecies is a Tasman. Their leader, Pastor Smith.' Williams paused. 'They've been after the original Black Book for ages, but we've got it in the National Museum here, across the square. Access allowed only to academic researchers. Incidentally, it does genuinely seem to be fifteen hundred years old. It's a battered old thing. God knows how it's survived this long. The Shining Light people say it's a miracle.' Shiva noticed that the clipped prose was gone, the commissioner's evident anxiety making him discursive.

'Some people wanted the damned thing destroyed,' Williams went on. 'Accidentally, of course.' He smiled tightly. 'Well, it's gone now. A week ago someone broke into the museum, smashed in the watchman's skull and stole it.'

Shiva's mind clicked into investigative mode. 'How securely was it kept?'

'Very. Locked away in a combination safe. But the Black Book people probably have an expert on safe codes amongst their growing congregation. Recently they've been flying recruits from here and America who are specialists in all sorts of technical fields out to the Tasman Islands.'

'They *fly* them there?'

'As part of the Tasman Islands quota. The Black Book people have friends in government.'

'Why do that?'

'We don't know. They've even brought some nuclear scientists, though there are no nuclear facilities or even uranium down there. The immigrants say they want to be near their leader. Pastor Smith. He keeps himself apart in some secret sanctuary, directing his political and religious activists. Incidentally, there seems to be an unusually high death rate amongst the foreign recruits. Sudden strokes and heart attacks. Usually with death certificates signed by a doctor who's in the movement. The Black Book people are almost a state within a state down there.'

'Maybe they think when the rest of humanity is destroyed, an educated elect would be useful.'

'But they don't believe *anyone* will be left. They think when the End comes they'll be raptured, as they put it, up to heaven.'

Shiva did not reply. In the context of the struggles to survive humanity had faced, and still faced, the idea seemed unbearably repellent.

'When they got going twenty years ago they formed a political party. The Shining Light Movement. Their support got up to twenty per cent in the 2120 election in the Tasmans, but no other party would go into coalition with them and since then support has dropped away. These days their campaigning seems half-hearted. But they are still bringing in scientific experts. They're very wealthy, by the way: every member has to give ten per cent of their income to the Church. For poor people that takes them near the breadline, but they still do it. The Tasman government's been wondering what they're up to, where all that money's going, and so have we and the Americans.'

'A coup?' Shiva suggested.

The commissioner shook his head. 'They don't seem interested in infiltrating the police or army. Although if they did take over the Tasman Islands, we could live with that. It's very far away. But we can't have them murdering an EU citizen and stealing that book. The End of the World, by the way, is prophesied for some time this year.' He leaned forward, businesslike again. 'But now a chance has come up. To infiltrate them.'

'Me?' Shiva asked.

'You.' Williams smiled tightly.

'It couldn't work, sir. I could never pretend to be a religious fundamentalist.'

'You won't need to.' Williams bent to a file on his desk. He passed a photograph to Shiva. It showed a woman in dark clothes, wearing surgical gloves, disconnecting wires in a junction box on a wall. She was in her early thirties. Her long dark hair was tied back in a ponytail; her features, caught in an expression of fierce concentration, were the same light brown colour as Shiva's.

'She managed to disable the power system to that part of the museum. We also have a film of her working on the safe. She was there for three hours. We got the pictures because the museum surveillance system has a backup, a security camera with a battery that activates on movement. She missed the lens poking out of the wall. By then she'd already killed the security guard, a blow to the head from behind. The last photographs are of her taking the book from the safe and leaving.'

Shiva looked at the woman's face. The eyes were narrowed with concentration, the mouth tight. In repose the face was probably attractive.

'The Americans tell us her name is Parvati Karam.

Family were Indian shopkeepers in San Francisco before it was inundated. Moved up to British Columbia, grandfather did well as a wholesaler. Young Parvati is a mathematical wizard; spent ten years designing security systems for the Federal Reserve. In the meantime she got herself involved with the Shining Light Movement, and two years ago they invited her to emigrate to the Tasman Islands. Government in Dunedin were happy to take her on as a security systems adviser. And so the Shining Light Movement gained another expert.'

'Do we have back-channels to the Tasman government?' Shiva asked.

'A few. We're wary. Not all the Shining Light people declare who they are when they take civil service jobs. But the Tasman government doesn't know what they're up to, though they think something is going on.'

'I should say, sir, I've never done any political work.'

'I don't know if you'd call this political. We don't really know what it is. A murder, to start with.'

'Where is Karam now?'

'Back home, I'm afraid. The monthly flight to Dunedin took off the night after the book was stolen and she was on it. By the time our internet systems identified her, she was back in Dunedin.'

'Has the Tasman government been contacted?'

'Yes. But meanwhile Hardacre at internet decided to run an ancestor search on Karam, just to see what came up. And the system flagged up a connection to you.'

'But I've never done any ancestor research,' Shiva said.

'We have.' The old man smiled. 'On your behalf. We realized years ago that if we could find an ancestral connection between one of our undercover people and someone we were interested in, it would be a way of getting into their confidence. It's happened a few times, and now it's happened with you. Your great-great-great-great-grandfather and Parvati Karam's were brothers in the same Indian village. Both families emigrated in the 1940s, during the troubles when the British left. They were Hindus in the Muslim area. We want you to go out there, get to know her.'

Shiva nodded. But he did not feel the *frisson* of excitement that a new case normally gave him.

'We'll fly you to Dunedin on the next monthly flight. A transworld flight – I envy you that. You'll be a diplomat taking up a post at the EU embassy. Cultural attaché, tried and tested cover for spies. Contact her via her ancestor site e-mail, say you've been researching and found you were related, and ask to meet her.' The clipped, peremptory tone was back.

'When did she do her search?'

'That's interesting. Only a year ago, well after she joined the Shining Light. They discourage ancestor research. May indicate a vulnerability on her part.'

Shiva looked down at the photograph. 'She doesn't look vulnerable.' He hesitated. 'I've never gone under-cover to trap a woman before.'

'Will that be a problem?'

'No. It's just a question of . . . thinking around it.'

'Do that.' The commisioner nodded. 'When Karam was in Birmingham she stayed at a guesthouse in the suburbs. Witton. See what you can find out from the landlady. She's the only one we know who actually met her. I'll give you her file, and over the next couple of weeks you'll get some training about the Black Book and the Shining Light. I'll see you again.' He paused. 'You were brought up a Hindu, weren't you?'

'I was brought up in the old traditions. But my parents weren't really religious.'

'You'll have quite a bit to learn.' He studied Shiva. 'Yes, it's hard to pretend serious faith. We think when you meet Karam you should be sceptical but not hostile.'

'If she wants to meet me.'

'It will be very helpful if you can make sure she does.'

'And the Black Book? If I find it?'

Commissioner Williams's face darkened. 'Destroy it.'

Shiva had been given a guest apartment at the Commission. Tomorrow, books and papers would arrive, about Parvati Karam, the Black Book, the Shining Light Movement. His room was small, high up in the building. He had set the statue of Shiva on his dressing table. In the old days not many Indian boys had been called Shiva, but his parents had liked the statue. Shiva looked at his face in the dressing table mirror. It looked tired. It was a thin face, bony, clever – delicately pointed, Alice had once said. He looked at the statue. Sometimes he felt all the weight of India on him. Destroyed, massive inundations drowning half the Ganges valley in two years, while in the rest of the subcontinent the summer heat had risen to forty-five, forty-six degrees, more than humans could bear. There was no way out for the people; to the north lay only the bare Himalayas. What Indians were left now were scattered around the world, accepted or discriminated against in various degrees, depending on the country. Shiva thought of meeting this woman, another Indian. An enemy. He stared at the statue, trying to lose himself in its symmetry. The god's face was enigmatic as he danced, protecting the world, his foot on a demon from the underworld.

II

A week later Shiva walked out to the inner-city suburb of Witton. He left early, dressed formally in a cotton suit and wing-collared shirt. Shopkeepers were opening their shutters, the arterial roads filling up with bicycles and horses and carts and the electric cars of the rich. With a quarter of a million souls, Birmingham, high above sea level, was one of the few populous cities left in the world. It had been chosen as the new European Union capital over Berlin, now a coastal city still threatened by the rising seas.

For all that it had shrunk to a cluster of islands half its original size, Great Britain had fared better than most countries. It had an abundance of fertile land, only the Scottish and Welsh mountains requiring serious soil enhancement. No need in Britain for intrepid parties to brave burning deserts to raid the old cities' landfill sites for organic refuse to make artificial soils. Britain's island status, too, had protected it from the worst of the migrant wars.

Shiva stopped at a roadside stall to buy a coconut from a vendor. The tanned young man expertly sliced off the top with his machete. Shiva drank the cool milk gratefully, for after an hour walking on the dusty road his throat was dry. He walked on to Witton, an area of old back-to-back terraces, with south-facing windows now converted to solar panels. There was a small lake in the centre to take the monsoon overflow of the river Lea. The water was low at this time of year and lines of chimneypots from submerged houses broke the surface. Children were swimming in the brown water, calling out to each other in Brummie accents.

Around the lake new earthhouses had been built,

and Shiva headed for one of the larger ones, two storeys high, the thick walls and the frames of the solar panels painted bright blue. A sign was nailed to the wall by the door. GUESTHOUSE. VACANCIES. He knocked on the door and a small terrier began a frantic barking. A large, grey-haired lady opened the door. She wore a shapeless yellow dress, sweat-stained under the arms.

'Good morning.' The woman looked tense, worried. A Jack Russell ran up behind her, barking angrily. 'Sit,' the women snapped. The dog obeyed. Shiva stared at it; pets were an unusual luxury.

'Mrs Ackerley?' He gave her his most winning smile. 'My name is Inspector Moorthy. Wonder if I could ask a few questions?'

Her broad shoulders slumped. 'Come in. Sam, *away*!' The dog walked obediently off. 'It's about that woman, I suppose,' Mrs Ackerley said heavily.

'Afraid so. Expect you're tired of being questioned about her.'

'I had three officers on different days, asking me the same questions. They won't tell me what she's done.'

'Last time, I promise.' He smiled at her again.

She sighed and led him into a lounge, where canvas chairs surrounded an old wooden coffee table. The shutters were open, large windows giving a good view of the lake. The computer was on, a documentary about Antarctica. Five-mile-wide rivers crashed through a landscape of stone worn as smooth as glass by vanished glaciers. Mrs Ackerley bent stiffly and turned down the sound. 'You'd better sit down,' she said.

Shiva looked at the screen. 'Look at those rivers.'

'We'll all be drowned yet.'

'No, the ice sheet's nearly gone. The sea can't rise much further.'

'So the politicians tell us,' she replied darkly. She sighed again. 'Please, ask me what you want. The guests are out at work. I don't want them coming back to find the police here again.'

'Thought they would be out at this time of day. That's why I came now. It's mostly businessmen and officials visiting the city that you take in, isn't it? It's a nice house, nice view.'

She wasn't mollified. 'Aren't you a bit young to be a police inspector?' she asked.

'Thirty-six. Older than I look. Now, I don't want to trouble you by going over the whole ground again. I just wanted to ask what you thought of her. Miss Karam? As a guest. As a person. Your insight.'

The old woman seemed a little mollified. 'She appeared nice enough when she arrived. Very polite. But private. Didn't mix with the other guests.'

'Self-contained, then?'

'Guests have a right to be private. Though I would have liked to talk to her,' she added regretfully. 'Coming from so far away. I wanted to ask what the Tasman Islands were like. What it was like to fly, looking down on all the old dead places. But I could tell it wouldn't be welcome.' She shrugged. On screen a man in a jersey stood on the bank of a great river, a tiny dot, chunks of ice the size of houses sweeping by.

'I may be flying myself soon,' Shiva said, to engage her. Mrs Ackerley's eyes lit up with interest.

'How exciting. Is it to do with this case?'

'No. Something else. Tell me, what did she say she was doing over here?'

'A conference on computerized power systems. To help conserve the electricity.' Mrs Ackerley settled back into her chair, relaxing. 'The only real conversation I had with her was a few days later. She'd been working in her room and came down to make a cup of tea. I asked about her family. She said they were in Canada; she hadn't seen them for years. I told her my family had lived in Brum since the industrial times.' Pride entered her voice.

'Did she wear a cross?' Shiva asked. Most of the Shining Light people did, chunky wooden ones painted silver.

'No. I would have noticed. I wondered what religion she might be, as she was—' Mrs Ackerley flushed '—of colour,' she concluded, using the currently correct phrase.

'You said earlier that she seemed quite nice when she arrived. Did something make you change your mind later?'

'Yes. Sam. My little dog. I know people say pets eat scarce food, but it all comes off my rations.'

'People can be too strict sometimes.'

'He makes a lot of noise but it's only to protect me. He doesn't bite. I wouldn't have mentioned it, only one of the other guests saw what happened and told the police when they interviewed him.'

Shiva leaned forward. This hadn't made it to the report. 'What *did* happen?'

'One evening I was in here and I heard a yelp from the kitchen. I went in and poor Sam was cowering against the wall, howling. I could see he'd been kicked. And that Parvati woman was standing against the opposite wall, glaring at him. I shouted at her that he's only a helpless little dog. She was apologetic, said she'd been brought up in Canada and they have problems with wild dogs out there. One had bitten her once. But when I came in she'd looked angry, not frightened. I would have asked her to go but I need the money. One of the other guests heard us shouting and came down. Like I said, he told the police later.'

'Thank you. That's interesting.'

'Is it?' She fixed him with puzzled eyes. 'If she's done something bad enough to have the police coming here time and again, what does hurting a little dog matter?'

'Everything matters,' Shiva answered, retreating into his clipped official voice.

When he left he needed to think, to order what Mrs Ackerley had told him. He walked across to the lake and sat on a bench under a eucalyptus tree, out of sight of the house. Nearby, a little boy and girl stood in the shallows fishing. They wore dirty kaftans and broad-brimmed straw hats, like Tom Sawyer. Mosquitoes darted around, and he hoped the children had put on their repellent. These lakes were malarial.

Parvati Karam had been self-contained, Mrs Ackerley had said. That fitted with the information they had found on the databases. Her parents had been strongly atheist, like most people these days. Shiva's own parents had kept up the old Hindu customs through respect for tradition rather than real belief. A loner at school, Parvati had shown great mathematical ability and had gone to university in Alberta at sixteen. The interesting thing, Shiva remembered, was that at university she had joined the dog-hunting clubs. It was not only people who had fled northwards from the deserts of the old United States but dogs too, millions of pets that had formed predatory packs, reverting to old instincts. They were getting larger, reverting to their wolf ancestry, and in the many isolated settlements they were a major problem. Hunting them was encouraged. The reports said that Parvati Karam had headed a student team, which won prizes for the number of dogs they killed. Had she gained a fear of them that had led her to kick Mrs Ackerley's pet? Or was it hate?

The dog hunting had stood out because otherwise Parvati's life seemed so bland. She had worked on electronic security systems in Winnipeg after graduating.

Three years ago she had been converted to the Shining Light Movement, and in 2133 she had taken up a new job in New Zealand. Within the Church she seemed to be just an ordinary member, going to church, joining the party, paying a tenth of her salary to the movement. No record of any official position in Church or party, no active involvement in the campaigns against sodomy or abortion or eating pork. Yet a few weeks ago she had come up quietly behind the watchman at the Birmingham museum and expertly felled him with a blow to the back of the neck that broke it. Shiva had seen the photographs, the look of surprise on the old man's face. She would have learned techniques of stalking and killing in the dog hunts, he realized. He wondered if she had killed the man coldly, as though he too were a dog.

Across the lake a group of men pushed a boat into the water, unfurling a white sail. They carried fishing rods. Ripples spread across the water, making tiny waves at Shiva's feet.

'Them blastid men'll scare the fish,' the little girl said to the boy. They were very alike; they must be brother and sister.

'Na, they'll drive 'em this way. 'Ere, I've got one!' he shouted excitedly.

A struggle began with a small carp that had taken the bait and was struggling fiercely out in the water. The little boy gripped the rod tightly while his sister waded into the warm shallows, grabbed the line and began hauling in the fish.

Shiva envied their closeness. Like Parvati Karam, he was an only child. Large families had been officially discouraged since the Catastrophe, with so little good land to feed the survivors. He wondered: had her childhood been as lonely as his, had she too been driven to succeed by parents whose future she represented?

Shiva had also been an outsider, a small thin dark child in the Surrey town on the edge of Thames Bay. But he had wanted more than anything to belong. He had found his way in by attaching himself to children who were natural leaders, popular and charismatic, for charisma begins early. But often those leaders of playground gangs were cruel, and Shiva had always recoiled from cruelty, perhaps because he feared them turning on him. When he was sixteen the group he hung on to attacked and robbed an old woman; the leader of the group, Starkey, had planned it carefully. Shiva watched them while they divided up the money, then went and reported the crime to the headmaster. Starkey, a promising pupil, was expelled. Shiva's own part was kept secret; he was awarded detention with the lesser offenders to defray suspicion at his own request. His path had been decided then. Sometimes he wondered what had happened to Starkey. Perhaps he was in prison like Marwood.

'Buy a fish, mister?' A voice at his elbow startled Shiva. The two urchins stood beside him, the little girl holding up the carp, the sun reflected from its golden scales.

'No, thanks. I'm staying somewhere where they give you food.'

'Only one euro. Off the ration.'

'No. Thanks anyway. I have to go.'

He stood up and walked away. The sun was hot now, so he took his canvas hat from his pocket and put it on. Behind him the children argued about where to sell their fish.

Tonight he would send Parvati Karam his first e-mail. He had already done a genuine search on genealogical sites to find her, in case somehow she retraced his steps on her computer.

*

There were demonstrators at Birmingham airport; the few airports left in the world had permanent pickets. Shiva, watching the banners beyond the fenced-off enclosure, could understand their anger. Most agreed that the explosion of air travel in the years before the Catastrophe had hastened the warming. Now it was strictly rationed, limited mostly to politicians and diplomats who needed to travel to the Tasman Islands or Patagonia, and the scientists monitoring Antarctica. One could not get to the southern hemisphere by boat, for like the land the tropical seas were too hot for human survival. Luggage was limited on the plane; there had been no question of bringing his statue.

He entered the little airport building. It was hot and muggy outside and worse indoors. As he waited to be searched he looked through the far window. The plane was sitting on the tarmac. It seemed a small and fragile thing to take him so far. He looked around at the other passengers, mostly middle-aged and prosperous-looking.

When they took off and Shiva looked through the window, he felt the clutch of fear in his stomach they had warned him about. The world was spinning away, the city transformed into a patchwork of miniature houses in a sea of green.

'First time?' the passenger next to him asked sympathetically. He was a spare man with a grey beard, dressed less formally than most of the other passengers, a jacket over a white kaftan. 'It's a bit disorientating. At first.'

'Yes. I suppose it's a privilege, an experience.'

'I've done it nine times. It'll get boring. The refuelling stop in Tibet will come as a relief.' The man sounded weary. 'I'm a hydrologist, going to have another look at the Antarctic icecap. I'll be taking a second flight down from Dunedin.' He smiled sadly. 'It's hard on my wife and children.'

'Are they in England?'

'Leeds. Name's Bill Allen, by the way.'

'Shiva Moorthy. I'm a diplomat. Joining the embassy at Dunedin. Cultural attaché.'

'Long posting?'

'Couple of years.' He changed the subject. 'I hear the Antarctic rivers are still rising.'

Allen nodded. 'Inevitable now the icecap's melting faster – its area's a fifth of what it was. It'll be gone in a few decades, and then the sea will stabilize at last. But as the seas warm up down there, the heat's releasing more methane from the seabed, like we had in the north last century.' He looked at Shiva seriously. 'We're still not safe.'

'Will we ever be?'

'I don't know.' The scientist paused. 'I saw a methane eruption from the air once, miles of sea frothing and bubbling, even burning in places, throwing all that stuff up into the atmosphere.'

They talked a little more, about Antarctica and Dr Allen's family and Shiva's fictional job. Shiva used the scientist as a practice run for the story he would tell Parvati Karam, and related his fictional background in the civil service. After a while Dr Allen said there were papers he must study and left Shiva to look out of the window. They passed high over the fields of Germany, through a brief interlude of scrub, then into the great brown desert. Endless stony plains and mountains, the dried-up Danube and its tributaries visible as dry veins and arteries. He saw the jumble of an abandoned city beside it – Budapest, perhaps. Already it was hard to believe there were once great cities here. In time, as they crumbled away, perhaps people would forget they ever existed. He turned away.

Dr Allen had fallen asleep over his papers. Shiva reached into the bag he carried on his lap and brought out his copy of the Black Book. He had studied it carefully over the last few weeks, reading through the verses of prophecy. In the original book, which had been carbon dated to the seventh century, the verses had been in Latin. He was surprised that they still rhymed in English; surely the translator must have interfered with the verses' meaning. Most of the prophecies related to events in medieval and Stuart England, and all of them, the believers said, had come true. The verses seemed to Shiva to be no more precise than the rambling incoherences of the Book of Revelation, which he had read as part of his preparation. He read once more the final verse of the Black Book, which the Shining Light people said applied to the present day:

Five hundred thirty years, then God returns to save
His chosen, once the sinful have been purged.
Their wicked cities flayed by burning sun and drowned in purging flood,
And at the end a sun-bright fire of blood.

When it was first discovered, the book had been no more than a curiosity, until the Shining Light Movement had declared that the earlier prophecies coincided with real events, and that this showed that the book had been inspired by God. And this year, 2135, was five hundred and thirty years since the Gunpowder Plot that was the subject of the previous prophecy.

'And at the end a sun-bright fire of blood.' It sounded like a nuclear holocaust. But as Commissioner Williams had said, there was no nuclear power in the Tasman Islands – old arsenals enough in the north, but none down there and no way of getting nuclear equipment. The only physical communication with the north was flights like this one, every passenger rigorously searched – but for explosives, not books, which was how Parvati Karam had got away with the original Black Book. The Shining Light Movement firmly believed that the world would end this year but claimed not to know exactly how. That would be for God to reveal. But then why recruit these scientists and engineers? What were they planning? Shiva looked down at the cover of the book.

They were over blue water now, the plane casting a tiny shadow on the sea. There was an island in the distance – the Crimea, an isolated desert crag in the centre of the vastly extended Black Sea. Shiva returned his copy of the book to his bag. He thought about the religious dogma he had had to read about in these last weeks. In the years before the Catastrophe, fanaticism had been everywhere, in Islam and Christianity and Hinduism and in a secular faith too: the blind belief in pseudo-scientific free-market theories that had succeeded Communism. The globalizers had believed in endless growth, that in some mystic way technologies to defeat global warming would appear. Like Marx, they had talked of the inevitable destiny of mankind. Their dogmas, like their world, were dead now, and they were hated for the blindness their ideas had brought. Humanity was tired of faith; the world today was a practical place; it had to be if humanity was to survive. But now Shiva wondered whether perhaps that practicality was only skin deep, perhaps always had been, the urge for the simplicities of faith always ready to surface. Outside, the colours changed, from blue sea to the grey moonscape of the Caucasus.

The face of the murdered old watchman came to Shiva's mind. He had been a breadwinner, supporting two grandchildren in a crumbling Birmingham terrace. His life had been snuffed out like an ant's. Shiva promised himself that whatever else transpired in the Tasmans he would see Parvati Karam arrested and tried for his murder.

It was getting dark when they landed to refuel in Tibet, on the airstrip that had once served Lhasa. Here, at the southern end of the vast desert that stretched to the Chinese settlements in Siberia, a group of guards drawn from all over the world kept permanent watch over stores of aircraft fuel. Ten years ago a group of eco-warriors had got on to a scheduled flight and had managed to blow up the fuel dump. Nowadays the passengers were herded into a secure outbuilding while the plane refuelled.

Walking from the aircraft to the building, Shiva was amazed by the clearness and coldness of the air. In the distance, between a dried-out riverbed and huge mountains, he saw the ghostly jumble of deserted Lhasa and, above it, the old Potala Palace, tier upon tier of empty windows. He felt a sense of wonder at the journey he was making and was conscious of the huge distance he was from England, from all that he knew. The sun set behind the mountains, and the long shadows merged into darkness.

'Amazing sight, isn't it?' Dr Allen whispered beside him. 'Makes me want to cry when I think what we've lost. Better hurry up,' he continued gruffly. 'Don't want to catch a chill.'

The concrete building where they waited was another relic, faded pictures of drowned Chinese landscapes lining the walls. They sat on wooden benches, and a group of guards distributed rugs and bowls of soup.

'I didn't know it could be so cold anywhere,' Shiva remarked.

'We're very high. Over three and a half thousand metres. Makes some people ill. I don't envy the guards. A ghost city and no one else within two thousand miles.'

'No.'

'And we fly south over India next. The great jungles, all the new plants.' Enthusiasm entered Dr Allen's voice. 'Tree ferns two hundred feet high, huge sprouting flowers we don't even know the names of. The plants have adapted to the heat faster than anyone could have guessed. Pity it's too hot down there to do any proper scientific surveys.'

'What about animals?'

Dr Allen shrugged. 'People say there are big creatures down there. They see the trees move from the air. God knows what they are. Some people say there are even people on the Himalayan slopes.'

'Survivors?' Shiva asked eagerly. 'From India?'

The scientist looked embarrassed, no doubt making the connection to Shiva's ancestry. 'It's just that some pilots flying over thought they saw smoke rising from the jungle, like campfires. On the upper slopes it's not too hot for people to live. But condensation often rises from forests when they warm up in the mornings. It could be people, though, it could be. One day when things are more settled we'll go down there and find out.' He smiled uneasily. 'We're lucky in a way: we have a whole new world to explore.'

'Yes.' Shiva thought of people who looked like him, perhaps living a Stone Age life down there, cut off. If the Black Book was right, before the year's end God would kill the lot of them.

'What are the Tasman Islands like?' Shiva asked.

Dr Allen laughed. 'Prosperous. Busy. Old-fashioned. Very like the old world in a lot of ways. Dunedin's pretty, nice view out across the bay.'

'I hear they've got a big fundamentalist movement,' Shiva said neutrally. 'Gets a lot of votes in the elections.'

'Less than they did, thank goodness. Maniacs.'

They talked a little about the scientist's work, then he went to sleep again in his chair. Shiva looked out at the huge old palace, grey in the moonlight, high jagged mountains rising behind. He thought of the most recent message he had received from Parvati Karam: 'Look forward to meeting you on Thursday. Mackenzie's Café, George Street, Dunedin. 2.30.'

He thought of Alice, who had given him the radiation ring. It was two years since they had parted. She had loved him but he hadn't loved her back, or not enough. He often disappeared for weeks at a time because of his work, but she was always waiting for him on his return. There was something smothering in her devotion and in the old-fashioned way in which she wanted him, as the man, to decide and initiate things, even their lovemaking. Shiva hadn't wanted that sort of power himself. Strange, though, that it was always leaders – people who wanted or wielded power – to whom he had been drawn since school, mixed in somehow with a desire to bring them down, show their feet were made of clay. Like Marwood. He saw the fraudster's face again, heard him cry out that he was innocent. The case had affected him more than any other. There had been something in the way the man actually believed his own lies that had made Shiva ashamed to deceive him. Marwood had been generous, had desired affection. Yet that did not make him any less wicked than any of the fraudsters he had brought to justice over the last ten years. Marwood had deceived farmers who were trying to scratch a living from thin mountain soils, surviving on the edge.

He felt a similar unease about Parvati Karam, about using their own shared heritage to deceive her. He shook his head. These qualms didn't make sense in moral terms. He was just tired. Tired to the bone, he realized. He had spent sixteen years in the police, twelve in the fraud department. It was time to leave, he thought; he needed to change his life. But where would he go? An inspector he knew had retired early and gone to work in the refugee camps; a number of people did. But he didn't want to do that. He wasn't built for it, apart from anything else. He looked at his hands, thin and bony. His parents had called them Brahmin's hands, though they weren't Brahmins. A boy at school had once called them girl's hands. He could kill a man with them if he had to; he had been trained to do so long ago. That ability, though, was about knowledge of anatomy and lines of force, not strength. He leaned back in his chair and slept, a deep and dreamless sleep until a guard shook him awake. The guard was tall and stocky, with high cheekbones and slanting Asiatic eyes. 'Time to get back on board, sir.'

It was still dark when they flew over India, so Shiva saw nothing. There was turbulence that the pilot said was tropical storms below. He slept again and awoke, eyes sore, to find they had crossed the Indian Ocean and were above a red desert stretching endlessly to the horizon. Australia, once partly inhabited but now the hottest desert in the world. A few hours now and they would be there.

In his mind he reviewed his correspondence with Parvati. He had started with a tentative e-mail saying he had found they were distantly related. Her reply, his first words from her, had been equally tentative, but he fostered the correspondence, feeding her information about his family, a mixture of truth and invention. When he had said he was coming to work in Dunedin, where she lived, she had said that was a coincidence.

Shiva had wondered whether there might be any underlying suspicion there but decided it was imagination. He sensed an underlying keenness to meet him. When he gave her the date of his flight, her next reply had been enthusiastic, asking about his life in England. She said her own was dull: 'I work long hours, boring computer stuff for the government, but I have a nice house overlooking Victoria Bay and the islands. Work for my church takes up my leisure time.' She suggested they meet in a café near the EU embassy once Shiva had settled in.

His first meeting with Alice had been in a café, set up through a dating site. He recalled sitting in the little café, batting off mosquitoes, sweating because it was just before the monsoon, annoyed that the pretty white girl opposite him looked quite cool. He wondered where she was now.

The engine note changed, the front of the plane tipping slightly forward. Dr Allen leaned across Shiva to look out of the window. 'That's Dunedin,' he said with satisfaction. 'Nearly there.'

Below, Shiva saw a coastline. The plane circled lower, and for the first time since passing over Germany he saw a green, cultivated landscape, little fields marching up hillsides, mountains in the distance. Then, once more, houses again, perched above a bay with islands beyond. Humanity, clinging determinedly to its last fragments of the earth.

III

The old city of Dunedin lay beneath the waves, and a new town had been built on the hills behind. Most of New Zealand's mountainous South Island had survived, though the Canterbury Plains were gone. As the bus from the airport drove into town, Shiva saw rows of colourful earthhouses with elaborately carved wooden frontages. It was the gardens that amazed him, full of roses and flame trees and carefully cultivated palms. In Europe there were few gardens, only endless vegetable plots. But the Tasman Islands were the richest nation in the world, with plentiful hydroelectric power, large areas of mountain land that was potentially fertile but had never been cultivated, and a homogeneous, highly educated population. As he watched the healthy-looking people, many wearing shirts rather than kaftans, their long hair often braided into elaborate designs, Shiva wondered how such a people could have turned to an organization like the Shining Light Movement in substantial numbers.

The bus dropped him in the town centre, near the embassy. Dunedin was built around a large eight-sided roundabout called the Octagon, a reconstruction of the one that had existed in the old city, and Shiva took a road named George Street. The new town had re-created the design of the old, just as the original Scottish colonists three centuries before had named the streets after those of Edinburgh. It was midday, but the heat was bearable. A cool breeze wafted up from the sea, whipping up dust. In England at this time of day, people would be hot and sticky, searching out vestiges of shade, but here they walked about in the sun, relaxed-looking. Shiva carried his luggage to the embassy, which stood in a street of four-storey wooden official buildings, rising high above the one- and two-storey earthhouses in the surrounding streets. The doorpost was elaborately carved with what Shiva guessed were Maori carvings, intricate designs surrounding grimacing faces.

He was taken to a room on the third floor, a large room with a wall of windows overlooking a sea dotted with little islands. The embassy intelligence officer was a dapper man in his forties, immaculately dressed in a dark suit and high-collared white shirt. He wore black-leather shoes, polished so they shone. Shiva knew his name was Rodriguez. He rose from behind a large desk, where papers stood in neat piles, and shook Shiva's hand, his grip dry and strong. On the wall behind him was a map of the Tasman Islands; Tasmania and the South Island of New Zealand relatively little changed from their old coastline except that the North Island was now split into two. Above Tasmania, a corner of Australia showed at the edge of the map, the endless desert coloured orange in contrast to the green shading of the Tasman Islands.

Rodriguez poured Shiva a glass of fruit juice and invited him to sit down. 'You look tired,' he said in a strong Spanish accent. His own eyes looked deceptively sleepy.

'Yes, sir. My body thinks it's the middle of the night.'

'Flying is not a natural way to travel. Once was enough for me.' He smiled, showing white teeth. 'We have a small house for you a few streets away. You can get some rest soon.'

Shiva noticed that though Rodriguez' tones were formal, he did not use the clipped speech of the official classes at home. Was that only an English affectation? He had never been abroad, so he didn't know.

Rodriguez smiled at him. 'Well, what is your first impression of Dunedin?'

'It seems prosperous, everyone looks well fed. They have space for gardens.'

He nodded. 'Compared with most places last century they were very lucky. By the time the great inundations came, most Australians had abandoned the continent; it hadn't rained there in thirty years. Those left went down to Tasmania, or came here. There were the usual refugee camps and starvation and disease. But the population's up to eight million now – impressive when you think there are fewer than thirty million in Europe.'

'It is.'

'They've planted everywhere except the high peaks and the western fjords. They've been very successful. Of course, it helped that the islands were so isolated. And they had a navy. They blew refugee boats coming down from Indonesia out of the water.' A trace of bitterness entered Rodriguez' voice. Perhaps he was recalling when Spain turned to desert, the migrant wars in the Pyrenees.

'It's surprisingly cool,' Shiva observed.

'The water around the islands is cold. Ten years ago there were still icebergs drifting up here from Antarctica. In time, it'll get hotter.' He leaned forward and smiled, his eyes not sleepy any more. 'Have you made an appointment to see that woman?'

'Tomorrow.'

'Good. Get some sleep before then. And watch your step. The Shining Light are tricky people. They show three faces. On the one hand the church services and the evangelization drives, on the other the politics, the pressure for religious laws. But the third face is the hidden one. They are very good at infiltrating key points in state and private institutions with people, hiding their allegiances. The civil service is full of them.'

'I understand they're not as powerful as they were. Politically.'

'No. There was a movement here a few years ago to privatize some of the public services, like the railways and the water supply. People looking to make easy money out of facilities it took the government fifty years to re-create. The Shining Light people jumped on the bandwagon; their programme of going back to biblical morals hadn't done very well, but taking the lead in the privatization campaign brought them votes. For a while.'

'Only for a while?'

'Yes. They privatized the railways and it was a disaster. No coordination, fares through the roof. The Shining Light people got blamed.' He paused. 'Companies they run still own several railway lines, though. Make a tidy profit. There are lines pushing everywhere into the hills as people settle them.'

'I was told their leader is reclusive.'

'Ah, yes. Dr Brandon Smith.' Rodriguez shook his head. 'They have a hideaway somewhere in the mountains in the south-west. They bought a lot of land there, and no outsiders are allowed there. Smith disappears for months, then appears at the climax of some evangelization campaign. Seems to show himself less and less these days, but still turns up now and again standing on a box in a town centre somewhere. Promises everyone salvation if they join the Church, everlasting fire if they don't.'

'Have you ever seen him?'

'Once, here in Dunedin. He's very dirty and ragged, looks like an Old Testament prophet. But he runs everything from behind the scenes. He used to be a schoolteacher until God told him he was destined to be a great prophet.'

'Why have they had so much success here? There are a few of them in the north, but they're a joke, a little sect.'

Rodriguez shrugged. 'Perhaps people here feel guilty about the degree of success and prosperity they've regained, feel it can't or shouldn't last.' He leaned forward. 'Whatever the reason, the Shining Light people feel they are special, chosen ones. That always makes people dangerous. And we've seen from the theft of the book how ruthless they can be. And this Parvati Karam—' Rodriguez grimaced '—the Shining Light think women should be subordinate, stay in the home. To rise to a position where she was trusted with a task like stealing that book, Parvati Karam would have to be very good.' He raised his eyebrows. 'Be careful, Inspector Moorthy.'

He met her at a café near the Octagon two days later. He was tired; it had taken his body a long time to adjust to the experience of flying over the world. Unnatural, as Rodriguez had said. He was glad to get out of the small, bare house they had assigned him. Without his statue of Shiva, he felt curiously vulnerable and edgy. He had bought a shirt and light trousers like the locals, and as he walked to the café the wind from the sea was refreshingly cool, though the sun was hot.

The street was crowded, the faces nearly all white except for a few brown-skinned Maori. About ten per cent of the people wore white-painted wooden crosses that marked them out as members of the Shining Light Movement. He noticed more of the elaborate hair designs. It seemed to be the better-dressed people who had them; perhaps it was a sign of status. But the streets were like those at home, beaten earth. Pedestrians walked at the sides; bicycles and tuc-tucs and a few electric vans drove down the centre. For a moment he thought he saw Marwood in the crowd and jerked his head around, but it was only some man who looked a little like him. He thought, That's never happened before. I'm getting burned out. This is the last undercover case I'll do.

Mackenzie's Café was a small place that sold coffee and drinks and little cakes. Most of the customers were elderly. He saw Parvati Karam at once, sitting at a table facing the door, looking straight at him. She was not as attractive as he had thought from the photographs, but it was a softer face than he had expected. Her long dark hair was drawn back in a severe ponytail. She wore a white-painted wooden cross at her neck. Her expression was expectant, slightly nervous, and when she saw him she stood up.

'Mr Moorthy?' There was eagerness and interest in her voice. She had a slight North American accent, softer than the hard Tasman drawl.

'Yes. Miss Karam?' Shiva held out his hand, and she took it. Her grip was light and moist. He looked into her brown eyes. They were unreadable.

'Can I get you a cup of tea?' he asked. 'Juice? A cake?'

'Just a tea, please.' She sat down again, and Shiva went to the counter. While he was waiting to be served and pay, he looked around. Parvati was staring back at him intently. She smiled.

When he sat down, she asked how he was adjusting after the flight.

'Still a bit tired. There's an insecticide they've told me I must wear in the evenings. Something about a new type of biting insect down here.'

'Yes, they're vicious and carry malaria.'

'All the animals and insects are changing, aren't they? Adapting, I suppose. They say that in India there are big animals no one's ever seen. We passed over it on the flight.'

'What did you see?' she asked curiously.

'Nothing, I'm afraid. It was dark. There was turbulence, big storms under the plane. A man I travelled with, a scientist going to Antarctica, said some people think there are survivors in the Himalayan foothills. But they're not sure.'

'Life for them would be very primitive, very hard.' She shook her head. 'Hardly worth living.'

'Things seem good here.'

'Everyone works hard. Planting is going on everywhere in the mountains. No one talks of anything but making better artificial soils. It is a materialistic place,' she said with a sudden hardness.

Shiva looked around the shop. 'We're the only brown faces,' he said.

'Yes. There are few Indians in the Tasmans.' She smiled wryly. 'People take me for a Maori.' She looked at him. 'Thank you for getting in touch. I thought there wasn't anybody left from my Indian forebears apart from my parents.'

'I only did a search recently. Felt it was something I ought to do. We shouldn't forget them, should we? Those civilizations only live on in people like us.' He smiled. 'Isn't it a strange thought, those two brothers in that Indian village who went to England in – when was it? – the 1940s?'

'They left because of the violence between Hindus and Muslims when British rule ended. The British were Christians. I think they tried to reconcile them, but they weren't strong enough.'

'I heard the British cut and ran, left them to it.'

'They had to preserve themselves. They were Christians and that's a Christian's duty. It's like the Great Catastrophe; it's really only Christian nations that have survived in any numbers. It's part of God's plan.' She spoke the hard words gently. 'So my Church teaches.'

Shiva thought suddenly of the dead watchman. He looked at Parvati's hands. Slim and delicate. Yet she had taken some blunt instrument and killed the man.

'What about the Chinese?' he asked. 'They seem to be doing quite well.'

'It can't last. They won't survive up there on the

permafrost. And God won't help them. Not heathens.'

'That's a very harsh doctrine.' Shiva smiled to defuse the words.

Parvati smiled sadly. 'I know. The truth is harsh. However you might wish it wasn't.'

Shiva looked at her. He could not reconcile this rather sad, pensive woman with the killer. If it was her, and it had to be, her act was as good as Rodriguez had warned. Better than him. He thought about the dog hunting. She didn't look as though she could have done that either, but she had.

'If you believe India's destruction was ordained by God,' he asked, 'why go back and look for ancestors? Why answer my e-mails?' He still spoke gently, smiled again.

'I don't know. I've always had a sort of . . . sense of grief. I suppose I wanted to assuage it. Since my boyfriend died in a car crash. In North America.' She frowned hard.

'When was that?'

'Four years ago.'

'I'm sorry.' A year before you joined the Church, Shiva thought.

'Are you married?' Parvati asked suddenly.

He looked at her, puzzled by the unexpected question. 'No.'

'I'm sorry.' She smiled and nodded at his left hand. 'I thought that might be a wedding ring.'

'No, it's a ring to measure radiation. It goes pink if the level is dangerous. Most people wear them in England. Because of the old flooded power stations.'

'I see.' She frowned again. Perhaps they hadn't warned her to take that precaution when they sent her to Europe.

'I just wondered if you had children,' she said. 'I don't think I'll ever marry now.'

'I nearly did once. Maybe one day.'

'I hope you didn't think me impertinent.'

'Not at all. Which Church are you in?' he asked. 'You didn't say.'

'The Shining Light. They saved my life after Steve died.'

'You believe the end of the world is coming, don't you?' he asked.

'Yes, we do. You should read the Book of Revelation, Shiva, and the Black Book.' She sighed. 'There was such an opportunity down here, survivors with a Christian heritage in a plentiful land. But they've kept the old materialism, spoiled the last chance they had to be . . . pure.'

'I'm not sure what I believe,' he said.

'That's the same as unbelief. Belief isn't easy, but it's right, it's true. And our leader, he's a great man, a prophet.' She spoke with quiet certainty. Then she looked at her watch and stood up. 'Well, it has been nice to meet you, Mr Moorthy. But I think I ought to go.'

'Already?'

'Yes. I'm sorry. I think coming was perhaps a mistake. My Church teaches that we should forget the past.'

He rose and followed her to the door, surprised to see how small she was. 'Perhaps we could meet again some time?' he asked. 'I don't know anyone in Dunedin . . .' He heard his voice stumbling as they stepped out into the street, less crowded now as darkness fell. He turned to face her.

Then from further up the street came the frantic blaring of a horn, and shouts and cries. Before Shiva had time to react, Parvati grabbed him by the shoulders and, with surprising strength, swung him around and shoved him against the wall of the shop. The wood creaked and shuddered. He stared past her. A yellow van, its horn still blaring, had passed over where he had just been standing and was careering on down the street. Pedestrians leaped aside and cyclists wobbled away. The van struck the side of a blue tuc-tuc, knocking it over with a crash, then barrelled into a side street. People ran over to the tuc-tuc as the driver and passenger climbed groggily out. 'Fetch the police!' someone called. Shiva turned to Parvati, who stood breathing heavily, looking more shocked than he was. 'Thank you,' he said. 'I think you just saved my life.'

'I saw it coming. You had your back to it – thank God.' She leaned against the wall, shaking slightly.

Shiva looked at the tuc-tuc. People were helping the driver and passenger. The driver was looking miserably at his overturned vehicle. He was big and dark-skinned, a Maori.

'The van driver must have lost control,' Parvati said. 'Pray Jesus he hasn't knocked anyone else down.' But Shiva was thinking that he had heard no electric hum; the van's engine was off. But if it had broken down, that wouldn't stop the driver from steering it. He meant to knock me down. And her? But for her quick reactions, Parvati would have gone down too. Where had she learned to react that quickly? The dog hunts in America, perhaps.

'I think we could both do with a drink,' Shiva said. 'Is there a bar around here?'

'I'm sorry, we're not allowed to drink.'

'This would be medicinal.'

She shook her head and smiled. 'I can't.'

He took the opportunity the narrow escape had provided, and said: 'Well, at least let me take you out to dinner, to say thank you. Anywhere you choose.'

She lowered her eyes. 'Thank you.' It would have been rude of her to refuse now.

'Tomorrow night, perhaps.'

'Tomorrow's Sunday. We don't go out on the Sabbath. But perhaps the night after. There's a place not far from here, in Charlotte Street. They serve nice food.'

'My treat. As a thank you.'

She hesitated, then smiled again. 'All right. Will you be able to find it?'

'I've got a map.'

Two policemen on bicycles rode past them, halting by the overturned vehicle. Shiva shivered at a blast of cold wind from the sea.

'Are you all right?' Parvati asked. 'Perhaps you should go and lie down.'

'I think I will.'

'I never asked anything about yourself, your work. I'm sorry. I don't think I'm quite myself these days. It's coming up to the anniversary, you see – Steve's death.'

'I'm sorry.'

'We can have a proper talk on Monday.' She smiled. 'About ourselves.'

Shiva looked at the policemen. 'Let's go,' he said. 'I don't want to get caught up in enquiries.'

Parvati looked at where the policemen were helping the driver to heave the vehicle upright. It looked badly dented. 'Poor man,' she said.

Lying on the bed in his house, he thought more about the van. It could have been an accident, but all his training told him it wasn't. That meant that someone, somewhere, knew who he was and why he was here. Had someone betrayed him? Someone back in England, perhaps? He thought of the cynical, epicene old commissioner; he could hardly see him as a secret member of the Shining Light Movement. Perhaps it was someone in Rodriguez' office. Rodriguez had said the Church had tentacles everywhere in the Tasman Islands. He thought about Parvati. She had been nothing like he expected, with her quiet, sad certainties. But it was her in the photographs. He thought again of the old man with the beaten-in head, the man he was determined to avenge. He would have to tell Rodriguez what had happened. He wished he had his statue with him.

IV

Rodriguez sat behind his big desk, considering what Shiva had told him, his fingers steepled together and his eyes half-closed. On the map behind his head the long, deep inlets of the fjords bit into the western coast of South Island.

He looked up. 'I will send a message directly to Commissioner Williams. And I will have the security protocols here checked. But neither the European Commission nor the embassy would ever let a Shining Light sympathizer near a confidential post.'

'Someone could have converted after joining the embassy, sir. You said yourself, sir, that sometimes they hide their membership.'

'We do thorough vetting where sensitive material is involved.' He looked at Shiva. 'Of course, it might have been a genuine accident.'

'What do the police say?'

'They haven't found the driver. And no one got a numberplate. But if it was a genuine accident, the driver would have every reason to keep quiet. He'd lose his licence, could even end up sorting waste in prison.'

'It just seems too neat. She rescues me and that way builds a bond, gets me to trust her. And she was looking at her watch just before we left the café. She asked to leave quite suddenly. She said she felt guilty about coming, her Church wouldn't approve.'

'If the intelligence services have been infiltrated, we have a major problem. But I'm not convinced they have been yet.' Rodriguez thought a moment. 'Do you want a minder, someone to watch your back discreetly?'

'No, thank you. If they're as clever as they seem to be, they'd know. That would be the end of my cover.'

'Don't be too brave for your own good. Or ours.'

'I'll take care, sir. The next meeting should be safe enough. It's in a public restaurant.'

Rodriguez nodded. He turned in his swivel chair and looked out of his window. In the bay, a large ship was winching a big net aboard, full of whitish material. Seagulls whirled and screamed.

'They're dredging the landfill site from the old city,' Rodriguez said. 'Organic material for the artificial soils. How we persist, humanity, how we struggle against extinction. Will we succeed, do you think?'

'We've come a long way in the last fifty years,' Shiva replied, echoing Commissioner Williams.

'But no one knows when the temperature will stop rising. There are nuclear power stations under the sea. Populations rising, still not enough soil.' Rodriguez smiled sadly. 'Forgive me, I am a Spaniard, we have a fatalist streak. But, yes, things have been getting better, and I pray that may continue.' He looked at Shiva. 'Do not worry, Shiva, I am not a follower of the Shining Light, merely a rather puzzled Catholic. And we have eschewed politics since Rome was abandoned.'

Shiva spent Sunday working in the embassy, answering letters for the cultural secretary, part of his cover job. There was a tiny air travel quota for cultural exchanges, and he had to field competing requests for Shakespearean actors, academics and musicians to be sent out. The Tasmans still revelled in their British heritage, more than ever in this age obsessed with history. He left at six so he could get back to his house in daylight. He walked carefully, alert for anyone following, but there was no one.

As he turned into a street near his, he heard voices from a long, low, earth-built building on the corner. A large sign, black letters on white, was fixed above the door: CHURCH OF THE SHINING LIGHT. A boy of around eighteen, neat in shirt and trousers, stood in the doorway. He smiled and nodded at Shiva. On an impulse, Shiva turned and went in.

The interior was a sparsely decorated hall. There were posters around the walls: stylized pictures of Jesus, a halo around His head, performing miracles. One poster showed a dark, tattered-looking book. Underneath, in large letters, THE BLACK BOOK, THE LOST PROPHECIES.

The hall was crowded, neatly dressed men and women of all ages sitting in rows of canvas chairs. Hairstyles were neat, unadorned. Nearly everyone wore crosses. They spoke in soft voices, glancing at a large empty platform where three chairs were set.

The boy who had been at the door had followed Shiva in. He was tall and thin, his face speckled with acne. Shiva quickly looked around, wondering if Parvati might be there, but could not see her. He thought, This is reckless; I shouldn't have come in here.

'Is this your first time, sir?' The boy's Kiwi accent turned *this* into *thus.* 'Why don't you take that seat?' He indicated two empty chairs at the end of a row. 'I'm Michael, by the way.'

'Peter.' The false name came to him instantly. He hesitated, then took the last seat in the row. Michael sat next to him. He realized that these arrangements had been planned; the boy had been placed at the door to encourage newcomers. On the floor at Shiva's feet was a Bible. He picked it up. After Revelation, at the end, the Black Book was printed:

Five hundred thirty years, then God returns to save
His chosen, once the sinful have been purged . . .

All along the rows, the hubbub of conversation died. A door to the platform opened and three men stepped in. Shiva wondered if one might be the Leader, but there was nothing of the Old Testament prophet about any of the men, who took seats facing the audience. All were middle aged, well dressed in dark cotton suits, happy smiles above white clerical collars.

One of them got up to speak. He said how happy he was to see so many worshippers tonight, here in God's house. The sermon that followed, about the works of Jesus and His Passion, could have come from any evangelist church at any time. Occasionally, someone in the audience shouted out 'Yes!' or 'Amen!' Shiva found his mind wandering. He was aware of Michael looking at him occasionally, but he avoided meeting the boy's eye. The pastor sat down and they sang some hymns, Shiva forcing himself to join in. After the singing had finished, Michael leaned towards Shiva and said: 'Pastor Henry is going to preach now. He has great truth.' There was a catch of excitement in the boy's voice.

A second pastor, a short, stocky man, got up to speak. His voice was loud and ringing.

'St John of Patmos told us in Revelation that in the last days there would be great calamities. Earthquakes, plagues, great battles. And it did happen, just as the angels promised St John. The Great Catastrophe. The vials of God's wrath have been poured out in full measure.'

'Hallelujah!' someone called out.

'Yet is it not true that those left after the Catastrophe, in these islands and far away in the northern lands, remain as sinful as ever men were, breaking the laws God set down in the Bible, to his just anger? It is true, but God has set out their punishment, their final End. He has given us the prophecies of Brân, the Black Book that in fact contains the Shining Light of truth. The book that has proved its truth by prophesying many events that came to pass in history, and at its end we find the promise of the final catastrophe, bringing the End of the World and the Last Judgment; when the last sinners go to hell and the righteous are raptured up to heaven, to worship Jesus for ever and ever. And we have the date: 2135, this year.' The pastor's voice had grown gradually softer, more intense; now it rose again as he approached the climax.

'We are the righteous. Our duty in these last days is to bring to truth those who will listen, but above all it is to know that we are the Saved, alone in this wasteland of sinners.' His voice was shaking with emotion now. Triumphant joy, but also, Shiva thought, a callous fury at the disobedient world around him. 'Any time now the world will end in the blink of an eye – and then we shall be in heaven!' He ended with a shout, followed by a chorus of hallelujahs and amens.

Shiva had to resist the urge to get up and walk out, but that would have made him conspicuous. He sat through more hymns, a reading from the Black Book with explanations of how its previous forecasts had come to pass, of wars and plagues and rebellions. At the end Pastor Henry asked for people who wished to learn more about the Church to come forward. Two did, an old woman and a young man, and the pastor blessed them and said the Church would consider them for membership, for a place in heaven. Then there was a final hymn, and the service ended. Shiva walked quickly out of the hall. He caught a glimpse of Michael's disappointed face.

The following evening he went to meet Parvati. He wore his suit – a white linen jacket and trousers – and a high-collared black shirt. It was raining, a heavy tepid rain that drummed on the solar panels on the town's roofs. The restaurant was in a side street near the Octagon, down a little alley. Darkness had fallen, and Shiva looked around carefully. Still he had seen no sign that he was followed.

The restaurant was long and narrow, lit by candles, with a seagoing theme: nets hanging from the ceiling, fish in ancient glass cases. He was early; Parvati wasn't there yet. The clientele was well dressed, mostly young, wearing shirts and kaftans with elaborate designs, hair piled up in loops or hanging down in plaited braids. No one here wore a cross. The manager, a coldly formal man in a dark suit, led him to a table for two. Shiva thought he looked at him dubiously and wondered if it was because of his colour. At the next table, two men with elaborately styled hair were eating, whispering softly to each other and laughing. One was short and dark, the other older, blond, his coiffed hair covering a bald patch that shone pinkly through.

Parvati arrived shortly after, wearing a plain white dress, her dark hair hanging loose and her cross conspicuous at her breast. The younger of the men at the next table glanced at it, frowning at her slightly as she sat down.

'I hope I haven't kept you waiting,' she said to Shiva.

'No. I was early.'

'I haven't been here before, but it's supposed to be very good. I thought you might like it.'

'Shall we order some wine? No, I'm sorry, you don't drink. Shall we have water?'

'Yes. Thank you for remembering.' She leaned her elbows on the table and looked at him. She seemed more confident tonight, more settled. 'Tell me about Europe,' she said.

He told her about the big cities like Birmingham that had survived, how every speck of land was cultivated, the hard work and long hours people put in to grow food, the attempts to green the Norwegian mountains and the bare rocks of Iceland.

'Are there many people from India?'

'A few. There was a lot of violence against minorities during the wars of the last century, but things are better now. My parents followed Hindu ways, but it was just a matter of keeping the old culture alive, rather than from belief.'

'Mine didn't believe at all.' Her face clouded. 'I don't see them now.'

'Mine are dead.'

'I'm sorry.'

'We'd grown apart too.' That was true – all he had said so far was true – but he went on to relate his cover story: how he had joined the civil service from school, worked in administrative posts for years, then joined the diplomatic service in the hope of travelling to the continent of Europe, and had been delighted to be sent to the Tasmans. 'I was never technically minded,' he added. 'Sometimes I feel guilty that I can't work on something useful, like energy efficiency or soil enhancement. I just haven't got that sort of mind.' It was true: when he was training he had had to learn about the types of bombs and explosives that robbers and terrorists used; he had found it almost impossible.

'It doesn't matter how much technical skill you put into it,' Parvati said, 'or what systems you develop, northern North America will never be made fertile.

Most of it is just peat bog, melted permafrost. People live on stupid dreams.'

'You have to try.'

Shiva saw that she wasn't concentrating any more. She glanced frowningly at the two men at the next table. A young waiter, a good-looking blond boy, had brought their main course, and the two men smiled at him suggestively as he served their food. 'We'll call you back if we want anything,' the younger called after him as he left. The boy blushed and walked away faster. The man laughed. His voice had a drunken slur.

Parvati leaned forward and spoke in a low, angry voice. 'It should be made illegal, what these people do. Yet here they are flouting it in public.'

'Ignore them.'

The two men had heard and turned their heads towards them. Parvati took a deep breath, returning to their conversation. 'And in the Rockies, some of the mountain land is just too steep. Like in Fjordland here. They can never cultivate there.'

'I hear you have problems with dogs in North America.'

'Filthy things. I hate them. A pack of dogs killed a young cousin of mine. They had a farm out in the wilderness. Just took her one day when she was out playing, tore her to pieces. We try to kill them, but there are millions of the things.' She laughed bitterly. 'Some people still keep dogs as pets. Pretend that animals can give them affection. But they're just things; they don't have souls.'

Her anger was showing through now, Shiva thought. The blond young waiter came to take their order. They both asked for trout and sweet potatoes. As the waiter left, the younger man at the next table said in a loud, mock-hurt voice: 'And I thought he was coming to see us again.'

'Oh, for goodness' sake,' Parvati breathed. She gave the pair another nasty look but controlled herself. 'There are animal problems here in South Island too,' she said to Shiva. 'Keas.'

'What are they?'

'Native parrots. When the kiwi went extinct they were made the national bird. They were protected for a time and the population soared. They're a real pest in the countryside now.'

At the next table, one of the men made a little squawking noise, like a parrot. The other laughed and joined in. Parvati ignored them, and, leaning forward towards Shiva, said: 'We try to kill them with traps,' she said. 'It's starting to work. They're intelligent, but they're greedy too.'

'What a bottom that waiter's got,' the younger man said loudly. The remark was meant to provoke; the two were looking at Parvati's prominent cross.

She turned around and, suddenly furious, said: 'Be quiet! You filthy animals!'

The men's expressions changed at once to anger. 'You watch your mouth, lady,' one said.

Shiva stood up. 'Let's cool things down,' he said quietly.

'They're filth!' Parvati seemed to have lost control completely.

The older man stood up.

'Look, I'm sorry,' Shiva said.

'We've nothing to be sorry for,' Parvati said.

'Fundamentalist bastards.' The blond man stood, raised his arm and took a swing at Shiva. He dodged, grabbed the man's arm and suddenly they were struggling. They both fell to the floor. Shiva could have dealt with him easily but dared not show it in front of Parvati; he was supposed to be a cultural attaché. The younger man stood up, egging his friend on. 'Show him, Dave!' Other diners stood up. A woman screamed. The manager appeared. 'Stop this!' he shouted. 'Stop it!' Shiva disentangled himself from the blond man and got to his feet, but the younger man grasped him around the waist, unbalancing him so they both fell backwards into Shiva's table. Parvati took the jug of water and threw it over the younger man's head.

'Get out!' the manager shouted. 'All of you! Get out! This is a civilized restaurant!'

Shiva found himself released. The two men glared at them, then threw some money on the table and stalked out together.

'I'm sorry,' Parvati said.

Shiva was angry with her now. She had been provoked, but it was her outburst that had turned things to violence. 'It doesn't matter,' he said coldly. He apologized to the manager and led the way outside.

The two men were waiting for them, one on each side of the door. They grabbed Shiva from behind, pinning his arms behind his back, and dragged him around the side of the building into a dark alley. Shiva struggled but realized that he was dealing with professionals, not amateurs. The younger man held him fast and the older stood in front of him. His expression was cold and clear; there was no sign of drunkenness now. He reached up and took something from his shirt pocket.

Shiva glanced around. He saw that Parvati was standing at the entrance to the alley, looking out on the street. She turned and stared at him with a blank face, then nodded to the man. Shiva looked fearfully at his hand, expecting to see a knife, but it was a cloth he held. He pushed it into Shiva's face. When he breathed in it was as though a horse had kicked him. He was conscious of falling, then everything went dark.

V

Shiva awoke to find himself lying on a wooden floor, his hands bound behind his back. His left shoulder hurt badly. He became aware that his body was rocking gently to and fro. An electronic hum vibrated through the floor. He was on a train.

Painfully, he tried to sit up. A booted foot on his chest pushed him back.

'Let him up.' It was Parvati's voice.

Strong hands lifted him into a seat. He almost cried out at the pain in his shoulder. He shook his head to try to clear it. He was in a small railway carriage, empty apart from him, the two men from the restaurant and, sitting opposite, Parvati. He glanced out of the window. Spectacular mountainous countryside, ploughed fields and olive groves outside the train. Some way off, in the foothills, he could see people working, clearing squares of land, laying new soil, creating fields.

The two men were wearing crosses now, and their elaborate hairstyles had been combed out, leaving scarecrow-like shocks of hair. He looked at their faces properly for the first time. There was a similarity in the cast of their features and their sharp blue eyes that Shiva had missed; he realized they were probably brothers. He turned to Parvati. She wore a confident expression now, her eyes fierce. It was as though a different person had taken over her body. She was a very good actor.

'You were easy to capture,' she said. Her voice was different, the enunciation slow and cold and clear.

'Where are you taking me?' Shiva's voice came out as a croak, and he realized he had a raging thirst. His shoulder throbbed. They must have twisted something, hauling him about when he was unconscious.

'The bottom end of South Island,' Parvati said. 'To meet the Leader.'

'Your friend's in for a surprise, isn't he?' the younger man said, and both laughed. Parvati shot them an annoyed look. 'This is serious,' she said. 'We have to find out what he knows.'

Shiva glanced up and down the train. From the speed at which it was moving up a very steep slope, he guessed there was only one carriage. 'You have your own train?' he asked.

'We do,' Parvati replied. 'A private company run by our nominees controls all the railways in the south-west. And we built this one for ourselves, out to the far west where nobody goes. Our Leader is a great strategic thinker,' she added in her new, didactic voice.

'This is the train we bring the scientists on.' The dark-haired young man had the air of someone enjoying telling a secret.

'The scientists you got to emigrate here? Where do you take them?'

'Same place you're going. You'll see.'

'What happens when we get to this mysterious place?' Nobody replied. Shiva swallowed. 'Can I have some water?'

'We'll be there in an hour,' Parvati said. 'You can have some then.'

The train rattled on, the engine humming. It slowed as they climbed higher into the steep mountains. In the far distance Shiva saw men labouring like ants on what looked like a new hydroelectric project. Then there were no more people, only bare, impossibly steep mountainsides rearing high above into the blue sky.

Shiva must have been still groggy from the drug they had given him, because he slept. He was jerked awake by the train coming to a halt, clanking and jolting. His thirst was terrible now. He was hauled to his feet and cried aloud at the pain in his shoulder. The two brothers walked him down the carriage and out of the door. He saw what was outside and his jaw dropped. The two men let him stand and look. Parvati stood next to them, arms folded, a sardonic smile on her face.

They were standing on scrubby grass, near the edge of an enormous cliff falling perhaps a thousand feet to a sheet of still blue water. They were at the head of a long fjord, huge mountains rising sheer out of the water on both sides, some far higher than the cliff where they stood. The peaks were reflected in the water. The fjord was perhaps two miles across, running in a straight line to the distant blue line of the ocean. The almost sheer sides were nearly bare, brown scrub clinging to ledges here and there.

Shiva had seen Milford Sound in documentaries, a landscape formed aeons ago by giant glaciers. In the old days it had been a place of tourist pilgrimage. Shiva remembered that it was in Fjordland, where Parvati had told him the land was too steep to cultivate. Once Milford Sound had been a wet place with vegetation clinging everywhere to the cliffs, but now it was bare, the air hot and dry.

There were gaps here and there in the cliffs, circular depressions cut into the hillsides by ancient ice, inaccessible except from the water. On the edge of one of these Shiva saw a little complex of wooden buildings, some of them little huts but others the size of warehouses. A big wooden jetty had been built out on to the water. At the end of the jetty an enormous, dark grey metal thing, three or four hundred feet long, lay half-submerged. It was shaped like a cigar, a projecting tower near the front and a fin at the back. A submarine.

One of the brothers reached into his pocket and pulled out a large army knife. Shiva thought for a moment they were going to kill him now, but the man reached behind him and cut his bonds. Shiva gasped with relief and brought his hands carefully in front of him. His shoulder throbbed.

'We've got a bit of a walk, Parvati said. 'It's steep. You'll need your hands to balance. Don't think of running – there's nowhere to go.'

But Shiva was looking at the ring on his right hand, where inside the gold setting the disc had turned pink and was growing darker, edging towards red. He looked at Parvati. 'This place is irradiated,' he said.

'I know,' she said simply. 'It doesn't matter.'

They went down a steep narrow path, little more than a ledge. One of the brothers walked behind Shiva and the other went ahead, behind Parvati. They needed to hold on to the nearly sheer cliff to their left. To the right was a drop to the still waters hundreds of feet below. A warm breeze rose from the sea, making Shiva's suit jacket, dirty now, flap around his chest. The other three were wearing shirts.

A pair of stocky grey parrots eyed them from a small ledge above. As they approached, the birds took off and flew around them, dangerously close, showing the brilliantly coloured underside of their wings.

'Take your jacket off!' the man behind Shiva ordered. 'It's the movement that's attracting them.'

Shiva pulled off his jacket and threw it over the side of the cliff. It spiralled down to the sea, and the two birds flew after the strange object, calling loudly.

'Wretched things!' Parvati's face was angry. She looked around at him. 'That's a pair of keas.'

They scrabbled along, moving slowly downwards. 'How deep is the water?' Shiva asked the man in front of him.

'Couple of thousand feet,' he replied over his shoulder.

Shiva could see the submarine more clearly now. People were climbing in and out of it; a group was studying a large chart laid on boxes on the jetty beside it. A pile of small torpedoes stood on the jetty. A group of men appeared to be taking them apart, removing the detonators. He saw a name painted in large white letters along the landward side of the hull: *Patriot.* Beside it was a small Union Jack. He knew now what the craft was: one of the nuclear submarines from the last century which had disappeared during the methane hydrate eruptions. Several were presumed to be lying on the ocean bed. He looked again at his ring: a light red; not immediately deadly, perhaps, but a dangerous dose.

They came to the end of the path and walked on to the jetty. Shiva saw more of the keas flying around, people shouting and waving at them to go away. One stood on a nearby post, picking at coils of rope wound around the top. It looked thin and hungry, its plumage ragged. Probably dying from radiation poisoning.

They came to a halt near the pile of torpedoes. The men studying the chart and the others on the jetty looked at the little party curiously. The giant submarine loomed ahead. One of the brothers said, 'I'll get some water,' and walked off.

A kea landed on the pile of bombs, and one of the white-suited men shouted angrily and waved his arms until the bird took off.

'They should shoot them,' Parvati said.

'Can't risk that with those bombs opened up,' the remaining brother said.

'How long before we die of radiation poisoning?' Shiva asked Parvati bluntly.

'A long time. The Leader will tell you more. Perhaps

you'll even understand, though I doubt it.' She gave an angry little laugh.

The man brought back bottles of water and passed them around. Shiva was so thirsty it hurt to drink. When he had finished he looked at Parvati again. 'Who betrayed me?' he asked.

'Mary Ackerley is one of our people,' she replied stonily. 'She's been one of us for a long time. We got her to open up a guesthouse for visiting officials; it is a useful way of finding things out. And somewhere for me to stay, where I knew I'd be secure.' She inclined her head. 'And she's an old lady; people don't suspect old ladies of being spies. You told her you were going to be making an air journey soon. Then you contacted me. We put two and two together.'

She broke off then, looking behind Shiva. He saw that all the people on the jetty had stopped work. Many wore hats, and now they took them off and stood, silent, looking at a man approaching from one of the large buildings. He was large and roughly dressed, with an untidy white beard, and he walked with a stick, a heavy rolling gait. A canvas bag was slung over one shoulder.

'Back to work,' the man called as he approached. His voice was deep and loud, with a North American accent. He walked right up to Shiva and looked him in the eyes. His face was lined and weatherbeaten. His eyes were blue-grey, intense and alive, seeming almost to glitter. He smiled. 'Inspector Moorthy.'

'I've told him how we got to him,' Parvati said.

The bearded man nodded. 'Yes, God was with us that day.' He looked hard at Shiva. 'Well, Mr Moorthy. Do you know who *I* am?'

'The Leader? Brandon Smith?'

'That's right. Now, first question – it's been on my mind. How did you find out that it was Parvati who took the book? Was it a camera she missed in the museum?'

He did not reply. Smith smiled, showing bad teeth. 'Not talking? You will.'

'You realize you're all slowly dying of radiation poisoning?' Shiva said.

Smith nodded. Like Parvati, he did not seem to care. 'There was a small leak in the reactor. It's closed now, but it polluted the area badly. We're all dying, I guess, like the birds, but we've time for what we need to do.' His look at Shiva was cold and hard.

Shiva took a deep breath. 'There are others waiting for me to report back, in Dunedin. My movements were being watched. They'll know where I am.'

Smith smiled again. 'Don't try to fool me, son. Have you any idea how remote this place is? There's only one way in, on a train we own, on a line we own. No one saw us put you on it. And we have watching-posts all along the way. We've had only three visitors in the five years we've been here, wanderers who wanted to see the Sound, and even they were captured a few miles off.'

Shiva said nothing.

The big man nodded slowly. 'We need to find out just how much you do know. That's why we brought you here. And we will. You'd be best to cooperate, son,' he added in a heavy, paternal voice.

Shiva looked at the great bulk of the submarine behind Smith. It was so big and so close he had to bend his neck to look up to see the conning tower. He decided to ask a question of his own. He had already guessed that they would not allow him to leave here alive; he saw only one slim possibility of escape.

'How did you get the submarine?' he asked.

Smith smiled heavily. 'We didn't get it, son. God led us to it. The first man to come here in decades was one of us. He felt called to come out into the wilderness to listen to the voice of God. He found the submarine beached just where it sits now. It's an old British one. It must have been caught in a methane upwelling in the last century. All the crew were killed – just skeletons when we found them – but the hull wasn't breached.' Smith looked down the fjord to the sea. 'The sub just drifted here and sat here for eighty years until God brought us to it. Isn't that something? The crew managed to close down the nuclear reactor inside before they died, but it's still functioning, the missiles and warheads intact. Four Trident Five missiles that can reach a target eight thousand miles away, each carrying a warhead that'll atomize everything for miles around the impact site.'

Shiva felt his face tighten in horror. 'But I thought you were dismantling them.'

Smith laughed. 'Hell, no.' He glanced at the bombs on the jetty. 'Those aren't the missiles; the missiles are huge. Those are just a few conventional torpedoes they had on board. We don't need those – hardly likely another submarine will attack us, now is it?'

'You . . . you'll kill millions.'

For answer Smith reached into his canvas bag and pulled out a small black book. It looked incredibly old; the covers were wood, battered and stained and peppered with nail holes. The Leader held it up. A ragged clapping sounded from the workers who had been watching. Smith held the book up so they could see it.

'We're nearly at the climax now,' he told Shiva. 'In a few weeks we'll be ready to sail the submarine away. As far north as we can go. Then we'll fire the missiles, at Birmingham and Berlin and Winnipeg. The Europeans and North Americans will think the Chinese are making a pre-emptive strike, like they did at Russia during the Catastrophe, and they'll fire back. Then the prophecy will be fulfilled, and in the midst of the last war Jesus will return and we will be raptured up to heaven. So you see, son, the radiation doesn't matter.' He raised the captured book above his head again and the people clapped and cheered. So these scientists and engineers were willing to go all the way, Shiva thought. The others, the ones who died mysteriously, must have refused.

Smith opened the book carefully and turned the thick, ancient parchment pages covered with handwritten Latin script. He placed a thick, grimy finger on a passage near the end, then read aloud to Shiva. '"A sun-bright fire of blood",' he intoned. There was something in his hard, passionless delivery that made Shiva despair, made him realize that nothing and nobody could move this fanatic from his course.

'We wondered how the end would come about,' Smith went on quietly. 'Then we found the submarine and realized what the prophecy meant. Sometimes God requires men to act, to bring His wishes to fulfilment. When the Jew Oppenheimer exploded the first nuclear bomb, he quoted your namesake, the pagan god Shiva: "Now I am become death, the destroyer of worlds." He was afraid of what he had done, but we are not.'

'That was Vishnu, not Shiva.'

Being corrected seemed to annoy Smith more than Shiva's pursuit of them or his lies about others coming. He frowned. 'All these Hindu gods are aspects of each other, don't you know that? You skinny little heathen thing.' He returned the book reverently to his knapsack and turned to the two brothers.

'Have him questioned. Don't worry about the methods. We need to know if we have a real threat here.' The Leader turned and walked away without a backward glance.

*

They took Shiva up the jetty to the wooden buildings set against the cliff. Looking up, he saw more of the sickly-looking parrots sitting on ledges. The brothers tied his hands in front of him with more rope, then opened the door of a small, solid-looking shed and hauled him inside. The floor was of bare rock with an iron ring bolted into it, the end of a length of rope secured to the ring. The brothers bound Shiva's hands again with a thin but strong rope, binding them separately, a strand of rope about an inch long connecting them, like handcuffs. Then they tied the strand to the length of rope connected to the iron ring. He cried out as they jerked at his shoulder, but they paid no attention. They tied his feet together, then left without looking at him again, shutting the door and turning a key.

He sat up painfully. The shed was dim, with only a tiny unglazed window less than a foot square at the back, facing the cliff. Shiva leaned against the wall to give his hurt shoulder some support.

He knew they were leaving him to reflect before the interrogators came. Don't worry about the methods, Smith had said. He took a deep rattling breath. He considered his story about people in Dunedin ready to follow him. With practised speed he developed it in his mind, building it up to sound consistent, true. Even if they believed him, he realized, they were hardly likely to delay the project; they might even speed it up. But he had to try to scare them. His life didn't matter. Even if by some miracle he did get out of here he might be badly affected by radiation already.

He had one hope of escape. In the restaurant he had deliberately concealed that he was trained to fight. Even with a strained shoulder, he thought that if he could get free of these bonds and into single combat with one of them he might have a chance. But they were well tied. He struggled with them for a while before giving up. Even if he could escape, he realized, he could never make it across these trackless mountains with people who knew them in pursuit. But he had thought of something else he could do, if he could get free. He thought about it hard and sweat ran down his brow, because he knew that if he succeeded he would certainly die.

He jumped and whirled around as a sound came from the barred window and a shadow fell over the room. One of the grey parrots was there, its clawed feet on the sill, looking in with bright beady eyes above a sharp, hooked beak. It glanced at Shiva, then peered over the floor. Shiva realized it was looking for food; the keas must live by scavenging the camp. When the bird saw there was nothing to eat it flew away. It had looked sick and scrawny, like the one on the post. Shiva glanced at the circle in the centre of his ring again. It seemed red now, though it was hard to tell in the dim light of the shed.

Shortly after, the brothers returned. One carried a large leather bag. With them was a tall, craggy-faced older man who walked like a soldier. Shiva was surprised to see that he held a bowl of food in one hand, a spoon sticking out. He could smell something like chicken. In his other hand the man carried a bottle of water. He laid both beside Shiva.

'Hungry?' he asked. He had a Tasman accent. 'I guess you're thirsty too?'

Shiva picked up the water, drank it, then took the bowl clumsily on to his lap. It was difficult to hold the spoon in his bound hands, but he managed, though he spilled some food down his shirt. He ate the meat and started on the thin, fatty stew underneath, but after a few mouthfuls he felt nauseous and had to put the bowl down. He wondered if it was a sign of radiation sickness.

The man turned and nodded to the brothers. They left the room, the one who carried the leather bag putting it on the floor. They locked the door behind them. The soldierly man sat on his haunches in front of Shiva. His eyes were calculating. 'My name is James,' he said. 'I want to ask you some questions.' His voice was gentle. 'How are you feeling? They said you hurt your shoulder on the journey?'

'Yes.'

'OK.' James nodded, then turned and picked up the bag. He pulled out a rope and a knife. He used the knife to cut the bonds on Shiva's left hand, then quickly and expertly, giving him no time to react, he hauled Shiva's left arm up behind his back, looping a second length of rope around Shiva's neck and securing it to his wrist, fixing his left arm up behind his back. He cried out at the pain in his left shoulder.

James leaned back on his haunches. 'An incentive to answer my questions,' he said in the same quiet tones. 'Now, how did you find out about Parvati Karam?'

Shiva had been taught about dealing with torture. The main point was that in the end nearly everyone gave in. The pain in his shoulder made it hard to catch his breath as he told the story he had formulated. To begin with, what he said was true: how Parvati had been seen through the camera at the museum, how he had been picked because of their shared ancestry to start an internet correspondence with her, his journey to Dunedin.

James's face twisted with contempt. 'Shared ancestry. When I was young I was in the police in the refugee camps, when rations were so short some of them turned to cannibalism. Don't think they bothered much about shared ancestry. I saw what people without God are like there. It's finished, it's all finished. Don't you understand that?'

Shiva took a deep breath. 'The Tasman government have suspected for some time you were planning something big. There were people tracking me everywhere I went. They knew what they were doing. They'll follow that railway of yours. The best thing you and anyone else in this place who still has a foot in the real world can do is run.'

James looked at him steadily for a long moment, then he shook his head. 'It's not a bad story, but I don't believe you,' he said. 'We were watching you carefully all the time you were in Dunedin, and we saw no one following you. We don't think anyone there has the faintest idea of what we are planning. We're better organized than you seem to think. You probably think since we're Christians we're naive and badly organized, but we're not.'

'And you go in for torture and murder,' Shiva said, gasping at the pain in his shoulder.

'Read your history,' James said contemptuously. 'And don't try to distract me. I think you came here to hunt down Parvati Karam. I think you're pretty much alone.'

Shiva did not reply. 'I'm right, aren't I?' James asked, then rose to his feet. Shiva flinched. 'I'll leave you for a while. When I come back I'll have you standing with both arms tied up behind your back. That'll be worse.' He looked at Shiva intently. 'So have a good think about whether you want to stick to that story.' He untied the cord around Shiva's neck and tied both hands back to the rope fixed to the ring in the floor. Then, without another word, he left the shed.

An hour passed. It began to get dark, the light coming through the little window fading. Shiva twisted and manoeuvred to find a position that would ease the pain in his shoulder. He knew that when James came back, before long he would tell him the truth. He thought about the ancient monk who had written the verses. If he had not written that wretched book, none of this would have happened; he would not be here. 'Couldn't you see people would do something like this with your book, you fool?' he asked aloud.

He heard a fluttering sound. One of the mangy-looking parrots was at the window again, perhaps the same one. It stood on the sill and looked at Shiva, then at the bowl on the floor. It must have smelled the congealing remains of the stew but was obviously frightened to fly into the shed. Shiva looked at the hooked, sharp beak and remembered the one on the post that had been chewing at the rope. Very slowly and gently, so as not to startle the kea, Shiva edged painfully over to the bowl and, gritting his teeth, put his bound wrists inside it. He dipped the piece of rope connecting them into the watery mess. The kea watched intently.

Shiva hoped its hunger was stronger than its fear. He lifted his hands out again and managed to pick up the bowl. He shuffled back against the wall. He put the bowl on his lap, held his roped wrists beside it. The bird twisted its head from side to side, assessing what was going on. Parrots, Shiva knew, were intelligent birds.

'Come on,' Shiva said encouragingly. 'Come on.'

It hesitated, then fluttered down to the floor. It stood there out of reach, studying him without moving. Shiva closed his eyes and leaned his head wearily against the wall. This wasn't going to work.

He felt a wind, then sharp little claws on his thigh. He opened his eyes. The parrot was perched on his leg and had put its head into the bowl. A dark little tongue flickered out of the open beak, greedily licking up the remains of the stew in the bottom of the bowl. He saw how thin it was. The bird kept one eye beadily fixed on

Shiva. When it had finished, it jumped into the empty bowl and looked at Shiva's bound wrists. There was a little of the stew on his fingers, and he feared the bird might bite them. The kea looked up at his face uncertainly for a moment, then stretched its head forward and began picking at the rope.

Some instinct to grub and peck had been stimulated, for the kea bit and tugged, swallowing pieces of rope as well as the stew smeared on it. Shiva sat as still as a stone, enduring his pain. The bird bit his wrists several times and blood began to flow, but he gritted his teeth and made no sound that might startle it. After about fifteen minutes the bird suddenly stopped, then flew up, perched on the windowsill for a moment, and was gone.

Though it brought pain to his shoulder, and to his wrists too now, Shiva tugged at the ropes. The strand linking his wrists was almost severed, and the kea's pulling and pecking had loosened the others. He felt something give, and pulled his right hand free. He looked at his wrists; his hands and wrists were dotted with sharp little cuts, many bleeding. With his free hand he began picking at the ropes until both hands were free, then his legs. He arranged the ropes so it looked as though his limbs were still tied, then leaned back against the wall, breathing hard, trying to pull himself together. He arranged his hands in his lap so it looked as though they were still tied. Then he leaned back against the wall again, grateful for the dim light. The trousers of his best suit were dark with grime and dust now.

This time it was only a few minutes before he heard footsteps approaching the hut. The key turned. But it wasn't James who came in, it was Parvati. She carried a gun, a large old revolver that looked huge in her little hand. In her other hand she carried an olive-oil lamp which she laid on the floor. She stood looking down at him. Her expression was annoyed, irritated.

'Did he hurt you?' she asked.

'Yes.'

She looked at his bloodied hands. For a second Shiva was afraid she might guess the truth, but she must have thought James had cut him, for she said: 'So I see. He doesn't think you've told him the truth. You should, or he'll hurt you badly.'

Shiva laughed. 'Have they sent you to play nice policeman to James's nasty policeman?' He looked at her. 'Bad choice. Nice is the last thing you are. I thought that ever since I saw the photographs of that murdered watchman in Birmingham.'

'Everything I've done has been for the Shining Light. That old man would have died soon anyway. He just went to hell a little early. The end is almost here.'

'You're bringing it.'

'We're fulfilling the prophecy. It's God's plan.'

'Your God. How cruel and vile He is.'

She laughed contemptuously. 'Who are human beings to set themselves up as more moral than Jesus Christ and Almighty God? He led Pastor Smith to the Black Book. Many others have had the book in the past, and none realized its significance. We are the instruments God has chosen to bring His plans to pass. The whole purpose of the prophecies was to give us, here in the Last Days, proof of what God wished us to do. And it was He that brought us to the submarine.'

'There were several nuclear submarines never accounted for. I bet there are others washed up on uninhabited shores around the world.'

Her voice took on a note of cold intensity. 'You're saying it isn't strange that an undamaged, fully armed submarine should be washed up on the remotest shores of the country where the Shining Light burns strongest, where one of us found it? No, this was meant.'

For a brief moment Shiva wondered if they could be right. But even if they were, it didn't matter. Shiva knew what he must do now. Looking at Parvati, he knew he could kill her and do it with little feeling. And then he gave a long, shuddering, involuntary sigh.

She misread what the sigh meant. 'You're afraid of James coming back?' she asked. She made her voice gentle. 'There's no shame in that. Tell me the truth, Shiva. Nobody's coming after us, are they?'

Her body had taken a relaxed, unthreatening posture, and Shiva saw her hold on the gun relax a little. He kicked out with his right foot, the ropes flying away, knocking it from her hand. Parvati gave a cry of astonishment. He launched himself from the floor and butted her in the stomach. The gun dropped to the floor as Shiva's weight toppled her over. She gagged and gasped for air as he pressed his elbow on her windpipe, but she still struggled fiercely, trying to get her arms free. Shiva reached for the gun, picked it up and smashed the butt down on her forehead. She gave a little grunt and went limp. He brought the gun down on her head twice more, until he was sure she was dead.

He stood up shakily and leaned against the wall. While attacking Parvati he had felt no pain, but now it washed over his shoulders and cut hands in waves. He felt faint and sank to the floor again, allowing himself a few seconds' rest. Then he got up, walking around the room a couple of times to test the strength of his legs. Not looking at Parvati's face, he bent and felt in her pockets for the key to the shed.

Now he must be quick, not hesitate for a moment. He took a few more deep breaths and felt himself fill with purpose, certainty. Hold this feeling, he told himself, hold it to the end.

He put out the lamp and opened the door quietly, just a crack, holding Parvati's gun behind him. Lights shone out into the darkness from the buildings around. Though he had feared James might be coming back, the complex seemed deserted. The night air was warm and still. From somewhere he heard singing, hallelujahs, God's elect preparing themselves for the End. He looked down the length of the jetty, the submarine visible as a black shape in the moonlight against the beautiful vista of Milford Sound at night. A full moon was reflected in the still water. The missiles the men had been dismantling had been covered by a tarpaulin. He made out two guards standing there, wearing dark kaftans. One looked young, slim and slight. The other was larger, older, and carried a rifle.

Shiva closed the door again and stood thinking. Somehow he had to disable the guards without shooting them, for the sound would bring people running. Then he would fire the gun at the detonator of one of the torpedoes. The whole lot would go up, and so would the missiles on the submarine. This corner of South Island would probably be devastated, but there were few people here and he hoped that the gigantic natural funnel of Milford Sound would absorb much of the energy. And the whole world would not go up in a nuclear war that devastated, shrunken humanity could surely not survive. And if God meant that he should fail, at least he would have tried, and if he found himself at some seat of judgment and an angry God thundered at him and asked if he believed that his morality was greater than God's, Shiva would answer 'yes' and go proudly down to hell.

He opened the door again, just a crack. The guards looked bored and listless. Shiva slipped the gun into his belt behind him, then opened the door and stood in full view. He raised his hands above his head and started walking slowly towards them.

They looked at him in astonishment. The one with the rifle raised it and pointed it at Shiva. He was in his fifties, fit-looking. The other guard was just a boy. He reminded Shiva of Michael at the church in Dunedin. He felt sorry for what he must do.

'Stop right there!' the older guard called. Shiva slowed his pace further, to a shuffle, but still walked on. 'I want to confess everything,' he said. 'I've seen the light.'

He was still too far away for the guards to hear properly. 'What?' the older one asked.

'I have to tell you. God himself has visited me. See, my bonds are gone. See the stigmata, the blood running on my wrists.' He made his voice tremble with emotion. The guards looked at each other. Shiva knew he sounded convincing; he had always been able to sound convincing. Even his clothes, ragged and dirty and torn now, added to the image. It was enough to throw the guards off balance. He came to a halt, perhaps twenty yards from the tarpaulin. He had walked at a slight angle, taking him near the water. He stopped and the two guards came slowly up to him.

'How'd he get out?' the young guard said. He sounded afraid. They both stepped right up to him. Shiva was in great pain, but he turned quickly and threw all his weight against the older man. He gave a shout and toppled into the water with his rifle, hitting it with a loud splash. Shiva pulled the gun from his waistband and pointed it at the young guard. 'On your knees,' he said. 'Hands on your head.'

The boy obeyed. 'Please,' he said. 'I'm not ready. I'm not prepared yet. This isn't the time.'

Shiva swiped him across the side of the head with the

gun and he went down with a groan. Shiva rolled him over and over until he too fell into the water. He could hear splashes and gurgling cries from the other guard, but there was no way for him to climb up again.

Shiva walked over to the tarpaulin and pulled it away. The pyramid of ugly, snub-nosed bombs lay there. Shiva picked one up and laid it on end as he had seen the technician do earlier. He had a momentary fear that he would not be able to unscrew the top, but it was surprisingly easy. He looked at the complex mechanism. The guard in the water was shouting now, loudly, his voice carrying far in the clear night. Shiva heard the singing stop. It must be now. He hesitated, then out of the blue remembered the two children fishing in the lake at Birmingham and felt a sudden overwhelming love for poor, fractured, weak, helpless humanity. God help them all, God *should* help them all if He existed.

He stood right above the bomb, aimed downwards and fired.

He saw a red light and then a blinding white light and in the middle of the white light the figure of Shiva, dancing in his circle of fire to keep the world in being, his face impassive.